HORROR WRITERS

DEATHPORT

EDITED BY
RAMSEY
CAMPBELL

POCKET BOOKS

New York   London   Toronto   Sydney   Tokyo   Singapore

The sale of this book without its cover is unauthorized. If you purchased this book without a cover, you should be aware that it was reported to the publisher as "unsold and destroyed." Neither the author nor the publisher has received payment for the sale of this "stripped book."

This book is a work of fiction. Names, characters, places and incidents are either products of the authors' imaginations or are used fictitiously. Any resemblance to actual events or locales or persons, living or dead, is entirely coincidental.

An *Original* Publication of POCKET BOOKS

POCKET BOOKS, a division of Simon & Schuster Inc.
1230 Avenue of the Americas, New York, NY 10020

Copyright © 1993 by The Horror Writers of America, Inc.

All rights reserved, including the right to reproduce this book or portions thereof in any form whatsoever. For information address Pocket Books, 1230 Avenue of the Americas, New York, NY 10020

ISBN: 0-671-69575-4

First Pocket Books printing September 1993

10 9 8 7 6 5 4 3 2 1

POCKET and colophon are registered trademarks of Simon & Schuster Inc.

Cover art by Ben Perini

Printed in the U.S.A.

Copyright Notices

Introduction © 1993 by Ramsey Campbell
Echoes © 1993 by Chelsea Quinn Yarbro
Jet Lag © 1993 by Ron Dee and P. D. Cacek
Cleansing Agent © 1993 by Don D'Ammassa
Thank Your for Your Patience © 1993 by Matthew Costello
The Man in the Mirror © 1993 by Les Daniels
55-Gallon Drums Along the Mohawk © 1993 by Gregory Nicoll
To Feed the Sun © 1993 by David Niall Wilson
Tire Fire © 1993 by Nancy Holder
War Cry © 1993 by Edo van Belkom
When Prayers Are Answered © 1993 by Roberta Lannes
Consent © 1993 by Nancy Baker
The Man in the Moon © 1993 by Michael Arnzen
Bruja © 1993 by Kathryn Ptacek
Beneath the Tarmac © 1993 by Lawrence Watt-Evans
In Country © 1993 by Peter Crowther
Just a Few Drops of Blood © 1993 by Dawn Dunn
The Smoking Mirror © 1993 by Dan Perez
Sacred Wheel © 1993 by Patricia Ross
Buzzkiller © 1993 by Clark Perry
Sacrament © 1993 by Brian Hodge
Passing Through © 1993 by Steve Rasnic Tem
The Telltale Head © 1993 by Adam-Troy Castro
Piranha © 1993 by Stephen M. Rainey
Soul Catcher © 1993 by Wendy Webb
I Am No Longer © 1993 by Nancy Kilpatrick
Plane Scared © 1993 by Douglas Hawk
Scalps © 1993 by Chet Williamson
In the Still, Small Hours © 1993 by Charles Grant

Contents

CONTENTS

CONTENTS

Introduction

Where *do* we get our ideas?

That, with variations, was a question I asked myself quite a few times while trying to produce the germ of this book. Chelsea Quinn Yarbro, then the President of the Horror Writers of America, had coaxed me into conceiving the third of the anthologies intended as a showcase for the members of that body. As its name suggests, most of them are American, but I am not, and I wanted to come up with an idea which would inspire contributions from both sides of the Atlantic. I was also aware of following two excellent concepts for anthologies by Robert McCammon and F. Paul Wilson. I've found few combinations of requirements more inhibiting, and several months later I still had no response ready to Quinn's invitation. Then I found myself trapped at the Manchester airport en route to NECON, the annual convention in Providence, during one of those apparently interminable and pointless preludes to a flight, and by the time of boarding I knew what the anthology was to be about.

In the preface to my first book I made the mistake of describing all the settings, and other inventions too, instead of allowing the reader to encounter them in the stories. I won't do so here, not least because the central notion and its ramifications are no longer only mine. Far be it from me to deny the reader of the present book the pleasure of discovering what Dry Plains International is and what it has become. The stories offer different possible resolutions—in alternate worlds, perhaps—of the series of events.

INTRODUCTION

I think the book fulfills its intentions—to display the range of talent, skill, imagination, and style representing the Horror Writers of America. I thank every one of the contributors for helping me achieve that goal, and I thank Marty Greenberg for doing far more work than I did.

Ramsey Campbell
Wallasey, Merseyside
3 December 1992

ECHOES

Chelsea Quinn Yarbro

"THEY WERE MUCH WISER THAN WE ARE, YOU KNOW." SHE STOOD behind the gift counter at the Dry Plains International Airport, a woman with shag-cut, grey-struck hair and enormous light-blue eyes behind small wire-rimmed glasses; she looked as if she had been stuck in 1967 for the last quarter century.

"They?" said Philips absentmindedly as he paid for the two magazines of local interest; one boasted a long section on the delights of Mexico, just over the Texas border, the other had a gorgeous series of photographs of restored turn-of-the-century houses in Dallas and Houston. He wanted to keep his mind off Dry Plains—the place gave him the creeps, always had.

"The Comanches. They used to live around here, long ago. Sometimes, at night like this, I think they're still here. They were a very spiritual people." She beamed at him, handing him his change with an expression that said "Have a nice day," though it was now twenty minutes after two on a windy autumn night.

"I don't know about Comanches," Philips said, his manner suggesting that ignorance was just fine with him.

She smiled and indicated some of the Indian necklaces in the display case—Hopi and Navajo, for the most part, and with very unspiritual price-tags—with a gentle sigh of approval. "The native Americans understand nature so much better than we do. They're so empathetic, so much in

1

tune with the earth. It's part of their way of life, not like us at all. They respect everything in nature. You can see it in everything they do."

"Thanks," said Philips, moving a short distance from the counter so as to end her version of small-talk. He paid no attention to her, choosing to put his mind on the superior photographs of the magazines. After a little while he wandered out toward the lobby area for private and corporate airplanes, half-reading the first of the magazines and trying to decide if he ought to call the Trager International office in Dallas before they called him. Just because it was the middle of the night didn't mean that Trager wasn't barrelling along. He decided that he ought to get another cup of coffee so he wouldn't be tempted to doze.

He had taken a seat on one of the high stools at the only snack counter open at that hour and had just been handed a large, biodegradable cup filled with lukewarm coffee when he heard his name on the PA system. He picked up the carry-out cup and hurried toward the nearest courtesy phone, preparing to defend his decision to land here rather than at Dallas/Fort Worth. "Galen Phillips here," he said as he lifted the receiver.

"A call for you, sir," said a woman's voice with a faint Spanish accent. "I'll put you through."

"Thanks," he told her in order to be polite. He waited, wondering who would be on the other line.

"Philips!" boomed D. A. Landis, as if in the middle of the night he was ready to participate in a jousting tournament or emcee a banquet for a thousand people. "Good to talk to you this way."

Philips sighed. He had a strong distrust of the hearty, venal Landis who ran the Trager division in Chicago. "Good morning, D. A.," he said, trying to infuse a little good fellowship into his voice.

"I had a call from the maintenance people there about half an hour ago." He made every word portentous. "They told me that you had to be one lucky son of a bitch to bring our company jet down without any harm, considering the malfunction of the instruments. We ought to listen to you veteran pilots more often. Your hunch about the plane was right. If you'd tried to push on, you might have crashed;

that's what the night supervisor just told me. We can't have that."

"I guess not," said Philips, his guts feeling suddenly hot, then cold.

"You experienced flyers, you've got instincts." He coughed once. "You better lay over there until the plane is fixed. They say it shouldn't be much more than two days. They can start work on it in the morning; their night crew is just a skeleton, a shift of five guys. They can't handle the trouble, and according to them it'll take a day at least to check it out. Hell, we can spare you from the roster that long. Besides, you're due for some ground time, aren't you?"

"Pretty much," said Philips.

"Too bad we don't have a corporate apartment there you can use—there's no reason for it—but find yourself a hotel and get a good room. Not the most expensive suite in the place, but we don't want you camping in a broom closet, either. Looks bad to the stockholders." He had a plummy chuckle that sounded like ripe fruit bursting. "Put it on your corporate account. We'll cover anything reasonable like car rentals and meals, providing you don't eat steak and lobster three times a day, or drive to Nevada."

"Thanks," said Philips, feeling a bit dazed by his good fortune and suspicious of it all at the same time.

"Use this as your long rest time. You're supposed to take three days off at the end of the month. You might as well do them now." He sounded more hail-fellow-well-met with every word, and Philips distrusted that.

"Why now? I've got other flights logged." He did his best to sound mildly curious instead of worried.

Landis did not answer him. "Oh," he said as if it had just occurred to him, "would you mind sticking around the airport until the morning maintenance crew comes on? Stay with them while they go over the report on the plane? You were there when the trouble started and you know the right things to ask. They'll be able to give you a better picture about the repairs, and you can relay that to me when you get to the hotel."

Philips swallowed hard. He knew that the morning crew at this airport arrived at six, which would mean he would have to wait another three and a half hours to talk with them. He was glad now that he had bought the magazines. "Sure. No problem."

"That's terrific," said Landis. "That's just fine."

As reckless as it was, Philips could not keep himself from asking, "What about the Amsterdam flight? Who's going to cover for that?" He was scheduled to leave late tomorrow afternoon with a group of executives bound for a crucial meeting in The Netherlands.

"We'll find someone," Landis told him confidently. "We can probably bring Chapman back from vacation a day early."

"I could take a commercial flight up in the morning, after I get the report on the plane. I could be out of here by noon," Philips suggested. He did not want to admit that he hated this place and the thought of being here for more than a couple of hours made him edgy. "I'd have enough time for sleep and sufficient hours off to make the flight."

Again that high-calorie chuckle. "I wish more of our people had your dedication, Philips."

He wanted to say it wasn't dedication, it was dread, and a sense of being drawn here, as if the very place itself were reaching out to snare him. But such an admission could earn him a psychiatric evaluation and enforced retirement; he was close enough to that already. "You know me. I like to fly, and Amsterdam is a great place. I had some plans for the trip, that's all. I was hoping to get in a little . . . play."

Now the chuckle had a licentious spice in it. "I enjoy playing in Amsterdam myself. I can't blame you for wanting to go there. Maybe we can arrange for you to have a couple of extra days there when this is over." The offer was a sop and both men recognized it for what it was. "Let me know what the maintenance people tell you, and we'll figure out what to do next. How's that?"

"Great," said Philips, who thought it sucked.

"I'm relying on you," said Landis, and went on to assure Philips that he would be sure to credit him with saving the company's second-largest jet, and planned to inform the Board of Directors that there ought to be a bonus in the deal for him.

When Landis had finished finessing Philips, he hung up abruptly, leaving Philips to stare down the long, empty corridor toward the main part of the airport. From the air, he thought it looked a little like a lopsided galaxy, with four spiral arms stretching out from the center. Now he had the disquieting impression that he was at the edge of a whirl-pool, turning and pulling, turning and pulling. He wanted to avoid the center as long as possible, for once there he would not escape. It was hard for him to shake off that irrational sensation as he went back to the snack counter to buy a couple of stale doughnuts.

The woman from the gift shop was there, getting a cup of herbal tea. "You're still here," she said in that lilting way that brought back memories of flower children. "Are you waiting for a connecting flight?"

"No," he said. "Worse luck."

If she noticed his terseness it made no difference to her. "At night like this, there aren't many flights coming in on this arm. It stays quiet here. Over there"—she cocked her head to the south where the international flights arrived—"there's things going on all the time. People leave at one in the morning and land at three. But here, we don't see much of that. They try to keep traffic to a minimum after nine." There was a faint, romantic smile on her face. "I used to work in the International shop, but they moved me over here a couple of years ago. It was exciting, seeing all those strange things in the shop, and meeting people from all over the world. Don't you think it's exciting to meet people from other countries? Isn't it wonderful to learn about them and the places they come from?"

"I guess," said Philips, who had no desire to talk.

She beamed at him and held out her long, slim hand, nails unpainted. "I'm Senta. It's a pleasure to meet you. I don't often get to talk to people, working the night shift. But most of the staff don't like working at night, even though it pays better."

Reluctantly he took her hand. "Galen Philips."

Her eyes brightened behind the granny glasses. "You fly for Trager, don't you?"

Since the badge on his jacket was embossed with the Trager logo—a sixteenth-century merchant ship called a hulk—he only nodded.

"I like the way Trager planes look," she said. "You can

always spot them, with their wings and the tail painted red and the ship in black. It's very distinctive." Her expression changed, became distant. "When I first worked here, Braniff had jets painted neon orange and shocking pink and bright lime, colors like that. They were beautiful, like huge butter-flies. I loved it. No one does that anymore."

"I remember them," said Philips, drawn by the memory. "The first time I saw one I thought I was hallucinating."

She laughed, sounding much younger than she looked. "So did I. I was still doing mushrooms then, so it made sense. Still, it was a relief to know that I wasn't just seeing things. Sometimes, around here at night, I worry about that." She glanced in the direction of the gift shop, then looked back at him. "I'm sorry. This is great, talking to you, but I've got to get back to work. There's nobody here, but I have to stay in the shop. We have rules. Things could happen. You know how it is."

Now that he had the opportunity to get away from her, Philips decided he would rather talk a little longer. "I'll come with you. I haven't anything to do until six, anyway, and if I read I'll probably doze."

She looked mildly surprised. "That would be nice," she said with curious formality. "My relief comes on at eight. But things pick up before then. The first of the commuter flights arrives just before six. The first is from Atlanta, and then the one from Chicago, and then two from New England—Boston and Hartford, I think, or maybe Providence—and then L.A., St. Louis, Seattle, Omaha, Atlanta again, Salt Lake, Albuquerque, Buffalo, San Francis-co, and Cleveland, and that takes us almost to seven. I guess you'll be gone by then."

"You've memorized the schedule," said Philips, wonder-ing if there was somewhere he could sit in the gift shop.

"After all the time I've worked here, it would be hard not to. I know some of the regular passengers now. There's a man who comes in on the seven-ten flight from Denver. I've seen him twice a month every month except December ever since I've been working here. He told me he's a courier for some international outfit. He always dresses in expensive suits; he carries a briefcase handcuffed to his wrist. He buys

6

the local paper, a couple packages of gum because he gave up smoking, and he says something about the weather. Every time. It's unreal. And one of the men on the L.A. flight makes the trip on the first Monday of every month. He's some kind of attorney, real flashy. He always comes in, picks up magazines and the paper. Another one, on the seven-forty-nine from Dulles, stops in to ask about traffic. He talks fast, in bursts. He's a kind of a flirt. He's the assistant to the Congressman in this district." Her color was heightened, like a girl boasting about her suitors and not a middle-aged woman discussing her regular customers. "They have news, sometimes, but not like over in the international arm. It's not as exciting here. Those people were real different."

"Because they're from far away?" Philip guessed.

"Oh, yes. They're out doing all kinds of things, things you can't imagine; they're seeing things." She gave him a winsome smile, the kind of smile that usually fades by the time a woman reaches thirty. "I used to like the trans-Pacific flights, because everyone was trying to figure out what day it was. No one has that trouble over here, except sometimes when we have real bad weather." It might have been a joke because the lines around her light-blue eyes crinkled.

"I suppose not," said Philips, who decided her conversation was a welcome distraction after all; it muted the gathering sense of disquiet that Dry Plains International roused in him.

"I did a little traveling when I was younger. I wanted to go to India, but I ended up getting six weeks in Spain and Portugal, right before I dropped out of college. I did two years, and my grades were good enough, but it didn't seem relevant to what was going on in the world. You know how it was, back then?" Her hands moved quickly and delicately, reminding Philips of small, industrious birds. While she talked she rearranged the jewelry display, shifting price tags and merchandise into an arrangement that drew more attention to the case. "I had friends who were killed in the Vietnam war, and one of my cousins was shot during a riot. He wasn't even part of it, he was just watching the news people set up their cameras, and bang. I didn't think that getting a degree in English Literature and then getting my teaching credentials made much sense. There had to be another way, you know?"

"And you ended up here, instead of teaching," said Philips, being careful to make this not seem to be critical of her.

"After about four years of just checking out the country, yes. There was a *feel* to this place. I felt I could live here because of the feel. I'd be in touch with something important." Her chuckle was self-deprecatory. "I know how that must sound to you, but—"

He interrupted her. "No. I agree. Dry Plains has something about it." That was as far as he was willing to go.

She rewarded him with another winsome smile. "You're real nice," she said with earnest sincerity. "It *does* have a feel, and I couldn't get away from it, you know? I tried a couple of times—I spent a year in New Orleans when my kids were little—but I came back here."

Philips was mildly startled to learn she had children. "How many . . . kids do you have?"

"Just one now," she said, with a trace of sadness. "My daughter. My son died of AIDS three years ago. He was twenty-two. He worked here with me for two summers when he was in high school. Doing loading and unloading in the back, stock work, that kind of stuff. He got injured in one of those freak accidents that . . . The paramedics got here right away but they had trouble stopping the bleeding. It turned out the transfusion they gave him was bad. It's funny, you know? We thought at the time it was saving his life." The lightness went out of her, and she struggled to recover it. "My daughter's twenty. She's in college in Oregon, where her father lives. She says she's going to get an engineering degree." Now her smile was puzzled, as if she could not imagine any child of hers wanting to be an engineer. "I thought she'd want to be an astronomer. As a kid she liked the stars so much. She knew where all the constellations were. She would sit out at night and watch the sky, making up stories about what she saw up there. Some of them were pretty far-out. Monsters and massacres. You know how kids love gore."

"Not really." Philips, who had lost touch with his ex-wife

fifteen years ago, shook his head. "I don't have any kids." He could not imagine raising children anywhere near this place. The thought of what they might see in the sky around here made him wince. "Your kids grew up? . . ."

"Mostly around here. I settled here just before Kirsten was born. Her father got a job at the local newspaper as a photographer, but it didn't work out between us." She looked a little sad and more nostalgic. "He left the area twenty years ago. He said the place was wrong for him, that it made him want to get violent, and he was a pacifist. When we had those bomb threats, five years ago, he said I should get out of here, too. He said that there were too many dangerous people using airplanes—terrorists and crazy people. He's not a very open person."

"And you raised the kids?" said Philips. "Here?"

"Sure. He helped some, taking the kids during the summer and all, and sending money when he could. He got married about four years ago." She shook her head in remembered incredulity. "I never thought Bram would get married." She left the jewelry alone and turned to the shelves where a number of hardback gift books were for sale. As she rearranged the titles so that the ones dealing with Indians and Indian lore were most prominent, she went on, "Some friends of mine and I got a place out toward Santo Muerto—it's not far from here."

The name made Philips start. "Santo Muerto?"

"It's one of those little villages that's turning into a suburb, about a mile and a half from here. It used to be off on its own ten, twelve years ago. We ran a thirty-acre farm there for a couple years about ten years back; it's the richest soil in this part of Texas, and we wanted to use it right, at least at first." She felt evident pride at this. "We studied all the old ways, the way the Indians did it, planting the right kind of crops and raising them with all-natural fertilizers and like that. But we had some hard luck. It happens to farmers when they're not in tune with the earth, you know, and Kevin lost sight of that. He began using pesticides after the first two years because we had a lot of insect damage to our plants, and it kept getting worse. And something went wrong with the stuff he used. He got sick, and some of the people who ate our produce got sick. So we had to close the farm down and sell off half the land. Kevin's got cancer now. He's been in the hospital for the last five weeks."

"That's too bad; I'm sorry," said Philips, his heart thumping. This place is rotten, he thought, rotten to the core. And it pulls on me like an unholy magnet.

Senta looked up suddenly. "I've been prattling at you. I'm sorry." She gave him a direct, uncomplicated stare. "You're a pilot. That's got to be a lot more interesting than working at a gift counter at an airport."

Philips almost said, Not *this* airport, but managed to stifle the remark. "It's a job I'm good at," he said. "I've been doing it for what feels like forever."

"Have you always worked for Trager?" she asked, concentrating on his answer.

"Pretty much. I flew for TWA when I started out, but Trager made me a better offer after my second year, and I took it." He glanced toward the waiting area, and noticed that there was an indistinct figure at the far side of the cavernous space. The sight of that lone figure made him apprehensive.

She saw where he was looking, then showed him a reassuring smile. "It's just one of the airport staff. They have to check all the stations out before the airline people arrive."

"Oh," said Philips, with the unsettling feeling that this facile explanation was not entirely accurate.

"It's funny how the eyes play tricks on you," she went on, soothingly. "I thought I saw an Indian out there, late one night about six years ago. It was probably one of the security people checking out where the 747 crashed earlier in the day. It was because of the storm, they say. A terrible thing, you know? The storm knocked out all their instruments and they never realized how close to the ground they were as they came in. Almost everyone in the plane was killed, and two of the fire fighters too. I wasn't here when it happened, but I saw some of the wreckage, and it was on the news." She saw the revulsion in Philips' eyes. "Oh I'm sorry. I didn't think. You pilots probably don't like to hear about crashes, I guess."

"Don't things like that ever get to you?" Philips asked, suddenly appalled by her.

"Oh yes," she said. "If I'm not careful, any sad thing makes me lose my centering, you know? And I have to work hard to restore my balance, my proportion. I have to think of all the other people who die in senseless accidents and put that behind me before I can clear the negative things from my mind." She glanced in the direction of the shadowy figure again. "Sometimes, when I'm here alone at night, I use the time to meditate, to get in touch with my higher centers."

It struck Philips that there were few places in the world he would like less to meditate in than this airport, if he were into meditation. "I hope it helps," he said to let her know he was listening.

"Sometimes," she answered, and switched her attention to him again. "So I guess you don't live around here?"

"No," he said, adding silent thanks to himself.

"Where do you live?" she persisted, her bird-like hands now picking through the gum and candy, restoring order and improving the display.

He hesitated. "Not much of anywhere, really, except on Trager planes," he said. "The corporation rents apartments for their pilots in a dozen cities. Most of the time I stay in one of them. I'm registered to vote in San Diego and I carry a California driver's license. I get most of my mail through Trager's Chicago office. I get three weeks' vacation every year; usually I go deep-sea fishing." He admitted this apologetically, as if his way of life required it.

Senta's eyes were bright again. "That sounds like a wonderful way to live, just going anywhere in the world you want to."

"Not quite that," said Philips. "I go where Trager orders me, and I go when they tell me. It's a pretty rootless—"

"But still, they're all over the world, aren't they?" She did not wait for his answer. "I bet you've been to India."

"A few times," he said, and did not add that the poverty of the people and the unfamiliarity of the culture bothered him. "To Calcutta and New Delhi. Trager has projects in both places."

"That's wonderful." Her hands were more animated. "Have you ever been to China?"

"Yes," he said, finding her fascination flattering and

amusing. He had not thought of his life as adventurous in a long time.

"And Tibet? Or Katmandu?" She leaned forward for his answer.

"Neither; sorry." He hated to disappoint her. That sudden realization shook him and he watched her more closely. "I've been to Sri Lanka once, does that help?"

"I'll bet it was beautiful." She directed her gaze at him with such intensity that he thought she was trying to absorb his memories of the place with her eyes.

"It was very hot," he said. "I didn't see much of the place; I was taking a couple of company vice presidents to a meeting there, that's all."

"I met someone from Sri Lanka once, when I was working over in the international arm. That was before they moved the customs area, so I got to see more of the foreigners. Now all you find in that part of the terminal is returning Americans and people getting things at the duty-free shop before they leave." She braced her elbows on the counter and stared at him. "You've been everywhere, haven't you?"

He shrugged. "Mostly I've been in the cockpit of a plane," he said.

She clearly did not believe this. "But you get to *see* things, to watch the whole world."

"Sometimes," he admitted. "When there isn't too much cloud cover, or it isn't dark." Or when he was not approaching such godforsaken places as Dry Plains International Airport with the electrical system on the fritz and the controls sluggish as they were tonight when he landed, he added to himself.

The figure at the far side of the waiting area had vanished.

"You must have a copilot," she said suddenly.

"Yeah," he said, "and a navigator."

She looked around as if she expected to find them. "Aren't they with you?"

He sighed. "My copilot went into the city to get some sleep and my navigator's down at the medical station. He's been having stomach trouble." Poor Conrad had been bent nearly double when he got out the plane, breathing in gasps because of the pain. "He thinks it's a bad case of turista. Maybe it's a bad case of flu." As he said this, he found it harder to believe than he had when they landed: Philips had seen lots of cases of turista over the years, but none as severe as the case Conrad had. It was this place, he thought, this damned airport.

"I hope it isn't anything worse," said Senta, picking up some of his anxiety. "We had an outbreak of food-poisoning here last year. There were hundreds of people getting sick."

There were so few times that he had the luxury of unscheduled rest, thought Philips. Why did he have to be here when the opportunity struck? It didn't surprise him that there had been an outbreak of food poisoning here: He would not have been amazed to hear that the airport had anthrax, or bubonic plague. "What did you do?"

"We had to quarantine part of the airport, and some of the planes that had left reported that their passengers were sick. In fact the whole flight crew of one KAL came down with it." She heaved a gentle sigh. "There was an investigation, but nothing was ever proven. Accidents like that happen."

And they happen here more than any place he had ever been, thought Philips. "Doesn't that ever worry you? A place like this is so . . . unprotected. Someone could come through with a deadly disease and the only way you'd know would be when people start dying."

She did her best to look philosophical. "I don't like to let that bother me. I mean, if you think about it, anything might happen. Last week a guy lost control of his car on the upper deck and it smashed into the rail and crashed onto the road below. There was a big fire when the gas tank exploded. A couple of people said that he'd swerved to avoid a man standing on the road, but . . ." She shrugged. "It could have been that or a flat tire or anything. It was right during rush hour, and I was late to work because of the traffic. I didn't know what happened until I got here and the afternoon girl told me." She lowered her eyes. "I hate it when bad things happen. I just hate it."

Philips wanted to know why she worked here, of all places, if that was how she felt, but he managed not to speak his thoughts aloud. "I know what you mean."

Suddenly she looked at him, and there was a fanaticism blazing in her faded eyes. "I want to be more like them, you know? Like the Indians who lived here. They were good people, and they . . . they were *better* than we are. If you go out in the fields at night, in Santo Muerto, you can feel them all around you, strong and . . . real. Sometimes they seem more real than most of the people getting off planes. You know?"

He dreaded to think that he did, and yet he could feel some of her yearning in himself; he recognized it with repugnance. "I've noticed something like that, around here."

She moved as near as the counter between them would allow. "It used to frighten me. When I first got here, it scared me. I felt . . . out of my depth, you know? But not any more. Now I know how wonderful it is, to be near all the knowledge and the power."

Philips shook his head. "If you like it, I guess—" He stopped abruptly.

Senta went on as if she had not noticed he had left his thoughts incomplete. "I used to worry about all kinds of things, little things. But since I've learned how it was here, how they were wise enough to have something to die for, I've been . . . oh, I don't know. Maybe eager, or envious that they were so much more true to themselves than regular people." Her gesture took in the empty waiting area. "After my son died, for a while I couldn't stand this place. I blamed it. I thought that it had caused the trouble with the blood, that there was a plot or conspiracy or something. But it wasn't that, not really. It was that none of us were worthy yet."

A few times in Philips's career he had had conversations like this one, deep discussions with near-strangers about matters he would not discuss with anyone he saw regularly. It struck him that this was one of those conversations, and that in spite of the repellant aspect of the airport, this soft-voiced woman was drawing him toward her, as the tarmac drew his plane. "How could worth have anything to do with what happened to your boy?" He did not want to reveal his thoughts for fear of what the place would do with them, but he wanted to offer her sympathy or some consolation in this terrible place.

"I know that's the trouble," she said earnestly. "Because I

don't know anyone who has something they're willing to die for, not any more." Her smile was short and wistful. "I thought I had, once, but I don't know."

This confession only strengthened Philips' resolve to do what he could to show her she was wrong. "You're being too hard on yourself, and too easy on this place."

"Don't say that," she said to him, putting her hand out as if to close his mouth with it. "This is a special place, remarkable and special, and that makes ordinary things more obvious for what they are."

"No," he protested. "That's not it." He wanted to argue with her, but all the coffee he had drunk was making demands on his bladder he could no longer ignore. "I'll be back in a moment," he said and went out to the men's room.

Standing in the empty room, he stared at the white surface of the urinal, taking care not to look in any of the mirrors in the room. He had done that once here, and the memory of the hideous thing he saw could still sicken him. He closed his fly, washed his hands with his face averted from the mirror, and reached for a paper towel. Out of the corner of his eye a reflection caught his attention, but he refused to look at the image in the glass, and left with only a vision of a head with eyes removed and blood running down the hollow cheeks. I've got to get out of here, Philips thought as he rushed out the men's room door. I've got to get out of here.

"You look tired," said Senta as Philips came back to the gift shop. She was aligning the paperback books now, putting the ones with the brightest covers at eye level. "I hadn't meant to keep you up."

"I have to wait, anyway," said Philips, thinking that his expression had more to do with what he had almost seen than with the hour. "I'll get a chance to rest once I talk to the day crew about the plane."

"That'll be pretty soon, then, I guess," she said, giving him another of her smiles. "It's wonderful having someone to talk to. Most nights I'm lucky if I have a dozen customers, and most of them don't have anything much to say. The administration talked about closing this shop down, but they decided against it. They want one service and one food area open on each arm, all the time, and for this arm—this was the best offer for me." She gestured to indicate the little shop.

"I hope they pay you very well," said Philips with feeling.

"Pretty well," she said. "Better than the waitresses and like that. And I'm bonded. They pay for that, too." She came back toward him. "You know, talking to you, I can't stop thinking about traveling again, going all those places I've always wanted to go. I think you're the luckiest man in the world, flying everywhere, seeing everything."

"It's my job," said Philips, who did not think he was as lucky as she did. "It's demanding, and it's pretty solitary, when you come right down to it."

"This is solitary," she said. "You're free."

Philips did not want to dispute the matter. "I suppose it looks like that," he conceded.

Her eyes brightened again with excitement. "I wish I could go with you when you leave. Just fly wherever you're going—"

"Chicago," he said.

"Chicago, Boston, Montreal, Hawaii, Melbourne, it doesn't matter. Houston would be different." She recited the names as if they were her saints and she their acolyte.

"You can go there, Senta," he said with a sudden welling of kindness for this woman. "Take a weekend, or a vacation, and go anywhere you want to go."

She turned to him. "It wouldn't be the same, going by myself. It would be a trip, not . . . not a journey. Don't you see the difference?" She held two paperbacks in her hands, one promising the bloodiest secrets of organized crime, the other offering the thrill and titillation of the sexual peculiarities of the very rich.

He had to answer honestly. "No, not really."

She gave a short sigh. "No, you probably wouldn't, because you do it all the time. You think it's ordinary, not special. But you're wrong." She put the books into the wire racks and came up to him. "You don't go places for vacations, or to be a tourist, you go there for the going. That's what makes you special. It's what I wish I could do."

"It's not . . . the way you think," he said, looking down at the hope that still shone in her eyes.

"But it is," she said. "I wish I could prove it to you."

Impulsively she reached out and took his hand. "I wish I could go with you. I mean that." She saw his doubt and released his hand. "For years I thought I couldn't do anything, that I had to stay here, because I had so much to do here, with the kids and all. I have a home and . . . things. Just things. But if I could be really free, then I'd chuck it all for it."

Before he could stop himself he asked, "And what about being worthy?"

She beamed at him. "But I would be, don't you see? I'd show that something meant more to me than this place, than the things I have, than any of it. I would be worthy then. I'd be able to die for something."

The alarm Philips felt was so great that he had to make himself remain where he was instead of fleeing. "I don't think," he said, each word separate and distinct, "I don't think it would be the way you imagine it would."

"I know it would," she said with serene confidence. "Five years ago I might have doubted, but since Eric died, I've known that if I could just find a way to be free . . ."

The silence between them lengthened, widening like a chasm.

"Maybe Trager'll let me take you up to Chicago," he said at last, in an effort to reach her. At the same time he called himself a fool for making such an offer. "You'll have to find your own way back, but I guess you could arrange that, couldn't you?"

Her grin was wide and delighted. "You *mean* that? Really? *Really?*"

While he was not convinced it was true, he said, "Yes. Sure."

She reached out to take his hand again, faltered, and stepped back. "That's wonderful of you. Wonderful." She looked away, speaking more softly. "If you can't do it after all, that's okay. I won't mind. It's enough that you offered, you know?"

"I'll ask when I call in my report." He did his best to sound emphatic. "It'd be nice to have company, other than the copilot and the navigator."

She clasped her hands together to avoid reaching out to him again. "That's wonderful. Just wonderful."

"I'll let you know," he promised her. He felt restless again, antsy, and he looked out through the huge shop windows to the boarding area.

Two figures waited there this time, but they were both carrying cases and had the unmistakable look of early travelers struggling to wake up.

"It's twenty to six," said Senta, observing him. "Probably time for you to go down to the repair hangars."

"Yeah," he said, aware that the sky was lightening. He turned and stared at her. "I will ask, and if they say yes, I will take you up to Chicago. I mean it."

She nodded once. "Thanks." After a moment she added, "This is a hard place to leave. You know?"

He hesitated, thinking there ought to be something more that he could say; then he strode off toward the central terminal, still feeling the airport all around him like a clammy odor. He wanted to get away from the place, and the sooner the better.

Just as sunset slipped into dusk the next evening, the Trager jet rolled out onto runway Number Four of Dry Plains International Airport. Galen Philips was at the controls; his copilot was David Reissman and his navigator was Jose Aguerrez. They flew an empty plane because D. A. Landis had refused to allow an unknown passenger on board.

As they rolled past the arm where Senta's shop was, Philips could not help glancing up, wishing he had been able to take her along. It was such a minor thing, and it would have meant a lot to her, or so she said. He thought that maybe if she had been able to leave Dry Plains for a day or two, she might have realized what a pernicious place it really was.

There was a figure in the vast window fronting the waiting area, and a single figure stood in it, a shadow of greater darkness than the shadows around it. As Philips watched, he saw the figure raise an arm and wave to him.

"Senta," he said, and against all his professional impulses, waved back. It was the least he could do, after he had failed to get approval to fly her to Chicago. It was only

Chicago, he said to himself. It's not as if I asked to bring her along on my next flight to India.

He never saw the landing 737 skid out of control just as its wheels touched down. There was a dull sound as the 737 exploded, lifting back into the air in the midst of flames, and then pinwheeled toward the Trager jet.

"What the—" the copilot began.

The explosion reached them, slamming the plane into the side of the airport arm a quarter of a second before the ball of flames engulfed them, bursting what the impact had not broken.

In the gift shop at the far side of the boarding area, Senta lifted her hands to her face and screamed as the window erupted in fire and glass.

JET LAG

Ron Dee and P. D. Cacek

FROM 37,000 FEET, THE HAZE-COVERED METROPOLITAN AREAS looked like just so many tiny dots tossed across the landscape.

Dillon Stuart hated flying—he hated the idea of hurtling through the air inside a hollow wrapping of relatively thin metal, glimpsing (though he always tried not to) the looming clouds that swept past and the ground so far below.

It made him dizzy.

It made him *ill.*

Like now.

He hated paying for the privilege of making himself sick by traveling this way, and was barely grateful for the new low airline rates that made this torment slightly less betraying . . . rates so gentle he was surprised a whole planeload of tickets could even pay for the fuel. The airline had begun the program for infrequent travelers. No discount points offered.

But Dillon had no desire to be a frequent flyer. It was bad enough that he had no way to avoid this trip. His boss insisted on the international meeting at Helsinki, but to Dillon it was a trip to Hell . . . even the airline had agreed, abbreviating Helsinki's name to *Destination: Hel.*

Any place would feel like hell by the time he finished this damned flight!

The airline's motto: *We give you what you want at the lowest rate you can afford and get you there in one piece.*

One piece. He would be lucky not to leave his entire stomach on board.

To begin this rare flight, Dillon had bravely stared out the porthole and tried using the swizzle stick from his second vodka collins to connect the city-dots below.

But it hadn't been anywhere as easy as connecting the dots on his latest business triumph, the Ked-Corp acquisition.

He gagged again to keep himself from throwing up, then did his best to ignore the piggy-eyed glare from the aisle seat beside him—an aging biker in stained jeans and a faded concert T-shirt. These cut-rate flights had attracted some of the lowest scum he could imagine.

Sweat was beginning to dribble down Dillon's hot face, and his stomach was twisting harder.

Not even the success he'd had swallowing one of the most promising biochemical companies made it better. Not even the sight of the approaching dark-haired stewardess in her tight, tiny uniform—

"Sir? Are you all right?"

Dillon was holding his mouth with his hand now, wanting to make a grab for the upchuck bag in the seat compartment ahead of him, but—

She was attractive. Tall and lithe, black hair sexily tapered around her cheeks and forehead.

"Sir . . ."

He swallowed the first saliva of illness willfully, keeping his eyes on her and trying to distract himself by imagining the body under her uniform. The feel of her breasts under the name tag: *Lillis.*

But he could not get up much interest in even that.

"Can I get you anything, sir? Are you feeling ill?"

"I think . . . I'm okay." He dropped his palm and sat up straight, drawing a snort from the biker.

"I think I want another seat," the biker said.

Lillis glanced through the plane and nodded, pointing out an empty chair two rows up. The biker unbuckled and left with a taunting glare of disgust.

Lillis sat down in the empty seat.

Dillon smiled the best he could, trying harder to ignore the way his stomach was dive-bombing him again.

"There's been some very slight turbulence . . . barely enough to be noticable, but sometimes it bothers people who are especially sensitive," she smiled, her eyes on Dillon's. "I guess you're a sensitive kind of guy, huh? Maybe we should get together sometime . . ." Her smile grew. "Would another drink make you feel better?"

He felt the blood drain out of his face and tried to pretend he hadn't seen the twinkle it brought to her eyes. "I . . . don't think so . . ."

The intercom gave off three airline gongs and Lillis looked up at the lighted warning sign.

Dillon felt the jet's tremble battling the tremors in his stomach. "God—"

Lillis leaned closer and dropped her hand over his seatbelt buckle, making sure it was fastened.

"I guess it's getting a bit worse," she spoke calmly. "Don't you worry a bit, sir. We'll take good care of you—it's our motto to give you what you want." Her fingers dropped two inches and disbelievingly, he felt the gentle stroke she gave him. Felt her kneading fingers curl around him through his slacks.

But she winked. "Let me know if you need anything, sir."

Nodding as best he could while the plane rolled and the engines shrieked, he swallowed bile once more and—

Felt the plane fall out from under him.

Screaming.

Dillon was gasping, feeling his own warm, wet illness covering his shirt and tie . . . smelling it and wanting to be ill all over again.

He coughed and sprayed, but managed to steady himself as he focused on Lillis and another stewardess. They were doing all they could to reassure the other frantic passengers. The noise all but drowned out the low voice of the captain over the intercom.

A calm woman's voice broke out more loudly on that speaker: *"Ladies and gentlemen . . . the captain assures me that everything is under control. We are currently experiencing some Clear Air Turbulence . . . a condition known as 'CAT.' There is no reason for concern—"*

The chaos of voices ebbed slowly.

"I must ask you to remain in your seats with your seatbelts secured until the captain turns out the sign—"

The rest of the unknown woman's words were lost on Dillon as Lillis sat back down beside him and wrinkled her nose. He blushed.

"What a mess you are," Lillis smiled.

Dillon's face got hotter. "I . . . I need to clean up—this is a five hundred dollar suit—"

"Calm down, sir. Everyone *must* keep their seats now—"

The smell of his vomit was only making his need to repeat it worse . . . like a perpetual motion machine. "I have to clean up—*give me what I want!*" His shuddering fingers released the catch on the safety belt and he grabbed her wrist, fighting the bumps and rolls to stand—

—as the plane roller-coastered.

—sucking Dillon's stomach inside out.

The wild tug threw him against Lillis and his forehead smacked hers painfully. She went down and Dillon barely managed to hold himself up by grabbing an old lady's arm, ignoring her squeal that was only one of dozens.

Keeping himself steady by reaching his hands to the chairs on either side of the aisle, Dillon gurgled the liquid stench surging up his throat and kept his jaws tightly shut, making his slow way to the back section and the restrooms.

"Sir!"

It was Lillis. Already, he recognized her cool voice.

But he kept on.

"Sir—it is dangerous for you to be standing!"

By the time he reached the two closet-sized cubicles at the back wall, Dillon's hands were shaking so badly he wondered if he would be able to open the nearest door.

But he did.

"You must return to your seat *immediately,* sir!"

But as the plane bucked up and down, back and forth, Dillon was thrown into the tiny restroom. Once more, he threw out his hands for support, turning.

He saw the rows of passengers, some with heads bowed in prayer, some with faces plunged into their sick bags . . . their open mouths silent in the whine of battling engines and the crackling, indecipherable voice of the intercom.

Lillis, her smooth walk somehow unaffected, came right towards him.

"Sir!"

Kicking the door with one hysterical foot, Dillon slammed it shut in her face . . . felt a new flood of hot bile creep up the back of his tongue.

Sliding the "occupied" latch into place, he slumped back against the flimsy press-board, gulping air like a suffocating trout.

The gentle rap on the door seemed louder than the constant roar of the jets.

"Are you all right, sir?"

Kneeling in front of the stainless steel toilet, he held tight with one hand and ran his other through sweat-slick hair. Just in time, he dropped his face into the bowl and heard the wet splash of his retch.

And then another.

It went on forever.

Empty and weak, Dillon pulled the handle to open the suction release and fell backwards, banging his head on the door, crumpled against the tight confining walls as he tried to lie as flat as he could . . .

When his eyes opened again, it was almost as though it had all been a nightmare—

The screams and cries had stopped. Silent except for the jets.

Dillon felt his heart thudding painfully against the inside of his ribs and remembered . . .

Long ago.

He had found a bird torn open by his cat . . . held it in his hands as he tried to find help—his mother—

Its heart had been beating just as hard as the wings that flapped around his fingers . . . right before it died.

Maybe . . . maybe *he* was dying . . .

Closing his eyes again, Dillon let the plane rock him in its now-gentle arms.

A second later, the door's support of his neck disappeared and he was falling again. His head dropped to the hard floor. *Crash.*

Stale, foul air swam up his nose, taunting him with the need of a revived nausea.

Dillon choked and gasped.

A hand clutched his shoulder.

"Sir?"

Lillis.

Her arms went around him and she helped him stand.

"What—*happened?*" he gurgled.

She pressed him back inside the stall and entered with him, then shut the door tight, latching it.

Occupied.

"What . . .?"

"What a *mess!*" Lillis giggled, her voice sweet and light. Saccharine.

He saw the splotches of the sickness he had infected her white uniform with when he had fallen against her. She stared down at herself with him. "Both of us—*what a mess, huh?*"

His bobbing stomach was empty.

"Let's get out of these and clean up . . . and get you back to your seat, all right?"

Dillon couldn't reply. He wanted to vomit again so badly he would have sold his soul, but nothing but painful upchucks of air would come out.

He stared at her. Her back . . . at the shapely ass facing him as he crouched up against her. Her cool fingers touched his and lifted them to the zipper at her neck.

"Unzip me please."

"I—"

"*Now.*"

Her voice was firm . . . as firm as the globes of her cheeks. He felt her skin tighten under his fingers as he lowered the zipper and wished he could feel the interest he wanted to have.

The nightmare hadn't ended. He knew he was still trapped inside a dream . . .

She slipped out of the dress, braless and naked, tilted her face to the side and pursed her red lips. "Now you."

He didn't resist. Knew this wasn't possible . . . wasn't real.

But he shivered as the goose bumps formed on his bare skin.

"Why . . . what? . . ."

Lillis stroked him even though he was too disoriented and ill to react. "We had a small problem with the atmospheric pressure, but there's nothing to worry about now." She picked up her dress and all his clothing and stuffed it all into the waste door, piece by piece.

We'll get you there in one piece . . .

His Brooks Brothers suit. Even his shoes.

He could barely hold himself up. "I—"

Her lopsided grin was full of fun, and she pressed it to his lips, leaning back onto the sink cabinet and parting her thighs.

"I don't believe this . . ."

"Anything to keep you calm and happy, sir."

She pulled him against her . . . inside her.

The sickness disappeared and they struggled together in the tiny room as best they could, forgetting comfort in the need that was growing hotter inside him.

All too soon, it was over . . . and Dillon felt sicker than ever.

She took his hand briskly. "Come on now, sir. You've had your pleasure and taken care of your business, right? Now let's get back into our seat like a good boy and strap ourselves in, all right?"

Following her tugs, he knew this was one hell of a dream . . . the *worst* nightmare he'd ever known: Here was the fantasy of fucking a stacked stewardess brainless and he was too sick now to revel in it—to even *want* to believe it had happened!

She led him up through the rows of seats, both of them still naked.

He was blushing, hoping that this *was* a dream where no one would notice.

But then he saw that all the others were naked, too—saw another stewardess climbing off an old man's lap . . . a steward kneeling between a fat woman's bulging thighs . . .

"What?—"

And then he noticed the air-mask hoses hanging down, leading to the masks covering every passenger's face—the new improved masks that even covered the eyes.

"You'll need to wear your mask, too," Lillis sighed, glancing back at him. "Captain's orders."

"But—"

She was practically dragging him now.

He tried to hold himself back, but couldn't. Only long

enough to stare at a skinny teenage boy who was frantically banging his head against the back of his seat. A stewardess was fulfilling his dreams too, and dismounted him a moment later.

But there was something else wrong with the picture: Through the clear plastic mask the boy's eyes were flying open and clamping shut again and again as vivid spasms rocked his body—

As the plastic on his face turned red with the syrup that coated his features . . . as the dark liquid was sucked up into the air hose . . .

Into the plane.

"Christ!"

"Don't trouble yourself, sir. Everything's under control."

The icy fingers clamped over his wrists were unrelenting.

With an effort, Dillon looked back and saw the final drops of red from the teenager disappearing up the hose into . . .

The plane.

And then he saw another passenger. Focused on her gaunt, shapeless face that was pale and loose as though the mask hanging on her face had slurped the very life out of her.

And the man beside her . . . and in the row ahead of her . . . and beside him.

The whole fucking plane!

"Noooo!"

He hit Lillis with a wild punch and felt his mushy fist crumple against her bare flesh; fell back . . .

Into the hard, bony lap of what had once been a woman. Dillon tore at her mask and wanted to retch more than ever when he saw the hole it had left in her face . . . a raw, gaping wound in the outline of the mask—

Warm crimson dots splashed all over Dillon.

The mask leapt up on its own and flew against the splatters on Dillon's chest, and he felt the urgent suction of hot desire dragging his own skin.

"God damn it—"

He pulled away and felt the first layer of his flesh tear and shred as he escaped . . . the mask dancing in the air as it tried to pull loose from the jet's ceiling to come after him.

"Calm down!" commanded Lillis, clawing Dillon brutally now, pushing him ahead of her and into his seat.

Dillon saw the biker in the rows ahead, pale and lifeless in his new chair . . .

"Please—"

Lillis pulled the mask hanging above him closer . . . and he saw the double row of curving incisors edging it . . .

"Ple—"

She laughed brightly and shook her head. "Seatbelts first! I'm sorry, sir. You've confused me. Let me help you strap in—" Her strong hand pressed him back into the surrounding cushions and she locked the belt around his middle, shocking him with the cold buckle.

"Now—"

"You . . . you *can't*—"

Her hand dropped to squeeze him again . . . her other hand pushing the mask to his face . . .

She held his arms tight against the armrests.

Cold air that tasted of machine staleness filled Dillon's lungs as the mask grew tighter around his cheeks and forehead . . .

Then the air was pulled back . . . becoming a suction . . .

He felt his tongue pried out of his mouth . . . the skin of his face separating from the bone . . . his eyes—

His eyes.

Dillon opened his mouth wider to shriek the incredible agony as sight popped out of his head and he went blind, feeling the eyeroots tugged out . . .

. . . as his lungs decompressed in a drowning flood of blood that shot up his throat like the vomit he'd longed to be free of only minutes before.

He felt his heart tearing itself from its cavity . . . his teeth . . . his brain . . .

Seeping through the holes where his eyes had once been . . . through his open, gagging mouth.

"It's so much faster this way," Dillon heard Lillis saying distantly as he left life behind. *"So much more efficient! I'm even getting a paycheck now!"*

He suddenly knew why the airline didn't offer frequent flyer points.

CLEANSING AGENT

Don D'Ammassa

IT WAS IMPOSSIBLE, BUT DANNY HEARD A TOILET FLUSH IN ONE OF the empty stalls.

He jumped at the sound, whispered "What the fuck?" under his breath, wishing he had a weapon, the Magnum he'd lost in a poker game, a knife, even a wrench. He'd just finished checking out the entire men's room and knew there was no chance that he might have overlooked anyone, and the fixtures were so primitive, there couldn't have been an automatic timer.

He moved to the far wall, where a row of filthy sinks underlined a murky mirror. There were six stalls; he counted them again just as he had the first time, when he'd swung each door open in turn, revealing nothing more alarming than wads of damp toilet paper lying on the floor, dangling from the fixtures, or draped over the cracked porcelain seats. Each door remained open as he'd left them, the sound of rushing water coming from somewhere near the far end, one of the last two.

"Anybody in there?" His voice sounded unnaturally hoarse, an old man's querulous inquiry, totally inappropriate for someone who had celebrated, after a fashion, his twenty-first birthday only a few months earlier. And a lifetime ago.

Another step and fresh pain blossomed just above his groin. Danny ignored it as best he could, trying not to remember the mass of bruised flesh that girdled his body, already turning grey and purple and yellow. He had no watch, and when he'd regained consciousness, there was only the vaguest sense of the passage of time. Minutes, or hours? He'd been too busy to worry about it, too busy taking inventory of his battered body and shattered self-confidence.

They were supposed to be his friends, the foursome who'd turned on him treacherously just as he was about to divide up the spoils of their cooperative effort. Only Tanya had made him uneasy at times; she always looked at him as though he smelled bad. But Buzz and Dylan insisted it was all an act with her, that everything was cool, and Lizzie, well, she'd been giving him the eye a little when the others weren't looking, as though she were interested in something more than business but not sure enough to act right out in the open. He'd played it cool and waited for his chance, thinking he was about to score big with one of the best-looking chicks he'd ever been close enough to touch.

Well, they'd touched all right. He particularly remembered the expression on her face when she stood over him, kicking his ribs so hard it must have hurt her as well, but with a face so full of the pure joy of inflicting pain that he wasn't surprised when she kept right on with it, probably even after he'd passed out. Afterwards, they'd bundled him into a narrow closet and left him to recover or die on his own. There'd been an ominous amount of blood in his urine when he'd pissed a few minutes ago, sitting in one of the stalls, trying to pull himself back together.

The final gurgles subsided and silence returned. Danny walked to the far end of the room, supporting himself with one hand brushing across the rims of the sinks. There was no one there; he was alone in the bowels of the airport.

Danny was good at his chosen profession, a natural talent he'd nursed from a smoldering ember to a raging fire. While his newfound business partners were distracting people with their outrageous appearance and language, he moved among the crowd, collecting wallets almost at will, so many that he'd worried a security guard would notice the bulges in his intentionally voluminous clothing. But everyone was preoccupied, still wondering what had caused a passenger flight to crash on the main runway earlier in the day, and he'd been amazed at how easily things had gone.

He had removed all the cash and had been about to count the not inconsiderable evening's take when Buzz hit him from behind, and the money was falling from his numb fingers as Tanya pivoted on her heel and kicked him in the balls. It still hurt to think about it, not just the terrifying, utterly devastating pain, but the expression on her face as she did it—not cruelty, not anger, not anything he could live with. Tanya looked as though she'd turned over a rock and found something too loathsome to tolerate, something that needed to be squashed, destroyed, utterly expunged from the world.

The stalls were still empty, all of them. There was no place to hide, no utility closet, ventilation duct, or any other feature that might conceal an unseen lurker. He was alone in the restroom just as he had been ever since he'd regained consciousness in the maintenance closet and staggered here.

There was a sudden twist in his gut and Danny turned, leaning over the sink, waiting for his gorge to rise. But although he tasted the bitterness of bile at the back of his throat, his stomach lacked the contents, or the strength, to follow through. When he was sure the spasm was over, he splashed lukewarm water onto his face, blinked rapidly, trying to evaluate himself in the steamy mirror.

He couldn't believe how humid it was down here; the walls were dripping with condensation, as though he'd stumbled into the stomach of some plastic-and-concrete behemoth. He used his sleeve to clear a roughly circular spot in the mirror, brushed at his clothing. There was blood, but not a great deal of it, and the stains were already dried. His padded vest was reversible and he shrugged it off, moaning briefly as bruised ribs protested this exertion. Bruised or broken? He didn't want to deal with the second possibility.

With the lighter side of his vest showing, he was satisfied that his appearance was sufficiently acceptable that children would not run screaming from his presence. Danny turned away from the mirror and had actually started toward the exit when the toilet flushed again. But this time the sound was different, not a flush exactly, more like a prolonged swallow. There was something about it that suggested a living creature, something that Danny was not sure he was willing to face. Without glancing toward the row of stalls, he took a deep breath and crossed to the door, swung it open, and stepped out into the corridor.

There was a painting on the facing wall, one of a number of poorly rendered murals that were sprinkled throughout Dry Plains International Airport. Danny was aware of their presence without having taken conscious note of their subject matter, but this particular mural was so grotesque, so out of place, that he stood transfixed for long seconds.

His eyes were drawn initially to the small pile of bones in the exact center of the scene, a horned head vaguely reminiscent of a steer, although there were subtle differences which might have been attributable to careless artistry, or which might have been designed to imply something else entirely, a species driven to extinction, or perhaps one that existed only in legends.

The bones were flanked by scattered cacti and dead trees, and in the branches of those trees sat four starkly rendered, ominous creatures—vultures, wings held close against attenuated bodies, long beaks, scaly talons clutched tightly around their perches. There was something vaguely familiar about them, so tantalizing that Danny stood transfixed, staring, until he decided he was interpreting the painting through a filter of his own preoccupation. Certainly one vulture was holding its head at the same odd angle that Dylan used when he was contemplating mischief, and another stared with the same intolerant expression he'd seen in Tanya's eyes, but that couldn't be anything other than simple coincidence.

Danny forced himself to turn away and headed toward the staircase that led up to the main concourse. He could hear the sounds of human activity, muffled, like distant thunder. Earlier, the five of them had slipped past the ropes and signs indicating that this section of the airport was "Closed for Renovation," secure in their belief that no one would be working in the small hours of a Sunday morning, that they'd be uninterrupted.

There were featureless doors on either side of the corridor, differentiated only by small signs with block lettering. ELECTRIC, he read; PERSONNEL, MAINTENANCE, LOST AND FOUND, SATISFACTION, and SUPPLIES. Danny was several meters beyond before the oddity registered. Satisfaction? He stopped, half-turned, squinting to reread the sign in question. It still bore the same letters, clear and enigmatic at the same time.

Danny backed up and knocked hesitantly, then said "Fuck it!" softly and tried the knob. It turned easily. The room beyond was dimly lit and unfurnished. The walls were plain and unadorned, no windows, not even a calendar to break up the smooth plains of off-white, softened even further by the inadequate illumination provided by a single fluorescent light. A table stood in the center, covered with dust so thick that Danny almost failed to notice the faint outline of two objects, a torn scrap of paper and a small metal key.

He leaned forward and blew the worst of the dust away, then picked up the paper using just the tips of his fingers, shaking it until it was relatively clean. It was a detailed black and white map of the airport with a single black "X" marked near the upper right-hand corner. Danny folded it carefully and slipped it into his hip pocket, then picked up the key, still bright and shiny despite the layer of dirt, engraved with the number 216 along its stem.

There were several rows of short-term rental lockers near the gift shop upstairs. Apparently one of the keys had been misplaced a long time ago. With any luck, the locker was back in service and might well contain something Danny could use, preferably cash or something he could hock, although he wouldn't have minded even a fresh set of clothing.

He closed the door behind him when he left.

It seemed as though there were far more steps leading up than there had been coming down, one short flight after another, interspersed with gently inclined ramps. Danny felt as if he were plodding an endless treadmill, wondering if his strength would hold out long enough for him to reach the upper levels. And just as he was considering stopping for a while, to catch his breath and will away the throbbing pain in his ribs and thighs and the center of his forehead, he found his way barred by an imitation velvet rope, pale yellow, draped from stanchion to stanchion like stringy intestines.

There were people beyond, but fewer than he expected, most sitting or standing in small, isolated clusters throughout the concourse. The concessions were all closed except for a small coffee shop at the far end, whose lights blinked irregularly. No one sat at the counter, although a hunched form was visible in a corner booth, motionless, perhaps asleep. A uniformed man with a fixed expression of disinterest was pushing a wide-headed broom across the floor, leaving small piles of debris at odd locations, following no pattern, never clearing any of the accumulation away.

Danny stepped over the cordon and pushed forward.

The locker was on the rear side of one row, facing the wall, sheltered from observation. Danny inserted the key and twisted, half expecting the lock to have been changed, but there was a slight, distinct click and when he pulled on the handle, the door slid smoothly open. There was a small paper bag inside, the open end folded over and stapled shut.

Disappointed already, Danny ripped the paper angrily, expecting to find a couple of magazines or an embossed sweatshirt or something equally useless. What he did find was a snub-nosed pistol, clean and well-oiled, and loaded with six cartridges. He glanced around nervously, made certain that no one was watching, then slipped the weapon into the inside pocket of his vest, adjusted the way it fell until he was confident no one would be able to see it.

The presence of the pistol was like a powerful analgesic and much of the pain receded, his back straightened, and he raised his chin, drawing from this newfound source of strength. Satisfaction, the sign had read, which right now meant revenge, and he had the instrument of that imperative at hand. Buzz and Dylan, Tanya and Lizzie, yes, most of all Lizzie, with her treacherous unspoken promises, they were all fair game now. All he had to do was find them. It never occurred to Danny that they might have left the airport, dispersed to whatever crumbling tenement they called home. He knew with absolute certainty that they were still around, still within reach, believing him unconscious or even dead back where they had dumped him. He even fancied he could detect a faint trace of Lizzie's perfume in the air.

But how was he going to find them?

Danny returned to the concourse, strolling with deliberate casualness in a great circle. Most of the handful of people he passed turned away rather than meet his eyes; a few stared back defiantly. The man with the broom was making a fresh circuit, rearranging the small piles of candy wrappers, cigarette butts, claims stubs, and other debris into fresh patterns no less confused and useless than before. If Danny had been in a more settled frame of mind, he might have wondered at the air of lethargic chaos that reigned tonight, might have noticed that all flights, both incoming and outgoing, were labelled on the overhead monitors as "Canceled" or "Delayed." But his own preoccupations were paramount.

He climbed an open-railed staircase to the observation deck, found it abandoned, crossed to the wall of reinforced windows and stared down onto the airfield proper. Two planes were snug up against one wing of the airport off to his left, but their lights were all off and there was no flurry of baggage handlers and mechanics, no indication that passengers were boarding or disembarking. In both directions, the umbilicals designed to offload passengers were partially extended, making gentle curves like the talons of a vulture.

No, he told himself, almost speaking aloud. More like the fingers of a sleeping child. The airport is a body, he realized, and tonight he'd crawled out of its very bowels, no, its heart, an antibody of some kind, a white blood cell on a mission to seek out and destroy invading parasites. That's what they were, all right, Dylan and Tanya and the others. Parasites. Danny had always thought of his own thievery as a game, sleight of hand, his wits and skill and agility pitted against those of his victims. No one was ever hurt, not really, just inconvenienced. And he passed over those who looked as though they couldn't afford the loss of a few dollars, telling himself he acted out of compassion, never admitting that the truth was that the small potential gain was not worth the risk.

Danny had teamed up with others in the past; it always helped to have a distraction, a loud and carefully staged argument, hot coffee spilled over someone's tailor-made suit, even once an impromptu folk-singing duet whose talents might well have been more profitable had they been directed toward a more constructive goal. He'd always worked out the split in advance and never backed away, even on those occasions when he could have run off with the entire take. Danny had standards, what he thought of as his personal code of honor.

He'd made a mistake in allowing himself to become involved with the foursome, but they'd made a bigger one in letting him survive the encounter.

The airport complex seemed even larger from up here, sprawling in several directions, the original building lost in a complicated series of additions, modifications, and then abbreviations as certain underutilized areas were closed off, their functions consolidated elsewhere. It was a bewildering maze taken as a whole, and Danny felt a brief moment of despair when he realized how easy it would be for the others to conceal themselves. There were multiple walkways between the main structures, a system of veins and arteries that rivalled the human body in scale.

Then he remembered the map.

It was still in his pocket and when he unfolded the creased paper, the semblance of a living creature was even more obvious. The two parking ramps at the south end could be legs, although certainly not those of a human—they were more insectlike, with sharp angles at the joints and a length disproportionate to their width. The passenger terminal made up a stubby torso, no real arms although it was possible to imagine them tucked close to the chest, with only the hands and fingers extended. The cluster of restaurants, gift shops, and other concessions formed a misshapen head.

The "X" he'd seen earlier was drawn precisely over an unlabelled square next to the shallow garage where the baggage trucks were parked. Even from the observation deck, and despite the floodlights spaced evenly outside the building, Danny could barely distinguish the garage's roof from the surrounding shadows. But it felt right.

It took several minutes to discover the small accessway, an unmarked door whose lock succumbed to one of Danny's other acquired skills. He descended a short ramp covered by a flapping tent, realized the wind had picked up outside, the hot, dry air filled with particles of dust that stung when they struck unprotected flesh. Hunching his shoulders, he stepped beyond the fabric, blinking as he reoriented himself.

There! The building was surrounded by a hurricane fence, but the gate was unlocked. He removed the pistol from his vest and held it against his hip as he moved quickly to the side of the windowless building. It was loud out there, he realized, not just the wind but a rhythmic thrumming that came from the external blowers of the airport's ventilation system. Canvas had been stretched between two posts to break the force of the exhaust, and the fabric billowed out, then fell back, then out again in a regular pattern that reminded him of a breathing creature.

Someone laughed inside the building. He barely heard it above the din, but never doubted the evidence of his senses. It was the familiar, unpleasantly nasal sound Tanya made when she was amused. The strangest things amused her he'd learned, usually things that he found sad or repulsive. His fingers tightened around the reassuring solidity of the pistol and he edged around the far corner and saw the door just a yard or so ahead.

As far as he knew, none of the others carried anything more dangerous than a pocketknife, but they'd deceived him on so much else, he wasn't prepared to take any chances. When he reached the door, he hesitated, assaulted by doubts. Did they know he was there? Were they waiting for him to come inside so they could finish what they'd begun earlier? Even if he surprised them, could he subdue all four before they could react and take the weapon away?

For a few seconds, his resolution faltered. He took one step back and relaxed his grip on the pistol, but as he did so the pain returned to his body with such immediate, overwhelming force that he doubled over, barely managing to retain his hold on the weapon. It was a clear message, but from whom?

"Okay," he whispered. "I won't chicken out." And as quickly as the pain had returned, it was gone.

They were sitting in a circle playing cards when he came through the door. Dylan looked startled, his face twisting into a defensive smile as he recognized Danny. The first bullet shattered the smile forever and the second quite unnecessarily struck him in the chest. Buzz and Lizzie were already diving for cover, but Tanya jumped to her feet and lunged forward, her eyes still filled with a raging contempt that only disappeared when she fell to her knees, staring disbelievingly at the small entry wound in her chest.

"You shithead!" It was the last insult she'd ever deliver.

Buzz and Lizzie had disappeared, concealed behind a pile of wooden crates and several pieces of machinery covered with tarps. This was a storage shed of some sort, Danny noted disinterestedly, as he moved slowly to one side in an effort to spot his prey.

A dark shape leaped out of the darkness, swinging something wildly as it came. Danny fired without conscious thought, then a second time when the shape continued to advance. Buzz slammed into him, still moving, but fell away before Danny had time to react further, dead before he hit the floor, a length of chain still clutched in one hand.

He found Lizzie crouched in a ball behind the last row of crates.

"Don't you come near me, you goddamned asshole!"

Danny stood just out of reach, the pistol angled toward the floor but ready to rise. He wondered now what he'd ever seen in her. There was a certain wild attractiveness, but the long black hair was unkempt and unclean. Lizzie deliberately wore excessive makeup and it was badly smeared, her cheeks wet with tears, forehead glistening with sweat.

"Come out of there." He said the words softly and she ignored him, so he raised the pistol and repeated the order, this time with clear menace. "Come out of there now."

She hesitated for only a second, then stood up, her arms pressed tight against her breasts, shivering slightly despite the heat. Danny gestured toward the door and followed her out, noticing that she carefully avoided looking at the bodies of her late friends. No, not friends, companions. People like Lizzie didn't have friends, as he'd so recently realized.

"What are you going to do?" She was making some effort to regain her self-control now that she realized he was not going to kill her out of hand. But what *was* he going to do? Danny suddenly realized that he'd spared her, up to this point, without a conscious plan. Did he intend rape? He considered it briefly, but the idea was unappealing. Lizzie revolted him now, her breasts and thighs were alien shapes, concealing alien pleasures.

"This way." He gestured toward their right, where a

walkway ran parallel to the main building, then angled in under an overhanging roof.

"Where are you taking me?" Strength was flowing back into her voice with every passing second. Enraged, Danny lunged forward, swung the butt of his pistol in a short, vicious arc that intersected with Lizzie's shoulder blade. She stumbled forward with a sharp cry, nearly fell.

"Just do what I tell you," he warned when she turned to face him, torn between fear and anger.

He used the last bullet to shatter the safety glass in an unmarked door, but Lizzie didn't seem to have been counting his shots and made no effort to escape. "Unlock it," he ordered and she reached carefully through the broken glass and did as she was told.

There was another door beyond, and this one opened into a familiar corridor. Lizzie reluctantly led the way past a double row of familiar doors, then around a corner into a dimly-lit dead end.

"Look familiar?"

Lizzie turned to face him, anger gone. "Listen, I didn't want to stiff you like that, Danny, but the others made me do it. I always kind of liked you, and I thought, you know, maybe we could've been better friends if Buzz and the others hadn't've been around." She tugged at her blouse, trying to look casual as she pulled the material taut to emphasize her breasts. "Won't'cha give me a chance to prove it?"

Danny felt a momentary weakness, something inside that wanted to believe her, but he remembered the expression on her face as she had kicked him again and again and knew her words were false, another lie, and rage was a bright flame that drove away his uncertainties just as it had dulled his pain.

"Come here," he said quietly, lowering the empty pistol to his side, trying to reshape his mouth into a smile.

Lizzie nodded, still hesitant, faltered after a single step. "You wouldn't hurt me, would ya, Danny? I mean, we're gonna be, like, friends and all. Partners maybe. Without the others, there'd be less to split."

"Sounds good to me," but as she advanced within reach, he swept his arm up and smashed the cold metal into her left cheek. Lizzie twisted as she fell away, landing on her stomach, moaning, trying to get back to her feet. Danny let the pistol fall to the floor and moved to her side.

When his right foot began to hurt, he used his left, continuing long after he had broken all of her ribs, even after she had finally slumped to the floor for the last time, motionless, unbreathing. There was surprisingly little blood, but then most of her injuries, like his, were on the inside, where they didn't show.

Once his breathing returned to normal, Danny suddenly became acutely aware that he was standing next to the evidence that could send him to jail for the rest of his life. Or was there a death penalty here in Texas? He couldn't remember. This part of the airport seemed deserted, but he couldn't count on that indefinitely. Besides, he'd already decided on a fitting resting place.

He dragged her by the heels to the maintenance closet door behind which he'd regained consciousness some indeterminate time earlier that evening. Had it been only minutes, or hours? Danny had no watch, nothing with which to measure the passage of time. The door was latched but not locked, and he pulled it open, prepared to bundle her into the tiny space within, among the mops and brushes and cleaning supplies.

But he couldn't carry through with his plan because there was already a body inside. It seemed to be a young man, about his own age, slumped forward with head on knees, wearing baggy clothing and a vest with very large pockets. The vest was virtually a copy of his own; in fact, so were the shirt and pants.

Danny staggered away, Lizzie's body forgotten, and raised the back of his hand to his mouth, stifling what threatened to be a cry of outrage and shock. "What the fuck's going on here?" he managed at last, but neither of the two dead people answered.

He was tempted to reach forward, lift the man's head, and examine the face. But every time he started to do so, his muscles cramped and his stomach threatened to rebel, and he realized he really didn't want to know anyway. With a small, inarticulate cry, he turned away and ran back down the corridor, running so fast that he caromed off one wall, stumbled over his own feet, continued forward off-balance for several steps, then crashed full length to the floor, knocking the wind from his lungs.

When Danny had the strength to rise, he felt emotionally parched, and his legs were so unsteady that he pressed both palms against the wall while his self-control slowly returned. He raised his head, found himself staring into the same mural he'd examined earlier, four vultures holding watch over the remains of a past meal. No, it couldn't be the same, because there were no bones visible in this one, just a bare patch of sand. And the carrion eaters were drawn differently as well, alert, attentive, as though a fresh meal awaited them.

Danny tried to straighten up, but discovered that he couldn't lift his hands away from the wall. Mystified, he lowered his eyes, then gasped when he realized his forearms disappeared where they touched the plaster, as though his body was being absorbed into the wall. That's when he remembered his high school biology class and what happened to white cells once they were no longer needed, but his subsequent frantic attempts to pull free only caused him to fall forward into the wall.

He tasted hot sand in his mouth in the instant before sharp beaks and talons touched his flesh.

THANK YOU FOR YOUR PATIENCE

Matthew J. Costello

SHE CHEWED HER LOWER LIP, LOOKING AT A MONITOR, THEN at all the monitors that said the same thing.

Please see an airline representative for current flight information. Thank you for your patience.

She heard the whirring, a buzzing in her ears. Ellen Wright turned around and saw a man coming up to her in a wheelchair. He had a full beard and flashing blue eyes, and Ellen thought he didn't look sane. He brought his chair to a sharp stop next to her.

"Damn stupid thing. 'See an airline representative' . . . Stupid . . ."

Ellen looked down at the man.

"Do *you* see any representatives around? Well, do you? This part of the terminal is deserted."

Ellen looked around. When she had arrived, so many hours ago, everything looked okay, simply the normal bustle and confusion of the Dry Plains International Airport. It was supposed to have a frenetic feel, all the hub airports are like that. Ellen *knew* that.

The big airports *always* looked as if they were filled with panicked people. Here, it hadn't looked so much different. Not at first . . .

"Maybe," she said quietly, looking back at the monitor screens as if they might quickly flutter, change, and give her a glimpse of what time her plane would taxi up to Gate D-23, what time it might take off . . .

"Maybe someone's going to come."

She heard the electric engine of the man's wheelchair whirr and then she saw him roll away. She wondered how he got his chair here . . . whether he was going to take it on a plane.

"Right. Sure, someone's going to come. You can believe that if you want, babe, but I watched everyone, all the different airline employees moving the hell out of this concourse, away from the gates. Last I heard they were huddled down in the baggage area . . . some kind of meeting or something. It's a goddamned strike . . ."

A strike, Ellen thought. Well, that would explain it, wouldn't it? There's been a strike. And—she guessed—there'd be people to take the places of the strikers. Of course there would have to be. People from the front office would come.

She spoke to the man in the chair. "I guess that's why there's a delay."

He laughed.

"Right. Sure." He laughed aloud, and Ellen thought that she should walk away from this annoying man. Maybe he wasn't here for a plane. Maybe he was one of these cripples who sold things. Except they weren't called cripples anymore . . . they were—what?—"challenged" . . .

She took some steps away.

The man and his engine followed.

"Look around. You see everyone waiting, right?"

Ellen thought that she should call a security guard . . . if there were any security guards. But there were only the other passengers, and not as many before. The few passengers still waiting sat in the plastic sculpted chairs, Walkmen attached to their ears, buried in paperback books.

"They're all waiting, except there aren't as many of them as before."

Well, of course not, Ellen thought. The man made his chair keep pace with her. Not as many—because some have gone down the concourse from the D gates, back to the main terminal. Looking for answers, looking for help . . .

She wished the man would leave her alone.

"They'll come back," Ellen said. "As soon as they know when their planes will take off."

The man abruptly shot in front of her, cutting her off. He

43

looked up at her, his eyes wide, his full beard bristling, reddish under the direct glare of fluorescent light.

"Then why haven't *you* gone down there?"

She stopped walking. Ellen looked at him and then down the long arm of D Concourse.

"Well," she said.

People have gone down there. That was true. Looking for information, maybe a voucher for free travel if they were going to get bumped from their flight today.

"I don't know. I guess—"

"Guess *nothing.*" The man's voice was loud and a woman sitting in a chair by Gate D-22 looked up. Ellen looked at the woman, not really pleading for help with her eyes. After all, the man in the wheelchair was just talking to her, that was all.

"You haven't gone down there because you don't know what's down there . . . waiting."

Ellen turned around, looking toward the main terminal. The electric walkways were off. That might simply be a energy conservation feature. So it would be a long walk down there. But that wasn't all.

"Kind of quiet down there, isn't it? Quiet and, damn if it doesn't look dark, as if . . ."

Ellen walked away. The man was crazy. He was one of those crazy men you meet at the airport, selling flowers, wacky Bibles . . .

She saw a silhouette for the women's room. She'd get rid of him that way. He wouldn't follow her in there.

She walked in, hearing the whirring behind her, and then nothing . . .

It was so bright in the bathroom. She heard a flush and then a gray-haired woman, looking shriveled and washed out under the terrible light, came out of a stall. She didn't look at Ellen.

Ellen wanted to say to her, *be careful.* There's someone out there. Some guy. I think that he's crazy. Instead Ellen moved into one of the stalls. It seemed as if that's what she should do.

She shut the door and pulled the metal bolt.

She heard the water being run in one of the sinks. They

were run by electric eyes, as were the toilets. You need not touch anything. Ellen liked that. You didn't have to touch anything . . . and nothing touched you.

She stood there, waiting until the woman left. The water stopped spattering. The air blower came on. Ellen stood there. She hoped that the man in the wheelchair was gone.

How did he get his chair here, she wondered? The airport had wheelchairs, all folded neatly, waiting for a squad of . . . the challenged. But this man had his own chair, a motorized chair. He was making this wait, the terrible wait for the flights to resume, so much harder to bear . . .

There was no sound outside. The women's room was empty.

Ellen took a breath. She could leave now. It wouldn't look odd to leave now. She grabbed the silver metal bolt and slid it to the right.

It didn't move. It was stuck. So she applied more pressure to the bolt, grunting.

"C'mon," she said. "Move. C'mon. Damn—"

She didn't like to curse, though it wasn't the worst thing that you could do. No, there were many other worse sins—pride, greed, lust. None of those troubled her, but when she got sc—

When she got *worried,* sometimes she'd say "damn." It was a weakness.

The bolt wouldn't move. Then she heard water splashing into one of the sinks. She hadn't heard anyone come in—but perhaps they could help her. Silly thing, she thought, the way the bolt won't move.

No—how could anyone help her? That was impossible. She'd have to just keep tugging on the bolt. It couldn't be stuck *that* badly.

But the more she tugged, the more she dug a pencil-thick red ridge into the pads of her fingers. The more she tugged, the more she was faced with the fact that the door wouldn't open.

She took a deep breath.

There was more splashing, more sinks coming on. Still, she hadn't heard anybody come into the women's room.

She looked down to the tile floor. It looked clean. She chewed her lip—a habit. The floor looked clean.

Still, she didn't like the idea of getting down on her hands and knees and crawling under the door. She'd have to get right down on her belly to get out. She knew that. *Right on her belly* . . .

The floor looked clean . . .

She tried the bolt one more time but now it felt welded.

"D—" she started to say again, catching herself.

She knelt down.

She felt the lip of the toilet bowl brush against her leg. It felt cold and slippery. The day had been hot, too hot for stockings. But the airport was cold, frigid. The feel of the porcelain bowl made her shiver.

But then she was on the floor. She looked ahead.

The door was so low. This would be like crawling under a guillotine. That's what it looked like, the door like a huge razor blade, poised to chop down.

She was breathing so fast now and chewing her lip, gnawing at it as if it was a piece of rubbery rawhide.

Maybe I should try the bolt again, she thought. Get up again and—

No. If it didn't work she'd have to get back down on her knees again, get on her belly. That had been so hard to do.

She lowered her head to the floor, her cheek touching the tiles. They had looked clean, but now she smelled the cleaner, the pungent bite of ammonia still clinging to the tiles.

She inched forward.

When she heard sounds from behind her.

No, that's impossible, Ellen thought. Not behind me . . . someone came into another stall and—

She heard a flush. It happened automatically. There was no handle. The toilet flushed, as of someone had been sitting on it. Then it flushed again, and then again . . .

A roar. Right next to her ears.

Ellen kept crawling forward, grunting, moving her head under the door, seeing the sinks splashing on, first one, then the other, then another.

As if someone was darting in front of them, sticking hands under the electric eye.

But there was no one there.

And still there was the sound of flushing behind her, and then a bubbling noise, and wetness, touching her ankles, her calves . . .

"No, oh no . . ." she said, thinking, *I'm getting all wet. When my plane comes, I'll be all wet.*

She grunted, pulling herself out, then up, snakelike, squirming out from under the stall, her legs wet from the overflowing toilet water, the bottom of her dress sopping.

She stood up.

The sinks stopped shooting on and off. And Ellen looked down at her dress, her legs, covered with icy water from the toilet. It made her stomach go tight.

But it wasn't the clear sheen of water she saw on her legs, matting down the fine hair on her legs, making her madras dress go dark.

It was a thin film of red, thin and slimy.

Ellen shook her head. Her first thought was that she had started menstruating. But that wasn't possible.

She touched the blood.

No, that was still *weeks* away. Then—this must—

She imagined someone using the toilet, clogging it with a bloody tampon, each flush stirring the mixture, making it swirl.

Ellen ran to one of the sinks, her stomach heaving. But she hadn't eaten or drunk anything in such a long time that she could only hack at the bowl.

She stood there a moment. Then she stuck her hands under the faucet, in the path of the electric eye. She was going to clean herself.

Somehow, she'd clean her legs, even her dress . . . somehow.

Nothing happened. She moved to the next sink. Nothing happened. She went back and forth, up and down the line of sinks that had been splashing—I heard them, Ellen thought —but now they were silent . . . as if the water had been shut off.

She stood there a moment until she realized that she'd have to go outside to find some water, to see whether everything was getting back to normal. She looked in the mirror. The person there looked *sc—*

The person looked *worried.*

Ellen turned and walked out to the terminal.

There were even fewer people waiting, a small circle of them gathered tightly around, listening to the man in the wheelchair.

Ellen started walking toward the people, hearing his words.

"You *can't* go down there," he was saying. "Look, has anyone come back?"

"Maybe it's only a power failure," a woman said in a tiny voice. Ellen kept walking, no one taking any note of her, not yet. "They've lost power, and what with the strike and all, and—"

A man at the outside of the circle turned and looked at Ellen.

"Hey," he said. Then again, louder. "Hey, where'd *you* come from? Were you down there?" Then there was that whirring noise. The crowd parted and Ellen was face-to-face with the man in the wheelchair.

"The hell she was. She was in the women's room." He jiggled the controls of his chair and made it inch close to her. "And I bet that was fun, huh babe? Bet you had a grand old time in the lavatory . . ."

Ellen shook her head. "Wh-what do you mean? . . ." She felt as if she was going to cry. I just want to get my airplane, she thought. Fly out of here. Get home and—

Another whirr. "Did you call on Jesus in there? Did he appear in the mirror to help you?"

Ellen shook her head. She looked at the crowd, looking for a sympathetic face, but they all seemed aligned with this man.

She shook her head, then, to the crowd she said, "I got blood on me. There was—" She looked down to her legs, her dress. They were wet, nothing more.

The woman with the tiny voice said, "I—I saw my husband. He was hurt, bleeding. He wanted me to come with him . . ."

Someone else said, *"I* saw something in a mirror. I screamed. I couldn't—"

The phone rang, a pay phone only feet away from the

group. Ellen looked up at the monitors, which still suggested that she *Please see an airline representative for current flight information. Thank you for your patience.*

The phone kept ringing.

"Why don't you answer it," the man in the wheelchair said. "Go on. *Pick it up.*"

Ellen turned and looked at the phone. Maybe it will stop ringing, she thought. She walked to it slowly, thinking—with every step—that it would surely stop ringing.

But then she was standing next to it. She reached out and picked up the handset. She brought it slowly to her mouth, her ear.

"Hello," she said. It must be airport security, checking on us, telling us where to go. We probably have to leave the D Concourse and go—

"Hello?"

For a second there was a hiss, as if the line had gone quickly dead. But then there was—so faint—these voices, high-pitched, squeaky voices, chattering away.

They were going at the wrong speed, chattering, laughing, squealing.

The crowd was watching her. Ellen shook her head.

The voices slowed down, the pitch lowering, until she heard—clearly now—a low, gravelly voice, struggling to get the words out.

"Come . . . here . . ."

Ellen smiled.

"It's the airport. We're supposed to leave here. Go down—"

She turned and looked towards the other end of the D Concourse. It was so dark down there, certainly darker than before, as if it was shut down for the night. A power outage, Ellen thought. They're waiting for us past there . . . back at the main terminal.

In her mind, she heard the whoosh of jets taking off, the screech of brakes as they landed . . .

Though in truth she heard nothing.

"We have to go down there."

The man in the wheelchair made his chair jerk forward once, and then turned it again.

"The fuck you do. Something's wrong here. This area

49

used to be filled. *Something's wrong here,* I don't know what. But our moving like sheep into the darkness isn't the answer . . ."

Ellen looked at him, his eyes wild. She let the handset slip through her fingers. It was only a week ago that a plane had exploded here, sitting on the tarmac. There were live TV photos of the bodies, hanging from the plane, draped, like meat curing, and other bodies crumpled on the runway, bits . . . and pieces.

She looked at the wild-eyed man. And she backed away.

She asked God for strength. Please, God, she prayed.

"I'm going down there. And if anyone—" her voice rose, as if she was speaking to a group at her church, calling on them to come forward, to declare their lives in trust for God, calling them to get up, to feel the joy, *the power—*

"If anyone who wants to come with me, I'll lead the way!"

The group seemed frozen, but then a middle-aged man, all dressed up in his business suit with nowhere to go, came forward. "I'm coming with you," he said. He was followed by two women, maybe sisters on vacation, and—Ellen waited a moment.

Then the man in the wheelchair spoke quietly. *"We're going to go out that way,"* he said, pointing to the end of the D gates. She saw an exit sign. "That way, and get the hell out of here."

He's crazy, Ellen thought.

And she turned and started walking down to the main terminal, three people following her, the light growing fainter as they moved towards the dark end.

There were no lights on and everything seemed shrouded.

"It's the terrorists," the middle-aged man said. "I bet they've taken the airport."

Ellen kept walking. She had seen blood, on her dress, on her legs.

She took a breath. No, I *thought* I had seen blood. I was scared, I was—

Hysterical.

It grew darker still, until the giant panes of glass that looked out to the runways showed only blackness, the darkest of nights.

"I don't like this," one of the women said.

When, from ahead, from the nearly total blackness, a voice said. "This way. That's okay—keep coming—"

"Oh, yes," the woman said. "Oh thank God, there's *somebody.*"

And in the darkness, Ellen saw someone standing there, a face lit up as if the person was holding a flashlight up.

Ellen saw a woman, an airport representative, her hair lustrous, the wave perfect. She was smiling. A pretty smile with perfect teeth.

"Sorry for the problems, but . . ."

The middle-aged man, then the women, hurried to the representative, to her face, glowing in the darkness.

And Ellen stopped. *Sorry for the problems.* But . . . but . . .

But what? Ellen thought. Why is it *so* dark here and why is it night outside, a night with no stars, a night without any lights glowing in the darkness, total night, and—

The voices from the phone rumbled through her head, the high, squeaky voices, the laughing, that terrible giggling, the ringing that went on forever—

"Thank God!" the middle-aged man said. "What's going on here? This is a total—"

The flight attendant's voice seemed to freeze. Now the face was a still picture, suspended in the darkness. Ellen opened her mouth to call out to the others. Better stop. Better stop right there . . .

Then the face—and Ellen knew that that's all it was— started to fade. It began to vanish, fading to a pale, milky color, then a sick washed-out yellow as if the batteries were dying.

No, Ellen wanted to say. But she looked around. She stood alone in the darkness.

Saying no wouldn't do any good, would it?

She backed up.

"Hey, what the—" she heard the man's voice, the friendly representative's face fading, faded to nothingness.

Ellen backed up another step.

The man screamed.

I've never heard a scream like that, Ellen thought. He is

experiencing something I've never felt, something so *bad* that it takes the voice places it's not been before . . .

Back. Another step. Another. She didn't look behind her.

The two women cried out. Oh . . . God. Like human kittens, being held by something, held and slowly crushed, their voices pitiful, mewling—

Ellen cried, "No." Still backing up. Then there was a chorus of noise. Snapping, breaking. A last mewl. Wet sounds, a floor being mopped, and then—

The high-pitched laughter, the chatter, slowing down, struggling to be intelligible, struggling to say, low, rumbling, gravelly—

"Ellen—"

She turned, and, though surrounded by the blackness, she ran.

Until, as if through a film, she saw fluorescent lights, the monitors, mocking her.

Please see an airline representative for current flight information. Thank you for your patience.

The phones were all ringing now.

She stopped. Now there was only a small part of the D Concourse that wasn't dark, that hadn't been hit by the . . . power outage.

And the people were gone. Ellen cried, thinking, *they got away.* And way down at the other end, she saw the open exit door.

She walked there, slowly because it didn't matter. Not really, she knew that now.

It was only a matter of time.

She got to the door. It was open.

They got away, she thought. And if they got away, maybe I can.

She went to the door and looked outside.

And she saw, below her, a bit of the tarmac, yellow lines to guide the planes to their proper gate. An abandoned luggage cart. But beyond, looking left and right, up and down, was the perpetual night, a dark bubble encasing the nearby gates.

Is everything normal in the rest of the airport, she wondered? Are people still getting on planes, taking off? Are there still announcements, reassuring voices telling people that "flights will resume . . . in just a few minutes . . ."

She touched the door frame. There were metal steps down. Did they get away, she wondered?

But then, she heard something. A familiar whirring noise. She spun around, expecting to see the man in the wheelchair.

Surprise! Happy birthday!

But no—other than the darkness creeping closer, there was nothing.

She looked down, past the door. And now she saw, just below the stairs and tucked under the metal stairs, the wheelchair. The electric motor was still running and one wheel was spinning.

She looked up, both hands holding onto the door frame.

She thought of the children's story about the Pied Piper.

Everyone's gone, Ellen thought. Everyone except me.

She turned around and looked at the fluorescent lights close to her, starting to fade.

Everyone's gone except me. So she started to pray.

She prayed, and she waited . . .

THE MAN IN THE MIRROR

Les Daniels

LACKLAND TRUDGES ACROSS THE INDUSTRIAL-STRENGTH ORANGE carpet, his future hanging from his hand. He slows down when he reaches the airport's security checkpoint, just like everybody else would if anybody were around. He's acting naturally, but the palms of his hands are sweating and slippery, and it's not that easy to hold on to his suitcase; for the first time in his life he's grateful for the coarse grain of the leatherette handle that hurts his fingers and leaves red marks on them whenever he carries the damned thing. It won't do to drop it now. He doesn't want what's inside scattered all over the floor, not when he's so close to finally getting out of this hellhole for good.

He tries to keep calm, but he's dripping like a cold bottle of beer on a summer day. His old Palm Beach suit is damp around the crotch and armpits, and his little straw hat is a greasy oven clamped to the back of his head. This is worse than nerves, or hangover, or even both at once, and he should know because that's just what he's got. It's actually a relief when he realizes that what's happening is not entirely his fault, because the air-conditioning has broken down again. Yellow light pours through the plate glass walls.

Somehow the heat is the true horror of the place, worse than all the wild stories whispered in control towers or shouted in the pages of supermarket tabloids. "AIRPORT OF THE DAMNED," they'd say, or "ANCIENT CURSE PULLS PLANES FROM SKY." It's easy enough to laugh at headlines like that, Lackland thinks, especially since he

54

wrote them himself, but when artificial cooling kisses Dry Plains International good-bye, it feels like all the forces that turn a stretch of land into a desert are conspiring to crush this outpost of civilization back into the ancient sand. This whole structure of steel and glass and concrete, with all its life and noise and motion, is just a temporary aberration, a monument to human vanity that will never stand the test of time. People had to be crazy even to try to carve a habitat out here, to build and irrigate and refrigerate, when it's so obvious that they aren't welcome at all.

At least that's what he kept trying to tell the readers of *The National Buzz,* and maybe they believed him. They believed a lot. His public. He spent years goofing on them, coming up with such preposterous crap that they must have known it was all a joke, but they bought it. He even used old movie titles for headlines so the hipper people who bought the paper for laughs would know where he was coming from: "I WALKED WITH A ZOMBIE." "I MARRIED A MONSTER FROM OUTER SPACE." Nobody ever complained.

But ultimately the real joke was his life. When he and a bunch of other dopers started *The Buzz* twenty years ago (actually it was longer, but that was too much to deal with), they were Atlanta's radical rascals, proud to be more idealistic and more cynical than any other humans in recorded history. The paper was their primal scream, a shout of defiance against the way of the world. When the world got worse anyway and all hope died, they started printing lies as the only way to even suggest the truth, and for some reason circulation skyrocketed. They got a national distributor, and went into the business of bullshitting. Somewhere along the line he got a haircut and lost the bellbottoms, then gave up pot in favor of bourbon. He didn't need wild ideas anymore as much as he needed a way to make them stop.

Now he's stopped himself, waiting for permission to get on the plane. His suitcase sits on the conveyor belt, and a stumpy blonde with bad skin is running her metal detector up and down his leg. She doesn't get a ding. He's thrown away everything that might slow him down, from his belt to his pocket change, so technically he's clean. It's not metal that will cause chaos, though. It's meat.

He takes a couple of steps and he's on the other side of the invisible barrier, and his little gray suitcase is swishing through those gray rubber ribbons, and the X-ray or whatever it is didn't see anything evil inside. He grabs it with one hand and fumbles for a cigarette with the other, moving down the corridor while he lights up for the last time for a while. He's got his ticket in his hand, but he's not in the smoking section because there is no more goddamn smoking section. The government thinks it can protect his fellow passengers from him, but it's not going to work. Lackland is puffing away like a lunatic as he reaches the last line of defense and hands his packet of cardboard and tissue paper to the kid with the blow-dried hair and the little blue uniform. Let him shuffle the papers. The boy in blue lets out a little cough to tell Lackland it's time to grind out that butt in the standing ashtray, but the whole area is already hazy with nicotine so no one notices the faint wisps of vapor seeping from the seams of the suitcase.

Lackland is on his way. A taller blonde stands at the entrance to the big bird, a fixed grin on her face, her big white teeth like a row of Chiclets. Her smile is so intense that it looks painful; the corners of her mouth are actually turned down, not up. She's happy to be getting out of Dry Plains, that goes without saying, but she'll be even happier at the other end of the run, when she's safely somewhere else. Then she'll be standing in the same spot with the same scene running backward, and she'll be saying "Bye-bye, bye-bye, bye-bye" like some sort of tape loop, and her troubles will be over. That's what she thinks; Lackland can see it in her eyes. Her face is a mask of makeup: lipstick and eyelashes and some sort of orange powder that's clotting up with sweat. For a second she reminds him of his new editor, the one who was sent in when the conglomerate took over *The National Buzz.*

Jackie Jimenez, the one who didn't get the joke. She came roaring in with her big hair and her big shoulder pads, and in a few weeks she turned everything around. No doubt that's what she was getting paid for, but no doubt she really enjoyed it, too. No more "BIGFOOT IS AN ALIEN." Jackie wanted shit that smelled real, and she wanted Lackland digging around in the sewers for it. Instead of getting himself half in the bag and dreaming up something wild, he was expected to go out on the road and talk to mothers whose babies belonged in bottles, and babies whose mothers belonged in jail. People were getting killed and crippled and corrupted everywhere, and Jackie loved it. Lackland was expected to love it too.

For a while, he didn't understand. Once upon a time, *The Buzz* had been his paper as much as anybody's. People like him handled the writing, and the ones with no imagination got stuck selling ads. Yet somehow those people, the ones who really had nothing to do with what it was all about, ended up owning the whole show. He found out too late that counting ad pages was worth more than writing. Lackland had started wearing a white suit as a gag because it reminded him of the reporter in that TV show about vampires, but he didn't realize soon enough that he really was battling bloodsuckers on the job. His friends from the old days sold *The Buzz* to a multinational for a lifetime supply of free money, and all at once he was working for the very humanoids he hated and feared.

A few months later they had fired him, and that's what set him on the path to an airport on the sorry side of Texas. As much as it sickened him to admit it, he had really wanted his job back. He might not have been much good at it anymore, but he certainly wasn't good at anything else, and Dry Plains looked like a story. The way things turned out, of course, was absolutely unbelievable, and now he's got a one-way ticket for Mexico City.

With the suitcase safely stashed under his seat (paid for with an employee discount, it pleases him to recall), and the DC-10 rushing forward on its sprint into the sky, the high-pitched whine of the engine has him gritting his teeth, and the strain of the takeoff forces his body back. He feels sick and scared the way he always does, but for the first time in his life he's loving it. He's not hot anymore, and he won't be kissing ass where he's going. Or cleaning toilets either.

When he hit Dry Plains for the first time, he had signed on as a janitor. The job was no picnic, especially in a place that was hopelessly understaffed, but he consoled himself with the thought that he was doing undercover work. He refused even to consider the idea that this was all he was good for now, but the paycheck didn't hurt, and he'd drunk up his unemployment long ago.

For a while, it had looked like he wasn't going to learn anything but how to push a broom. He tried questioning his colleagues in the mop 'n' slop brigade, but most of them didn't speak English, and they acted like they didn't want to talk anyway. Illegal aliens, probably, more frightened of losing their lousy jobs than of any abstract doom that might be hanging over their heads. There was only one old bastard who had anything to say, and he dropped dead before he said much. Cashing out in a public men's room wasn't a great way to go, but at least the guy's life hadn't been totally wasted: he gave Lackland a lead just before he collapsed while trying to rub a stubborn spot off a mirror.

"The more I rub it, the bigger it gets," the old man complained.

"That's what she said," Lackland answered from across the room, and punctuated the remark by flushing a urinal he'd just finished scrubbing. The noise drowned out whatever happened next, but when Lackland turned around his informant was down on the tiles, kicking and twitching. He'd cracked his head on the floor as he fell, and Lackland saw blood. He just stood there for what seemed like a ridiculously long time, looking back and forth from the man to the mirror, as if the most important thing was finding out if he'd had time to get it clean.

The spot was still there, vaguely gray and misty, and it seemed to be spreading like the puddle of blood on the floor. Lackland stared at it, his eyes blinking and his mouth hanging open, while the blotch smeared its way across the mirror until it obscured the reflection of his face. He didn't even notice when the old man stopped moving, and didn't listen to the last sound he made, which was something like a backed-up drain. Lackland's feet were pulling him toward the mirror, even while his mind was urging him to flee. His hands reached out to grasp the rim of the sink in front of him, and his face thrust forward toward the polished glass. He looked like a man trying to see if there was something in his eye, except that he was screaming at the top of his lungs.

The airport was nearly empty at that hour, but Lackland's howls attracted two other night-shift janitors, and they pulled him out of the echoing room. In the story he wrote later, Lackland claimed it was the sight of the dead man that caused so much of the cleaning staff to quit, but these were poor Mexicans to whom death was no stranger. What really frightened them was Lackland himself.

He didn't remember too much about the end of that night's work, but a few drinks eventually calmed him down, and he did recall the one key point of the conversation that had taken place before the old man started swabbing that spot. Lackland had been digging for ideas to explain the jinx that seemed attached to Dry Plains International, and of course he'd heard the stories about an Indian massacre that had taken place in the area. That was the closest thing to a stock explanation for what might be no more than a run of bad luck, and no doubt it would be good enough for the readers of *The National Buzz*, but Lackland wasn't really satisfied, and the old maintenance man had agreed with him.

"Nothin' to do with the Comanche," he said. "Nothin' at all. That's what people hear, and what they hear is about all they can hold on to these days. Nobody reads anymore, but any fool could find out about it at the library. Nobody bothers, though. They're all watching that damn box. I'd rather read, myself. I read a lot. And I can tell you one thing about what's happening here: It's a lot older than the Indians."

Lackland eases his seat back into the reclining position, careful not to disturb the plastic tray that's balancing two baby bottles of bourbon. Both of them are empty, but he is not. He shuts his eyes and listens to the reassuring rumble of the engines. The plane has leveled off now, miles above the clouds, and Lackland is at peace with the world he's left behind. It's not worth worrying about anyway, because he knows he won't be back. Neither will anyone else on the plane, but he hasn't told them yet. They're nervous enough, suspended in midair between their glee at getting out of Dry Plains and their fear that they won't get where they're going. As if they knew.

He's a bit disappointed that there aren't more people on the plane, but it's convenient to have the seat next to him empty, especially since his suitcase seems to be leaking a little. He counts twenty-two passengers, not to mention the crew, and that should be enough for quite a party. To tell the truth, he's lucky to have as many traveling companions as he does. Even when an airport's popular, Lackland tells himself, you can't expect to find too many Americans trying to get to Mexico, except for tourists. Most of the migration is in the opposite direction, as his colleagues on the cleaning staff could have told him. And as he found out at the public library, it had been going that way for centuries.

After the old man died, Lackland faxed a story, an eyewitness account of the sudden death complete with embellished last words, to Jackie Jimenez at *The Buzz*. She bought it, but not for much, and told him he would have to wait for the check like everybody else. He was a stringer now, not staff. Lackland gritted his teeth, reminded himself this was only a start, and didn't smash the receiver against the wall until after she'd hung up.

He visited the library the next day, and found a middle-aged woman who seemed to know just what he was looking for (actually, she couldn't have been much older than he was, but he certainly felt younger). She came up with a little book, privately printed, and shyly confessed that her uncle had written it. Lackland, who already liked her far better than Jackie, fell halfway in love when he realized what a treasure trove she'd handed him. He thought about inviting her to lunch, then thought again. She might have been as eccentric as her uncle, whose anecdotal history of the region was hardly a work to inspire confidence. As fodder for a tabloid, however, Uncle Elmer's *Dry Plains Destiny* could hardly have been improved upon. A compendium of weird rumors and crackpot theories was just what Lackland had been hoping for.

What Lackland learned from Uncle Elmer confirmed the words of the other dead old man. The place had been bad luck for as long as anybody had been around to notice it. The story about a local tribe being massacred was true, apparently, but a footnote made the point that if dead Indians were all it took to create a curse, there would hardly be a mile in the whole country that wasn't haunted. The Comanche had been butchered in retaliation for a raid on a wagon train, which old Elmer ascribed to a fever which "drove the Red Men mad." And the fever was caused by a famine, caused by a drought, caused by a dust storm, and so it went. The root cause, according to *Dry Plains Destiny,* was an ancient invasion by Aztecs, and when Lackland saw that, he sat back and smiled.

He didn't know much about Aztecs, but he knew the magic words that would get him back on *The Buzz:* Human Sacrifice. Ancient Gods. Blood Lust. And he remembered that classic headline, the nine immortal syllables from the days when every tabloid preferred gore to gossip: "I CUT OUT HER HEART AND STOMPED ON IT."

Lackland's own heart fluttered. This was the sort of stuff that brought in the bucks. He didn't know much about the Aztecs except for the bit about cutting out hearts on top of pyramids, but that was enough to get started on: "PYRA-MID POWER FUELED BY HUMAN BLOOD!" He did vaguely remember something from another one of those old black-and-white movies that they wouldn't even show on the tube anymore: a really rotten rubber monster that zoomed through the sky on an all-too-visible wire. *The Flying Serpent.* Maybe someone could dig up a still.

After deciding that the Aztecs were ancient enough to wait for a while, he spent the afternoon going through newspaper files, taking notes on every mishap or near miss connected to Dry Plains International. He managed to compile quite a list, starting with two fatal accidents during the airport's construction. Near closing time he wrangled a library card out of his lady friend, checked out every volume he could find about the Aztecs, and rushed off to catch the bus that carried him to work. He stashed the books and his white suit in his locker, climbed into his overalls, and resumed his disguise as a member of the working class.

Judging from the untouched time cards in the rack when he punched in, he was just about the only one around who needed a job. And for some reason he couldn't explain, Lackland wasn't afraid. He even pushed aside a pair of sawhorses that barricaded the entrance to a certain men's room, which visitors were informed was out of order. He had no real reason to go in, unless it was to prove to himself that there was nothing strange about the place, so he passed the time staring into the mirror that shone over the row of sinks. He didn't bother to notice how long he spent there, but the night seemed to hurry by.

He didn't feel tired when he finished his shift, so he decided to catch up on his reading. Sitting on the bed in his seedy furnished room, with books spread out around him, Lackland boned up on the Aztecs. They'd been wiped out centuries ago when the Spaniards arrived, but according to Uncle Elmer, a group of Aztecs had escaped and made their way to what was now Dry Plains. Lackland was willing to take that on faith; what he was looking for as he skimmed through countless pages was a list of juicy bits.

One book was full of weird old drawings of gods and monsters and bloody rituals; some of them looked like cartoons, but they gave him the creeps anyway. Evidently the sacrifices, which occurred with appalling frequency, were intended to please a bewildering array of deities. Among them, Lackland recognized his old friend Flying Serpent, also known as Feathered Serpent. He knew he'd heard somewhere that birds were just reptiles with feathers instead of scales, but it seemed pretty clear that this thing called Quetzalcoatl was meant to be more than just a big bird. And strangely enough, the book said it was benevolent. There was another god who was not, and when Lackland saw its name he put the book down on his blanket and closed his eyes. This dark god was known as Tezcatlipoca, but in English its name was Smoking Mirror.

He should have slept, but instead he pulled out his little portable typewriter and banged out another story at fever pitch. His bedside radio was running to help keep him awake, and when a bulletin came on about a pilot who shut off his engines and refused to fly, Lackland thanked whatever gods there were and incorporated the incident into his story. He knew he was on to something good, and he felt as if his fingers were on fire.

He finished the piece, faxed it off to Jackie from the machine at the corner copy shop, and then dragged himself into work. Discipline was deteriorating at Dry Plains, nobody seemed to be in charge, and Lackland was exhausted. He needed rest, and he couldn't think of a better place to hide than the barricaded men's room. Keeping it closed for so long was crazy, but then again the whole airport was falling apart, and there were plenty of other places where people could take a leak. Maybe somebody was scared. Maybe everybody was. Lackland, on the other hand, was just a happy man who needed a nap. The worse things got, the better he would like it, and if something interesting happened while he slept, it would probably make enough noise to wake him up. He looked at the man in the mirror, and the man in the mirror smiled at him. He curled up in a corner, nestled against the shining tiles, and slipped into a dream. . . .

And now he's dreaming again, leaning back in the padded seat and flying through the air. He can't believe how relaxed he feels, how easy everything is. The idea startles him a little, and he sits up suddenly, rattling the plastic tray in front of him. He's got to stay on top of things for a little longer. He checks his watch and realizes there's not much time left before they're scheduled to land, so he rings for the stewardess and orders one last drink. He doesn't know if he'll be able to get bourbon where he's going, not that it matters too much. There's sure to be something. He should have done more research on his destination, but there really wasn't time. Everything happened so fast toward the end.

He pulls a folded copy of the latest *Buzz* out of his jacket pocket and opens it up in front of his face. He hardly needs to read it at this point, but it's the issue with his story featured on the cover, and he's expecting it to make an impression when his drink is delivered. There's a nice collage of an Aztec mask hovering in the sky over a stricken airliner, and inside there's an old engraving purporting to depict Tenochtitlan, the island capital of the Aztec empire that later became Mexico City. Lackland loves looking at it, and inwardly congratulates the art department on their fine work, but he's a little less satisfied with the article he wrote. It may be hot off the press, but he wrote it almost a week ago, and he knows so much more today.

Jackie bought the story, but she still didn't offer more than what she called "our standard rate," which he knew was a lie. He'd practically started the paper, and now she was quoting prices to him! He was almost certain he could have sold his stuff for more money to someone else, but he had to beat *The Buzz*. They had to know that they needed him, even though the job itself no longer seemed quite so important to him. For the first time in years, he cared more about the story. He felt exhilarated, like a man who has suddenly caught sight of his goal after he'd almost forgotten he had one. He felt like a kid again, maybe even a kid who'd dropped acid.

He had begun hanging around the airport even when he wasn't on duty, and he realized that nobody noticed him. A maintenance man in overalls was almost invisible, and so was the men's room he'd converted into a private office. The gates nearby had been shut down as flights were canceled, and people just stopped coming around. The emptiness of the area gave him an eerie feeling from time to time, but if anything was haunting this part of Dry Plains International, it was Lackland himself.

Occasionally he'd wander out into the main concourse, where people still appeared, and once in a while he struck up a conversation. When he found someone who was interested in what he had to say, he was happy to take them under his wing and give them the guided tour. A few of them even got to see his mirror. There was hardly any point in going home anymore, except that his typewriter and his books were there. And another mirror.

His third story, which unfortunately went unpublished, was Lackland's masterpiece. He wasn't writing much about what happened at the airport anymore, or even getting old stories out of the books, since he'd discovered how much he could learn from holding those ancient pictures up under his eyes and reading their reflections. There he could interpret the strategy of Smoking Mirror, the entity from another realm of being who was twisting time to preserve the ancient empire of the Aztecs, five centuries after it had been destroyed. Lackland could see the plan in his photographs of old stone calendars, where there were predictions that a white man would come to herald the arrival of The Flying Serpent. That was why the Aztecs had welcomed Cortez and his invaders, and now only a true manifestation of the sacred serpent could set things right. That's what the man in the mirror told him. Someone had to prevent the Spanish from crossing the border, before they stole more jobs from honest, hardworking Aztecs. There must be a return.

This was the pattern that Lackland laid out in plain and simple terms that anyone could understand, and at first he was more baffled than indignant when Jackie told him it wasn't what she had in mind. He explained to her quite calmly that anyone could keep count of deaths and disasters, whereas it took a real investigative reporter to determine the meaning of it all, and it wasn't until she hung up on him that he realized just how confused she was. She didn't even understand the danger well enough to stay away; in fact, she announced that a story this big would require her personal attention. She didn't give him time to argue with her, and she barely gave him time to meet her plane. He thanked the serpent that it was so easy to get in and out of his overalls, then called to reserve a ticket to Mexico City. He'd have an hour between her arrival and his departure, and that would give him a chance to show her a few things about Dry Plains.

Of course she was crazy to think he wouldn't realize that she had not only fired him again, but stolen his story. And she hadn't even mentioned the checks for the ones she'd already published. The funny thing was that none of that mattered anymore. The only important thing was defending the border. He spent a few minutes looking for his suit and his suitcase, and laughing at a language that made it sound like one might be inside the other. What a mess that would make! Eventually he remembered that everything was at the airport, and he hurried off to catch his bus.

He was a bit surprised that Jackie's plane was on time, and not surprised at all that she didn't recognize him. He had to take her arm to get her attention, and when he did, she jumped. For a second he thought she might make a scene, and if she did, he'd lose the power of invisibility. So he whispered his name in her ear, and that seemed to calm her down a little, but she still gave him the impression that they had nothing to say to each other. She wanted to interview officials (as if they knew anything), but finally agreed to give him a few minutes when he told her he was leaving for Mexico to follow up a lead. He knew she was humoring him, and he didn't care.

She let him carry her suitcase, and with it in his hand he became transparent once again, a faceless functionary doing his duty. In spite of all his explanations she didn't really want to see the mirror, yet she followed him toward the unused gates, and even made a little joke about a woman venturing into a men's room.

He'd promised her something worth writing about, and he could tell she was impressed when he opened the doors to the four stalls and showed her what was sitting there. He started to unzip his overalls and then realized he could keep them on. In fact, it might be better if he got them soiled. That way, his name would be in the paper even after he was gone. And Jackie's too, naturally. He had to give her that.

The flight to Mexico City isn't a long one, and Lackland can feel the plane dropping down as they approach their destination. Up ahead, the blonde stewardess with the big white teeth is moving down the aisle toward him, collecting plastic cups and urging everyone to fold their trays up into the seats ahead of them.

Lackland is ready for her. He drags his steaming suitcase out from under his seat and props it up on his tray. It knocks his little bourbon bottle into the aisle, and that catches her eye. Clouds of vapor roll out when he pops open the suitcase, and as it clears away, the bed of dry ice glistens like the shards of a broken mirror. He isn't very good with a knife, really he isn't, but four of the hearts are neatly trimmed. Only Jackie's, which he had to do in a hurry, has its symmetry marred by the stumps of those big ropy veins, or arteries, or whatever they are.

His offering gets a big scream, and right away chaos sets in, but that's all part of the plan as far as Lackland is concerned. He's not so happy about having half a dozen people descend on him with fists and feet and elbows, and he can't understand why they're so angry at him already, when they don't even know what's going to happen. Some of those punches really hurt, but the main thing is that the pilot's still flying the plane, and they're coming in for a landing, and Lackland's the only one who knows that they won't be touching down in Mexico City, or at least not the Mexico City they expect. His five hearts, one for each century they had to travel through, are scattered down the aisle and trampled underfoot, but they've had time to do their job.

The plane lurches and screams and rolls to a halt, and

THE MAN IN THE MIRROR

Lackland is quite impressed with the pilot's skill in negotiating a water landing in unfamiliar terrain. He almost wishes the man didn't have to be sacrificed along with the others, but a deal is a deal, and it's a small price to pay for changing the course of history. He wonders how the Aztecs feel, seeing this huge roaring monster descend from the sky, but surely they'll recognize it as The Flying Serpent, just as they'll recognize him by his white clothes. He can hear the welcoming trumpets now, a sound like sirens, and in a moment he'll see Tenochtitlan. They're dragging him out of the plane now, these people who think they are his captors, but before they know what's happening he'll be released by a golden tribe with ebony eyes, and he'll climb to the top of the pyramid, and the serpent will gaze into the mirror, and the whole world will be one.

55-GALLON DRUMS ALONG THE MOHAWK

Gregory Nicoll

THE COMANCHE'S GLEAMING METALLIC SKIN WAS RED AS A SUNSET in Monument Valley. It stood proudly between two Chero-kees, brandishing an immense tomahawk from its rear wiper. Yellow warpaint splashed across its sides spelled out the words GO BRAVES! ATLANTA #1!

As Johnny Ray Lonebird stepped closer, the Comanche let out a fearsome war cry that echoed off the concrete walls of the parking garage. *A-whoop-a-whoop-a-whoop-a-whoop. . . .*

The boy leaped backward, took cover behind a nearby Mustang, and glanced over his shoulder. *Shit!* he cursed to himself. *Just my luck that the damn thing's wired with one of those novelty alarms. Sure hope the uniforms don't hear that . . .*

Sensing his retreat, the big red Jeep's alarm switched itself off in mid-cry, and fell silent: *A-whoop-a-whoo—*

The sound of a hot Texas wind whistled through the long gray concrete corridor on Level 7 of Dry Plains Internation-al Airport's long-term parking deck.

Johnny Ray walked back to the corner and sat sullenly upon his Ford Pinto. The air stank with fumes of gasoline, diesel, and leaking motor oil. Somewhere, three or four levels above, an airport security motorbike sputtered and backfired as it slowly descended an access ramp.

Time to move along. Johnny Ray fired up his Ford and rode the Pinto down to Level 5, parking it in a shadowed corner near a massive Winnebago. He leaned back to wait.

The Pinto's little engine ticked as it cooled. Another hot wind gusted through the corridor.

Looking around, Johnny Ray noticed some graffiti sprayed in dripping brown letters on the closest of this level's concrete support pillars. It said, THIS LAND BE-LONGS TO THE NU-PIONEERZ—ALL OTHERS STAY AWAY.

Johnny Ray sneered; he knew who *all* this land really belonged to, from sea to shining sea. And some new street gang—especially one that the Mohawks and the Sidewinders had never heard of before—had no right to claim otherwise.

As he stretched out across the bumpy vinyl seat, a small sheet of brown paper crumpled in the pocket of his denim vest. He carefully removed it and spread it on the seat beside him. In bright red ink, the scratchy handwriting of Thomas Sevenkiller spelled out a now invalid set of orders:

FIND:
COUGAR
THUNDERBIRD
FIREBIRD

Johnny Ray folded the paper and stuffed it back into his vest pocket. He'd keep it as his main souvenir, he thought, of his three weeks in the Mohawks. His second souvenir—the street gang's trademark extreme haircut—was well on its way to growing back now. From beneath the band of the tight denim cap he wore to cover it, a bead of sweat rolled down his cheek.

Stupid for a Comanche to have a Mohawk haircut anyway, he thought. *Better to let it grow, to let Gramma Lonebird put it back into the long, black braids as before . . .*

Nevertheless, Johnny Ray knew he'd miss belonging to that Native American street gang, drinking and hanging out with other boys of Indian blood—Kiowa, Cherokee, Mescalero, and Apache. He'd especially miss cruising with them on their "wilding" nights, their hot-rod Ford lowriders circling the city square like a war party on the prowl.

Last spring he'd stalked a Cougar for hours here in the airport deck, finally spotting a gleaming brown XR7 on

Level 4. He would've scored it, too, if not for the security blues discovering him. Johnny Ray's stainless steel slim-jim was stuck in the big cat's door, halfway to slipping its lock, when its alarm let out a piercing animal screech—and a dozen of the uniforms surrounded him.

First offense, the court called it.

Thanks to a judge named Lukas Muledeer, Johnny Ray checked out of the Crossbar Hilton in just three months—but the Mohawks wouldn't have him any more. Bad medicine, he was. They'd waited just long enough for his prison-shorn mohawk haircut to grow back. Then Thomas Sevenkiller had stripped him of the gang colors in front of them all, and sent him walking.

He wiped the sweat from his cheek and adjusted the cap, pulling it down more tightly over his compromised hair.

The denim jacket he wore today wasn't technically the Sidewinders' colors, but it was close enough to keep some of the street heat off his tail till he was accepted as a full member. The only thing Johnny Ray still had to do for his Sidewinder membership was bring them a late model Jeep Comanche, ideally one with a killer stereo and new tires. Their sergeant-at-arms had even painstakingly showed him how to get around the EVS II Keyless Entry alarm system that came with most of the cars. Nothing to it, now.

But is it all just a mean joke? he wondered. Were the Sidewinders taunting him, semi-secretly humiliating him by forcing him to steal a vehicle named after his own Native American tribe?

Though the question worried Johnny Ray Lonebird, he tried to ignore it. More than anything else, he wanted *to belong.* There was power in being part of a gang's numbers . . . any gang's numbers.

Belonging. Yes, that's what he wanted—and what he needed. *Just to belong . . .*

Johnny Ray ducked as a Plymouth Arrow flew down the ramp and into an empty parking space opposite him. An overweight white couple noisily emerged, their flabby bellies distended under Washington Redskins T-shirts. Straining at the weight of their many suitcases, they argued openly about their flight to Buffalo as they passed. The concrete walls echoed with the slapping of their grotesque, awkward city-white-men's footsteps and the booming syllables of their quarrel.

As the din gradually faded, Johnny Ray once more heard the puttering of a security motorbike a level or two above. Cursing, he started up his Pinto again and rode it down the ramp. At the turn onto the Level 4 landing, another security bike was waiting with its engine switched off. But the uniform who rode it was busy writing up a citation on an illegally parked Buick Wildcat, and didn't notice Johnny Ray as he passed.

The boy kept rolling.

As Johnny Ray drove quickly by the glass booth at the deck's entrance/exit on Level 3, he saw that the same chubby black attendant was still sitting on duty there. The old fellow wore a Red Man Chewing Tobacco baseball cap, and was amusing himself by watching an old John Wayne movie on a small, flickering black-and-white TV. The sound of Indian drums boomed from the set's little speaker, tom-toms beating out background music as the Big Duke and Jeffrey Hunter stalked through a herd of bison.

There were more drums as Johnny Ray descended beneath the earth to Level 2, then deeper toward Level 1—but these were 55-gallon drums, enormous barrels painted bright orange and ringed in white. They alternated with herds of sawhorses and constellations of flashing yellow warning lights. Many long, buzzing, white fluorescent tubular bulbs still clung for dear life to the remaining ceiling. They flickered, adding to the weird strobe effect of the yellow flashers.

Dimly, Johnny Ray recalled hearing of some minor disaster that happened recently here on Levels 2 and 1—a large section of the concrete flooring gave way, crushing an airport fuel handler as he got out of his car in the specially reserved employee parking lot, down on the deepest level. There'd been talk of shutting down that part of the deck . . . but, after all, this *was* the busy season, and the airport had to use whatever space it still could.

Stupid white men, he thought. *No respect for their own dead . . .*

He rode his Pinto down into Level 1, past the huge EMPLOY-EES ONLY—DO NOT ENTER sign, and pulled it up to a sputtering idle near a smaller one which cautioned, SPECIAL PARKING PERMIT REQUIRED. The 55-gallon drums down here surrounded a huge area of shattered concrete flooring—the impact zone. Broken sections of the roof which had fallen down from Level 2 now lay helter skelter, many of them embedded deep in the exposed Texas soil. Arriving cars were guided around the mess by rows of small rubber traffic cones, which stood proudly like a miniature wigwam village.

But what caught and held Johnny Ray Lonebird's attention was not the evidence of the white men's misfortune. It was the *cars* here on Level 1—the place was a Happy Hunting Ground stocked from wall to wall with 4x4's.

Sneaked between the Pontiacs, Cadillacs, and Alamo rental cars there seemed to be at least two of everything an off-roader could want: Ford Broncos and Rangers, Nissan Pathfinders, Mazda Navajos, Isuzu Troopers, Dodge Dakotas, and Geo Trackers. And there were Jeeps in abundance as well: Wranglers, Cherokees, Comanches, Comanche Pioneers, and Comanche Chiefs—even one tall, magnificent red Comanche Grand Chief. It was as if the actual spirits of the frontier had personally guided the Dry Plains International Airport employees in the selection of their own vehicles.

And best of all, Johnny Ray knew that the security here on this level was the most relaxed in the whole deck, apparently because there was less outside traffic, less coming and going all day. And also, there was something sort of spooky about the place—all dark and underground—that seemed to keep away the casual prowlers.

His hands grew sweaty on the wheel as he anticipated stalking and winning his prize. He pulled his Pinto into one of the few vacant spots and killed its engine. His heartbeat quickened as he slipped from his mount, moving graceful and silent across the broken terrain. He reached for the gleaming steel slim-jim swinging in his jacket pocket, his red fingers closing around its long, smooth wooden handle.

"Hold it right there, you redskin bastard!"

The voice came from the far corner—young, white, and hot with anger. Its shout was punctuated by the distinctive metallic *clack-click* of a Winchester rifle chambering a bullet. The sound reverberated in the hollows of the gray concrete corridor.

Johnny Ray froze. His belt knife would do him no good against a firearm. No doubt about it, this white asshole had him. At least for now.

Footsteps plodded nearer, slapping on the concrete. There was a short burst of radio static and then the voice spoke again. "Crockett, this is Wild Bill. I got the shithead in my gunsights here on Level 1. You can bring the boys on down now."

Johnny Ray turned slowly to face his captor.

The kid was a thin white skinhead with bad teeth and a complexion to match. He wore black Doc Martens laced all the way up, and filthy bluejeans torn in three dozen places. His pale and hairless chest was partially covered by a loose brown vest with a long buckskin fringe. The lever-action .30-30 carbine he pointed at Johnny Ray looked at least a hundred years old, like a prop from a Clint Eastwood western. In contrast, the tiny walkie-talkie transceiver hanging on the lapel of his vest could have been stolen from the Starship *Enterprise*.

"Make one move," Wild Bill said, "and you're dead as General Custer."

Johnny Ray narrowed his eyes and watched, waiting.

Engines rumbled from above. Then, sweeping down the ramp came a caravan of the weirdest vehicles Johnny Ray had ever seen. All five of them were light-brown Ford Rancheros with wooden panelling on their sides, and mounted over the open pickup bed of each car was a huge white fiberglass shell shaped like the bonnet of a Conestoga wagon. Custom wheel covers gave their narrow tires the illusion of being supported by yellow wooden-spoked hubs.

Johnny Ray couldn't help but stare.

The cold steel muzzle of Wild Bill's carbine poked at him.

"So you like our prairie schooners, huh?" asked the kid. "Well, do ya?"

Johnny Ray didn't answer.

There were about twenty gang members here, an even mix of boys and butch females. One of them remained behind the wheel of each customized Ranchero while the others climbed out and encircled their Indian captive. They were all young whites, with heads shaved smooth. Most of them wore brown buckskin-fringed jackets or vests, and several had coonskin caps tilted at odd angles on their heads. They were armed with a variety of weapons, from knives and flintlocks to Winchesters and Uzis. One stocky girl carried a long white rope, its end coiled into a hangman's noose.

A tall, thin boy in full buckskin gear stepped forward, brandishing an immense, gleaming Bowie knife. His head was shaved and coiffed so that his hair formed a natural coonskin cap, complete with a carefully dyed "tail" hanging down his neck.

"Good work, Wild Bill," said the tall boy to the skinhead with the Winchester. He turned to Johnny Ray. "My name's Crockett—and me an' my people here, well, we're the Nu-Pioneerz."

Johnny Ray's heartbeat quickened again, but he said nothing and did not move. Crockett grinned and prodded at Johnny Ray's right hand with the tip of the Bowie knife.

Johnny Ray released the thin metal slim-jim and let it fall to the ground. It made a tiny *clink* as it struck the concrete. The sound seemed small and far away.

"Thought you were gonna score y'self some white man's wheels, eh, red boy?" asked Crockett. "Well, the Nu-Pioneerz are here to see that these parts are kept safe from heathen savages like you. Fact is, for quite a while we've been wise to what y'all Sidewinders and Santa Annas and Mohawks and all the rest have been doin' here. Y'all just *don't belong here,* and we reckon the time's come for a little payback."

The rest of the Nu-Pioneerz stirred with excitement. "Payback! Payback!" they began to chant.

Weapons slipped from creaking leather holsters. Knives hissed from sheaths. Safety switches snapped off. Rifle levers *click-clacked.* One skinhead began scraping a long, thin knifeblade across a whetstone, sharpening its already razor-fine edge. The beefy girl with the noose stepped up beside Crockett.

Johnny Ray noticed that two Nu-Pioneerz were busy fastening the other end of the rope to the rear bumper of a prairie schooner.

"What we're gonna do, Red," said Crockett, grinning, "is make an *example* outta you. And it's gonna be an example that all the others like you won't soon forget."

One of the gang girls let out a shrill laugh. A bareheaded boy near the front of the group hollered, "Damn right about that!"

"So," Crockett continued, "have ya got anything to say, Red, b'fore we start dispensatin' some frontier-style justice?"

Johnny Ray swallowed a lump in his throat. *Fuck it,* he thought. *There's nothing I could say that wouldn't just get me in more trouble with these assholes . . .*

He glanced left and right. The barrier of 55-gallon drums and sawhorses was very close. *Maybe if I broke away suddenly, and ducked there for cover . . .*

Without any further hesitation, he did it. Blood pounded in his ears like war drums as he ran, crouching low, moving silent and sure.

Shots rang out, and bullets whined past him. They ricocheted noisily off the orange-and-white 55-gallon barrels up ahead, leaving jagged parallel scars that looked like silver warpaint.

In an instant Johnny Ray was past the row of brightly colored drums. He ducked under the sawhorses and set out across the chaos of fallen, broken concrete slabs. Graceful as an antelope, he darted over the exposed Texas soil.

And then he was hit.

The slug caught him in the shoulder with the force of a speeding locomotive and knocked him forward, face down in the dirt. He tasted the crimson earth, and watched in horror as blood jetted out from his wound. It splattered to the ground—the life essence of a Native American returned to its roots.

There was something else here in the soil—something wide and white, like part of a gigantic spoke. He studied it in distracted fascination, remembering Gramma Lonebird's stories of the Indian medicine wheels from long ago . . .

"Hey, Crockett—look at his hair!"

The force had knocked off Johnny Ray's cap, exposing the remnants of his mohawk cut.

"Now *that* scalp's gonna be a purty fine addition to the

collection," said Wild Bill. "Looks like we got us a gen-u-ine mohawk injun."

Johnny Ray fought for his breath. *"C-Comanche,"* he choked.

"Get him on his feet!" boomed Crockett's voice.

Four rough hands hoisted Johnny Ray upright. He was nearly blinded by the glare from the wide, stainless steel knifeblades flashing near his face. It seemed that one of the Nu-Pioneerz must have lit up some sort of herbal cigarette, for a peculiar burning smell crossed his nostrils and he saw a thin wisp of smoke swirling up past his face.

"Hey," said a small, rough voice that Johnny Ray hadn't heard before. "Hey, Crockett. Looks like there's smoke comin' from the ground over here."

"That's just dust, ya damned fool—dust from where he fell."

Johnny Ray blinked, trying to clear his vision. He felt lightheaded, stunned by the shock of his wound and his fall—and by the gnawing fear of whatever violent plans this gang had for him. His head reeled at the weird burning smell, at the flashing yellow strobes and winking fluorescents reflected in the many knifeblades.

And then there were the drums.

At first he thought it was the gatekeeper's TV set, turned up too loud. Indian tom-toms beat out a fearsome rhythm. *Or is it just the blood pumping in my ears?*

"Hey Crockett!" shouted the unfamiliar voice again. "Look at *that!*"

At the same instant another voice asked, "Hey man, what's this funny *smell?*"

The stink of burning was intense, dark, and musky. Like the accompanying drum beats, it seemed to come from everywhere at once.

"Holy shit . . . ," gawked one of the Nu-Pioneerz.

Johnny Ray sensed his captors releasing their grip on him. Still feeling lightheaded and weightless, he started to fall—but caught himself before he hit the earth. He looked back over his shoulder and was amazed at what he saw.

A thick cone of sulphurous white smoke spumed up from the dark, broken soil—and an immense white horse stepped from the misty clouds.

On the horse's back sat a fearsome Indian warrior, with streaks of warpaint on his weathered cheeks and a bow and arrow ready in his hands. His color was pale, almost white, but it changed as he rode from the mist. His skin tone glowed to a coppery red. His hair grew black and shiny, the decorative eagle feathers long and brown. And the translucent arrowhead poised on his bow became a solid, dark flint. The Indian drew back the bowstring and let the arrow fly. It sailed silently through the air.

And went straight into Wild Bill's throat.

Screaming and coughing, with blood pouring from his lips, the young skinhead dropped his carbine in the dirt and struggled to pull the arrow free. He collapsed to his knees, delirious with shock and pain.

Gunfire from the Nu-Pioneerz crashed like heavy artillery as its sound boomed off the concrete walls. A flintlock rifle let out a plume of smoke, Colt revolvers and Winchester long guns spat lead, and a rattling Uzi emptied its clip with the brutal efficiency of a high speed drill. Hot brass cartridge casings jingled to the concrete, smoldering like cast-off Marlboros.

But the mounted Indian warrior nudged his horse and rode forward, notching another arrow on his bow. He was joined by two more braves, whose color changed from ghostly white to murderous crimson as they rode from the smoky mist. They nimbly steered their galloping mounts across the broken concrete pillars, over sawhorses, between the 55-gallon drums, and out onto the concrete.

What great riders, Johnny Ray Lonebird thought as he watched them. Then he realized what tribe they must be from—the legendary horsemen of the plains, just as Gramma Lonebird had so proudly described them to him time after time.

Comanches . . .

Something stirred deep in his blood. A primordial memory. A tribal spirit.

Crockett beckoned and shouted commands to his awe-struck, scattering gang. "Fall back! Get the wagons in a circle!"

The Nu-Pioneerz scrambled to their vehicles, which the drivers now noisily fired up. Spoked wheels crushed dozens of the teepee-shaped traffic cones as the prairie schooners rolled into a ragged loop. The gang took cover behind, and frantically passed around extra weapons and ammunition. The shooting began again, the Nu-Pioneerz spraying gunfire indiscriminately in the direction of the circling Comanche warriors.

The bullets seemed to pass right through the Indians. Many of the shots zinged off the walls, breaking away chips of concrete. Others punched into the parked automobiles, shattering glass and triggering a variety of car alarms which added the whooping, chirping, ringing, beeping soundtrack of a video arcade to the bloody encounter.

The sound of war drums was even louder now. The frightening rhythm blended with the chaos of shouts, shrieks, hoofbeats, and gunblasts.

The Comanche war party was now twenty strong. They rode easily around the ring of wagons, launching arrows and casting war lances with deadly precision. One of them hurled a tomahawk which struck Crockett hard in the face, cleaving his nose.

Four airport security motorbikes puttered down the ramp and into the fray. One of them steered too wide on the turn, crashing into a pair of blue Isuzu Troopers and a single white Ford Ranger with black-masked windows. Car alarms went off, the two Troopers blowing a cavalry charge, and a voice-synthesizer on the lone Ranger letting out a mighty cry of, *"HI-HO SILVER!"*

The uniforms drew their pistols and opened fire on the Comanches. Within seconds, a responding volley of lances, arrows, and tomahawks had silenced all four of the men in blue.

Johnny Ray, still lightheaded from the shock of his wound and his fall, took a step backward. He nearly tripped over something large and smooth behind him. Turning in place and looking down, he was stunned by what he saw lying in the Texas soil.

It was himself.

Johnny Ray Lonebird—dead at age nineteen from a .30-30 rifle slug fired in the Level 1 employee parking deck of the Dry Plains International Airport.

He reached out to touch his own face and felt his hand

pass through it. The body in which he now stood was translucent white, but slowly its color began to return—a deep, *deep* red.

He felt something heavy in each of his hands. In his left was a long stone knife. In his right was a tomahawk adorned with brown eagle feathers.

A pinto pony whinnied impatiently nearby. It stamped the earth with its right front hoof and whinnied again.

Johnny Ray walked up to the animal, stroked the dense fur of its white and brown coat, and then vaulted effortlessly up onto its back.

The Comanches were moving in for the final kill now; and the Nu-Pioneerz, overrun by the braves, were making their last stand. The Indians set to the work of slaughter, rape, and trophy-taking. Two of them drew their knives and began to remove Crockett's unique scalp.

Johnny Ray nudged his pinto and rode proudly forward, with red blood surging in his heart and Indian war drums pounding mightily in his ears.

Here, amidst the blood and the smoke and the screams . . .

Here, with the earthy scent of warpaint in his nostrils . . .

Here, with his brothers . . .

Here, at last, Johnny Ray Lonebird *belonged*.

TO FEED THE SUN

David Niall Wilson

JULIO'S STEPS ECHOED LOUDLY THROUGH THE NEARLY DESERTED airport, accompanied by the loud squeaking of the wheels on his mop bucket. It was late, too fucking late to be cleaning up after a bunch of fat, inconsiderate people. He wouldn't have been there at all, but Margarita, the maintenance supervisor, had offered him extra money for taking the late shift.

"The others," Margarita had said, "they do not like this place, Julio. They will not come in the night, some not even in the day. They say there are spirits . . . Aiii! We have an airport to clean, and they tell me we cannot do this, because there are ghosts in the baño? You do this for me, Julio, and I give you two more dollars an hour. You are a strong boy, not afraid, eh? Maybe one day you'll have my job? Eh?"

She sounded just like his mother, but two dollars more an hour was a lot of money. So here he was. A few minutes earlier he'd walked through the large first-floor men's room and made sure that all the stalls were empty. His bright yellow SECURED FOR CLEANING sign hung from its little frame in front of the door, and he pushed it aside so he could roll the mop bucket through. He planned to make quick work of this. Cleaning bathrooms was not high on the list of things he wished to accomplish in life.

As he entered the brightly lit, yellow-tiled room, he let out a curse. Down at the end of the row of sinks, which, he noted with disgust, were filthy, stood a man in a rumpled suit. The man was shaving, letting the hot water run freely down the drain.

"Hey," Julio called out. "Can't you *read*, man? This place is closed!"

Startled, the man slipped, drawing the cheap plastic razor in his hand roughly across his chin and releasing a trickle of blood. With a few choice words of his own, the man reached for a paper towel, dabbing at his wound and turning to glare at Julio.

"What the hell is the *matter* with you?" the man asked, his face reddening in anger. "I'm just trying to shave, for God's sake. I have a flight at 1:00 A.M. and . . ."

Julio didn't really hear the man. He was watching the blood. It ran slowly down the man's chin and dripped to the white porcelain of the sink, missing the paper towel altogether. Julio shook his head slowly, but the sight held him with an eerie fascination.

It wasn't the blood itself; he'd seen plenty of that. It was the way it steamed when it hit the sink, like it was hitting a hot frying pan in his mama's kitchen. And the guy didn't even seem to notice.

Wherever a drop of the blood hit, smoke rose. Not small wisps, but in steady streams, like those smoke bombs called "snakes" that were sold before the fourth of July. It wasn't until the tendrils of mist reached nearly to the guy's nose that he finally spun back to the sink and to the mirror.

"What?" the man said, barking the word like a startled dog. It was the last word ever to leave his lips. The smoke thickened around him as he tried to backpedal, swirling and coalescing, one stream for each drop of blood, blending like a small, impossibly thick whirlwind. Julio wanted to back away, but he could not. It was like watching a horror movie, or riding a roller coaster. The fear was there, cold and biting, but he could not turn away—could not escape.

There was a gurgling scream. Julio knew it must be the guy in the suit, but he could no longer make out any details. The fog-like mist had filled the room, cutting him off on all sides. Then the air before his eyes began to clear again, and what he saw in front of that damned mirror just wasn't possible.

There were two men there now. The newcomer was shorter than the first, but powerfully built. His hair flowed down over deeply-tanned shoulders, and his chest was adorned with strange, painted designs. He held the other man's limp form by the throat with one hand. The other hand was raised above his head. As the vision continued to clarify, becoming more distinct, Julio saw the man bring that second hand in a vicious downward swing, saw at the last second the thick, wooden head of a club, feathers trailing in its wake. He tried to move, to scream, but his lungs seemed to be filling with the mist, and he could not control his limbs.

The club met with the skull of the man who would never make his 1:00 flight. Bright blood spattered the room—hanging impossibly from the mist. The short man with the club turned toward Julio, catching him in a fierce, challenging stare. He wore a strange cape—it seemed to be made solely of feathers. The man began moving forward with slow, predatory steps. Terrified, Julio saw that the man was now backlit by an incredible glare of sunlight. It filtered through a line of trees that were outlined by a clear blue sky, not yellow tile and fluorescent light. His vision blurred once more, and the room seemed to spin beneath him.

He felt his elbows brush the floor, then he felt the sharp crack of his head on the tiles, but it was as though the pain was far away, a memory, or someone else's. What Julio was concerned with was not what he felt, but what he saw. The mist, swirling once more, was reforming into the shape of a small tornado, and the base of that twister was headed for his face. Before he could even try to move, to escape, the thickened, whirling fog entered his mouth, trailing a few wisps up through his nostrils, and sucked itself inside him as though he were a vacuum. It filled his lungs until he thought they would burst, stealing his oxygen. Then there was blackness, cool and deep, and he saw no more.

It was nearly five in the morning before another passenger entered the first-floor men's room of the airport, frowning and sidestepping the cleaning sign. It was another twenty minutes until he managed to get hold of anyone in authority, and another five before the police were called. Meanwhile a large crowd had gathered, all trying to squeeze far enough forward to get a glimpse of the body.

"They say his head's caved clean in," a short, bowlegged man in a faded black T-shirt confided to his neighbor. "Say it was some Mexican cleaning kid—must've used a baseball bat or something."

"They caught the guy?" another asked.

"Not so's I've heard," the man in black replied, enjoying his moment of slight notoriety. "Hear tell he's loose in here somewhere. Police'll roust him, I reckon."

Almost as if in answer, sirens rose in the background, lending an eerie accompaniment to the babble of voices. Julio heard it all from his concealment in the shadowed stairwell that led to the building's lower levels. He did not feel fear. His eyes had taken on an intensity of purpose, almost a glow of growing strength and inner power.

The sun was just rising; he had glimpsed it through the large glass windows at the front of the airport. It was pale, not yet filled with the strength of the day. He knew what must be done and done quickly. There was little time to waste.

He hardly resembled the boy who had gone into the men's room so short a time before. He had ripped the restraining shirt from his shoulders, knotting a strip of it in a band across his forehead. He had cut the seams of his jeans so that they flapped loosely from the knees down, giving him more freedom of movement. On his belt, the flap of his buck knife sheath was loose. He had a vague desire for another sort of knife—dark, like glass—flashing with captured sunlight, but he shrugged it off as unimportant.

Through the windows, along with the rising sun, he'd seen the gleaming white stone of the control tower across the runway. Stone steps wound around the outside of the building—leading to the roof, where maintenance workers could access the antennas for the various radar and communications gear. Another vague flash of memory intruded itself on his concentration—wider steps and towers narrowing at the top—and again he shrugged it off. He must not grow confused or slow, not now. Pulling himself even deeper into the shadows, he waited.

* * *

"I don't see why they're so certain that this kid is still hanging around," Officer Jim Rainey whined to his partner, Tom Groton. "Don't even see why they're so certain he's the killer. Odds are we'll find him tucked away, chopped into pieces, while the real killer walks on out with the security guards."

"Cut it out, Jim," Tom answered sourly. "Just keep your damned eyes open. You may not have noticed it, but that guy's head was smashed like a pumpkin. You might want to see this guy before he sees you, if possible."

"Shit," Jim replied, obviously not convinced. He'd been at Dunkin' Donuts twenty minutes before, working eagerly on his second creme-filled doughnut, and he had no patience for this type of nonsense. He moved his imposing, 250-pound-plus form as stealthily as possible, but his heart wasn't in it.

They were moving slowly down the stairs to the basement level of the old building. The lighting was dim, casting shadows in all directions like cold, silent sentinels. Nothing moved, and the air was chill and somewhat damp. They never heard a sound.

Julio moved without thought, bringing the knife up in a fast, short arc that caught the shorter, slimmer man directly in the throat, dropping him with a strangled, gurgling sound. Whipping around with astonishing agility, he sidestepped the collapsing body of his first victim and slid quickly back to the shadows. The large, fat one stopped, staring in disbelief at the fallen body of his partner, outlined in a growing pool of blood. The hesitation was a mistake. With cold precision, Julio brought the hilt of the buck knife down across the back of the man's skull, dropping him instantly beside his partner, still breathing.

Now every minute would count. Outside the sun was rising rapidly to its throne in the sky, and there would be others following these two—more enemies. He pulled the bloody corpse of the thin man into the shadows, relieving the body quickly of its gun, which he tucked into his own belt. He silently cursed whatever gods had sent the smaller man down the stairs first. His task would not be easy, working alone, and this had complicated it even further.

Grabbing the unconscious body of the second officer

beneath the arms, he began to drag him slowly toward the maintenance elevator along the far wall. It was no easy task, and sweat coated his brow in a fine sheen, leaking into his eyes to burn him. He shook it off, unwilling to be distracted. Just as he heard a fresh set of voices at the stairs, calling into the darkness, the elevator doors closed quietly, cutting off all sound.

There was a dolly in the elevator, used normally for hauling luggage out to the jets on the runway. He maneuvered the man onto it as quickly as possible, removed the handcuffs jingling on the officer's belt, and fastened the larger man's hands behind his back securely. He might not be unconscious long, and there would be no time for dealing with him once they were out in the open—beneath the sun, bathed in its primal strength.

The doors slid open again, and Julio moved out, not even waiting to see what he would face on the other side. It did not matter. Whatever he faced, he would deal with it. He felt the comforting weight of the gun against his hip and smiled grimly. For a moment, he felt an odd, uncomfortable sensation—the gun seemed to fade from his thoughts— something about a club. He shook it off, concentrating on the tower ahead of him. It shimmered in the growing heat of the sun, glistening white and silhouetted against a clear blue sky.

He was barely aware of his surroundings. Nobody, at this point, had taken any notice of him. Ground crews went about their own business and porters scooted about on their separate missions, none immediately taking heed of yet another figure who moved as though he had a job to do. Julio was nearly halfway to the tower before a maintenance crew chief spotted him.

"Hey," the man called out in irritation, "get that cart out of here! Don't you know where the hell you're going? That's a damned runway; you want to get killed?"

Then the man grew silent, realizing three things all at once. One, Julio was not dressed in anything resembling a uniform; two, the "luggage" on the cart was a man, not moving, and for all he knew, dead; and three, there was a gun pointed directly at his face. Julio never hesitated. The .38-caliber slug caught the man in the right shoulder, narrowly missing his neck, and spun him around as though he'd been struck. He fell roughly to the tarmac, blood already soaking the right side of his shirt and pooling on the runway beneath him. The man's screams had alerted the rest of his crew, but they were none too eager to move in on an armed lunatic. Julio ignored them. The sight of the man he'd shot, blood glistening on the ground, feeding the sun, strobed through his mind, setting up a rhythmic beat that pounded through his veins, lending him new vitality, clearer purpose. He turned back to the tower and moved off as rapidly as possible.

The tower loomed above him, bright and glistening, a mountain of white stone . . . the temple. The sunlight was filtered through the waving branches of trees that lined his path on either side. The ground was soft and grassy beneath his feet. His prisoner groaned, shaking his head groggily from side to side as he tried to orient himself. Julio gave him no chance. He placed the black, obsidian blade of his dagger against the man's throat and beckoned with his eyes toward the tower.

In the distance, his pursuers were only indistinct blurs—somehow blending with the tree line, their voices a murmur of incomprehensible sound. He ignored them, dragging his enemy roughly to his feet and shoving him toward the tower. The two of them mounted the wide, seemingly endless steps and began to ascend.

The man tried to speak, to beg, but Julio silenced him with pressure from the knife. There was no time, and he had no patience for the weakness of one who would grovel before an enemy. It was an honor being bestowed, a sacred duty he performed. He would not allow this fat outsider to mar the moment.

He could feel the man's fear. He pressed himself against the man's sweat-soaked back, controlling him with the dagger, moving him relentlessly forward. The sun was beating down upon them in strengthening waves—he felt invincible.

Strange sounds reached him from far below—from the base of the stairs—but they were too late. He could see the temple's top level; he was approaching it rapidly. They were too slow. As he shoved his prisoner over the last few steps and watched him collapse on the shining stone, Julio raised his arms to the sunlight, drinking it in, becoming one with its power and light. He could see his enemy's eyes as he fully comprehended the moment, could taste the fear and the helplessness as his dagger plunged downward—could feel the rending of the fat, worthless flesh as he offered its blood to the sun. . . .

There was a scream and a flash of light. Pain exploded through Julio's back, radiating from the left side outward, and he staggered forward, leaving the dagger firmly imbedded in his enemy's chest. Turning, he saw—hazily—figures pouring onto the rooftop. Something deep inside reached up and out, and he suddenly remembered the gun. He pulled it free, pointed it at his enemies, and emptied it as they dove to the sides, screaming.

They were too many. He would not escape, but neither would he be a slave. Turning his back to them in contempt, he ran as quickly as his injured side would allow toward the far side of the temple. With a final scream of defiance, he leapt into the bright blue of the sky, feeling more fiery jolts strike his body as he hit the air. Behind him cries of anger and dismay trailed after him, but he was concentrated. The sun filled his eyes, drenched him with power. He soared, an eagle in flight, a spirit—an arrow aimed at the heart of his enemies. It was the grandest of deaths, the holiest of visions . . . Below, the tarmac waited, gleaming and hungry.

Those below saw the body arcing gracefully into the air, saw it plunge downward to embrace the ground. The crowd scattered, screaming. From above, the police and security guards had rushed to the wall, gazing downward. When Julio struck, spattering blood against the side of the building and over an incredibly wide stretch of runway for only one body, a strange, misting smoke arose. It seemed to whirl like a small vortex, rising from wherever droplets of his blood fell. Then it was gone, sucked into the ground as though by a giant vacuum, leaving no trace.

When questioned, airport officials stuck to their story. The reports stated that a young man, probably on drugs, had killed three men, committing suicide immediately after the last two. There was also no mention of the strange blade—black obsidian—that the police found protruding from Officer Jim Rainey's back, or how it had smoked, flared, and been replaced by a simple buck knife.

None noticed that the sun seemed to shine a bit more brightly.

TIRE FIRE

Nancy Holder

ABOUT SIX MONTHS BEFORE DWIGHT SELF-ACTUALIZED AND ATE Angelo, his blood brother, he and Angelo fell into the same mood one night after their show at the Dry Plains Dome (great gig, thousands of Texan cats screaming "Yee-ha!"). They looked at each other and nodded. It was not their "Let's prowl" look. It was their "Hey, this is too much energy, too many blondes saying 'Y'all wanna blow job?', too much shit, let's split" look.

It took just a millisecond to flash this look between them—they were blood brothers, after all—because they both knew that somehow fame was not something bitchen tonight, just a goddamn gorilla riding their leather-clad asses. You dream, you get a garage band; you dream bigger, you go to Hollyweird. And all the dreams come true, but sometimes it's like someone turns on the dream blender—wheerreee!—and you get this goop that's kind of like nightmare purée cuz it's all too much. Hard to explain to someone who hasn't been there, but the cannibal cats both grokked it, and they knew they needed some space. Which Texas was supposed to have a lot of.

The after-gig bimbitas in the dressing rooms howled like banshees when the boys hopped on their Harleys, not realizing that Plan A was for their idols to have picked one of them and chomped her for a late-night snack. But the groupsters were saved—praise the Lord and the open road—when the boys put the pedal to the metal under the weepin', seepin' Texas moon. Which was Plan B.

They zoomed along to riffs of companionable gear shifts and bursting mufflers, Angelo pulling ahead like he always did. Dwight wasn't exactly thrilled to eat his dust, but he liked watching Angelo on his hog. They had both changed from rock-star performance leathers to rock-star high-performance leathers, and Angelo had righteous long black hair. Dwight was a redhead, kinda washed out. They went to a majorly expensive salon in the Hills to get their perms, but Angelo's hair held better. He'd always looked better, from when they'd met in high school and found out they were cannibals, to the struggling days in Hollywood before they got their record contract. And now that they were hotter than—what? Hotter than any fuckin' thing you could name, buckwheat—hotter than a tire fire—

—shit, Angelo looked much better in black leather than he did—

—And Dwight knew it. Well, what the heck. Angelo had put the whole thing together anyway, from the group to the deal. He deserved a little extra, Dwight supposed.

Angelo swerved around something. Dwight slowed. Jackrabbit. Dwight was surprised. Lots of times, Angelo just ran over stuff. Live stuff. Like he ate it.

Alive.

Like he ran over anybody who got in their way.

His way.

Dwight shifted to catch up. Angelo didn't look back, didn't need to. He knew Dwight lived in his brake lights.

But that would've been okay if Angelo hadn't eaten the only girl Dwight had liked—correction—the only girl who had liked him: Alice, their girl singer early on. An angel. And Angelo—what a name for him—had done her, alone, not even sharing; and probably cuz he knew Dwight liked her.

Dwight sped up. Faster. Faster.

Angelo left him in the dust. Dwight could swear that over the roar of the engines, he could hear the asshole laughing.

The moon was a big fat tit hanging in the sky, squirting out stars. Dwight thought about that for a while; there was a song in there somewhere, yessir. He'd have to tell Angelo. Angelo wrote most of their songs. He played lead guitar, too.

Dwight could do bass, but mostly he strutted in the laser light and dry ice and smoke, digging his image, even though part of him knew it *was* just an image and he was one meat-eating Cinderella for whom it all came down, as in tumbling, around four or five every morning.

Well, you couldn't have everything, and he had a lot. He and Angelo were fuckin' millionaires, with ancillary merch out the yin-yang, dudes like Jack Nicholson hanging with them. Anything they wanted, they snapped their fingers and the Japanese gangsters who owned their record company brought it to them wrapped in silk. So what if he felt like he didn't deserve any of it? Angelo kept telling him that would come in time. But how would *he* know, anyway? Angelo had been born feeling like the world owed him.

Angelo turned and waved. Dwight felt a rush of shame. Shit, if it hadn't been for Angelo, he'd be dead by now, beaten to death by his old man, same as Daddy had beaten Mom (bullshit that she fell down the stairs—No one on the dog-eat-dog planet believed that number, but no one could prove anything, either). And he also wouldn't know that he was a cannibal.

Which wasn't the coolest thing to know about yourself.

And mucho hard to deal with.

But still, you had a nature, it was good to admit it and do something about it. Kind of like Cannibals Anonymous, only he and Angelo weren't into stopping, no way; cuz they couldn't eat anything else anymore, and you do what you have to do to survive: twin lessons courtesy of their appetites and the music industry, dig it.

Plus, of course, there was no taste on earth like human flesh. Psychedelically delicious space food from heaven, amen.

They drove on, Dwight falling farther behind—what was it, the way he shifted? His choice of gas?—and the black-licorice road cut through sand and sage, an occasional picturesque cactus. Tumbleweeds, dig 'em. They sure had come a long way from their hometown in Ohio.

Angelo swerved again, in a major way this time, sailing off the road and managing several rotations through the sand before the bike skidded sideways and he flew off like a crash-test dummy.

Dwight shouted, "Oh, shit!" and raced to aid his blood brother.

He got there in no time—he wasn't that far behind after all—and Angelo was already on his feet, dusting the sand off his leather jacket and pants, swearing.

"Goddamn! Did you see that fucker, Dwight?" He threw his helmet in the sand and thrust his head up, hands on his hips. The moon shone on his profile.

Dwight unstrapped his helmet and laid it on his seat. "Angelo, man, what's wrong?"

"Didn't you see it? It was right there!" Angelo jabbed at the sky.

Dwight looked up. The stars, the tit-moon, the black velvet. He looked at Angelo.

"Um, like what?"

"Jesus, Dwight! How could you miss it?" He moved in a circle with his head up, like he was playing some kind of Blind Man's Bluff without a blindfold. "How'd it move so fast?"

Dwight shifted his weight on his hip. He wondered what Angelo was on, and why he hadn't shared. They were blood brothers; they were supposed to share everything.

Yeah, a voice inside him said. *Like Alice?*

"It was just here." Angelo scratched his head, careful not to disturb his curls even though the fall had done a righteous job of that. "Didn't you see that plane?"

Dwight said nothing, only shook his head. Angelo murmured, "God*damn*. There was a plane up there, Dwight. It was way big. Maybe a jet. It just swooped down—" He stopped talking and looked just about as sheepish as Angelo ever did. Which wasn't very.

"I thought I saw one, anyway. It seemed like it was diving straight at us. That's why I swerved."

"The second time," Dwight said, remembering the rabbit.

"Yeah." Angelo grinned. "Didn't want to mess up my wheel."

Of course not. It really had nothing to do with the rabbit.

"Well." Angelo walked over to his bike. "Help me?"

Together they righted his bike. Angelo checked it over. Wheeled it back toward the road.

It suddenly occurred to Dwight that Charlie, their road

manager, would be worried about them, or pissed off, or both: they had to haul ass to Houston for tomorrow's gig.

"I guess we'd better get back," he ventured.

"Little mama. *Mamacita.*" Angelo grinned. "You're so responsible, Dwight."

Dwight shrugged. He'd much rather be irresponsible.

"I guess I just had a flashback or something." Angelo scanned the sky. "But that was fucking weird." He shuddered. "Scary."

"Bummer," Dwight said, and mounted his Harley.

Waiting for Angelo, who got on, kick-started, and zoomed off.

Leaving Dwight in his dust.

But the road had changed, or something.

Or something.

It wasn't the same road at all. It wasn't straight, and it zoomed up and down a bunch of hills; and it wasn't leading anywhere near the Dry Plains Dome. It veered to the left—only way to go, no choice, no fork, fork you—and Angelo slowed so Dwight could catch up.

"What the fuck's up?" Angelo shouted. "We miss a turn?"

Dwight let go of his handlebars to make a shrug. He shook his head, too, in case Angelo didn't get it that he didn't get it.

And this time, while Angelo was looking at Dwight, and not the road, a jackrabbit felt the need to bound across the road and didn't make it, not by a mile of intestine, dude; because that little sucker shot straight up in the air while it exploded from the impact. Just *boing!* with all its guts flying out like New Year's Eve streamers, guck, guck, guck, spraying Angelo, who flew like a guided missile up, up and over, and smashed face-first onto the berm at the side of the road.

The truth of the matter was, that along with the shock, horror, and terror that raced through Dwight, trotted a fleeting, mean, nanosecond of a thought that said, *Now he won't be the best-looking one;* and later on, Dwight would fix it mentally so he didn't believe he'd actually thought that. He might be kind of dumb, and not very handsome, but being a cannibal cat had taught him excellent denial skills.

Before he knew what he was doing, he half-stopped, half-dove off his bike and flew to Angelo's side. He dropped to his knees with his hands halfway to Angelo's body, like a surgeon about to plunge into the left ventricle.

Holy shit, was if he was dead?

"Holy shit," he said aloud. "Angelo, Jesus! Holy shit!"

He didn't know what to do. Turn him over? CPR? Touch him at all?

He pressed his hand on Angelo's back, dirtying their rocker, which read "The Tokers." The logo was a pair of fat lips like the Rolling Stones, smoking a hand-rolled joint. Not too politically correct.

He didn't feel a heartbeat, or lungs chugging, nothing. But he didn't know if he could feel those things through the thick leather, anyway.

"Angelo," he said. "Man, can you hear me?"

Nothing.

"Angelo." He leaned his head next to his hands. Brushed some of Angelo's hair away. Maybe he was suffocating in the sand. Gingerly Dwight dug next to the side of Angelo's face. Then he crouched with his butt straight up to the stars and stared at Angelo's temple.

"Here goes," he muttered, and turned Angelo's head.

It came easy. Maybe too easy.

Angelo's face was covered with blood. His nose was smashed in. His lips—Dwight couldn't make them out. Fear and anguish made him want to puke.

"Angelo, Angelo," he whispered, placing his finger under the ruins of Angelo's nose. No air. Down at his mouth, or where it might be. No air.

"Oh, God," Dwight went for it, rolled him over, grimacing as he pictured Angelo in an iron lung or a wheelchair or something.

Angelo was a rag doll; he was a sack of flour. He was a body.

Oh, Jesus. He was fucking dead.

Dwight sat motionless with shock. It couldn't be. It couldn't be. Part of his mind sped ahead, to a funeral home and mortuary services, picking out a coffin (bury him in leather? in a suit?).

To interviews ("How Dwight Jones Is Taking the Blow"; "Dwight's Solo Career—How He Feels About His New-found Success"; Arsenio, Jay, David).

To tears. Tears splashed on his leather jacket. Snot. He threw back his head, wailing, rocking back and forth. It couldn't be. It could not be.

"Angelo," he whispered. "Angelo, man, I'm sorry." Because he was, for every resentment, every karmically uncool thought; for being pissed about Alice. For thinking Angelo was a dickhead, which he *had* thought, on occasion.

He was mortally, horribly sorry.

Angelo lay there with stuff pumping out where his nose had been, like all his innards were body boogers and he was cleaning himself out.

To Dwight's own personal disgust, he began to salivate. Two gigs, no food. He was hungry. But goddamn, this was his blood brother! That was one of those fancy Greek-god crimes, brother-eating!

Yeah, and some pygmy tribes ate their dead relatives. He and Angelo had read up on that kind of stuff.

Tears streaming down his cheeks, he dipped his forefinger in the chunky stuff and tasted. Closed his eyes as he reeled. Psychedelically delish. Oh, God. Oh Angelo, man, you're the best.

Surreptitiously, as if the tumbleweeds or the vultures might catch him at it, and narc, he swiped up another taste.

In the distance, he heard a roar, like that of a plane.

He tipped back his head. Angelo had seen something up there, freaked him out so bad he lost his traction.

But Dwight saw nothing. The tears careened down his face as he searched the sky.

Nothing.

Yet the roaring continued. Loud, rumbling, vibrating the desert floor around him. Grains of sand hopped up and down like Orville Redenbacher's Popcorn.

Angelo's hair flew around his massacred face as if he were still peeling down the open road.

Dwight half-stood. He looked to his right, at the thin line of asphalt.

A huge black bike flashed toward him. Behind it, another, another, another. Holy shit, there were a dozen of them. No, twenty.

He got up and ran to the road, flailing his hands. "Help! Help!"

They flew closer. The lead driver was a woman. Under a leather jacket, she wore a black bra top and bike pants. Jesus, high heels. Backless ones. Close-cropped black hair and cocoa-colored skin. Shades that wrapped halfway around her head.

She raised a hand and the convoy slowed. Stopped her bike, put down the stand, and threw her leg over the saddle. Stood facing Dwight.

"Yeah?" she said.

"My—my partner. I think he's dead."

She nodded. She had on hot pink lipstick. How he could see this all so clearly he had no idea. The moon, yeah, but it was like all his senses were heightened. Angelo's hallucination—had he taken something so powerful that Dwight had ingested it with his two swipes of blood?

"Get him," she directed the other riders.

Big guys, bad dudes, some with spiked Nazi helmets, got off their bikes. They were brown, too, with long black hair that trailed over their shoulders. One turned; his rocker read, "The Comanches."

They ambled like apes over to Angelo. Before Dwight could say a word, one picked him up and hoisted him over his shoulder. Ambled back to his bike, sat, and waited.

"I—I—" Dwight stammered.

"Get your bike. We're riding," the woman told him.

"But—"

"Get on and shut up."

She didn't even wait to see if he obeyed. Cuz it was like that, an order, not a suggestion or even a fuckin' request. Numbly, Dwight did as he was told—didn't he always?—and got on his bike. He wondered about Angelo's Harley, then wondered why the fuck he was wondering about something like that. His best, his only friend in the world, had augured in.

By the time he had it together enough to start up his bike, the leader of the Comanches, her band, and Angelo—as usual—left him in the dust.

He roared around behind them. The wind howled and clouds gathered; there was going to be a major storm and it wasn't going to wait for no funeral procession. The road wound and twisted, going nowhere he had been before—grok it, James T. Kirk—and he was getting so freaked he thought about splitting off and going the other way. But they had Angelo, and he couldn't leave him now.

He heard another roar, from above, and looked up. A plane. Another. They must be near the airport. What was the name of this hellhole? This goddamn awful place they should never have come to? He couldn't recall. Angelo had called it Dry Hustle. Dry something.

Shit, he would never stop crying. Never in his life.

Past tumbleweeds, past acres of moonlit sand, and all of a sudden the whole posse made a sharp right onto the sand and rode along as fine as you could want, like Jesus walking on water or something, dig it; Dwight stopped and cut a wide swath like a hockey player.

At the front of the line, the woman glanced at him but didn't put up her hand and shout "Wagons, halt!" or anything, just went along like she didn't give a fuck if he stopped here and dried into bones like those zippy cow skulls people used to stick in their front yards with orange gravel and cacti and shit.

So he figured, they could do it, he could. But he was pretty much wrong. It was a major hassle, getting through the grains, though it wasn't as bad as he would have expected. About this time, Dwight figured either these guys had special wheels, or something majorly strange was going on.

And then they all kind of shimmered, or rippled; they got vague, like. He could see through them!

The stuff in Angelo's blood, the stuff in Angelo's blood, he chanted over and over, until it sounded like, Follow the yellow brick road.

They turned sort of silver, and Dwight heard whoops and war chants, Indian-style, echoing off cliffs he couldn't see. The thunder of horse hooves—

Overhead, another plane angled downward for a landing at the airport.

Wherever the hell the airport was.

Angelo was dead. Follow the yellow brick road. Angelo was dead.

Dwight wept uncontrollably.

They made another one of their most bizarre lefts and sped up. Dwight limped along, squinting at a massive shape in the distance. Airport, he guessed.

Junkyard was the right answer. The motherfucker of all junkyards, with stacks of cars ten, fifteen high, and gigantic rolls of wire shit, and rusty things and stinky things and things that crunched when you rolled over them.

And riding the piles of crap like a trio of surfers, the hugest tires he had ever seen in his life.

The convoy stopped without a word from the woman. They dismounted. The man who carried Angelo broke off from the rest and laid him semi-gently on a torn-up mattress splattered with black stuff.

The woman strode up to Dwight, who was having trouble with his kickstand on account of he couldn't see so good, with the tears and sand in his eyes; and also on account of he was so torqued out he couldn't even talk. This was one long fuckin' nightmare, as far as he was concerned, and he was just about to decide he had finally wigged out from the stress of being a cannibal, or that all the drugs he took had like mixed together and caused a massive power failure in his brain.

The woman stopped in front of him with her legs wide apart. She was all muscle, hardly any tits. She had on gloves, took them off, and rippled long, shocking pink nails at him. Didn't take off her shades. Shit, how could she see?

Dwight felt like a little kid around her. Cinderella, the gig was over and he was still just Dwight the Dweeb, while Angelo, who acted as the cover for his friend's nerdhood, lay on a scuzzy mattress sleeping the big sleep.

"Hi," she said.

Dwight swallowed. "Hi."

She grinned at him. She had big-bad-wolf teeth. Really big ones. "C'mere."

Oh, you gonna eat me, he wanted to say, but he did as she said. Trying for some show of machismo, strut, strut, and failing, utterly.

He walked up to her. She put her arms around his neck and opened her mouth. Her pink tongue snaked out. He bent toward her, thinking she wanted a kiss, wanted to slip him some of that tongue, but she threw back her head and laughed. Slapped him on the back.

"Waking Nightmare!" she called.

"You got that right," Dwight mumbled.

Her smile was almost awful to see. "That's the name of my lieutenant. We're the Comanches."

"Mmm-hmmm."

"This is our sacred territory."

Uh-oh, and they had trespassed. His hair stood on end. They had brought him and Angelo here cuz they were going to kill him!

"I didn't know. We didn't. We're—we're singers. We were tired, is all."

She cocked her head. "Sit down with me."

They walked to the mattress Angelo lay on, sat on the edge next to him. His face was still pumping, probably from being upside down on the dude's shoulder.

One of the riders came over, pot belly, T-shirt, big boots. He cast a sour gaze at Dwight before coming to attention in front of the woman.

"Some firewater, Waking Nightmare."

They both laughed. Dwight didn't have the heart to join in.

The man walked away. The woman put her hand on Dwight's thigh.

"You're cute," she said. "Aren't you famous?"

"Sorta." He shrugged. His thigh was tingling. "Well, yeah."

"You and him."

He couldn't look at Angelo's body. Nodded. "We're . . . we were . . . blood brothers." His voice broke.

"Yeah, I know." She leaned back on her hands, thrusting her breasts forward. Crossed her legs and dangled her shoe from her toes. "That's why we came." She pointed a long nail at Angelo. "His blood." The finger swiveled toward Dwight. "Your mouth."

Had they seen him? "Oh, man, I . . ."

She rolled onto her stomach and ran her tongue along the back of his hand. "I can still taste him," she said. "I can smell blood in the air." She stared at him through her dark glasses. "You're practically part of the tribe, you know that? We'll call you Bloodsucker. You like that?"

"Um, yeah," he said quickly. He would like anything she said, if it would help.

"You want to join us?" Before he could answer, she licked his hand again. "You want to fuck me?"

Waking Nightmare returned with two bottles of tequila. She took them without thanks, handed one to Dwight, and raised hers in salute.

"To you, Bloodsucker. For calling us in."

"But I didn't—"

"Drink." She started ramming the tequila down her throat, chug-chug; Dwight's eyes bulged as he watched her. Like water.

He said, "I don't do too good with booze anymore." All he could take was water. Food these days was definitely out. He and Angelo had discovered that the hard way, puking their brains out after a dinner of raw steak. It had to be human flesh.

And it was better if it was still alive.

"You're just a baby." She reached out and tousled his hair. Her hand was icy. "I could grow you up, little man." She threw down her empty bottle and stood up on her high heels, bowing her back.

"You want him back," she said. "All right. It's only fair, since that's the way we got called in."

She cupped her hands around her mouth and made a funny, high shriek. All the riders started cheering, not like "Right on!" but like *"Ai-ai-ai!"* like they were real fucking Comanche Indians. They danced in little circles, rode their bikes in littler ones.

The woman picked up Dwight's full tequila bottle and held it out. Waking Nightmare got on his bike, rode over to her and grabbed it. He stuck a wad of material in it, rode for the nearest pile of tires, lit the material, and threw the bottle.

Ka-pow! The tires began to smoke. They all cheered again, *"ai-ai,"* and got on their bikes.

"C'mon." She started walking, gesturing for Dwight to follow. Got on her bike, indicated he should sit behind her. While they got settled—there was nothing to her waist, but her flesh was creepy, so cold and clammy—the other riders threw more bottles, burning sticks, and cigarette lighters at the pile of tires.

A thick black smoke burgeoned out from the pile, spreading fast and heavy. It mushroomed up, spread out; it was everywhere, and rolling toward them like a squadron of Stealth bombers.

Dwight covered his mouth. She laughed and said, "Hang on!"

With a loud whoosh, flames shot into the air, fifty, sixty, a hundred feet, more. The heat was intense. The smell, fucking horrendous. Dwight leaned to the side and dry-heaved.

The flames blazed higher, higher, then were lost in smoke. Dwight glanced at Angelo's body. It would be consumed.

"Now!" the woman shouted, lifting her hand.

Everyone screamed out of the junkyard, calling *ai!"* Dwight shut his eyes tight and held onto the woman. Fresh tears streamed down his face; he felt like he'd been dunked in teargas.

He kept them closed while they drove; the smoke was growing thicker. It filled his chest; he couldn't even tell if his lungs were working.

He pounded her arm. "Choking," he managed.

"Don't be a pussy!" She revved her motor. "This'll close it down, see. Then we'll have easy pickings."

"What?" He could barely hear her.

"Easy meat!" she shouted. "Ea-sy meat!"

He shook his head and huddled behind her.

They rode, and rode, through the oily, hot smoke. He couldn't see anything.

But suddenly he didn't feel like he was on a bike at all, no way; he was on a fuckin' *horse.* Feathers tickled his nose— what the hell?—as they galloped along. *Ca-rump, ca-rump;* and Dwight thought, Okay, this is it. I have truly lost my mind.

Then the smoke lessened; and he was on a bike again. He opened his eyes.

They were screaming through an airport. People ran every which way, and the riders charged after them; Waking Nightmare mowed down a man in a hat, a woman with a dog carrier. A dog popped out, ran away in time.

Waking Nightmare waved at the leader, who gave him the thumbs-up. Then she pointed to a man with a cellular phone.

Waking Nightmare returned the thumbs-up. Then he drove straight for the man, tilted sideways like a trick rider, and grabbed the guy under the knees. Slung him over his back the way he had Angelo. He must've popped the guy, cuz there was no struggle.

"Let's go!" the woman shouted. How anyone could hear her through the pandemonium was up for debate, but like one person, all the riders did one-eighties and headed for the exits.

Back into the smoke, the motherfucker killer of all smoke. Dwight had no idea how he was living through it, but he was grateful. He wondered if the other guy would make it.

Back to the junkyard. The smoke had risen up, and the air in the yard itself was clearer, though still thick and gray and vile.

The man on Waking Nightmare's back started screaming and pounding on his back. Waking Nightmare zoomed past Dwight and drove in spirals that grew tighter and tighter; then he stopped his bike. The other riders circled, shrieking and shaking their feets, like they had something in them—

—guns, knives, clubs—

Dwight didn't really know how hard he was clinging to the woman until she patted his hand and said, "Easy, little boy. Little Bloodsucker."

Someone rode up with a length of rusted pipe. Someone else dragged over a small tire, then another, another. They set them in a circle, stuck the pipe in the middle, propped it up with bunches of junk.

Dwight knew what **was coming down. He** didn't know how or why, but it was **majorly clear what the** scene was.

They got the pile of tires high; they got the pole steady. They tied the airport dude to it. He was screaming and raging worse than a record producer on coke, worse than anything Dwight had ever seen. The girls he and Angelo ate—and that was all they ate, was girls—they boozed them up, gave them grass, so when it was supper-supper-supper-suppertime, as Snoopy would say, they hardly even noticed.

This was a lot different.

"Tire fire!" someone yelled.

The man had worn himself out, plus he was tied up really tight. So when Waking Nightmare lit the tires, all the guy did was raise his head, let it flop back down.

The tires caught, and it didn't take more than two, three minutes. Just as quick, the Comanches doused the flames, only they didn't go out much. They worked on it a long time; water wasn't the answer, somehow. But after a while, Waking Nightmare scrambled over them and scooped up what was left of the guy, which was ashes and chunks of bone. He used a cracked pottery bowl—must've found it in the heaps of junk—and when he was done, he carried it to the woman.

She took it, said something weird, like in a funny language, and the others said something back. Then she unscrewed her gas cap and poured the ashes into her tank.

She motioned for Dwight to come to her. He did. She rubbed two of her fingers into the residue and streaked his cheeks with it. Said, "Look, paleface." Pointed toward the scuzzy mattress.

Angelo was sitting up with his head between his hands. Slowly he raised his face. It was still bloody, but nothing was pumping.

"Jesus, where the hell are we?" he said. His voice was slurry. He touched his jaw. "Fuck, Dwight. I broke a tooth."

Dwight cried *"ai-ai-ai!"* and ran to his blood brother. He couldn't believe it! He couldn't fucking believe it!

"Angelo!" He wrapped him in a huge hug and rocked him. "Angelo!"

"Hey, Dwight, don't go faggy on me." Angelo pulled away. "What the hell's going on? Where the fuck are we?"

Dwight rocked back on his heels. "They saved you! They burned up the dude and then—"

"Who did?"

Dwight stopped. He turned around.

There was no one there. No riders, no woman. Just a pile of tires that were starting to smoke up the place in a very bad way.

"But—" He blinked. His heart began to do the locomotion (yeah, like it hadn't until then). A cold sweat broke out on his forehead.

"Angelo, we gotta get the fuck out of here, now."

"Yeah, okay." Slow-mo, Angelo stood. Said, "Where's my bike?"

Dwight couldn't stop staring at him. Walked like Angelo, talked like Angelo, must be Angelo. But how?

"Um, we left it back a ways."

"How's come I don't remember?"

"You crashed." Dwight started to cry. "Angelo, you . . . I thought you had augered in."

"Fuck you," Angelo said agreeably. "Come on, we gotta go. Charlie's probably out of his fuckin' mind by now."

Dwight's bike stood beside the mattress, right where he had left it. He started to get on. Angelo stopped him.

"Lemme drive," he said.

"Hey, you're in no shape, dude," Dwight protested, but Angelo swung himself onto the seat and patted the space behind him.

"Come on, brother."

Dwight hesitated. Then he shrugged. He swung behind him and put his arms around his waist.

They roared off, on asphalt that hadn't been there a minute ago.

"I'm hungry," Angelo said over the roar of the engine.

"Me, too."

"Maybe some chick'll still be there."

"Yeah!"

The whole damn road was normal again, straight and narrow. Behind them, smoke rose into huge plumes and lathered the sky. It ran after them like a herd of—

—like a band of—

The thunder of horse hooves, the cry of *"ai-ai-ai!"*

"You hear something, Dwight?" Angelo asked.

"No, bro." He smiled wistfully to himself. If something was out there, or up there, hey, it was finished with them. It was their pal.

And next gig, maybe he'd ignite a Uniroyal in her honor.

"Let's burn rubber, white eyes!" he shouted, and laughed so hard he nearly fell off the bike.

Angelo shook his head. "God, Dwight, you're such a dweeb."

And that was true, and Angelo was a dickhead to mention it, but just at that moment, Dwight didn't fucking care.

Cuz love is a heat that burns like a tire fire.

(And so is hate, but that's another story.)

WAR CRY

Edo van Belkom

THE CAB DRIVER LOOKED INTO HIS REARVIEW MIRROR. "THAT'LL be fifteen seventy-five, ma'am."

Maria Bellissimo shifted her sleeping eighteen-month-old daughter, Alma, from her right arm to her left, then leafed through the thin stack of bills in her purse. She pulled out a twenty and handed it to the cabby.

The cabby took a few seconds to make change. Maria didn't bother waiting for it. By the time he turned around to give it to her, she was already getting out of the cab.

"Thank you, ma'am," the cabby said, tipping his Rangers cap at her. He pocketed the change and pulled into traffic.

Maria was left standing beneath the dim overhead lights outside the departure level of Dry Plains International with her one piece of luggage sitting on the curb and her sleeping child in her arms. She glanced at her watch. It was eleven thirty-eight P.M.

"Oh my God," she whispered under her breath. Her flight was scheduled to leave in twenty-two minutes.

She slung her bag over her shoulder and nestled her daughter's head in the crook of her neck. Then, making sure both her burdens were secure, she stepped through the automatic doors and into the crowded terminal. Once inside, panic rose up within her. She stood motionless a moment, unable to move, as a never-ending stream of late-night travelers flowed around her. *I'll never make it in time,* she thought. But as she looked down the long row of ticket desks lining the length of the departure level's far wall and saw the green, white, and red of the Air Italy logo, she once again had reason to hope. The three-colored, winged *A* wasn't that far off. She ran toward it as quickly as she could, trying not to bump into too many people, or wake her sleeping daughter.

Maria had to be on Flight 306 for Rome—just had to. Her brother Antonio had called earlier in the evening from the family home in Cesena. The news was bad. Mama was sick again. The doctors said that this time, at seventy-two, she probably wouldn't recover. And while Mama lay on her deathbed, she'd asked for nothing but to see her youngest daughter one last time, and her newest granddaughter—the one named after her—just once before she died.

The Air Italy midnight flight out of Dry Plains was leaving on shorter notice than Maria would have liked, but it was the only flight for Italy out of Texas until the next evening. Maria couldn't possibly wait that long for another flight, and from the sound of Antonio's voice—even through the poor overseas connection—Mama couldn't wait that long either.

When she reached the Air Italy departure desk the attendant smiled politely and said, "Ciao."

Maria took a moment to catch her breath, then said, "My name is Maria Bellissimo. I called—"

"No problem," said the attendant, a young man in his twenties with short-cropped hair and a double-pierced left ear. "We have your ticket already prepared. The captain has been notified that he'd have a late-arriving passenger."

"Thank you," Maria said, relief washing over her in a wave. "Thank you so much."

"Of course, you'll have to carry your bag onto the plane with you, but there are a few empty seats so you won't have to hold your daughter in your arms the entire flight." The attendant handed Maria her ticket. "Your flight is boarding on Gate 7. They're probably waiting for you. You'd better hurry."

"Thank you," Maria said, returning the attendant's polite smile. She glanced at her watch, tightened the grip on her bag and adjusted her hold on her daughter. Gate 7 was at the other end of the building.

Maria tried to run through the terminal without disturbing her sleeping daughter, but as she weaved through the crowds that filled the busy departure level, the jostling of the run proved too much for the child to sleep through. Within seconds, the girl's head rose up and twisted sleepily about.

Noticing her daughter had wakened, Maria quickened her pace into a full run. There would be plenty of time to sleep on the plane.

The automatic doors to Gate 7 were currently under repair and the entrance was half as wide as normal. To get to the gate, Maria had to run around two businessmen standing in place talking. As she brushed by the gray-suited one on the right, she ran straight into a group of teenage punks.

Maria tried to stop herself, but couldn't avoid colliding with one of the teens, knocking her to the floor. The impact had startled the baby, causing her to cry out in an unfamiliar voice. The sound her daughter had made—a strangely muted cry full of great pain and suffering—sent a shiver through Maria's body.

"I'm sorry," she said, trying to calm the baby while offering a free hand to help the girl up. "I didn't see you."

The punk was a girl about seventeen. The left side of her head was clean-shaven while the shoulder-length hair on the right side was dyed the color of orange flame. Her left ear was pierced four times, her left nostril twice. Two tattooed tear drops leaked from the corner of her right eye. She was one of the many youths that hung out at the airport in gangs the way teens in other parts of the country hung out in shopping malls. But unlike malls, Dry Plains was open twenty-four hours a day and was a place to spend the night for more than few Texas teenagers. After having them around for years, security guards on the short-staffed night shift finally stopped trying to chase the kids away.

The young girl got up without taking Maria's hand and brushed herself off. There was a dark wet spot on the front of her army-green tank top just below a line of chain-linked safety pins. One of the pins had opened on impact, drawing blood.

"Are you all right?" Maria said, seeing the dark stain on the girl's shirt. "Did I hurt you?"

The punk looked at Maria and her daughter with wide

green eyes outlined in purple eyeliner. "I'm fine," she said, cracking a slightly sardonic smile. "Enjoy your flight."

The girl had turned back around to share a laugh with her friends before Maria had a chance to say another word. If she hadn't been in such a hurry, Maria might have asked what was so funny, but as it was she had no more time to waste.

She ran through the gate, had her bag scanned by airport security, and was running down the companionway with scant minutes to spare. Fortunately, Alma had returned her head to the crook of her mother's neck and was resting in a drowsy half-sleep.

"Ah, here you are," an attractive dark-haired stewardess said in a distinctly Italian accent as she ushered Maria on board.

The cabin door closed seconds after Maria boarded and the plane immediately began moving. "Right this way," the stewardess said, taking Maria's bag.

As Maria walked down the aisle, the eyes of each and every passenger followed her, as if to show their displeasure and disappointment at being held up by someone who wasn't a professional athlete or movie star.

When they reached Maria's seat, midway down the airplane just behind the wing, the face of the stewardess turned grave. "What happened to your daughter's arm?"

"What? What is it?"

"It looks like a bad cut," the stewardess said.

Maria sat down, placed Alma on her lap, and looked at the girl's left, then right arm.

"Oh my God," she said.

The child's arm was covered in blood. There was a jagged cut about three inches long on the fleshy part of the forearm midway between the wrist and elbow. The cut was still bleeding, sending a pair of crimson rivulets streaking down the arm towards the fingers.

"I'll bring the medical kit," the stewardess said, already turning and heading for the back of the plane.

Maria wet the tip of a handkerchief with her mouth and began wiping the lines of blood from her daughter's arm. It had never occurred to her that the blood she'd seen on the girl's shirt could have come from anyone but the teenage girl. Until that moment, Maria had never seen her daughter bleed.

"Poverina," she said, passing a trembling hand gently over her head. The child opened her eyes, looked at her mother, then returned to a deep but fitful sleep. "Poverina piccola."

The stewardesses completed their preflight safety briefing and the airplane came to a stop at the end of the runway. A few moments later, the plane began accelerating down the runway. Once airborne, the dark-haired stewardess returned to Maria with the plane's medical kit.

"How did it happen?" she asked as she set to work cleaning the remaining blood from the child's arm.

"I was running through the airport to make it on time when I bumped into a girl. She had metal things on her clothes, pins and chains and razor blades . . . They must have cut my daughter's arm," Maria said in a slightly ragged voice.

"Quell'aeroporto maledetto," the stewardess muttered under her breath. She opened her mouth as if she had more to say about Dry Plains, but held her tongue. She finished cleaning the child's arm in silence. Fortunately, the cut turned out to be little more than a scratch. "The blood made it look worse than it is," the stewardess said.

Maria breathed a deep sigh of relief. "Thank you," she said. "Thank you for all your help."

"That's all right. It's part of my job." The stewardess reached up and took two pillows out of the overhead storage compartment. "Maybe you'd like to let your daughter sleep in this seat," she said, gesturing to the empty aisle seat on Maria's right.

"Thank you," said Maria.

The stewardess eased the seat back and Maria gently lay her daughter down on her side. She didn't expect the girl to stay asleep for very long, but the seatbelt would hold her for a little while and in that time Maria might get some rest herself. God knows she needed it.

The stewardess covered Maria and her daughter with blankets and for the first time in the past three hours, Maria had nothing to remember, nothing to check and nothing to do. Placing a hand on the gently rising and falling chest of her sleeping daughter, Maria's own breathing fell into a deep and regular rhythm.

Maria woke to the sound of her daughter crying. It wasn't the kind of sound she was used to hearing nightly around three A.M. when the child wanted her bottle. This was more like the sharp, choppy cries of her daughter being frightened.

Maria rubbed the drowsiness from her eyes and reached over to comfort her daughter. It wasn't until she had her comfortably cradled in her arms that she saw it.

The cut on the child's arm had become infected. It had turned a light shade of green and was oozing a thick, foul-smelling white pus. To make things worse, the girl had peeled back the bandage and had been fingering the wound with her left hand for who knew how long. The cut was more like a gouge now, twice as deep and a third as long as it had been a few hours before.

Maria looked at the arm, unable to speak or move. Finally she covered the arm with a blanket and began waving frantically for the stewardess.

"What's wrong?" the stewardess said when she arrived.

"The cut on my daughter's arm . . ." Maria stammered. "It—"

The stewardess looked at the child's arm. "I'll see if there's a doctor on board."

Maria held her daughter's head in her arms and began rocking back and forth in her seat. Alma's cries grew louder and more distraught. People in the seats around Maria began to notice her, casting looks of annoyance in her direction.

It was half an hour before the stewardess returned, with a young man who looked to be in his mid-twenties.

"I couldn't find a doctor," she said, apologetically. "But I did find a medical student."

"I've got another year to go," the young man said.

The look of concern on Maria's face disappeared for a moment as she flashed a polite smile at the young man.

"My name's Claudio," he said, opening the airplane's medical kit.

Maria pulled the blanket away from her daughter's arm. An overwhelmingly putrid stench rose up from the festering wound causing Maria and others nearby to hold their breath to stop them from gagging.

When he saw the girl's arm, the young man was speechless. The infection was obviously unlike anything he'd ever seen before, let alone studied. It was mottled green, gray, and blue and . . . was *moving*.

"What's wrong with my daughter?" Maria cried, trying desperately to hold back her tears.

The young man blinked his eyes, but his gaze was locked solidly onto the writhing flesh. "I . . . uh," he stammered. "I'm not sure."

"What do you mean you're not sure?" Maria cried. "You have to do something for her! Please!"

The young man took a deep breath and set about cleaning the wound as best he could. Each time he tried to touch the wound, the child cried louder. Each time he wiped away some of the pus, more bubbled up to replace it. In the end he could do nothing more than place a sterile cloth over the open sore and wrap the arm in bandages.

"There's nothing more I can do," he said at last. "She needs to be taken to a hospital as soon as we land in Rome."

"I'll tell the captain," the stewardess said.

Maria ignored the people around her. All she could think about was her daughter. All she could hear was the agonizing cries of her child in agony.

People in the rows ahead and behind Maria popped their heads over the tops of the seats to have a look.

"Can't you shut that kid up?" shouted someone from the very back of the plane.

"Yeah," someone closer added. "Some of us are trying to sleep."

The child's crying rose in pitch, grew louder.

Maria began to sob.

Rome was still over three hours away.

A newlywed couple sat side-by-side watching the in-flight movie, a romantic comedy starring Ted Danson.

The wife leaned on the armrest between them, roughly pushing away the arm of her husband.

The husband, jostled awake from a deep sleep, reached

over and slapped his new wife in the mouth, loosening two of her teeth.

Maria stirred in her seat, awakened from a shallow sleep by the high-pitched cries of her daughter.

"What's the matter, honey?" she said, trying desperately to comfort and quiet the child in her arms.

Her daughter's eyes opened, lids lifting to reveal glazed black half-shells bulging out of their sockets. The utter blackness of her daughter's eyes repulsed Maria and she unconsciously loosened her hold on the child.

The child's mouth opened too, letting out a shriek that cut through the air like a knife blade through smoke. The shrill cry was painful to listen to. Maria reached up to cover her ears, letting go of her daughter and allowing her to fall to the floor.

The volume of the child's scream doubled and its pitch rose twofold. It also grew raspy, as if the cries of others were being added one by one.

People around Maria were putting their hands over their ears, trying to protect themselves from the child's maddening cries.

Maria collected herself long enough to realize she'd let her daughter fall to the floor. She reached down to pick her up and saw through the torn bandages that the cut in her arm had turned as black as her eyes. Even worse, the oozing pus had been replaced by a more ethereal excretion. Instead of a stinking white slime, the wound was emitting a smoke-like vapor that rose up from the child's arms like threads that curled above the passengers, forming a thin white cloud.

Maria returned her daughter to the comfortable bed of her bosom and tried to comfort her, tried to quiet her cries, but the child was long past the point of consolation.

The dark black half-shells of her eyes had dulled slightly and now looked flat and lifeless against the pale white skin of her face. The "O" of her mouth was wide and gaping, blasting out what sounded like the anguished moans of a hundred slowly dying souls.

Above the passengers, the vaporous clouds flowed throughout the airplane from the rear exit doors all the way to the cockpit. Slowly, the vapors congealed, gathering into vaguely humanoid forms.

Maria felt one of the shapes brush against the back of her neck as it flowed past. The icy touch, piercing all the way through to her brain, was telling her something.

Kill.

And the piercing shrieks of her daughter were also cutting through to her brain, dulling her senses and bringing on the madness, making it easy for her to obey the slowly materializing forms overhead.

As Maria inched her hands towards her daughter's neck, she glanced to the right. A man in a tweed jacket was stabbing the elderly woman next to him in the eye with a ball point pen. When the woman slumped forward in her seat, blood flowing freely from her darkened eye sockets, the man held the pen in his hands like a dagger and buried its point deep into his own throat.

Maria's fingers curled around her daughter's neck, forming an ever-tightening circle until she'd closed off the child's windpipe and the maddening cries were little more than a muted wet gurgle in her throat.

As she squeezed the final bit of life from her daughter's ruined neck, Maria looked up . . .

. . . in time to see the young Comanche warrior bring the tomahawk crashing down on her skull.

Martin Braithewaite took another gulp of coffee from the paper cup in his hand. It was his fourth cup of the morning.

When the tape recorder was fully rewound, he depressed the play button and sat back in his chair.

The recording hissed with static.

This is DeSalles ATC. Come in 306.

The DeSalles air traffic controller's recording of Flight 306's last few messages were all Braithewaite had to go on. With the few cryptic words from the pilot, he was supposed to explain why a major airline's intercontinental jet would fly straight into the Atlantic; in perfect weather conditions and without any apparent mechanical malfunctions.

Everyone is going crazy . . . the madness . . .

There was a background noise to the recording, something sounding very much like a howling. A scream perhaps. Braithewaite had never heard anything like it before but knew it wasn't radio interference. The sound originated at the source. On the plane.

Repeat 306.

The transmission suddenly became garbled, everyone in the cockpit speaking at once.

They're here, all around . . . I'll ki . . . sonovabitch . . . Indians . . . the madness . . . ill you . . .

The recording degenerated into a mass of tormented cries, primal screams and unintelligible mono-syllables. In the background the howling was constant, rising in intensity until it drowned out all other sounds.

The tape suddenly became painful to listen to.

Braithewaite reached over and pressed *stop.*

He fished inside his pocket for a smoke. Lit it.

There were dozens of people waiting for him to give his opinion on the crash. After the airlines and the airplane's manufacturer, there would be news media to deal with and then finally the families of those who died in the crash.

He flipped through the thin file-folder on the table and read once more that 306 departed from Dry Plains. He was aware of the rumors surrounding the airport, even more aware of the alarming number of fatal incidents that could be connected to the place—both directly and by wild stretches of the imagination.

Was Dry Plains cursed?

Braithewaite had an opinion about that, but he knew no one would want to hear it. People wanted to hear about things they could touch, smell, see. A modern international airport was no place for the manifestation of ancient Indian legends.

He flipped a page and came upon the file of 306's pilot.

Roberto DiMaio was an Italian American from Brooklyn. He was a single man in his late forties with a hazy history of alcoholism. He'd flown nonstop from Toronto the night before taking off for Rome. He had been flying on less than four hours' sleep.

Braithewaite took the first sheet of paper from the file folder and uncapped his pen.

The crash of Flight 306 and the resulting deaths of all on board was caused solely by pilot error, brought on by mental fatigue, physical exhaustion, and possible substance abuse.

Braithewaite knew no one would question his conclusion.

It was what everyone wanted to hear.

Even if it wasn't true.

WHEN PRAYERS ARE ANSWERED

Roberta Lannes

FROM OBLIVION IT ROSE, WEAK, VAGUELY FORMED, ITS AWARE-
ness damped by a hundred years of dreamless sleep. Up
through rock and earth, dust and asphalt it floated until it
was free. It puddled on the tarmac behind a wall of colored
boxes, feeling the heat that the ground still held from the
day. It heard voices, footsteps, and retreated beneath the
boxes. A loud roar startled it. Thunder? Then another roar,
smaller, closer. Rumbling overhead. Suddenly the boxes
moved away on a thing with wheels, and it was exposed.

It straightened up and glided toward a huge stone structure with huge rectangles that reflected light from the stalks
that held the sun. When it stared at the rectangles, the
reflections diminished and it could see others inside. If it
could see them, they could see it. It hid behind a large silver
box, listening to far-off conversations it didn't understand.

A door opened on the opposite side of the box. Three men
came out arguing.

"No fucking way I'm going out there tonight. I saw that
thing."

"Saw what, man? After that six-pack you downed at
dinner last night, I'm surprised you recognized your dick
when you took a piss."

The other man laughed with his friend.

"It ain't funny. And I wasn't drunk. The thing was the
same color as a runway light. Flame blue. And it hovered
like an angel, only it looked more like a cloud with an angry
face in it."

"Look, man, everybody's tense around here since all this shit started. Hell, if you add up just the incidents that the ground crew reported, you could scare the whole fucking nation. Voices. Ghosts. Freak accidents. People flipping out, killing people. We gotta keep our heads on straight, man, or this place is gonna turn into an insane asylum."

"Yeah." The third man added. "It's mass hysteria."

"Fuck, yeah. You understand, man? It's like one guy says, 'Hey, wasn't that an earthquake?' and half the room swears they felt it even when the guy was joking. You're just joining the nutcases, man."

"If I'm nuts, that's all right just so long as I don't have to go out there with you guys tonight. I saw something and that's that."

"Well, we don't have any planes running out now. The only planes coming in now are flying at their own risk. So Meuller won't miss you."

"You won't remind him you left me back here, will you?"

"Naw. Hell, he's more scared than you. He told Shirley he was in the bathroom putting some shit on his hair implants so that they don't get infected, and he saw one of 'em was bloody. When he bent over to splash water on it, some guy bumped him so hard, he hit his head on the faucet and got cut real bad. So he whipped around to give the guy a piece of his mind, but there wasn't nobody there."

"No shit. Well, see what I mean? If I didn't need the money, I'd stay the fuck away."

"Awright. You just sit it out while Brennert and me go top off some of these tanks."

"Thanks. Later." There was the sound of footsteps and soft laughter. The man lit a cigarette and leaned back in a folding chair, nervously watching the night sky.

It smelled fire, then the aroma of burning tobacco. The familiar scent intrigued it. Moving stealthily, it found its way around the box to the far side. It could see the man, a paleface, sitting on a strange contraption. He held a white stick between his fingers and put it to his lips, drawing in the smoke and letting it curl out of his nose and mouth. It felt a hunger for the smoke. The man looked around quickly, moving the chair back behind the obscuring bulk of the silver box. It shifted, bent its formless body to avoid detection. A quick bass drumbeat sounded from the silver box as it leaned against it. The man's head jerked in its direction.

"Hey . . . You guys trying to fuck with me? Hey!"

It moved to the other end of the silver box, watching the paleface. The man began searching for his friends in the same area it had been hiding. He looked, blinked, then tried to back up too fast, falling onto the seat, which folded beneath him. The smoking stick rolled away.

"Oh shit!" The man struggled to stand, checking out his bloodied palm and elbow.

It saw the blood and felt suddenly stronger, vibrant. A seed, a sense of knowing grew. It saw the smoking stick, moved out from behind the box and reached for it, recalling a pipe. It was he, Lone Moccasin, calling for a peace pipe to be smoked, he who was called Moc by his warriors, making a false peace to weaken the enemy. The white stick burned at one end. He put the other end to his lips and drew in the smoke.

"Whoaaaah!" The man screamed as he saw it before him, the smoke wafting about its head, then turned and ran toward the door.

Moc grinned. This was as it should be. He felt the familiar rush from the nicotine in his lungs and the power of seeing an enemy retreat in fear.

"This is right. Soon, I will join the others. Then they will *all* run."

Joyce watched her son Kevin go off down the corridor with his grandfather just as her water broke.

"Damn." Her eyes went to the pearl gray industrial carpet turning charcoal beneath her feet. The baby wasn't due for another three weeks. Her husband's flight was arriving in less than an hour. If this child was anything like Kevin, she had hours before she needed to be in the hospital. But waiting like this was not going to be comfortable.

A skittish teenage girl, her hair twisted into a primitive style over wild eyes, walked by and noted Joyce's condition.

"You piss in your pants?"

Joyce stepped past the stain. "My water bag broke. I'm going to have a baby." She strained her head to the side in an attempt to see where her father-in-law had taken Kevin to the restroom.

"Bag?" The girl started to come toward Joyce, a hand with dirty fingernails and silver rings that reminded Joyce of gargoyles, going for her belly.

Joyce hurried past the girl before the girl could touch her, a contraction stiffening her gait for a moment. Where was that damned men's room? The airport was more crowded the farther away she went from the private carrier wing. As she neared the main concourse, she could feel the tension and craziness of the people. Packed in, waiting for flights out or for visitors that might never show up, they were agitated. *Manic* was the word she thought fit best. Their eyes showed fear, as some clutched bags, their mates, children, or as others gathered into cliques, their brows knitted, jaws set, full of menace.

She found the men's room and waited outside, staring at the door with single-minded determination, praying Kevin and Edmund would soon emerge. It would all be fine when Bill arrived and they could get to the hospital. Very soon.

Kevin burst from the restroom in front of his grandfather, hurling himself against her. Joyce gasped and buckled to her knees. Edmund grabbed Kevin and held his hand out for her.

"What is it?" Concern etched his handsome face, as he helped her up.

"My water broke," she whispered, leaning into him.

"I'll call Walter to bring the car around and take you to the hospital. We'll meet you there when Bill's in."

"Edmund, I have three or four hours before my contractions get close enough together to be anything to worry about. Maybe more. I want us to stay together. This airport is giving me the creeps and I won't leave you and Kevin here." She could see Edmund's look of incredulity. "Believe me, at the hospital they would just have me walking the halls for the next few hours until the baby gets into position. I'd just as soon be here, pacing."

"You'll tell me if things change?" She nodded. "The minute you begin to look ready, I'm calling Walter."

"Agreed." She reached her hand out for Kevin who was clinging to Edmund's pant leg. "Sorry honey, but Mommy's tummy hurts and we have to be careful around it, okay? You all ready to go back and watch for Daddy's plane to come in?"

Kevin nodded shyly. "Baby?"

Joyce smiled. "Yes, honey. Your little sister's coming."

"Or brother." Edmund added.

"Can Daddy see him?" Kevin looked up at Joyce.

"You betcha. He'd better be here to see him. I need my Lamaze coach."

"Mozz? Grampa, can I have some gum?"

Edmund reached into his jacket pocket and pulled out a half stick of gum.

"Not much attention span at four, huh? I've forgotten how quickly their little minds work." He handed Kevin the gum.

Joyce moaned. Edmund frowned at her. "Oh. It's *nothing*. A contraction. Come on. Let's go see Daddy."

Joyce followed Edmund, hand-in-hand with Kevin, past fidgeting bodies, jittering eyeballs, and fragile minds.

"Bill, we can't land at Dry Plains. Some kind of air traffic control shutdown."

Bill Sandler heard the pilot through his headphones. He was listening to Wagner's opera *Die Walkure* as the familiar voice cut in. Peeling the plastic headgear off, he glanced out the window into the ink of night and shivered. He had to get back. He walked forward to the cockpit of the private plane.

"Chas. What's this bullshit? We've got to land at Dry Plains. Joyce, Kevin, and my father are waiting. Hell. It's just extremely important."

"I hear you, Bill, but no can do. There's no one there to lead me in."

"Is there any other air traffic going in?"

"Don't know. Nobody's talking."

Bill stroked his chin. "I'm thinking that if they won't let us land, they're not going to let anyone else, either. That means nothing else in our way. Yes?"

"If everything's being rerouted, you're right."

"Can you check it out?"

"It's done."

Bill listened as Chas checked with other nearby airports

and landing strips. No one was going into Dry Plains. Chas agreed to fly in blind. Conditions were clear, and he was familiar with the flight path and the landing routine to get to the private leg of the airport hub.

Back in his seat, Bill drank down his third bourbon in an hour. He'd need it to confront his father. Bill let the conversation he'd had with his mother last Monday trickle back into the obsessive loop he'd been trying to escape.

She had come to his office, a sign that whatever she had to tell him was serious. She paced for a couple of minutes, shredding a tissue, before she had the strength to talk.

"Your father's been cheating on me."

He relaxed at her words. "Mom, I've heard this before. He has iron-clad alibis or real reasons that you've turned into paranoid delusions. There hasn't been a shred of evidence. Why do this to yourself?"

She stopped pacing, her body trembling with anger.

"You, always the lawyer. Well, he's doing it to you, too, sweetie."

"Sure, Mom. It affects all of us."

His mother's hands went out as if begging for his forgiveness. She began to tear up, her lower lip quivering around the word.

"Joyce."

"Joyce? Mom, you're nuts! Now I know you've lost it. That's so utterly ridiculous . . . She loves me more than I can stand, sometimes. She's devoted to me."

"She's devoted to your money. She loves how busy you are so she can carry on while you're minding your own business. And she loves your father."

"Now you're pissing me off. Show me some kind of proof or get out." Bill stood, his hands balled into fists on his desk.

His mother bowed her head, then bent over to produce a manila envelope and a videotape.

"I got it all. After so many years, with so many doubts, I had to know for sure. I hired a private detective. If only it had been some stupid bimbo. A stranger. But, this . . ." She handed him the stuff.

Bill held it a moment, then sat down. "This had better be good."

"It's the worst." His mother finally sat down and cried.

The photographs appeared, for the most part, innocent. Joyce with Edmund at L'Oiseau, coming out of his father's office building, in the Jaguar, in the limo—but there were others. Grainy pictures taken with long-range lenses of Joyce on top of Edmund, Edmund inside Joyce, oral sex which Bill had resigned himself to rarely receiving, and some kinky tricks that Joyce had told him were degrading to women. He put the cassette tape into his dictation machine and pulled on the headphones: Joyce telling Edmund that Kevin would be with the sitter in an hour and they could have four hours together instead of the usual hurried two. Phone sex. His father telling his wife what he wanted to do to her.

Bill stared at the videotape, shook his head, and pushed it across the desk toward his mother.

"How long has this thing been going on?"

"According to Edmund's secretary and other sources the investigator said refused to be identified, five years."

Bill leaped out of his chair. *"Five years!* Jesus, Mary, and God. That means . . ." He put his hands to his head.

"That he could be Kevin's father."

"Argh!" Bill pounded his desk, prompting his secretary to buzz him. He barked at her and went to sit down by his mother.

"I don't want to believe this, Mom. How could they do this to us? Why?"

She shrugged. "I tried to tell myself it was because you two had so much trouble conceiving a child. That Joyce lured Ed into making her pregnant and let you think it was you who got her that way. But it doesn't explain . . ."

"Why they've been fucking around for the last four years. Mom. I . . ." Then he wept in his mother's arms. Like a three-year-old.

He didn't go home that night. He flew to New York a day early. Made excuses and patronized Joyce during phone calls home. He even told Kevin to go ask his Grampa if he had any questions. Joyce sensed something but said nothing. He could tell. She knew him better than anyone else did.

The three days in New York were hell. Even two sets of tennis a day didn't ease the tension. He cried himself to sleep each night and wondered how he could have lived with a fake family for so long and not know.

Around and around it went in his head. The only respite came with the thought of killing them both. Confronting them first, then shooting them. He knew he could never do it, but the thought kept him off the carousel of pain.

Soon he would be there, standing before them, their phony innocence their only protection from his rage. Soon.

Moc moved through the open doorway and down the hallways lit with many little suns. The path was empty. Finally he came to a room where slabs floated over people's laps as they consumed food and drank from strange containers. He stood in the doorway. Their voices blended into a low din. No one took notice of him, so he moved on.

He saw a large half-open doorway ahead. He felt compelled to wait there, watching before exiting into the building's center. He slumped against the wall, eyes on the people sitting in the dimly-lit room.

He felt a presence before he heard the cry behind him. He let the smoking stick fall to the ground as he stood, ready to fight.

"Ahhhh! It is you, Lone Moccasin. It is you!"

Moc squinted in the bright light. A ghostly man floated by and stopped a few feet from him. It was Bright Eagle, his best warrior.

"Bright Eagle? How is it that we meet here?"

"I do not know, but it appears that we have been given a new call to battle. It is what we prayed for."

"Yes! You are right, Bright Eagle. I have forgotten much. I have been asleep for many years. This place was not here when what was left of the tribe laid us to rest. It is strange. The sun is everywhere. And they do not have pipes. They have these." He retrieved the cigarette. "And they smoke them without cause. But they fear us. This is good."

Bright Eagle nodded. "Do you feel stronger every breath you take, Lone Moccasin?"

"So it seems. I see the blood of the enemy and my heart soars, my head is clearer, and my feet long to carry me back into battle. The others . . . are they near?"

"I feel them, Moc. I see their eyes in the eyes of the strangers in this place. And I see the ghosts . . ."

"Of the enemy?" Moc frowned.

"The enemy is all around, only now it is not so easy to know him. He has many faces, but it is his hatred toward us that will expose him. I see few of our legion, but they are growing in number. Returning to know our blood triumph!"

Moc relaxed and leaned against the wall. "I must wait here."

"Then, I will wait, too."

Moc nodded to his companion, his ally, then turned to watch a child climb over the white-haired paleface beside the darkhaired women about to give birth.

"Kevin, leave Grampa alone."

"Joyce, it's all right. It's way past his bedtime. He's overtired."

"Me, too. He's making me nervous."

Edmund checked his watch. "Bill's late."

Joyce pulled her long fingers through her brown curls. "Shit. What now? Could things get any more complicated?"

"What are you talking about?"

"I told you. He seemed distant. Wary. Every time we talked on the phone. And your wife. Ruth was cold every time I called over to the house. When I asked her to take Kevin, she told me she was too busy. Then she hurried me off the phone. Neither one of them is usually like that. They know. I'm afraid for us, Edmund." She tensed for a contraction, then began her Lamaze breathing. Phew. Phew. Phew.

"Let me call Walter. An ambulance."

"Fifteen minutes. Give me that."

"Joyce . . ."

"Damn it, Edmund, I want my husband here when I go to the hospital."

"And what if he's figured it all out?"

"I hope he can wait to hate me until after the baby is born."

Edmund put his face in his hands and shook his head. "Us. He'll hate *us.* We really thought we were doing Bill a great service. Giving him a gift. *Your* choice of words, I recall."

"Stop it. Now." She gritted her teeth and frowned at him.

They sat in stony silence then, as Kevin began fishing for keys in his mother's purse.

Chas shouted back into the plane, "I've had to go in against the wind, so we'll be a few minutes late. I'm warning you though. If I'm charged with any FAA regulation offense . . ."

"I'll cover you. Every penny. And litigate my ass off if necessary. Good enough?"

"Enough. Buckle up. We're going in."

Bill closed his eyes as he fastened his seat belt, imagining his hands around Edmund's throat.

Moc's blood boiled. "I feel great anger and fear. We are near the plain of battle. I can smell it."

Bright Eagle grinned. "As can I. The taste of my enemies' blood is on my tongue, brother. The enemy will soon know our wrath."

"And the women will know our lust." Moc grabbed at his crotch over the loincloth in mock bravado.

Bright Eagle puffed out his chest. "When we are a great race again, we will take anything we want, when we want it."

"Our hungers, then, will finally be sated." Moc felt the desire for revenge in his heart, the longing for victory in his soul.

"He's landed." Edmund took Kevin up in his arms. "Daddy's home."

Joyce felt the contractions every three minutes. She was cursing her stubbornness. She tried to get up, but couldn't move. Breathe, she told herself. Phew, phew, phew.

"Daddy!" Kevin's voice was shrill in the growing ruckus of the airport.

Bill swallowed hard, both hands on the rails of the portable stairway. He wished his fury away, wanting to confront Joyce and his father with all the dignity he had in the courtroom. Damn it, he was famous for it. Bullet-proof poise, his opponents called it. Where was it now when his marriage, his life were at stake?

Each step closer to the tarmac, his throat tightened more, his heart beat more furiously. Sweat beaded on his forehead and upper lip. He gritted his teeth so hard, he could taste the crumbling filling he was digging up. His soft suitcase felt so light, like it weighed an ounce in his hand. His tennis racket banged against his thigh, but he felt nothing.

Step by step, he made his way up the concrete stairway to the lounge above. The words "How could they?" pounded in his head, a bass accompaniment to some escalating crescendo of madness.

He opened the door he'd opened so many times before, where each time he came home, they waited. In love. He paused.

"My father. My wife. My child." Heartache tore into his rage, and he crumpled. "Gone."

At once, his suitcase weighed a hundred pounds as he slowly made his way down the hallway.

Moc saw the large white man in the dark suit of clothes, carrying a satchel, as he grunted toward the door. Moc looked to Bright Eagle, who gave him a curious look, then nodded. Moc opened his arms to stop the man, standing in his way. But the man showed no fear and continued on, moving into Moc.

Moc felt a rippling of his skin, a tingling, as he became a part of the white man. He felt the man's grief and heartache, and willed them away with his own anger. As he did so, the man's anger was piqued and joined his. Moc felt a soaring of spirit such as he'd never known before. Together as one, he and the man strode into the waiting area, ready to confront the enemy and vanquish them.

The white-haired father stood by the doorway, the child in his arms.

"Daddy!" the boy squealed, eager to work his way into his father's arms.

"Bill, Joyce is going into labor. We've got to get her to the hospital."

Bill stared past his father and son at his wife. She smiled wanly at him, then grimaced in pain. He didn't care. He felt separated from himself, as if he was floating blissfully inside the hurt and angry Bill. He was free.

Reaching down to his bag, he pulled his metal racket from its Velcroed compartment. He took three long strides toward her and stared. She didn't seem frightened. She seemed annoyed. This enraged him. The whore.

"Bill, let's dispense with the usual pleasantries. My contractions are two minutes apart. If we don't go, I'm going to have the baby *here.*" She waved him off, holding her belly.

Bill grinned. Something inside pushed him past his fear and shame. He wanted Joyce and Edmund to grovel at his feet and beg his forgiveness. He wanted to see fear—no, terror—in their eyes. Even more, he wanted vengeance.

"Joyce. My wife. You want me to rush you to the hospital. To have *his* child. My father's child. My brother!" He laughed and it sounded like a battle cry, whooped over the noise all around him. "I *know* you're fucking my father."

"Bill . . ." She didn't sound scared. Or apologetic. She sounded harassed. She began to breath strangely. Phew, phew, phew.

The voice in his head said it so clearly, simply. No man's wife shall lay with another man, lest she be willing to lose her life and the life of the man she lays with.

With his vicious backhand swing, he whacked her belly. Her face went long, eyes wide, then rolled back into her head, a weak gasp escaping from her lips. He swung again and again, the racket slamming against her head, chest, belly. Her arms and legs flailed reflexively against the blows.

He was aware that sounds were growing all around him, but above it, he heard the shrieking of his son.

"Daddy . . . don't hurt . . . Mommeeeeee!"

Turning toward the voice, he saw the white-haired father watching, the boy struggling in his arms. Kevin kicked and fought, but Edmund stood fast, his face a mask of stone. Moc had seen that face before, as had Bill. The opponent always tried to make him think he was invincible by hiding his fear—any emotion. But he knew better.

A scream tore his gaze from the father to the wife. She was mumbling, her bloody hands pushing down on her belly, her legs splayed apart on the floor. Red seemed to obliterate her features so that she wasn't recognizable as Joyce any longer. Then he saw the baby, its head falling from under her skirt. He bent over and yanked the infant from the woman, holding it up like a prize.

"It looks just like Edmund, Joyce. See?" He tossed the child onto her chest. She was unconscious.

Bill swung the racket through the air until it sang. Moc liked its sound, though he knew it made a poor weapon.

"Now for you, *Dad.*" Bill rushed toward the man, racket flying through the air.

Edmund threw the boy down and stopped the racket dead in mid-air. Bill's fury was about to explode. Then the father spoke.

"Let's be done with these pathetic weaklings, Lone Moccasin. We have a greater enemy to conquer."

Moc blinked. Bright Eagle! He dropped the tennis racket and embraced the white-haired man.

"It is you!"

Bright Eagle nodded. "Yes, my Chief. It is I."

"Then we have a purpose in these bodies." He stared in wonder at himself, dressed in the dark suit, Bright Eagle, white-haired and handsome.

"That purpose is to mete out the death of our sworn enemy. Come. Your legion awaits you." Bright Eagle looked over Lone Moccasin's shoulder and nodded.

Moc glanced behind him. A motley crowd of white men, black men, yellow and brown, young and old, women, too, stood ready, their eyes wild with anger, their shoulders set with determination. In them, he saw his warriors, all risen from their deep sleep.

He strode toward them, Bright Eagle at his side, the answer to his prayers made so long ago, before him. He opened his arms and threw his head back to thank the Great Spirit for giving him and his people one more stand.

Bright Eagle stepped forward.

"Our Chief has returned. The Great Spirit is one with us again."

Lone Moccasin looked over his people, his hand on Bright Eagle's shoulder. Bright Eagle seemed suspiciously eager to speak for Moc. To step before him in front of his people. That was not done. Did he want what Moc had earned?

Maybe it was the body's thoughts, so wary was Bill of his white-haired father. So ready to make him suffer for his pain, which was now Moc's, too. In time, he thought. I will take care of the threat in time.

Moc eased Bright Eagle aside with a quick glance tinged with menace, then he faced the anxious crowd.

"Come," he shouted, as Bright Eagle frowned and made his way to the edge of the group. When Bright Eagle's head was bent in shame, Lone Moccasin felt Bill's resolve and his power return, and he was whole.

"Our enemy awaits us!"

CONSENT

Nancy Baker

THE PLANES COME IN, RUNNING AHEAD OF A FREAK DESERT ELEC-trical storm. Radios crackle with pleas and threats. From the exhaust trails, the subtle, sweet tang of blood and vengeance drifts down to touch the tarmac.

The airport lets them land.

"If they control our nightmares and dreams, they'll soon control our rational thoughts as well. It is our dreams—*and* our nightmares—that lead us to the truth, good and bad, of our humanity. It is our thoughts that give us the freedom we have waged wars to defend. If we surrender control of the expression of *any* of these things to someone else, then the true nightmare will have begun . . ."

The writer leans against the cold wall of the darkened hangar, hands tied to concrete blocks on either side, listening to his own voice coming from the tape deck on the floor in front of him. His head throbs from the blow to the back of it. His pride hurts more, for having fallen for the whispered promise of a private flight out of the strike-bound airport the storm had dumped him in. Bribes to the controllers had been paid by an admiring fan so they could take off despite the shutdown. He remembers the walk across the deserted runway to the darkened hangar, automatically noting the particular and peculiar smell of the air, gasoline and desert mingling, and the way the dim lights behind him had laid pale ovals that never quite touched onto the tarmac ahead of him.

He searches for endings to this strange scenario and wishes for once he did not have such a vivid imagination.

Something moves from behind the shadowed bulk of a plane, steps into the circle of light cast by a work lamp lying on the floor. For a moment, all the writer sees is a column of darkness stooping by the tape deck. His voice dies and the black shape dissolves on the concrete.

He squints and it resolves itself in a human shape, draped and veiled.

"You were very eloquent." It is a woman's voice, soft, with the faintest edge of something dark and sharp beneath its gentleness.

He gropes for something to say, some response to unexpected praise for a speech he finished only hours earlier, sitting before the long row of senators on the dais. "Thank you," he says at last, when nothing else surfaces.

"I'm sure it doesn't hurt your sales either."

"I don't know about that. My books have been taken off shelves in a lot of bookstores and libraries." Three years had not changed that and every time he spoke out it happened again. Somewhere.

"But you still testified today."

"Of course. If they legislate everything I do and believe in out of existence, it won't be because I stood by and let them."

"You are very passionate about it."

"Of course I am. I'm defending my life, after all."

"No, Mr. Donovan, you are defending your livelihood. Not your life. I don't think you know anything about having to defend your life."

"Who are you?"

"My name is Katherine Wingate."

Her face, blurred by newsprint, flashes through his mind, memorable only because of the ones who had preceded her. And the calls from the Charlotte police wanting to discuss his books. He remembers a woman with long brown hair, brown eyes, average features. Ordinary-looking. Forgettable. If there have been pictures of her, after, he has not seen them. "What are you doing here?" he asks. Being stranded in an airport with this woman, of all the women the world, is a coincidence so laughable he would be embarrassed to put it on paper.

"My plane followed yours from Washington."

"Your plane . . ." he echoes, trying to imagine this black heap on a commercial flight, stuffed into a too-small seat beneath the glare of the cabin lights, accepting foil-wrapped peanuts from a flight attendant.

"A private plane," she answers, sensing his confusion. "Good Nite's Rest Motels settled out of court. I suppose their lawyers finally realized that a jury would only have to take one look at me to decide that their lies about their motel's security were to blame for . . . what happened."

He remembers a brief article two years ago, noted and thrust aside with the turning of a page. The headline flashes across his mind: *Woodside Survivor Sues Motel Chain For $10 Million.* He wonders briefly how much she got—but does not ask. There is only one question he needs answered. He finds the strength to ask it.

"Then what do you want from me?"

"The police killed Jonathan Heller. Good Nite's Rest Motels has paid. You're the only one left."

"I wasn't responsible for Jonathan Heller!" The words come out harsh and ragged, scarred by the memory of the Woodside Killer and the sad-eyed bank clerk he'd turned out to be. He feels a sudden pain in his wrists and realizes he has lurched forward, trying to escape.

"No? It wasn't your books he read? It wasn't your murders he copied?"

"Jonathan Heller was crazy. He'd been crazy all his life. He'd have been crazy even if all he ever read were the Saturday comics."

"Maybe. But the Saturday comics wouldn't have taught him how to kill. The Saturday comics wouldn't have given him reasons and justifications for it. You did. You and all the writers like you."

"We don't tell people how to behave. All we do is report on the darkness inside human souls; we report the evil we are capable of. We don't make anyone become that evil." He has said these words a hundred times in a hundred ways, for articles and debates and Senate hearings. Practice overrides panic and gives him answers that he suddenly wishes didn't sound glib and rehearsed, despite all his belief in them.

" 'The blade slid in like it was a lost part of her, finding its way back inside, moving sweetly beneath the muscle and fat to touch the blackness inside. There was no blood, not with the silver hilt right up against her seamless skin. She screamed against the gag, eyes wide.' " Her voice is distant, distracted. "I memorized it, you see. He liked that passage. He would read it over and over while he tried to decide where the blackness in *me* was. It was from *Black Razor*. When he read, I could see your picture on the back cover, watching me. He'd already worked through *Red Night* and *The Watching Dark*. He was going to try to beat the killer's record of five days." There is a pause and he sees the veiled head lift a little. "Of course, he only made it to three with me before the police came."

"Ms. Wingate, I'm sorry about what happened to you. But what I write is fiction, just fiction. It's meant to entertain people, to give them a vicarious scare and to make them realize the dark side of our own natures. But it's never been meant to make anyone do what Jonathan Heller did to you and those other women."

"But that's what happened just the same. Because you told him it was all right. Your books and the movies and the magazines . . . they told him that it was just fine. We weren't *real*. We didn't *matter*. We weren't people. We were just things to use—and when that was done, we were just things to scream and bleed and die."

"I never . . ."

"No? 'Her eyes darkened and her throat fell back; the surrender of prey to predator, the consent of the deer to fall beneath the teeth of the wolf. He saw it over and over in the last moment—the willing yielding of their lives into his hands, the arch of their bodies onto the knife in voluntary ecstasy.' " She shifts to kneel, voice grinding out the words like broken glass.

"But in context . . ."

"Over and over again, you and all your friends tell them that it's all right, it's natural. The strong survive and weak surrender. The prey consents to be taken. The predator doesn't have to feel any guilt—it's the way of the world. But that's just the lie you tell to justify what you do—or what in your deepest soul, you *want* to do. And it is a lie, Mr. Donovan. No one consents."

Her voice rises, her hands clutch at the dark cloth concealing her.

"Do you think I surrendered? Do you think I wanted it? Do you think I consented to *this?*"

Cloth tears and the veils fall away. He sees her white skin, ribboned in red scars. One breast is gone, the other is nippleless. Angry, puckered lines drag her mouth into a sneer, wrap around her cheek and jaw, pull down one eye. Jesus, how had she survived? he wonders numbly. How had she endured it?

"Is it like you thought? When you were typing the words, is this what you saw? Did he get it right?" She spits the questions out sarcastically then draws the dark clothes over her burning white and red nakedness.

"I'm sorry, Christ knows, I'm sorry. But it wasn't my fault," the writer repeats desperately. Caroline's face flashes through his mind, standing beside his computer, reading the glowing words with a faint frown. He thinks of the killer and the room in the basement and words flowing like blood from his fingers and across the screen. He remembers the sharp, triumphant thrill of finding the perfect images, the perfect phrases, to express the visions flickering through his mind.

"It doesn't matter," she says softly, from behind the veil. "We can't change the past."

"No, we can't." He clings to the words, to the sweet rational sound of them.

"But I can't let you go on lying. I can't let you tell some other man how to kill." Her hand moves and something **flashes** against her darkness.

He pleads then, dragging up any argument he can find, from his wife and child to the legal and moral consequences of murder. But she can counter each of his future losses with her own past ones and brushes aside the promises of damnation and prison.

"I have five million dollars in a Swiss bank account and a plane to take me away," she points out calmly, crouching beside him. "I bought a house in Tripoli. The Libyans won't extradite me. And I have grown quite used to wearing veils."

"I don't consent, damn it, I don't consent. I don't fucking consent!" He flings her own words back at her—but knows that his lack of consent means no more than hers did. For one last moment he wishes that his fictions were as true as Heller had believed, wishes that there could be some semblance of safety in surrender.

"Are you sure?" she whispers and then the light breaks off the edge of the knife and blinds him.

The wheels of the jet roll across the slick tarmac. For a moment, the asphalt seems to suck at them, seeking to catch the plane and swallow it down into the tarry blackness.

In the dark hangar, something thrashes. If it had a tongue left, it might scream. If it had hands left, it might scrawl down the images of its dying in its own best-selling style.

The blackness beneath the plane releases it.

The airport lets it go.

THE MAN IN THE MOON

Michael A. Arnzen

1

MOMENTS—THOUGH IT SEEMED MORE LIKE YEARS—AFTER takeoff, when the plane finally came to a creaking buoyancy over Dry Plains International, Libby turned to face her daughter, wondering if they were actually free yet.

Free. From the pain. From the belt and the buckle which still buzzed its copper sting on her back. From the night-long terror, the fear of picking up the phone and dialing 911 or Papa or even Father Kreps. From the burning booze on his purple tongue as it spat curses at her and shoved its acidic way into her orifices. Free . . . from George.

"Look, Mom!" Stella bellowed, tiny fingers pressed against the small ovalish square of breath-fogged glass. "We're so close to the stars now! I can almost touch the man in the moon!"

"Quiet!" Libby hissed, tugging on her daughter's loose seat belt. "People are trying to sleep—it's late."

Stella leaned closer to the glass, pressing its coldness against her cheek, her head cocked awkwardly toward the ceiling. Libby watched her small eyes scanning the sky, her flitting black pupils reflecting the night: starry eyes, round and almost cartoonish in their innocence.

Libby looked around, abstractedly spying on the other passengers. There were about ten altogether. Few were actually napping on the flight to Vegas; most were looking out the windows just like Stella, though unlike her, their heads were nodding downward, toward the lighted land, the safe Earth below. Eyes silently watching Texas fade into a special effects carpet of tiny lights. Stella, on the other hand, preferred to look up—an innocent child with hope for the future, ignorant of danger and pain. Just enjoying the ride.

Libby thought about George; her husband's image was not shrinking in her mind at all along with the city below as the plane attained new heights, its wings now cutting sharply into grey clouds like two dull machetes. No . . . George was still down there, still as large and looming as always, as big as the world itself . . . and he would probably be waking up right now, tugging his leather belt free from the jeans that he wore every day to the construction site, slapping the buckle in a sweaty palm, searching the house for her and Stella. He might be punching walls. He might be throwing a bottle of Jim Beam against the sidewalk out front, right beside Stella's Big Wheel. Finding the Nova missing. His wallet empty.

And soon, he would begin his search for them. And someday he would find them. And he would beat her in more ways than one. Sooner or later. He would.

But for now, she was cushioned. She could see George doing all this in her mind, but there was time and space between them. She had a head start for now. Maybe there would be a chance to escape him forever. Maybe . . . if they kept on running. Kept on flying away.

Libby wanted to sleep. But she couldn't—he'd be there, too, she knew, in the land of dreams. He'd find her there for sure.

"Mom, did you say something?"

"No, Stella. Why?"

"What? I can't hear you!" Stella turned from the window and looked sadly at her mother, one eyelid scrunched painfully shut. A finger started digging madly in her ear. "I can't hear anything!"

"Shhh!" Libby said. "It's just your ears popping. You'll live, believe me."

Stella's face crinkled up in pain. "It hurts!"

Libby realized that it was Stella's first plane ride. The first time her inner cavities had experienced shifts in pressure, natural invasions. *Get used to it, child,* she thought.

"Can I help?" The voice came from a woman who was suddenly there next to Libby. A stewardess. A face of perfect makeup, straight brown hair. A plastic badge that said FAITH. A false white smile.

"No," Libby said, smirking as if insulted. "I can handle my own daughter, thank you."

"Okay," the stewardess smiled and nodded. "But if you need any help, just ring." She motioned at a button above their seats, and walked up toward the front of the plane, stepping behind a curtain that apparently led to the cockpit —glittering lights were in there somewhere, like hidden shining gems.

Stella had her hands over her face. Libby reached over and whispered into her ear. "Just hold your nose, close your mouth, and blow—like blowing up a balloon. Your ears will pop."

Stella tried, her cheeks puffing up. Libby could see tears welling in the corners of her daughter's eyes.

"Mommy, it's not working—"

"Shush!" Libby almost slapped her. "Keep trying, okay? It'll go away sooner or later. Give it some time."

Stella unlatched her seatbelt, climbed up in the chair, and pressed the CALL button before Libby realized what her daughter was doing.

Her arm lashed across Stella's face. She shoved the child down in the chair and buckled her in, tightly. "Don't you ever disobey again, do you hear me?"

The curtain opened. Faith was returning, curious, smiling.

Libby took a long deep breath as Stella bawled beside her, the stewardess leaning over her to help, assuming the tears were from the pressure inside the child's ears. Assuming the red welt on her face was blush-inflicted. Libby didn't watch as the much-too-young woman—a perfect stranger— mothered her child for her.

My God . . . I'm acting just like George. I HIT Stella; I didn't even know I was doing it. She closed her eyes, imagined him punishing her for mocking her.

She opened her eyes.

"Take this piece of gum and chew on it with big bites," Faith was saying, passing Stella a thin strip of Juicy Fruit. "Open your jaws like this when you chew." The stewardess made a face like she was at the dentist's office. "Okay?"

Libby looked over at her child. Stella was no longer crying; she was all wet smiles, eager eyes. She chewed the gum making monkey faces and giggling. "It works, it works! I can hear!"

"See?" The stewardess smiled, and grinned at Libby.

Libby smirked. "You really shouldn't be giving her sugar this late at night."

Faith shrugged.

"What's that?" Stella asked—almost too loudly, as if trying to wake up the whole cabin. She pointed a sticky finger at Faith's chest.

"These?" the stewardess asked. "They're my wings."

Libby looked at the metallic pin. "Oh please . . ." George had been Airborne in 'Nam. He *earned* his wings. This prissy bitch had earned nothing, nothing at all.

"They're for people who fly, just like you're doing right now," Faith was saying. "And from the looks of things, you've earned your own pair of wings. Would you like me to get the captain to pin them on you?"

"The captain? Wow! Yes!"

"Okay, angel, I'll be right back."

Libby did not want to be a part of this charade. She looked over at her daughter, saw the hope in her eyes, and held back anger.

And then she felt a familiar creeping wetness in her groin.

"Mommy, I'm getting my wings!"

"Yes, Stella, you are." She rubbed her head. "Mommy's going to go to the bathroom, okay? So be a big girl while I'm gone, and don't do anything wrong. Got it?"

"Check," Stella said, like a pilot.

Libby rolled her eyes and grabbed her purse.

2

The big pilot man, Stella thought, looked a lot like Daddy would if Daddy was an Indian. His face was sunburned like her Daddy's, only redder, browner. A larger nose and stiff black hair. If he wasn't wearing a funny-looking pilot suit, he might have looked like something in a cowboy movie.

He sat down next to her, where Libby had been sitting.

He cocked his hat up on his head—Stella saw that his hair was wet, sweaty. He smiled. "I hear you've earned your wings, young lady. Is this true?"

His voice was deep, warm. Stella felt her ears turn hot with blood. She was blushing. "I guess," she said, feeling silly.

"And what is your name?"

"Stella."

"Well, let me be the first to congratulate you, Stella." The pilot—whose big, shining name tag read JORGE—straightened himself up in the seat, and saluted her.

Stella giggled.

Military-style, Captain Jorge swung a free hand out, and Faith slapped a pair of silver wings in his palm like a nurse handing a surgeon his scalpel, and then she walked back to the front of the plane, leaving them alone. Comically, he pulled down his saluting hand.

He reached forward for Stella's blouse. Stella shifted in her seat, backing against the curved wall of the airplane.

Captain Jorge's hands pulled the fabric of her pink blouse away from her right breast. The captain smiled, opening the back of the wings with his fingers, getting ready to pin them on.

His hands were cold and she could feel the sharp nails of his fingertips slightly touching her breast. Her nipple felt funny; hot and hard, like a separate part of her body. She wanted to giggle. She wanted him to hurry up and get it over with.

"Ta-daaa," Captain Jorge said, finally getting the pin open and moving it toward her shirt. He looked up into her eyes. "With these wings, you are hereby a member of Flights America. Welcome!"

And he pinned them on—nipping the soft tip of her right breast with the sharp tip of the pin, drawing the tiniest line of blood.

"Ouch," Stella said, wincing from the pain.

"Sorry. But no pain, no gain!" He stood up, smiling at her. He looked somehow different. Bigger. Sweatier—new stains on his shirt and pants. "Now that you're officially a pilot, would you like to see the cockpit?"

"I can't," Stella said. "My mommy won't know where I am."

"Well, then," he replied, sitting back down next to her. "I'll just wait till she comes back, okay?"

Stella relaxed. She felt like an adult now. "Sure," she said, crossing her legs.

Captain Jorge just stared at her.

Avoiding his eyes, she looked out the window again, at the stars. They were so high up it looked like the plane was in outer space. "How high are we?" she asked, seeing one particular star that was large and glimmering . . . almost red. "I think I see Mars out there!"

"Well, Stella, we're pretty high up. But not as high as we're gonna get, though. What you see out there now is nothing." He leaned forward—she could feel his chin near her shoulder. "Why? You're not scared are you?"

She stared at Mars. "No, I kinda like it."

"Good. Because I might have to take those wings back, ya know, if you were afraid of heights."

She twisted around in her seat; he was closer than she thought. She could smell his sweat. "Afraid of heights? No way, not me. I'm gonna be an astronaut when I'm a grown up. I'm gonna go to the moon."

His eyes were glossy, spaced-out, reflecting the night. "Bang, zoom, straight to the moon . . . right Alice?"

Stella squinted. "Huh?"

"Never mind." He stared over her shoulder, searching the stars. "Why do you want to go to the moon?"

"The moon? Well," she said, stalling—she hadn't really thought about *why*, she just knew she wanted to go. "Because it's pretty. And I want to see the man in the moon."

His head snapped toward her. "The man in the moon? You don't want to see him. He'll eat you up! His mouth is one giant crater, full of humongous teeth! His eyes are pools of acid!"

Stella wouldn't let him scare her. "Don't lie. He's made of cheese. I like cheese. I'd eat *him* up!"

"Cheese? He'd spit on this very plane and kill us all if he

heard you saying that." Captain Jorge looked through the window again. Stella noticed that his nostrils were flaring like the nose of a horse. His voice drifted away as he spoke, deepening, changing, like an insane echo in her mind: "No, he is real. He is more real than you or me. A god. An *angry* god who watches with sun-blind eyes over Earth in the night. Angry because he is trapped in darkness. But my people knew how to please him. Long ago, my people did things to make him happy—things I cannot speak of. We worshipped him, and he was good to us . . . through us he could see, and through him we could see. He let us see in the dark when we rubbed the sacrificial blood into the pits of our eyes . . ."

She slapped him on the shoulder. "Oh, come on, silly! You don't scare me. It's only the moon."

The captain squinted, nodding slowly as he looked out the window, as if answering a question to someone outside. His eyes were red, as if on fire. "Tonight, my child, you will see."

3

Libby couldn't believe how much she was bleeding inside. It could have been the pressure from the flight—or the pressure from running away Texas—but more likely it was from something George had done to her in bed, the night before she had left.

She flushed and slid the latch on the door that said OCCUPIED.

As she walked up the aisle (past passengers who were now snoring), she saw some strange man in her seat ahead, talking to Stella. She deduced that it was the pilot, giving her her damned *wings,* filling her head with notions of unearned valor. She wished she hadn't taken so damned long.

An old woman stood up, suddenly blocking her way. She pushed a long cylinder on two wheels in front of her, a cart that had a hose on it, a tube that led to her snot-clogged, wheezing nostrils.

An oxygen tank.

There was no way around it. Libby held back a curse as

she backtracked to the restrooms, giving the poor woman plenty of space. The woman took her time, each step timed perfectly with each inhale and exhale. And Libby helplessly watched as the strange man talked with her child.

The old woman finally reached the restroom area, smelling of old fish and shit. Her skin hung around frail bones like bags of water. She did not look at Libby, only stared in front of herself behind bottle glass–thick eyeglasses.

That's probably me in ten years, Libby thought, feeling sick to her stomach. *If I live that long. If George doesn't get to me first.*

By the time she could get around the old woman and return to her daughter, the pilot was gone. Stella sat bolt upright in her chair, surveying the night sky. Libby cringed when she saw the metallic wings on her chest, wishing she could have stayed and protected her daughter from such nonsense.

"I see you got your wings," she said.

Stella turned to face her mother, smiling. "Yup. Captain Jorge gave them to me. He's *cool.*"

Libby felt blood rushing to her temples. She recognized that tone in her daughter's voice—the same glossy smile of infatuation that she herself had when she first met George. The blindness of hormones.

And it scared her.

A pressure welled up inside of her chest, throbbing at her temples.

Angrily, she reached forward and yanked the wings from Stella's blouse, the fabric tearing loudly in the silent plane.

"Mommy!"

Libby slapped her—harder than before—feeling the knuckles on the back of her hand against the soft flesh and bone of Stella's cheek. "Shut up, Stella. People are trying to sleep, damnit."

Stella's wail tapered into a barrage of snorts and sniffles. She covered her eyes with one hand, covering her chest with the other. "I can't have anything . . ." she said.

Anger still pulsed in Libby's temples. She could feel the beginnings of a migraine coming on. Her eyeballs hurt, pulsing as if something was trying to break out from her skull by tapping the orbs out of the sockets for exit. She closed the lids and massaged her temples while her daughter's sobs mellowed and faded.

And then her ears popped. Loudly, like a large drain gurgling open. She could hear Stella's cry again. It seemed too intense, loud enough to wake up the passengers.

She nervously looked over her shoulder. The other passengers were all asleep. The loudness was in her head.

And then her ears popped *again,* shutting out the noise like a door slamming shut. Her head hurt, the migraine coming full force now, her peripheral vision fading into tiny black pinpricks of pain. She dropped Stella's wings.

"my . . ." She barely heard, and turned to face Stella, whose cheeks were puffed up red, her eyes gigantic swellings. ". . . ears . . . hurt . . . again . . . help . . ." Stella unsnapped her seat belt and jumped up to press the button to call Faith. She punched it madly, over and over, the way she pressed elevator buttons sometimes.

Libby felt suddenly dizzy, drunk. She couldn't tell if the turbulence was in her head or from the plane itself—all she knew was that her world began to bob and weave involuntarily, that she had lost all feelings of security and control. Her stomach lurched and crawled up her throat.

The lights in the plane flickered, turned yellow. Stella was holding her ears in pain, tugging on the lobes. Libby, too, felt pain in the same spot, iron spikes in her ears. She plugged her nose and tried to blow as she watched her daughter's tears stream down her face.

And then she went deaf. As if at the flick of a switch, all sound clicked off. Nothing at all inside but the dull hum of her migraine.

She frowned and looked again at her daughter.

And Stella's ears quivered and spat. Small pink and yellow flecks of flesh landed on the airplane seat beside her: she had lost her eardrums.

In the window behind Stella's disbelieving face: stars. Too bright. Too close.

Oh my God . . . too much pressure. Too much altitude.

The panel above them flopped open and rubber masks and tubes dangled like snakes above them. Libby reached up, grabbed one, placed it over her face, and then quickly did the same for Stella, who had somehow given up to the pain and sat calmly in her chair, as if just waiting for the trauma to get over with. Libby snapped the oxygen mask on her, and Stella just turned and stared out the window, enjoying the sky.

Libby sucked madly on the plastic cup over her nose and mouth. The plastic bag that dangled from her chin did not expand and contract; she could feel nothing in her lungs but emptiness and the pain of swallowed needles, no taste in her mouth but the flavor of anxious spit . . . the masks weren't working.

Nothing was working.

Just when she had managed to break free from George, she and Stella were going to die.

I'll be damned if I'm gonna let that happen.

On instinct, she jumped out of her seat, rushing toward the back of the plane. It was insane, the entire hull brimming with madness. The other passengers had awakened, some gripping at their ears, others clutching their throats. A skinny man in a yellow polyester jacket was wrestling with the rubber hose attached to his face, pulling on the top of it, trying to milk air from its tubes. A woman had a ballpoint pen in her left ear, trying to dig out sound. Many people appeared to be screaming, but Libby couldn't hear anything now, her own ears blown and empty and pulsing with blood. She was dizzy now, more lightheaded than before, her legs wobbling beneath every step.

Libby kicked in the bathroom door, the panelling slamming against the fatty knees of the old woman inside. Her eyeglasses slid down her nose as her head lolled on its shoulders. Libby yanked the tubes from the woman's nostrils, trailing a yellow line of goo from her upper lip. The woman didn't move at all—she was already dead, no doubt—and Libby now found herself praying that she would be lucky enough to live as long as the old woman, diseased or not.

She shoved the tube into her mouth and sucked on it. The air felt like cool water coursing down her throat, and she swallowed it, burping on its gas. She yanked the oxygen tank from its cart, and cradled it in the crook of her arm, like a child. Like she once held Stella.

Stella.

She made her way back down the aisles. The insanity that writhed in the aisle around her faded, swallowed in the pain of her peripheral vision. She sighted Stella, still sitting calmly in her seat, looking out of the airplane window with the useless oxygen mask strapped around the back of her head. She couldn't see her face, and was glad—the look of innocence lost would be too much for her, she knew.

A hand reached up and tried to yank the heavy air tank from her grip. Libby brought an elbow down into the face of whoever it was, and then noticed that it was Faith, wrestling her way out from the grip of another man, clawing madly for oxygen.

She ran now, heading closer toward her daughter. She had to save her, to get her the oxygen quickly. They could share it, perhaps even last long enough to get into the cockpit and get control of the plane. She didn't know how to fly, but she was sure she could at least force the thing to point downward, towards Earth rather than out into space.

She reached Stella, who was turned away from her. Her senses were returning, the headache fading, though the intense pressure of the cabin still thrummed in her temples and groin. "Stella," she said, knowing her daughter could no longer hear. "Look over here. Mommy's got air . . ."

Stella turned. Her eyes were gone, empty sockets of red meat in their place. Her eyes had burst.

Libby was surprised more at her own lack of shock than from the horrible sight of her daughter's eyeless face. Libby no longer felt like even trying. Perhaps Stella had the right idea—to just sit and patiently wait for death to come.

Still, she sucked in a lungful of cool air, held it, and plucked the oxygen tube from between her teeth. Then she slipped the hose into her daughter's lips and turned away, not wanting to look at her anymore. She closed her eyes— they, too, would be bursting soon she knew—and wrapped an arm around Stella's neck, hugging her close. Waiting. Waiting for the ultimate freedom.

4

Stella reached up to her wings and caressed their silver feathers. She could not hear, but Mommy's heartbeat was loud and fast against her cheek. Slowly, she unsnapped the metal clasp from her blouse, and held the thin silver between her fingers.

She felt Mommy's arm, stroked it, looking for her elbow. When she found the crook of her arm, she dug the pin into the middle, where the doctor used to give her shots. Mommy didn't move. She was probably already gone.

The blood was thin and slick between her fingers, like warm ice cream. Stella scooped as much as she could into her palm and rubbed it into where her eyes were supposed to be. It felt mushy and weird, but good, too. Warm. Stella did it again, gathering up a handful of blood from Mommy's arm, since it was running quite a bit now.

Minutes later, she could see.

Black and white at first, then stars glistening amidst the black void of space. A large red flash in the middle of it all—Mars, maybe. Maybe something else. Something further away.

And she could hear, too.

Captain Jorge's voice came over the intercom: "Bang, zoom, straight to the moon . . . right Stella?"

Stella smiled.

And so did the gigantic ocean of white that suddenly eclipsed her newfound vision. It smiled and it winked as it got larger and larger, almost blinding in its whiteness. As if it was inside of her eyes and radiating out.

Cheese, Stella thought. *It's only cheese.*

But still she was smiling as she watched the stars glimmering around her. Smiling especially when she finally saw the tiny blue planet below.

BRUJA

Kathryn Ptacek

CHATO DEL-KLINNE LOOKED AROUND AT THE AIRPORT TERMINAL as he stepped out of the jetway. Not precisely Kansas, he could hear Sunny say teasingly as if she were standing next to him, and he would have smiled, except he didn't feel like it; he felt . . . uneasy.

Not precisely Kansas, no.

Southern Texas along the Mexican border, to be more precise. He'd been asleep on the plane, thinking he was heading back to Las Vegas when the captain announced that because of a vigorous storm system to the west, he had been ordered to change his route and land at Dry Plains International instead of Dallas/Ft. Worth.

"Vigorous." Chato shook his head. He just loved these euphemistic terms. Vigorous . . . meaning the entire western sky was painted a sickly yellow green, twenty twisters had been spotted between Dallas/Fort Worth and Amarillo, and if everyone was lucky, the tornados wouldn't remove the top six inches of soil throughout Texas, not to mention every single trailer park in the Lone Star State.

And so here he was. The airport was bigger than he'd expected. It was, after all, an international airport, but mostly he had discovered with great irony that in the southwest that term meant flights scheduled to and from Mexico. Period.

International. Yeah, right.

What he hadn't expected was the sheer chaos of the place. Many passengers milled around, while some clumped together to speak angrily about delayed or cancelled flights; somewhere someone was sobbing. Children darted back and forth, and several babies wailed.

He had the sense that something had happened, something horrible, and there was only one sort of thing like that that could make an airport chaotic. Yet the captain of Chato's plane had mentioned no disaster.

Maybe it had just happened now. No, he would have heard *something*. So, it—whatever it was—had occurred before his flight put down. It must have been after the one announcement, and it must have been too late for the pilot to go to another airport; jets had only so much reserve fuel, after all.

So, they didn't say a thing because they wanted to keep us from panicking, he thought grimly. Swell.

A youth hardly out of his teens and dressed in old jeans and a white T-shirt smeared with something dark walked by.

Chato grabbed the young man's arm. "Excuse me. What happened here, can you tell me? I just got off a plane from New York and—"

"A bomb!" the youth cried, his voice thick with fear and a West Texas accent.

"Where?"

The kid nodded with his chin toward the line of tall windows opposite the gate where Chato had disembarked. "Out there. Some terrorist had a bomb. I think it was one of them Eye-ranians. Blew up the whole plane right there on the runway. It was terrible, just terrible. They got firemen and ambulances out there, but I don't know if anyone's gonna make it . . ." The kid began sobbing and Chato let go and watched as he struggled through the crowd.

Chato was stunned. A terrorist here? He went toward the line of windows on the left, and now he could see the wreckage in the distance, maybe a quarter of a mile away. He saw emergency vehicles, and saw the flames and billowing black smoke, even in the daylight, and he wondered how his plane's pilot had negotiated the landing so that no one aboard had seen it.

Clever, real clever. Chato didn't much like being manipulated like that. Of course, what good would it have done to panic them while they were still in the air? Yeah, right; wait until we're on the ground, then we can panic.

Now he watched as people scrambled along the tarmac, some into ambulances, others standing with emergency personnel; he sensed futility. No matter what they did out there . . . it was too late. Inside the building men and women and children stumbled along, some pushing others, all of them close to panicking. The bomb had set them off, too, he knew; maybe they were afraid that there were other terrorists, perhaps even here in the building.

Terrorists. In a border airport in southern Texas. Sure. Dallas/Ft. Worth airport, yeah, maybe. But here? Something wasn't right.

He checked a monitor. Most departing flights were cancelled; his was among them. Of course.

Someone next to him started complaining that when he got home he was going to write to the president of the airlines about this incompetence—he had important business in Vegas, by God, and it had to be done on time, by God—and Chato was relieved he wouldn't have to fly all the way to Nevada with him; with his luck, the guy would have sat next to him and bitched during the whole flight.

Now that he knew he didn't have to rush for a connecting flight, he took time to study his fellow strandees. They were a mixed bag: young and old and in-between, a few in wheelchairs or with canes, a fairly equal combination of Anglo and black and Hispanic, with a handful of Asians. Knots of businessmen in anonymous grey suits and look-alike leather briefcases, and several elderly nuns in old-fashioned habits, a Dallas matron with bouffant hairdo and too much eye makeup, a black kid with gold chains and a gold front tooth to match, two little girls in matching pink and lavender outfits each clutching a stuffed animal, a tall Sikh in all white, and more, dozens more. These people didn't seem to know where they were going, only that they didn't want to stay here, didn't want to stay in one place for too long. And beneath the anxiety and disorientation . . .

He felt . . . *it*.

He supposed he'd been vaguely aware of it before this; perhaps it was what had troubled him when he first arrived.

But now that he stood there, not moving, he felt it, felt that touch of *something else,* of *somewhere else.*

He had had several close brushes with the supernatural before, and he knew its caress.

An Apache shaman, he had trained with his teacher long ago before leaving home; for a long time he had turned his back on his discipline. But in the past few years he'd gone through a lot, and his instruction had come in handy.

There was more here than just the explosion out on the runway. God knows that would have been enough for most places, but not here. There was more . . . much more.

Blood had been spilled here, he could smell it, and could sense, too, that something had awakened with the spilling of the blood.

He felt as if something shifted under his feet, but when he looked he saw nothing but the innocuous grey tile.

Sunny, he thought suddenly. He had to get to a phone and let her know that he was okay. He checked his watch. Six-fifteen here, which meant four-fifteen at home, and she'd be expecting him in a few hours. Only he wasn't going to be home in a few hours.

Mechanically he moved toward the phones, then stopped when he saw the lines there. They snaked back away from the handful of booths, back toward the waiting area.

Determined, he walked into another gate area, but the situation was the same there. At the newsstand no one stood behind the register. Several customers waited to pay, if only someone would appear; one guy was busy reading the *Wall Street Journal,* not even aware of what was going on around him. Behind him a short Hispanic woman stood with a magazine in her hand.

As he studied the area, he realized that since he'd arrived he hadn't seen a single airport employee. No one manned the ticket desks at the gates, nor had there been any announcements about incoming flights or departures. There was nothing but the damned Muzak inanely playing some cheerful mishmash of a Beatles tune.

He had the feeling that someone was watching him, but when he looked around he saw that everyone else seemed occupied in their own little drama. Still, he couldn't shake the feeling. The hair at the back of his neck prickled, and he rubbed the area. He tightened the band holding back his long black hair, then sighed.

Puzzled, he took the escalator to the lower level where the baggage carousels were located. The carousels moved, all right, going around and around, but no luggage shot out of the chutes. He checked the rental car desks: no one. No one stood behind the ticket reservation counters, either.

In fact, except for hundreds of panicked passengers the airport was deserted. He looked outside and saw no taxis waiting along the curb. There were no porters, either.

Where were all the airport employees? Off somewhere having a union meeting? On a mass coffee break, perhaps?

Or had they fled?

He thought he smelled burning french fries drifting down from the upper level, and he hoped that someone would go into one of the restaurants and investigate before the whole place caught on fire.

The music system was now playing "Raindrops Keep Falling on My Head." God, how he hated bouncy tunes like that. It was all so . . . pasteurized.

He went outside and winced as the oppressive heat of the Texas summer afternoon hit him. Then all at once he smelled the acrid fumes from the bombed airplane. He watched now as one of the ambulances swung around the building and shot out toward the highway. The vehicle abruptly began swerving back and forth; suddenly it flipped over onto its side and burst into flames. The second ambulance, following some distance away, stopped with a squeal of brakes, and the side and back doors flew open and the emergency crew raced away, just seconds before the vehicle exploded.

For a while Chato had thought about taking one of the rental cars—he couldn't call it stealing in an emergency situation like this—and getting the hell out of this weird place, but seeing what had happened to the two ambulances made him change his mind. Maybe it was just a coincidence, he told himself. And maybe not.

Maybe something didn't want anything or anyone leaving the airport area.

It wasn't a thought he wanted to contemplate for long.

He studied the countryside surrounding Dry Plains International. Well, whoever had named it had certainly gotten that name right. He didn't see anything except a flat brown expanse stretching off to the horizon, and above it a murky faintly blue sky, as if there was a haze. No mountains, no rivers or lakes, no buildings, no trees or bushes or strange cacti, no landmarks whatsoever. It was as if a tabletop had been swept clear and this airport plunked down in the middle. He had seen some desolate places, but man, this beat 'em all.

Comforting, he thought, real comforting. Just where the hell was this place?

To further increase his apprehension, a dry hot wind howled around the corner of the building, and in the wind he thought he heard voices, strange voices that seemed to whisper his name.

Quickly he went back inside through the automatic doors before the electricity decided to go off and strand him outside. He wasn't sure which was worse: being stuck outside or in. As if something had read his thoughts, the lights overhead flickered momentarily, and somewhere there was a high-pitched scream.

He decided right then and there to go where there were people. Safety in numbers? he could hear Sunny tease him. Damned right, honey. This level was far too deserted for his liking. Again, he felt like something was watching him, but again when he looked around, he saw no one.

The escalator stopped halfway between floors, and he was getting ready to walk up the rest of the distance when it started up again, only this time it went backwards. He managed to turn around before he got to the floor, then stood and stared at the slow-moving steps.

Well, he'd take the stairs now. Damned if he go on an elevator or try the escalator again.

As he walked toward the staircase, he thought he heard a sound like a moan. He stopped. There was no one near the escalator. Still no one at the car rental desks or airline counters. All that was left were two doors, each with its bland symbol symbolizing gender. He entered the men's restroom first.

"Hello?"

No answer. He checked all the stalls. Nothing.

He went next door to the ladies' restroom.

"Hello?"

He heard a movement in one of the stalls, and pushed open the door, which hadn't been locked. A young blond woman—she couldn't have been much over eighteen— huddled there. A very pregnant young woman, he thought, when she shifted.

"Do you need help?" he asked gently.

She nodded. When she looked up at him, he could see that tears had left mascara smudges down her cheeks.

"Let me take you back upstairs where there are other people," he said.

"I-I think the baby's about to come. I came in here. I didn't know what else to do," the girl said.

"Maybe there's a doctor or nurse on the second floor," Chato said as he took her by the hand, easing her to her feet. She shuffled forward a few inches, then groaned. He realized she needed to lie down right away, but he would have to get her upstairs for that. Maybe they could break into an airline lounge. Surely they had couches in there.

But once he got the girl outside the bathroom and halfway to the escalator, he realized they weren't going to get upstairs. She could barely hobble and kept crying the entire time.

While he had been looking around, he'd seen an area back of the stairs that made a protected nook. He took her there and told her to wait, then searched the lower level until he found a chair for her. She sank into it with a grunt.

"I need to go up and see if there's a doctor, okay?"

"No! Don't leave me!" She gripped his hand.

"Look, miss—"

"Gail."

"Gail," he said, trying to keep his tone reasonable. He needed to calm her, reassure her somehow that everything would be all right, when he wasn't at all sure himself. "It'll just be a few minutes. You're okay here. You've got this comfortable chair and—"

She squeezed his hand harder. "No, please, don't leave. I think someone's after me."

"No one can see you back here," he said. "It's out of the way. You can't be seen from the stairway or the doors or—"

"No, no, no! You don't understand. I've been hearing this voice ever since I got off the plane. Gail, it's been saying, give me your baby. I want your baby. I need your baby."

Chato stared down at her tear-streaked face, and knew then that this wasn't something she was imagining. She *had* heard the voice.

"Right. Okay. Look, give me a few minutes to scout around." He held up a hand when she started to protest. "I won't be long. But I want to see what I can find to make you more comfortable. Okay?"

She nodded.

"Just sit here and be quiet, and if anyone approaches . . . scream like hell, and I'll come running."

She nodded again, pressed a hand to her abdomen. "Thank you. You know, I don't even know your name."

"Chato."

He ducked out of the nook and glanced around the lower level. Empty as before. Or was it? The hairs along the back of his neck prickled again. Someone watched. He had thought that before. Now he knew he wasn't imagining it.

"Some Enchanted Evening" played on the music system.

That, he decided, could go off any time soon, and he'd be all the happier for it.

One airline counter over he found a door leading into an employee lounge. Lots to loot here, he thought with a wry smile. He dragged the seat cushions from some couches back to the nook.

"I would have brought a couch," he explained, "but I didn't think I could get it through the doorway. I'll be back."

He returned to the lounge and found a closet full of the lap blankets that flight attendants give passengers, along with a dozen or more small pillows. He took everything there he could carry back to Gail. He tucked pillows around her, and covered her with the blankets, and stacked some nearby.

Just in case, he thought. Just in case when the baby comes, and I have to deliver it. He felt a spike of panic. His shaman training didn't include lessons in childbirth. This he'd have to wing.

He'd been aware for some time of more noise from above, and it sounded now like screaming and shouting and assorted bumping and scraping. He wondered what was going on, but he wasn't about to go and investigate. And he hoped whatever was up there wouldn't make its way down here.

Not for the first time he realized they were virtually trapped in the nook. The safe place could become in a moment's notice a prison.

But what choice did they have? He didn't want to settle her in the middle of the deserted level, where anyone—or anything—could see them.

He went scouting again and came back with two fire extinguishers. Not the best choice of weapons, he told himself, but when you have nothing else at hand—well, that was not precisely true, he realized. He did have his Swiss army knife. Yeah, that would be a lot of use, wouldn't it? But if he had smelled something burning earlier, these canisters might come in handy. And if the electricity went off, he could always break the windows with them so they could escape outside.

He saw that Gail had fallen asleep, and so he sneaked back to the employee lounge. When he saw the vending machines again, he realized just how hungry he had was. He had slept through dinner on the plane, and hadn't had anything since he'd left New York City that morning. And he knew Gail would be hungry.

He reached into his pocket for change, but he didn't have enough for two candy bars, much less what he knew they'd need.

He studied the soda machine, then took out his pocket knife, selected a blade he thought would fit and began jiggling it back and forth in the lock on the front panel. Finally he was rewarded with a snick, and the panel opened. He did the same for the other machines.

Something thudded onto the floor above and he half-expected to see someone or something falling through the ceiling. But it held. For now.

He located several empty cartons and put all the cans of soda in there, as well as dozens of packets of cookies and potato chips and cellophane-wrapped sandwiches and candy bars. He threw in what paper napkins and plastic cutlery he found; he opened all the drawers and doors he could find to see what other goodies he could liberate. When he left, he thought the room looked like locusts had swept through.

He winced. Somehow he didn't like the imagery.

When he got back, Gail was awake and had struggled up to a sitting position. He put the boxes down with the others he'd brought back earlier.

"Hungry?"

She nodded.

He pawed through the contents of a box. "I have ham and cheese, or ham and cheese, or ham and cheese." She giggled and suddenly she looked much younger than her eighteen years. "Or the ever popular ham and cheese."

"It's such a hard decision. Umm. Let me have the ham and cheese, please."

"An excellent choice. And what will you have to wash it down with? Here we have more choice. Clear soda, orange soda, or brown soda."

"Orange, please."

Somehow he knew she would choose that. He opened the can and handed it to her. He was sitting on the chair now.

"I'll be back."

He went back to the airline counters and hunted around until he came to another fire alarm box. He took the fire axe. A better weapon.

On his way back he grabbed some pads of paper and pens. They might as well keep occupied while waiting for the baby.

He was heading back to the nook when he saw something on the now-stopped escalator. He edged closer. A thin trickle of blood dripped down from the floor above to the first tread of the escalator, crawled along the grooved metal plating, then dribbled down onto the tread below. Tread after tread, the blood dripped slowly down.

He backed away quickly.

"What's the matter?" Gail said, looking up from her sandwich when he came back.

"Nothing," he said with what he hoped was a steady smile.

"You're a bad liar," she said.

"I know. Sunny—my girlfriend—always says that."

He thought Gail seemed steadier now that she was eating and drinking something. Plus, he reminded himself, she wasn't by herself. That had to be a bit more reassuring, even if he didn't know what was going to happen.

"I don't know anything about you," he said after he finished his first sandwich and started on a second. He had never realized how good stale bread and dry cheese could taste. "You married?" She shook her head. "About to be?" She nodded. "And your boyfriend abandoned you, right?"

"Yeah, how did you know?"

"Lucky guess. Well, you're better off without him. He wouldn't have been much help now, I suspect."

"No, Randy said I was getting too fat and ugly."

"You're certainly not ugly. And you're not fat. You're pregnant. There's a big difference."

She flashed him a grateful smile.

"Where you going to?"

"Home to Omaha. I wanted to be with my family. My parents don't know about . . . my pregnancy. I guess my dad will yell a bit, but he really loves me, and my mom will just glare at him until he shuts up. It's the only place I can go. I was running out of money."

"Sounds like a good place, basically."

"What about you, Chato?" She was gnawing on her lower lip. She hadn't moaned for some time, but he knew she was hurting, by the look on her face.

"I live in Las Vegas; I was coming from New York City going to Dallas/Ft. Worth, but got diverted here. I do odd jobs, I guess you could say, sort of this and that. Sunny is a blackjack dealer at a casino. What else? Well, I grew up in New Mexico."

"And you're Indian," she said softly.

"Yeah. Chiricahua Apache."

"I went to school with some Sioux. There are a lot of Indians in Nebraska, you know."

"Yeah, I know." He paused as he thought he heard someone speak. Hadn't they said *Gail?* "Hey, I brought along some paper and some pens, and thought after we have our dessert of Paydays or Hershey Bars, we could have a rollicking game of hangman. How's that sound?"

She winced slightly from pain. "Great. I think I'm ready for my dessert now," she said. What were you doing in New York?" she asked as she peeled back the wrapper.

"Business. I was at some meetings in northern New York state."

"Are you an Indian activist?" she asked.

He was surprised by her question.

She smiled. "I heard about the protests up there with the Mohawks, and just wondered."

"Yeah, well, I was there at the same time, although for different reasons. I'm not really an activist." He didn't want to go into details of the matter he had handled; he thought it would be too upsetting for her now. There had been some misunderstandings, some deaths; nothing was ever as easy as he thought it would be. He rubbed at a scar on his arm, an angry-looking scar all too recent. He should know better by now; except that he didn't.

She sensed his reluctance and didn't pursue it. "How about that game now?"

"Fine."

He drew a hanging tree, and twelve spaces below it, then showed her the pad of paper.

"Twelve letters? Oh no! I was never good with long words!"

She had guessed eight of the letters when a really big pain shot through her, and she groaned so loudly he dropped the paper. He realized she'd been huffing her breath for the past few minutes, and he hadn't even noticed.

"Oh damn," he muttered when he saw her face, and leaped to his feet. The baby was coming.

Rolling up his sleeves as he dashed into the bathroom, he scrubbed his hands with soap and hot water, dried them, then came back to where Gail lay moaning softly.

He checked his supplies. He was as prepared as he'd ever be—rolls of paper towels, spare blankets, a bucket of water and sponges. Now if he just knew how to deliver a baby, he'd feel a little happier about the situation.

He helped her lay back down on the couch cushions and settled a pillow beneath her head.

"Okay?"

She nodded, her breath huffing faster. She seemed to be

counting silently. Then she said, "I have too many clothes on. You—you're going to have to help me."

He was embarrassed for himself and for her, too. He helped her remove her panties and push back her dress, and then he draped a blanket over her upraised knees.

Oh God, Sunny, he thought, where are you when I need you? He didn't know that Sunny had ever birthed a baby, but he wouldn't put it past her, and he knew she'd just stride into this little maternity cubbyhole, roll up her sleeves, and that would be that. Sunny would take care of everything.

Only Sunny wasn't here; he was.

"Oh God!"

Gail gripped his hand as he told her to push. That's what they did on TV, he told himself, so he assumed it was close enough to truth.

"Push again. Thatta girl. Good. Again."

The umbilical cord. What was he going to do about that? Oh Jesus, what had he gotten himself mixed up in? Then he remembered his pocket knife. He'd clean a blade off the best he could and he'd use that.

What if the baby died? What if Gail died? What if she bled to death right here? He'd have to go get help, he knew it. But upstairs . . . was there any help upstairs?

No. There was just him and Gail and a baby about to be born.

And almost before he knew it then the baby was coming, and he could see its head, and he told Gail to push harder and harder, and she screamed at him that she was, goddamn it, and he told her she was doing good, really good, and then all at once there was a baby in his hands. A tiny warm thing covered with blood, and the wrinkled face contorted itself, and he remembered some dumb medical show he used to watch, and he gently pried open the baby's mouth and removed mucus, and the baby coughed and started to cry.

Gail, her hair plastered dark against her forehead, smiled weakly. "Girl or boy?"

"Girl."

"Good. Boys are nothing but trouble. Does she have all her toes and fingers?"

"Sure does."

He cut the umbilical cord, and cleaned the baby gently with the paper napkins and towels, then wrapped her in one of the blankets.

Still holding the baby, he stared down at her and she blinked up at him. He felt an inane urge to grin foolishly. Babies did that to people, he knew.

He heard a sound behind him.

A small white-haired woman stood there. It was, he realized, the Hispanic woman from the newsstand.

"I will take over from here," she said softly, and her eyes were the yellow brown of a wolf's.

And he knew that this woman was the part of the reason for his unease. He knew in an instant what she was. Bruja. *Witch.*

Beyond her something shimmered, and at first Chato thought it was fog that had somehow crept into the terminal, but then he squinted and the fog coalesced. In the rippling light he could see figures that were there but not there, men from the past, dressed in feather headgear, cotton tunics, and shields. Their dark bodies glistened as if oiled, and the men grinned fiercely.

"These are my ancestors," the woman said. "They suffered much under the whites. And they are hungry for their revenge."

Chato didn't have to ask how they would be brought into this time. He saw the bruja eying the baby, and he knew without question she would take the newborn, would . . . sacrifice . . . it.

Not if he had anything to say about it.

Suddenly she leaped forward and grabbed the infant, and turned and ran.

"No!" Gail shrieked and tried to stagger to her feet.

"Stay there!" he yelled at the girl and he raced after the woman. For someone so little, she certainly ran fast. He risked a glance back over his shoulder, and saw that Gail had obeyed and was back by the nook. Good. He didn't want to have to worry about her as well. God knew what else was wandering around this airport.

This part of the building had grown darker now, as if it were close to nighttime, yet Chato knew it wasn't. He glanced out the windows as he ran and saw a gloom. But he didn't have time to think any more about it. He saw a door closing ahead, and knew the bruja had gone through it.

He stopped moments before he slammed into the wall, wrenched open the door, and stepped through . . .

. . . and fell down a steep and rough slope. He tumbled and twisted and bounced, and once slammed his knee against a boulder. Finally, he came to a rest at the bottom. Puffs of dust rose around him, making him cough.

Nothing vital, he thought, was broken, although when he managed to get to his feet he knew he was bleeding in several places; certainly he was bruised, and when he touched his side with his fingertips, he winced. He thought he might have cracked a rib or two.

Swell.

And just where the hell was he?

He seemed to be in a tunnel, rough-hewn from rock and the earth. The ceiling wasn't high, and when he lifted his arm, wincing with pain from his ribs, he found he could touch the surface easily. He was not given to claustrophobia, but he would have liked it if the place were a tad more spacious. The walls were scarcely an arm's length away on each side. The air smelled of must, of rich loamy earth . . . like a newly-dug grave.

The tunnel should have been pitch-black, but it wasn't. It was faintly lit, as though the earthen walls around him were phosphorescent. He scraped some of the dirt away, and his fingers glowed slightly. Quickly he wiped his hand on his jeans.

His eyes had adjusted to the semi-darkness now, and he could see that the walls weren't made of just dirt; objects seemed embedded in them. He stepped closer and brushed away some grime so he could better see. He backed hastily away when he saw the gleaming white of a human skull. The matrix of the walls was human bones: skulls and femurs, shin bones, and the thin bones of fingers and toes. Here and there stiff hair and parchment-like skin clung. Here and there he could see a bas relief carved, images of skulls and skeletons and pyramids of bones.

He looked back up the slope, but couldn't see the doorway. There was no way out there; that much was obvious.

He would have to go down the tunnel.

He didn't want to go down the tunnel.

No choice, old pal, he told himself, and it almost sounded like he had spoken aloud, although he knew he hadn't.

Something brushed by his ear, and he shook his head.

The floor, he realized then, was made up of crushed bones. Inside his boots his toes curled, but he had no choice. He had to walk upon the dead.

Carefully he moved forward, suspicious that there might be some trapdoor waiting for him; but the ground seemed solid enough. For now.

He noticed masks suspended from some of the walls—intricately carved images that leered or glared down at him with the countenances of stern-faced warriors and eagles and reptiles and pumas and other feral beasts. Masks with elongated earlobes, exaggerated noses and lips, eyes that were narrow slits, tear-shaped, or round as if with surprise. Masks hewn of coconut husk, of wood, of copper and silver and tin. Some had elaborate headdresses with the visages of jaguars and parrots. Bright feathers and plaits of human hair and strands of beads and teeth and shell dangled from the masks, and he saw the glint of gold and precious stones in the rings in the ears.

More light came from ahead, and he reached an opening on the right. There was a smallish room that seemed empty, and when he stepped into it, he saw himself as a boy of fourteen when his father had taken him to Ryan Josanie, his old teacher, the man who had taught him to be a shaman.

Josanie was showing the then-Chato how to control his dreams, and the youth was complaining that it was hard, and Josanie, not smiling, was saying that everything worth having is hard, and the then-Josanie glanced up and saw the now-Chato.

"Josanie." Seeing the old man brought him such sadness and regret. His teacher had been dead for years. Chato took a step forward, and with a shimmer, as if it were simply an image in water, the scene disappeared, and he was standing in an empty room.

He went out into the tunnel, which now turned to the left. Sometimes, he thought, the eyes of the skulls in the walls seemed to watch him, but he dismissed that thought. He was just getting spooked; that was all. Nothing was watching him.

Or was it?

He encountered another room. There he saw himself and Ross, his brother younger by three years, and they were at a state championship football game, and the then-Chato was in uniform, and Ross was saying how much he admired his brother, and Chato was laughing and telling him he'd know better when he got older, and Ross was saying he'd always respect his brother. Ross . . . whom he'd not seen in years, hadn't talked to for more than a year. Ross . . . they'd been close once. Now they had drifted so far apart.

Once again Chato took a step forward, and once again the image, as if mirrored on the surface of water, disappeared.

Out in the tunnel he grew aware again of a sound that had been with him since he'd entered this stygian world. Its rhythm was regular, he realized, and he thought it might be water dripping somewhere. No, it was more than that, And he recognized it then as the sound of a heart beating, and whether it was his or something else's he didn't know.

Some yards away he found another room, and this time he saw his mother and father working, working hard as they had always done to make a better life for his brother and him. They never complained, even though they often held down as many as two or three jobs at once, all so that their boys could go to school, would not live in the desperate poverty that they had known all too well.

In still another room he saw himself at the university, saw him getting his degree, saw his parents in the audience, and he knew their pride. He was the first in the family to go beyond high school. He was proud, and yet he felt as if he had lost something that night, something of his people, and he didn't know what.

In yet another room he saw a woman he had loved long ago; they had parted amicably enough; and then he saw his old house in Albuquerque where he had lived while he was a professor of geology there, and he remembered all the good times he'd had then, all the good friends he'd left behind long ago, all the memories that he had stepped away from.

Another chamber contained niches carved deep into the earth, and in the niches lay mummified bodies. Bodies that had been dead for decades, for a century or two or even longer. The dust was thick in this room, and he did not step inside. Here and there he could see a scrap of cloth still sticking to the leathery skin of the mummies, and the air smelled faintly of herbs. Something moved opposite him, and he watched a centipede crawl out of one of the body's eyes.

His stomach rebelled and he hurried away.

The path twisted to the right, and he stepped into the room and saw a man on a bed. The man was naked, and a blonde woman, equally exposed, sat astride him and ground her hips and moaned. Her hair was plastered in long sweaty strings down her back. The man on the bed reached up and brutally squeezed her breasts, and she cried out as she arched her back, and then she swiveled her head around and leered at him, and Chato saw with horror that the woman was Sunny.

"No!" he screamed. He stumbled from the room, and when he glanced back it was dark. No, no, no. Sunny wasn't with another man, wouldn't be; she loved *him*. Or did she? one part of him slyly whispered. She did, she did, she did. He repeated it to himself as if it were a mantra.

He rubbed his hand across his face, felt the sweat and grime there, and knew that what he had seen was false. He had been misled, deliberately. Whoever—whatever—was doing this wanted him to lose heart, wanted him to give up.

But he wouldn't.

He took a deep breath, and followed the curve of the tunnel which was now heading downward slightly, and he wondered how far below the airport he was now. If that was really where he was.

Abruptly the tunnel ended, and there before him stretched a pool of water. He edged closer and saw only himself reflected.

Now what? he asked himself.

He inspected the wall beyond the water, the walls alongside him. Were there hidden doors somewhere? No. He knew that this was the way.

But if he jumped in, he would drown. Who knew how deep this was? He might just sink like a stone, and that would be the end of him. Or perhaps there were . . . things

. . . slimy things waiting for him beneath the water, things that would suck the very breath from his body, and crush him with their rot-encrusted tentacles.

No, no, he couldn't do it. He had to go back, had to find another way to rescue the baby.

No, said a voice in his mind, and he knew it was old Josanie. *Think.*

He studied the water's tranquil surface. Nothing seemed to move below it. Nothing disturbed it.

Taking a deep breath, Chato took one step into the water and sank and sank and sank until he thought his lungs would burst from lack of oxygen, and then suddenly he was in another room, this one much larger than those lining the tunnel.

Firelight flickered, casting elongated shadows, shadows that seemed almost to move as if they were alive.

And there beyond the blaze stood the bruja, and she held the baby by its tiny heels, and dangled the child over the flames. The baby wailed miserably, and flailed its arms uselessly.

"You will pay," the woman whispered, and in that moment he saw she was not an old woman as he had first thought, but that her skin was dark and mottled, like that of a lizard, and her teeth were long and yellowed, with something red staining them. From her back arched wings of jade and ebony feathers, feathers that *moved,* from the lice and maggots that crawled across them. She looked like a feathered serpent.

He blinked, but the image stayed the same, and in that moment, he saw she wore his mother's face, then that of Sunny, then that of a girl whom he had known long ago at the university, and then it was the face of the old woman, but only as she must have been long long ago. She was at once beautiful and terrible to see, and he saw now that she was completely naked except for the necklace of bones draped across her full breasts, and her bronzed skin gleamed.

She smiled at him, and beckoned to him with one hand, and in that hand he saw an obsidian knife.

He remained rooted where he was.

Her skin was tattooed. At least he thought they were

tattoos. Tattoos of eyes, like the masks in the tunnel: mere slits, round, tear-shaped, and then with horror, he realized the eyes were watching him and that some had winked.

The woman's smile broadened. She raised her arm, the knife rising, and now he watched as the dagger came hurtling down and—

Without thinking, he threw himself across the fire. He was only dimly conscious of the sparks singeing his hair, burning his face and hands, and he grabbed the baby just as the knife slashed downward and pain shot through him as the obsidian cut through his sleeve into his flesh, and he yelled, and kicked out, and his boots connected with the woman, and she screamed as she lost her balance, and fell into the fire.

He scrabbled to his feet, the child cradled tightly in his arms, and watched as the woman writhed and howled as the flames licked up and down her body, melting the flesh away as if it were nothing more than thin tissue paper, and he watched as her bones burned, watched until there was nothing more than charred matter. Abruptly the fire died down, and there were only embers and what had been left of the bruja.

Tentatively he touched one of lumps with the toe of his boot, and he thought he could hear a faint cry.

He backed away from the fire, then examined the room. It was elongated, the now-dead fire at one end, a pool of water at the other. He had come *down* before. Would he have to go down again? It didn't make sense. After all, he wanted to go *up*, but then none of this made sense, at least as far as the rules of science went. This was a matter of something much darker, much older than science, after all.

The baby was whimpering, and he tried to shush her, and with a prayer that this was the right thing, he jumped into the water, and suddenly he was bobbing up and up and up through clear water, and his head broke the surface and he scrabbled out of it before the baby could drown.

Once more he was standing in the tunnel, and as far as he could see there was still no exit. But it looked like he'd have to head up that slope. There was no way around it.

He clasped the infant closer to him and started toward the slope. He ignored the rooms on either side of him; he didn't want to see anything that they held. The walls seemed to grow closer upon him, and things with long plucking fingers reached out and grabbed at his tattered shirt, his burned skin, and he gritted his teeth against the pain.

Finally he came to the slope. He started climbing up, holding the baby with one hand, helping himself find a purchase with the other hand.

What if, he wondered halfway up, what if he got to the top, and he didn't see a doorway, just like when he fell down the slope.

Believe, one part of his mind said, and it was his voice, not Josanie's.

He reached the top, and there before him was the door. He pushed it open, stepped through, and he was once more in the airport terminal, and when he looked back, there was only a smooth wall.

He hurried toward the nook, afraid now that he would find Gail gone, but she was there, sitting on her bedding. She leapt to her feet when she saw him and rushed over, and he handed the baby to her.

"What happened?" she asked.

He knew how he must look. His hair was partly singed, some of it laying in wet strands across his cheek and forehead. His face and arms were bruised, he had blood and cuts and dirt all over him, not to mention the burns and scorchmarks.

He grinned.

"It's a long story." He took a deep breath and felt the sharp pain in his ribs; he had forgotten about them during all this; now he was very much reminded. "I'm going to wash up in the bathroom, and then we ought to get the hell out of here. You agree?"

She nodded. "I agree."

When he came out of the bathroom a few minutes later, he found she'd made a makeshift bed for the baby from a small carton, and that she'd packed some of their things—mostly the food and drink and blankets—into a few other boxes.

"I didn't know how far we'd have to walk," she said.

"Walk? Hell, we're going to drive," he said, and he strode over to one of the rental car stations, and grabbed a handful of keys. "We're going to go to the rental lot, and find what fits where, and when we do, we're getting in and not looking back." He didn't mention the vehicles that he'd seen earlier, the ones that couldn't get out of the airport. Not now.

He wasn't about to stop for anyone or anything now, not after what he'd just gone through.

It took them half an hour but they found a blue T-bird, and got their boxes settled in. Gail strapped herself in, then held the baby tightly.

Chato got behind the wheel, put on his seat belt, adjusted mirrors and seat, and turned on the car, and without thinking, flipped on the turn signal. He grinned when he realized it wasn't necessary. Old habits.

Then they drove out of the deserted rental-car lot and into the outbound lane, and when they reached the shells of the ambulances, he saw that Gail started to shake as she realized what had happened earlier, and he said, looking into the rearview mirror and seeing the dark eyes of old Josanie, "I believe."

Chato drove away from the airport, away from the fire and the death, and it was only when they had driven over twenty miles that he remembered he never had picked up his luggage. He began laughing.

That was okay. He'd pick up some more bags. After all, he told himself as he look over at the sleeping mother and child, luggage was cheap; life wasn't.

BENEATH THE TARMAC

Lawrence Watt-Evans

THE HEARING PROTECTORS, WHICH LOOKED LIKE HEADPHONES without wires, were amazingly effective; they shut out the human world almost entirely. Murphy looked out across the vast expanse of paved ground and through the fence at the desert beyond, and he didn't hear a single human voice.

Oh, the jet engines penetrated all right, though they were muffled, but that whine and roar didn't seem like any part of the everyday reality of modern life. It was something alien, something primeval, something that sent shivers through him.

Murphy watched Delta 8806 taxiing out to the runway, its engines growling. Some people compared the big airliners to great silver birds, but he could never see the resemblance. Both had wings, and they both flew, but birds were curved and organically graceful, their wings warped and flapped and folded; the planes were stiff and straight and hard, the wings rigid. If they resembled anything that had ever lived, it wasn't birds; it was pterosaurs.

He had seen those in books, even seen a skeleton of one in a museum, the long, pointed, bony head thrust out like an airliner's nose, the trailing legs as complex as the tail assembly of a 727.

And pterosaurs were more appropriate out here, anyway —what kind of place was this flat, burning desert for most birds? Distant buzzards and an occasional roadrunner were about it, as far as birds were concerned.

Pterodactyls and pteranodons—he knew all the names—those belonged. A rhamphorhynchus would look right at home, out there above the parched Texas sand.

People, though—people didn't belong here. Not the ordinary travelers he glimpsed through the windows of the jetways and the planes, not the pilots and flight attendants in their tailored uniforms; they were civilized in a way this land would never be.

For himself, he was, perhaps, as alien and strange as anything else here, in his Day-Glo orange coverall, with his two red signal lights in his hands, guiding the great mechanical creatures to their nests, leading them out to fly.

He knew that most of the other traffic crew didn't agree with him about any of this; they didn't see how the land itself was rejecting them. When he shrugged off the bombed airliner and all the other recent disasters as an inevitable part of the land's struggle to rid itself of humanity, his coworkers shouted at him, told him he was sick, argued that he should back up his union, that it was all because management was doing something wrong, though none of them could define exactly *what* mistakes management was making. They didn't believe in the land.

He knew better, and even when he wasn't wearing the hearing protectors he could shut out the voices, could look out at the black pavement and the bleached golden desert beyond and know that those people didn't belong here.

Did he belong here himself, with his understanding of the land, and his inhuman appearance?

He wasn't sure.

Continental 3302 was down and coming to the gate, engines whining; he raised the lights and took his place on the tarmac, waving it in.

The pavement felt almost soft beneath his feet; the hot spell was in its third week now, sun beating down on the asphalt as the pterosaurian aircraft lumbered across, their wings casting mere instants of shadow, the weight of them pressing hot tires down into pavement.

That asphalt was made of the bones of dinosaurs, in part—oil and tar mixed with gravel, and oil and coal were the compressed and transformed remnants of the ancient fern forests and the beasts that once roamed them. Perhaps that was why it didn't seem like an intrusion on the desert—this was oil country, and the asphalt had come from ground much like this.

He backed up to the gate, arms waving in the come-along gesture, as he watched the giant pterosaur's claws . . .

No, he corrected himself, as he watched the airliner's wheels. He was letting his fancies run away with him. A little imagination was fine, he told himself, and his theories about what belonged here were all very well, but he mustn't let any of it interfere with his work. Safety first. Guide the plane in, get the jetway hooked on—*then* he could daydream about the desert, and the dinosaurs, and the pavement shimmering in the sun.

He got Continental 3302 in place without difficulty, helped guide the jetway up to the side, then stepped back and glanced at his watch.

His shift was over; Continental 4587 was late but that was too bad. Jerry would bring it in. He waved a farewell to the man driving the jetway, then turned toward the door in the terminal wall.

Then he blinked, and turned back.

Something had moved somewhere out there, on the broad asphalt-black and concrete-grey plain of the airport. He had seen it from the corner of his eye.

At first he thought that maybe 4587 had come in after all, and he'd just missed the signal, but no, there was no plane on the taxiways. A United DC-9 was lunging down Runway 22, starting its takeoff, but that wasn't it.

Had some kid gotten out there, perhaps? Had a cat or dog escaped from a pet carrier in someone's luggage? *Something* had moved, he was sure of it.

Where the hell was Jerry, anyway? Late again, of course.

Well, whatever was out there, it shouldn't be, and safety was his job. He turned off the red-capped flashlights, thrust them into the loops on his coverall, and marched out past 3302, trying to spot whatever he had seen.

There, toward the maintenance area—it had ducked around the corner, out of sight.

Nobody else would see it there, either, he realized; that

was a blind area. The main terminal was around the corner, and a blank concrete wall separated the maintenance area from the departure gates—it wouldn't do to have passengers watching as maintenance crews stripped down malfunctioning aircraft.

Except that the way the wall angled around, there was a stretch of empty pavement that couldn't be seen from the maintenance bays, either. It was roughly triangular, bounded on one side by that unnecessary blank wall, on another by an equally blank wall of the terminal, and on the third by a taxiway.

And whatever he had spotted, out here on the tarmac where it didn't belong, had just gone into that blind area.

He sighed, and headed in that direction.

Probably some lost kid, trying to get away from the noise, he thought. Or maybe there'd been another "accident," and the kid had panicked and run off to find somewhere safe.

Murphy didn't know exactly why there had been so many accidents lately; especially since the bombing it seemed as if safety had gone all to hell around Dry Plains International. Most of his union blamed it on bad management, but Murphy didn't see how management had gotten any worse lately than it had always been.

A few people had said it was some kind of Indian curse, but Murphy didn't buy that. Indians were just people; they didn't cast real curses.

It took something older and more powerful than just *people* to make a curse.

His own theory was that there *was* a curse, of sorts—or really, a rejection. The desert itself was rejecting the intrusions upon it.

Whatever the reason, there *had* been accidents, and Murphy didn't want there to be another, if whatever he had glimpsed turned out to be a scared kid who might panic and run out in front of a plane.

He rounded the end of the wall, into the blind area, and stopped, a little more abruptly than he had intended.

The pavement here had softened in the sun; his foot had sunk in when he took that final step. Carefully, he lifted it free.

Black gunk was stuck to the gum sole.

Murphy cursed quietly, then put his foot back down. It sank in again, but he ignored it; the damage was done. He scanned the triangle of black pavement.

No one was there—but as he watched, the movement came again. This time he saw it plainly.

The pavement itself was moving; it had humped up for a moment, easily a foot or two, and then sunk back down.

Murphy stared. What the hell could make it do *that?*

Forgetting about the softened tarmac, he took two steps forward. Both his feet sank into the asphalt, an inch or so down into the pavement; black goo oozed up around his shoes.

He looked down and cursed again. Some contractor had decided to save a few bucks, using cheap tar, he guessed— but south Texas was so damn hot that if this stuff had been up to spec, that hadn't been good enough.

That didn't explain that *lump,* though. He looked up, ignoring his ruined shoes for a moment.

The pavement rippled—not like a pond in the breeze, or like any sort of natural effect he could imagine, but as if something was moving beneath it and leaving a raised trail, about six inches high, that took a second or two to sink back. He stared.

What could do *that?*

Had he been out in the sun too long? Was he hallucinating?

Again, the pavement moved. Again, it looked for all the world as if something was *under* it, as if some beast or something was moving below the tarmac, that instead of a hard pavement he was watching something rubbery, something like a black tarp thrown over . . .

Over what? What was under there?

He pulled his foot up—it took a real effort to free it from the tar—and took another step forward, watching for movement.

The asphalt obliged him by humping up a mere yard or so away, then flattening again.

Murphy supposed he ought to be terrified, but somehow he wasn't. He had always said this place, this desert, wasn't quite natural. Besides, the whole thing seemed slightly unreal, those silent movements . . .

Then he realized that they might not be silent; he was still wearing his hearing protectors. He pulled the headset off.

The asphalt moved, a lump rising and crossing a few feet before him, then sinking again, and there *was* a sound, a sort of crunching, hissing sound.

That made it much more real, all of a sudden. He stepped back—or tried to; the tar held him fast at first. He had to pry his shoe free by rocking it back and forth, toe-heel-toe-heel, until it came loose.

He remembered those Indian scare stories, tales of dead savages buried beneath the airport's pavements—was that what was moving around under here? Was this neglected corner the sacred burial ground the rumors talked about?

It didn't seem very likely. And why would dead Indians be heaving up the tarmac in these random movements?

Another lump arose, and moved so close that the asphalt that held his right shoe twisted beneath him; he waved his arms, regaining his balance.

"Hey," he shouted. "Who's down there?"

For a moment, nothing happened; then, once more, the tarmac swelled upward. A much larger mound than any previous arose before him, and this time it didn't immediately sink back down; it stayed, a miniature hill, perhaps ten feet across and four feet high at the center. He could hear the asphalt straining and cracking; he could see seams opening where the hardtop split to reveal soft shiny black tar.

He still didn't see anything of whatever was pushing up the pavement, though.

If anything was.

He remembered his earlier musings about dinosaurs, and the oils and tars that they had become.

Could the pavement be moving itself? Could whatever force was responsible for the sightings of dead Indians have also brought back something far older, and far deader?

That was crazy.

He clipped the headset in its place on his coverall and took out, for lack of anything better, one of the directing lights. It was basically just an ordinary flashlight with a long red plastic cone over the top, but it was a foot and a half long, the most suitable thing he had for poking at the mysterious mass of pavement.

The red cap of the light tapped on asphalt.

Maybe, he thought, the desert was rejecting the whole airport, trying to throw off the asphalt covering.

Whatever was happening, he decided he didn't like it. Despite the hot sun, a chill ran down his spine. This was unnatural. It was dangerous. He should report it.

He tried to pull up his left foot, to turn around and go, but the sole had settled down even further into the asphalt—the black tar was started to close over the toe.

He reached down and grabbed his ankle with both hands, and tugged.

The shoe didn't move—but the tar did. It surged up, inched up over the instep, up the heel.

Panicking, Murphy yanked his foot right out of the shoe, despite the tight laces; his white gym sock tore open.

He didn't care; he put his left foot atop the empty shoe and quickly untied the right. As he pulled at the laces, he could see a tendril of the black tar creeping up toward his stockinged foot.

Then both feet were free, and he turned and realized that he was eight feet from the corner, and that even if he got that far, the asphalt extended well beyond. The entire apron, and the taxiway beyond, were all that same black asphalt—and he could see gentle movements in several spots now.

Why would this weird phenomenon, whatever it was, stay confined to one little corner, when there were acres of asphalt out there in the sun?

He imagined the great jet planes settling into the tarmac and being trapped, like pterosaurs caught in tar.

If he could get around the end of the wall, though, he would be in sight of the gates. He could call for help, he could wave, he could signal.

Where he was now, he could only be seen from planes as they passed by—and who aboard a departing airliner would see that he was in trouble, would be able to tell that anything was wrong? And what could they do if they *did* see?

He jumped, hoping to make it around the corner in a step or two, quickly enough that his feet would not have time to become stuck in the tar, but the instant his right foot—his leading foot—landed, he knew it wasn't going to work.

His foot sank right into the asphalt as if it were soft mud; by the time his left foot touched pavement, the right was sunk to mid-calf in sticky black tar. The left fared little better, and he lost his balance, sprawling forward.

The tar adhered to his coverall, from ankle to chest, and he was trapped, like a fly on flypaper—like, he thought, one of those animals long ago that had stumbled into a tar pit, and been trapped there until it sank and fossilized.

And even with his arm outstretched—his left elbow had landed in the tar and been caught, but his right was free—even with his arm outstretched, he could not reach the corner.

For a moment he panicked, thrashing wildly, but it did no good; he stopped himself just short of trapping his right arm as well.

He tried to calm down and consider his situation rationally—even though there didn't seem to be anything rational about it. Even if the tarmac had melted in the sun, how could he sink so far into it without hitting the ground beneath? And what about the moving asphalt masses?

So his situation wasn't rational, but still, rationality might help him get out of it.

Moving seemed like a bad idea; it seemed as if every time he moved, he sank deeper and got himself into more trouble. If he waited . . .

His first thought was that he would die of thirst, and his bones would be found years later, but then he drove that thought away. He'd had a drink of water from the cooler not half an hour ago, and the sun was well down in the west; even in the dry heat of the desert, he wouldn't be in any danger of death from dehydration until mid-morning at the very earliest. Hunger was even less of a problem.

Sooner or later, he would be missed—Jerry would show up and want to check himself in, check Murphy out. But would anyone think to look out here?

Probably not. And he couldn't think of any way to attract their attention; if he tried shouting, he wouldn't be heard over the racket of the planes.

But if he waited, it would be dark in a couple of hours,

and he had his lights; he could signal. Someone would be bound to notice. He could shine a beam that would reach around the corner. Then they'd come find him.

He wondered if anyone else was having trouble with the pavement, if there were tar pits appearing under planes or jetways, or out in the parking lot. A vision of cars sinking out of sight like trapped dinosaurs came to him, and despite his predicament he managed a smile. Cars like stegosaurs, airplanes like pteranodons, all caught in the tar pits.

And they'd named this place Dry Plains. Not so dry after all, perhaps.

If such things were happening, the rescue crews would be busy, it might be hours before they came for him; he would have to conserve his flashlight batteries carefully.

Sooner or later, though, if he had his lights, they would find him, and save him.

Perhaps the cool night air would harden the pavement again; perhaps he would be able to chip his way free with the butt end of a flashlight.

It was just tarmac. Even animated by some supernatural force, it was just tarmac, the remains of creatures dead for sixty million years. He could beat it.

All he had to do was wait for nightfall.

The roar of a plane's takeoff faded away into the sky, and he heard a crackling, hissing noise—the sound of whatever lurked beneath the tarmac, moving. He turned, expecting to see the big hill sinking away.

It wasn't; it was growing.

He choked with horror.

Making it till nightfall might be harder than he thought. If that thing fell on him . . .

Then the hill broke open, like an egg hatching, and the tyrannosaur's head rose up, eyes gleaming red in the setting sun. Its huge mouth gaped, revealing rows of razor-sharp teeth, and its ridiculous little foreclaws reached out in a swimming motion, pulling it forward through the tar.

It never tried to climb out. Murphy never saw most of it. He started screaming even before the jaws closed on his legs, but Delta 9016 was coming in just then, and the sound was lost in the roar of engines.

A hundred feet away, guiding Continental 4587 up to the

gate, Jerry Ingels wondered what had happened to Murphy; it wasn't like him to skip the check-in/check-out procedure.

If he wasn't careful, Jerry thought, Murphy could be in trouble.

Through his hearing protectors he heard the howl of 9016's jets—and for a moment he thought he heard something else, like the growl of some big animal.

He shook his head and got back to business, amazed at the odd fancies people came up with.

IN COUNTRY

Peter Crowther

A STRATEGICALLY-PLACED STREET LAMP BLOCKING THE SECOND
letter of the second word made the sign say:

DRY PAINS INTERNATIONAL AIRPORT
8 MILES

It seemed appropriate, and Robinson smiled into the
mirror at his wife curled up on the back seat, peering at him
from under the tarp. Only she wasn't really peering at him.

The sockets—he could only see one—simply glared at the
world inside Robinson's Chevy, glared around the bloodied
sheets of paper that Robinson had stuffed into them. The
sheets of paper that said sweet somethings. They also said
unfaithful and *two-timing* and *dirty, stinking, no-good
wetback-loving whore.* The sheets of paper that had hatched
a plan, delivered through the mails. A plan that said, *Hey,
let's run away together. Let's get on a plane and fly off into
the blue forever.*

Delivered through the mails. He gritted his teeth at the
thought of how stupid he had been.

Even the mailman had been in on it. Robinson had asked
him into the house before he left this morning and showed
him Ellen. Apologized for the mess and the fact that she was
leaking all over the damned carpet but, hell, it was so hard
getting a home looked after these days, wasn't it? So hard,
particularly when your Mexican-loving wife was busy pen-

ning sweet love-letters all the day long instead of fixing meals and keeping the place clean.

And the mailman had just looked at him. Looked at him like he was mad or something. The same look that the old woman had given him over by the side of the Song Tra Bong river when he'd cut up her husband and her two kids and thrown the pieces out, far out, into the muddy water. He'd done that for Shawaski.

Robinson shook his head and shifted his hands around the wheel. That was his biggest problem: too big-hearted, always doing things for other people. But he'd done Ellen for himself. After a while, a guy had to look after number one.

But the mailman hadn't understood. Hadn't even offered an apology. No *Hey, man, shit . . . I didn't know, okay? If I'd've known, hell, I wouldn't've delivered them letters. No way, nossir. You done right, man. She had it coming.* There was nothing. He just shook, wavered from side to side like a young tree. And so Robinson had chopped him down.

Put him out in the trash.

There was a lot of fucking trash out there.

He smiled into the mirror again.

Ellen Robinson didn't return the smile, just like she refused to meet his eyes. But then Robinson didn't expect her to. That was why he had stitched her lips together. To stop her smiling any more. To stop those *Oh, goshdarn it, Barry, you've made me all wet again, now. I guess you'd better stick the old ramrod into me one more time* smiles.

She was already dead and cooling off when he'd done it, when he'd stitched up the lips. He was taking no chances. Those lips had betrayed him, spoken softnesses—softnesses that should have been his alone—to Barry Martinez; kissed Barry Martinez's lips, big, full lips. Lips like Elvis, he'd said to Ellen when they had first met Barry. When Barry had moved into the neighborhood following his divorce. And they had laughed and sung "Don't Be Cruel" as they got ready for bed.

To a heart that's true.

Her heart. Robinson's left eye twitched and he lifted his hand to rub the eyelid. Her heart was now in the trash. Still, now, and silent. Beating for nobody at all. He'd cut the thing out, cut it clear of her body with his bayonet. Then he had used the bayonet on the mailman. Blamire's bayonet. One of many keepsakes from his time *in country*.

Robinson looked in the mirror at the roughly stitched slash below Ellen's nose, thought of it sliding open, all wet-lipped, wet-lipped and ready for that dirty bastard's mouth.

He wondered idly where that mouth had been on Ellen. But it made the headache worse. He figured he knew the places anyway. He had sanded them down, removed the taint. Tainted meat, his grandmother used to say. Good for nobody, not even a dog. Which was why Robinson had rejected his initial idea of feeding the heart to Mr. Ed, the trusty family labrador. And thinking about it had made him realize that even Mr. Ed couldn't be trusted. He, too, had been an accessory. Robinson knew that Martinez had been back to his house—his own fucking house, for crissakes—and Ed had settled down in his basket with a couple of Bonios while doormat-lips Barry Martinez mounted Ellen on the sofa and rode her to a wet and sloppy oblivion.

Et tu, Mr. Ed. Now he was in the trash with the mailman.

He wondered if Martinez had felt it when Ellen died. When she had finally drawn her last ruptured breath as Robinson stood over her in the living room. The living room. Robinson started to chuckle. That was some play on words. Living room. Hell, he'd made it a dying room. Taken his sweet time and spread the pain across and around her body until it spilled out and filtered into the carpet and the walls and the ceiling and all the shelves filled with her romance books and into the telephone receiver where she whispered her plans and into the drapes that she pulled shut to keep out all the prying eyes. He wondered if Martinez had sensed the removal from the world of that single, solitary, plodding beat. A beat that he had probably started to regard as his own property.

Ka-thump, ka-thump, ka-thump, ka—

He doubted it. Martinez would be there, at the airport, waiting for her. All greasy Desi-Arnez smiles and Copacabana limp wrist, like a young Xavier Cougat, decked out in one of those fucking ridiculous shirts that didn't have a collar. Made him look like he was protesting some goddamn draft. But Martinez was too young to remember that. Too young to remember the war. When Robinson was crapping in his Fruit Of The Looms because he'd just received his draft notice, old lard-ass Barry Martinez was only crapping in his diapers while he sucked on his mama's titties.

And while Robinson was crying to the wind and the rain as he scooped up Jimmy Shawaski's insides and dropped them back into the smoking hole in Shawaski's flak jacket, Barry Martinez was probably watching Rocky and Bullwinkle.

And when Robinson had come back to months of sleepless nights, when he'd wake up and see Sanchez and Termiton and Shawaski and Lunan and Blamire again, see them smiling through extra mouths and carrying their own legs and arms into his bedroom, holding whatever limbs they had left across their stomachs so's they could hold in their guts, and telling him, the way they always told him, *Get that ass off of that bed, boy, and let's go get us some gooks!* . . . when he was doing all that, where was old swivel-hips Martinez then? He was in first grade, the little slickback bastard.

Robinson had got himself some gooks now, sure enough. He'd got himself seven—counting the dog—and now he was going to get himself another.

He'd used the big, crooked needle that his grandfather used to stitch his nets with back in Ogunguit. To make sure Ellen's cheating lips didn't do it again. And her eyes had betrayed him, too, so he'd taken those out, dumped them in the trash with the two halves of Mr. Ed and all the pieces of the mailman. The fingers, too. The fingers that had stroked Barry Martinez's big, brown dick. In the trash. Along with the feet that had taken her to his house. All in the trash.

Trash. That was what Ellen was now. Refuse.

Robinson glared through the windshield and signalled to leave the freeway, muttering to the cold-eyed god of grunts everywhere of how he was looking forward to talking to Barry Martinez.

In the back seat, Ellen Robinson communed only with a couple of flies that had followed her and Robinson into the car. The flies now buzzed and dived, dropping into the sweet, iron-smelling wetness that seeped through the tarp

. . . the rich, deep red-blackness that had now run along and down the light-brown material, that had now pooled on the Chevy's old worn carpet and leaked through to floor panels rusted through by years of shot mufflers. There, it leaked out and ran along the underside of the car and dropped onto the blacktop, every few yards, in small, glistening, red-black globules.

The drips had been dripping for several miles but now, each time they hit the highway, the blobs seemed to sizzle, casting up a small puff of dusty air like bacon dropped onto a hot pan.

Robinson turned on the radio to see if there was any news about him. But it was only music. He figured that maybe they might have discovered the reason the general store at the end of Carmichael Street hadn't opened yet this morning. Actually, it *had* opened but it had closed early.

It had closed because they'd sold Ellen a pad of writing paper. They were in on it, too. He'd gone up there first thing (after the mailman), golf bag over his shoulder, and he'd asked the old woman if she remembered Ellen buying a notepad. And maybe some envelopes? Yeah, she remembered. She remembered selling her the stuff. And then he'd pulled out what he liked to think of as his driver, an M-16 gas-operated assault rifle, the one he'd brought all the way back from 'Nam and lovingly polished these past twenty years, and he'd given her a clean eight rounds in the gut and face. Then he'd given her husband two rounds in the head when he ran into the store from the back room.

Robinson had forgotten how sharp your hearing was when you'd fired your weapon. Some folks'll say how it turns you deaf but they don't know. Hell, they don't know shit. In 'Nam you don't have no time to be deaf because your ears are your lifeline. Your eyes are not much good, particularly in the night, when all you got for company are leeches and dysentery, webfoot and the shits, day in, day out. At times like that, the sharpness of your hearing could hear a gook's hand closing around a trigger a half a mile along the path. Could hear the last fart of a dead grunt as he rolled over in the brackish water.

Right then, in the general store, just after blasting the old woman and her husband, Robinson could hear the trucks moving along the interstate a couple of miles over by Rosewood Cemetery, could hear the shitty rap music pumping out at the filling station three blocks along Main Street . . . could hear, loud and clear, the sounds of material rubbing against material deep amidst the stock shelves of the store's back room. And so he'd gone through there, found the two kids. No more that fifteen, either of them. But being only fifteen didn't mean diddly. Over in 'Nam a fella was just as likely to get his balls sliced off by a kid as by anyone. So he gave the two kids he found in the back room the remaining ten rounds, five apiece. A neat job.

Then he'd moved the *Yes, we're open!* sign around so it said *We're sorry! We're closed! Call back soon!* and dropped the latch lock as he went out.

Robinson saw the sign up ahead, a right turn:

DRY PLAINS INTERNATIONAL AIRPORT
PLEASE DRIVE SAFELY

He slowed down obediently and checked his mirror. Behind him he could see a heat haze drifting up from the blacktop. He frowned. Strangest heat haze he'd ever seen. Looked more like a mist, spiralling up in thin plumes and then fanning out across the full breadth of the road. Must be hot enough to fry an egg out there, he thought as he turned the wheel and the Chevy moved onto the access road.

The radio sputtered and squawked. A man with an announcer's voice started to say that there were unsubstantiated reports coming in of problems at the airport. There was no real news yet, he said amidst crackles and spits, but the station had sent a team out to investigate.

Robinson saw the airport in the distance now. There were no planes to be seen in the air, either taking off or coming in. He smiled to himself. This was a stroke of good fortune. If there was trouble at Dry Plains then he was surely going to be able to get in there and take care of Barry Martinez without folks paying too much attention to him.

Behind Robinson, a mist was following the Chevy.

As he turned around a dense grove of trees Robinson saw

a thick cloud of black smoke spiralling into the air on the left. The radio sputtered and then cut out. Then he heard a sound from the back seat.

Robinson looked in the mirror and saw Ellen move beneath the tarpaulin. For a second, he lost control of the Chevy and lurched over to the right, narrowly missing an old man standing by the side of the road.

Robinson pulled the car over, keeping his eyes on his wife's body, and pulled on the hand brake. He turned around and lifted the tarp. She was still dead. Must have been the movement of the car or something. But now he saw that she was leaking badly. The carpet was stained nearly black.

He looked out of the car windows to see if he had attracted any attention. But there was nothing. Except for the old man, still standing in the same place, watching him. A mist was drifting along the road so that he could hardly make out the cars behind him. There weren't many cars on the road and, for a second, Robinson thought that was mighty strange. But the radio reports had probably persuaded people to keep away. Or maybe the police had stopped people pulling onto the access road. He chuckled. He was probably one of the last cars to get through.

Robinson turned around again and pulled the tarp back over Ellen's face. He got out of the car.

"Hey, old-timer," he shouted to the man. "Like to get yourself killed standing over there. What you doing, anyhow?"

The old man raised a hand, palm flat out, like he was saying *Peace* or something. Robinson shook his head. The old guy was an Indian. He could see that now. Hell, not just an Indian . . . an American. A real, bona fide US of A American. Just like me, he thought. Not some jumped-up, drug-running, wet-backed sonofabitch like Barry Martinez. Robinson raised his hand in response and said, "How!"

"You know how," the old man shouted back to him, and then the mist seemed to envelop him. It was the damndest weather.

Somewhere overhead, Robinson heard the drone of a chopper and, way in the distance, what sounded like the familiar soft whine of incoming mail. He shook his head and crouched down beside the Chevy.

The chopper appeared over the road and drifted across to Robinson's car. He waved up at the pilot, the pilot waved back. Then, when it was just a few feet above the sloping ground over the other side of the crash barrier, two men jumped out. He recognized them immediately: Hank Blamire and Jimmy Shawaski.

Shawaski ran over to Robinson and crouched down next to him, while Blamire waved the chopper away. In addition to the standard M-16, Shawaski carried an M-79 grenade launcher. In the holster by his side, Robinson could make out the telltale bulk of a .38-caliber Smith and Wesson. Blamire, now skidding into the dust beside them, carried a Claymore anti-personnel mine and a long strip of fragmentation grenades. In his hands he carried his trusty shotgun, sawn off, with strands of the barrel folded over to scatter the load with more velocity. On his belt was a .45-caliber pistol.

"Shit, guys!" was all Robinson could think of to say.

"Yeah," said Shawaski. He pushed his hands against his stomach and Robinson heard a dim squelch, kind of like the noise a drain makes when its full of sludge and leaves. When he pulled them away from his fatigue jacket, Shawaski's hands were dripping blood.

"We gonna party or what?" Blamire announced.

Robinson rubbed his eyes. He looked back along the road, saw the blacktop shimmering, saw the way the trees seemed to crowd in on the road as though there really wasn't a road there any more. But that was stupid. He'd just driven along there. It must just be one of those optical illusions. The curve of the trees he'd just passed, the tops sticking up just above the mist, made it look like there wasn't any road there at all. "Yeah," he said. "We're gonna party!"

Shawaski rose to his feet and pointed at something behind Robinson. "Who's the broad?" he asked. "There in the car."

Robinson turned around. Ellen was sitting up in the back seat, pulling pieces of paper out of her eye sockets with the stumps of her hands. Every now and again, she leaned forward and knocked her head against the rear window.

"My wife," he said. The words came out soft and hesitant.

"What a dog," Blamire said.

Shawaski laughed and started to howl like a coyote. He always drove the other guys nuts when he did that. Almost as if she understood what was happening, Ellen suddenly lay back down on the seat.

"We going, or what?" Blamire asked.

"Yeah," Robinson said. "We're going."

He half stood up and ran around to the driver's door, pulled it open. Blamire got into the back seat and crunched the butt of his M-16 into Ellen's face. Robinson heard her nose crack.

Shawaski got into the front passenger seat, gazing at the array of hardware that Robinson had brought. "Hey, you *are* going to party, man."

"Fucking A," said Robinson.

As the car pulled onto the highway, Robinson looked in the mirror and saw Blamire reach under the tarpaulin with a filthy hand. The hand was shaking ever so slightly. When he looked at Blamire's face, Robinson saw that the man was sweating. Outside the back window, the mist had reached the trunk of the Chevy.

There were more trees as they got nearer to the main terminal. Robinson didn't remember there being this many. They went right up to the runway at some points.

"Shit," said Shawaski, "will you look at that."

Robinson looked across the passenger seat. There was a solitary buffalo grazing beneath a sign that said:

TERMINAL THREE
TURN RIGHT

He swung the wheel. Blamire was grunting in the back seat and Robinson was aware of lots of movement, like he was fighting or something. But he didn't want to turn around and look. Nor did he look in the mirror.

"Pull over," Shawaski said.

Up ahead was a Plymouth station wagon, parked up against a public telephone. Out on the road an old man wearing a Yankee baseball hat was waving frantically for them to stop. Robinson braked and pulled in behind the

Plymouth. Shawaski leaned out of the window. "You havin' problems there?" he asked.

The man jogged up and leaned down. "There's something happening at the airport," he said. "Guy on the radio says there's been some kind of explosion and they're telling folks not to go in." He turned around and nodded disdainfully at the Plymouth. "And now I can't get the damned car to start."

"Yeah? Not your fuckin' day is it?" Shawaski said, smiling. He took out his .38 and planted a small hole in the man's forehead just below the brim of the hat. The man flew back and smashed against the crash rail, slid down to the ground in a sitting position looking surprised as hell. When the man slumped forward, Robinson saw that the entire back of his head, hat included, had gone.

"George?" A woman's head appeared over the other side of the Plymouth.

"I'll get her," Blamire said from the back seat.

Robinson was suddenly aware of a smell he hadn't smelled since back in high school. It was the thick musky aroma of unleashed pheromones and vaginal emission. He watched Blamire get out of the car, saw him pull up the zipper on his fatigue trousers, lift the shotgun and pull the trigger. The old woman who had stepped around from the back of the Plymouth shook as her head and right shoulder flew off in a spray of skin and bone fragments, then tumbled to the ground right where she had been standing.

"Neato," said Shawaski.

Blamire turned around and formed a circle with his thumb and forefinger. "Fucking A," he said and got back into the car.

Robinson pulled back out onto the road. In the mirror the mist gathered around the Plymouth like a pack of hungry rats.

It was another half mile to the terminal where Barry Martinez would be waiting. On the way, they saw a couple more buffalo, kind of indistinct among the paddies, grazing beneath the trees, and a few cars pulled over on the dusty side-road. They didn't see any more people. About halfway down the road there was a crudely constructed tower of sticks and blankets over to the right. At the top, Robinson could see a pair of feet protruding from beneath a fringed shawl. Leaning against the construction was a lance with feathers blowing in the wind.

The mist now seemed to be keeping pace with the Chevy, sometimes even drifting in front of them. Up ahead, the black smoke had dropped to the building tops, covering the sunshine behind the landing tower. "Damndest weather," Robinson said to nobody in particular.

Shawaski was singing. "Somebody To Love" by Jefferson Airplane. It seemed appropriate. In more ways than one.

By the time they pulled up to the terminal parking lot area, the light was almost gone. Shawaski rolled out of the car, cursing and holding his stomach, and ran to the shelter of the building. As he ran, he dropped small clumps of what looked like raw meat along the path.

A security guard looked around at him. "Boy, am I glad to see you guys," he said.

Shawaski put a finger to his lips and the guard nodded. Shawaski pointed over to the main doors and a man lifting a young boy onto a baggage cart. The guard looked around and frowned. Shawaski waved never-mind and pointed to himself. Then he pulled his gun from his holster. The first shot took out the kid, the second the guy. The guard span around, a look of horror on his face. That was when Shawaski put a shot straight into the guard's crotch.

Robinson opened the door and grabbed his M-16, trained it on the doors. There was no movement from inside the terminal.

Robinson watched Shawaski run over and put a single shot into the kid and the guy; then he saw him walk over to the guard and crouch down beside him. As Shawaski knelt down and buried his face in the guard's uniform, Robinson looked away. The mist had drifted right up to about twenty yards from the perimeter fence. It didn't seem to be moving any closer, probably because of all the air turbulence from the planes. But, looking up above the tower, Robinson saw that there were no planes in the air. More importantly, he saw that the mist, while stopping some distance from the fence, was drifting overhead as though it were out to cocoon the entire airport. Crazy idea, he thought.

Blamire ran over to join him, his feet squelching through the mud that now covered the paving blocks. Robinson broke out of his reverie and trained his M-16, did a 360-degree sweep.

The rear door of the Chevy creaked open and Ellen fell into the slime. He started to wonder where all that had come from and then noticed a long leech attached to Ellen's face which she was trying to sweep off with the stump of her right hand. Robinson took careful aim and shot the leech off. He took her cheek, right back to her ear, off with it. Ellen rolled over and tried to sit up.

Shawaski ran over and clubbed her across the face. The impact shook her brain out onto the paving slab and Robinson and Blamire watched in fascination as the thing scurried towards the terminal doors.

"Hell, let's get that fucker," Blamire yelled from over beside the car and, hefting up his .45, he took a shot at the brain. "Eeeehah!" he yelled. The first slug missed by a country mile but the second took a long sliver of grey out of the brain and Robinson was convinced he heard it cry out in agony. The thing, which for all the world looked just like one of the walnuts that Robinson's mother used to shell come Christmas time, now spouted a milky stream against the shattered glass. It didn't move.

Ellen, too, remained in exactly the position she had fallen though Blamire was now eyeing her with a fevered gaze. Robinson ran over and pulled down her skirt to cover the bruising. He didn't remember doing some of it.

Shawaski ambled over, sliding another cartridge into his .38. "That about wraps it here," he said with a nod.

"What do we do with her?" Blamire said looking at Ellen.

"We leave her's what we do," Robinson answered.

Over beyond the fence, the land had turned into deep bog. Robinson frowned and tried to recall seeing any rain. There was no longer any road to be seen. The skies hung with a thin curtain of rain, blowing across in sheets and foaming on the lake which had opened up on the plain and now stretched as far as the eye could see. Out in the water were small humps, like helmets floating on the surface, and each one had a circle of small red eyes that glowered in the gloom. Above their heads they heard the sound of engines racing, screaming for release. A plane was attempting to land in the gloom. Blamire ran to the car and took out his grenade launcher. He lay across the hood, his left side pressed onto the windshield with his head over the side, and hefted the launcher onto his shoulder. "Hey, Jimmy, come load me up."

Shawaski ran over and fumbled a grenade out of Blamire's bag, dropped it into the barrel. Blamire blew it out when the plane was directly overhead, about fifty feet up, and took a piece out of the undercarriage. The machine went another sixty to seventy yards and then buckled in the middle, fire and smoke belching out. Then it seemed to lose all forward momentum and just dropped, with more explosions rippling along its full length.

"Yay!" Shawaski shouted.

Amidst the noise and the smell of burning fuel, small, curled up, fiery shapes could be seen bouncing across the runway (which now looked very neglected and overgrown with clumps of weed). One or two of them touched down and started running but Shawaski took two of them straight away: Blamire let rip with his .45 and took out another three with six rounds.

"Check the water," Robinson hissed.

The other two looked over and saw that the eye-helmets were getting nearer to the shore. They were drifting into the long grasses next to the fence, where all the smouldering peasant bodies were stacked.

"What do we do, sarge?" Shawaski asked.

Robinson looked around. There seemed little alternative but to go inside. Inside! Barry Martinez! He had almost forgotten why he'd come here. "Inside," he yelled over the sound of burning metal and the screams of the dying.

As one, they turned and ran to the doors. On the way, Blamire took care to stamp on Ellen's brain. Robinson thought he heard it sigh, but there was so much going on it might just have been the wind.

Inside the terminal, people were crowded on the seats in the center of the departure lounge. Robinson, Blamire, and Shawaski stopped inside the doors and stared. The people stared back.

"Who we lookin' for?" Blamire hissed. His voice sounded

unfamiliar. Robinson glanced sideways and, just for a moment, Blamire's hair seemed to be longer than it had been.

"A guy," Robinson answered, "just a guy."

"Well, take your pick."

Martinez was standing over by one of the desks, dialing a number into a telephone.

"Wait here." Robinson ran across the lobby.

As he pulled up alongside Barry Martinez, Martinez said "Fuckin' telephones," and slammed the receiver on its cradle.

"Hello Barry."

Martinez span around and linked eyes with Robinson.

"Phil!"

"Surprised to see me?"

Martinez shrugged.

"Going on a trip?"

Martinez nodded and looked over Robinson's shoulder. "What you doin' here, Phil?"

"Brought you a message. From Ellen."

Martinez had finally noticed the M-16. "Hey, now don't do nothin' stupid, Phil." He pronounced "stupid" with a double-o, backing away from Robinson and raising his hands in supplication.

"You been fucking my wife, Barry," Robinson said softly. "I don't allow that."

"It—it wasn't nothin', Phil. I mean it. We was . . . we was just foolin' around. She di'n't mean nothin', honest."

Robinson reached out and took hold of the other man's shoulder, nodding slowly. "I know, I know," he said.

"What-whatcha doin' Phil? Whatcha gonna do, huh?"

"Let's go outside."

Martinez shook his head and pulled back towards the desk. "I ain't goin' anywhere with you, Phil." A woman appeared behind the desk and gave them a big smile. Robinson smiled back.

"Come on, Barry. She's outside."

"Outside? Ellen?"

Robinson gave a little nod, conspiratorially, chuckling. "Yeah. She's waiting for you."

"Phil—"

"Come *on!*" He grabbed Martinez's jacket lapels in one hand and pulled him away from the counter. As he did, Martinez thrust his hand into his pocket, pulled it straight back out and hit Robinson in the stomach. Then he pulled his hand away.

Robinson laughed, looked down at his shirt-front, saw the blood, frowned. Martinez hit him again. This time, Robinson saw the blade, saw it go into his stomach, saw the other man lift his hand high, heard him grunt, saw him take it out again, saw the blood and bits of stuff dripping from the blade. Then he felt the pain.

Robinson staggered backwards, bringing the M-16 up. He faltered, saw Martinez shoot a look to the left. He took hold of the barrel, steadied, and pulled the trigger. There was a burst of flame and sound and the woman behind the counter danced a jig, red blotches appearing across the front of her blouse. A little badge which said *Jackie* snapped in two and dropped to the floor. Martinez jumped sideways and started to run, crouched down, zigging and zagging.

Robinson steadied himself, looked back to the doors. Shawaski and Blamire had gone. But the old man was there. His hand was in the air, palm outstretched.

How!

You know how.

He turned around, saw Martinez running for the stairs. He fell back onto the floor, in a sitting position, and suddenly realized that something was dripping from his mouth. Martinez's figure was starting to blur now. He held the M-16 on his lap and, jamming two fingers between the trigger and its guard, he pulled, lifting the gun at the same time.

The first couple of shots took off the end of his left foot and he shouted. By then, though, the gun was up in the air. A whole crowd of people between him and the stairs started jumping around, blood lashing the desk fronts and the stair rails. Martinez took the last burst in his back and skidded the last few feet. He was still trying to regain his footing when his head hit the bannisters.

The magazine was empty.

Robinson looked down at his hands. There was a lot of blood.

Somewhere behind him, he heard the rhythmic beat of a drum.

When he looked around he saw the old man.

Walking towards him. Holding something.

That was one big knife! He fell back into the slime and waited. When he felt the hand grab hold of his hair and start to pull, he closed his eyes tight and bit hard into his lip. Back in 'Nam, they'd always said that when things looked bad you bit into your lip. Stopped the pain, they said.

They'd been wrong about a whole lot of other things, too.

JUST A FEW DROPS
OF BLOOD

Dawn Dunn

IT WAS JUST A FEW DROPS OF BLOOD. A PAPER CUT. KAREN OLSEN
pressed her index finger against her tongue to staunch the
meager flow, then glanced at the carpet where the blood had
fallen.

But it wasn't there.

She twisted around in the plastic chair of the airport
lobby and looked beneath her shoes because she was sure
she'd seen at least a couple of drops. . . .

Well, it was only a few drops; they must have soaked in.

She settled back into her chair and unfurled the magazine
she'd been reading, only to find she'd picked up the wrong
one. Her forehead wrinkled in confusion. She'd been reading the current issue of *Vogue*. How had she managed to lose
it? This one had no title, just some bizarre symbols—like
crude picture drawings—and the gory photograph of a
bunch of dead Indians all heaped in a mound. She noticed
that several of the bodies were headless, blood and entrails
coating the entire scenario. It looked too real to be faked,
and she was immediately disgusted. She shuddered and
thrust the magazine into the chair beside her.

Her copy of *Vogue* was nowhere to be seen.

"Attention, please." The PA system crackled. "We will
begin boarding Flight 287 to Los Angeles at Gate C. Would
those passengers requiring special assistance please come
forward now?"

Karen's attention shifted to the electronic schedule board
to see if her own plane was still on time. She'd been in Dry

Plains for a week, attending a computer seminar on the new mainframe her boss had ordered, and was anxious to get home to see her children—a little less anxious to see her husband. Jack could be a real asshole when he wanted to.

She waited patiently as information about the next two flights ran across the board, but her own wasn't listed. There wasn't any way she could've missed it; she'd been sitting here the whole time. It should be boarding soon. She checked her watch. It should be boarding *now*.

With a twinge of discomfort (flying always made her uneasy), she went over to the carrier's desk to inquire. Before she could speak, the woman behind the counter pointed at her and said, "Miss, you're bleeding."

"I know. It's just a . . ." Karen realized the woman was pointing at her sleeve and stopped in mid-sentence. A bright patch of scarlet, the size of a silver dollar, was spreading across the fabric of her blouse.

"My God." Karen touched the spot, but it didn't hurt.

"If you need medical assistance," the woman offered, "we have a first-aid station on the second floor."

Karen blushed. "No, it's nothing. Excuse me. I'll be right back." She pulled at the fabric as she turned and headed toward the nearest ladies room, still unable to feel any pain.

The stain had stopped spreading, but she slid into the first stall to slip off her blouse and examine the wound. Her fingers trembled as she fumbled with the buttons. What on earth had she done? How could she be bleeding? She pushed the blouse from her shoulder and saw that the bright spot of red had disappeared. The sleeve was pure white again, and her arm showed no sign of injury.

Karen rubbed her flesh inquisitively. This was just plain crazy. But the woman at the desk had seen it, too; she'd pointed it out to her.

What the hell was going on?

You're losing your mind. But she knew she wasn't.

She slipped on her blouse again, not quite sure how to explain it. But explanations didn't matter. She merely wanted to get out of here. Now more than ever. It was a feeling bordering on desperation.

She swung through the door of the stall and approached the sink. Her nervousness didn't show, and she smiled at her own reflection. You're all right, she told herself. Take a few deep breaths. She did, and then splashed water on her face, not caring about the make up she was washing away. There was no one to see her now. The seminar was over. All she had to do was concentrate on getting home. Kansas City, Missouri. Two kids, a husband, and a dog. *Please, God.*

She dried her hands and took another deep breath. She felt better, ready to give it another try.

Karen returned to the desk, but a different woman stood behind the counter. "Excuse me," Karen said carefully. "Could you please tell me about Flight 253?" She held out her boarding pass.

The woman eyed it peculiarly, as though she were somehow offended. "We have no flight number 253."

"What do you mean? Isn't that what it says on my ticket? This is the number they gave me when I checked my bags."

The woman's tone softened. "I'm sorry. I don't know what's going on here, but there is no Flight 253. You'd better check with the airport office. It's toward the front of the building. Security can help you find it."

Karen clutched her ticket and stepped back from the counter. No Flight 253. What the hell was she going to do? Somebody had obviously made an awful mistake. But she'd seen the sign when she'd first taken a seat in the lobby, and they'd had a 253 then. And it had been posted on the monitors downstairs when she'd checked her bags.

But it wasn't here now.

No.

Stay calm. Someone has made a mistake, but it can be rectified. You have your ticket, that's all the proof you need. Just find the goddamned office and give 'em hell.

Anger was building alongside her fear because they were scaring the shit out of her. No one had the right to put people through this kind of trauma. Someone was going to pay. A sob broke through the thickness in her throat. All she wanted was to go home and see her babies.

She located a security guard at the inspection point and asked for directions. He pointed her through the hub of little shops and restaurants, back toward the area where she'd checked in.

Karen thanked him, trying not to cry, but it was getting

harder. She was tired and overwrought, her mind stuffed with data on how to operate the new system. It had been a long week. She was almost dazed when she spotted a trickle of blood oozing down her ankle.

She blinked in disbelief. It couldn't be real. She rubbed at her nylon, smearing the blood but feeling no pain. And finding no wound. Like before.

Oh dear God.

She glanced around the terminal in panic. There was a row of phones over near the gift shop. She'd call home. Jack would know what to do. She didn't even care if he laughed, if he called her crazy or any number of other unpleasant things—as long as he got her out of this airport.

She slipped into one of the telephone cubicles, then punched in her calling-card number.

"I'm sorry," a prerecorded voice stated, "but that is not a valid number. Please, hang up and try again." She punched the number in a second time . . . and a third, receiving the same stupid message.

"What the fuck is wrong with this company?" she muttered, and banged her fist against the face of the machine. *Stay calm.* She dropped a quarter in the slot and spoke to a live operator. "I'm trying to call home. There's something wrong with my card. Could I make a collect call?"

"What number, please?"

Karen gave it to her and waited as the operator rang her house, then came back on the line. "That number is not in service."

"What do you mean?" Karen screamed. "I live there!"

"I'm sorry, that's all I know. If you'd like to speak to the supervisor—"

"Yeah, I'd like to speak to your fucking supervisor." This was too much.

Karen listened as the man explained that there was a disruption in the lines between here and there, and therefore the number was listed as being out of service. They were working to correct the problem. She argued but it did no good; they couldn't get through.

She sat in a daze on the stool, then picked up the receiver again, determined to make them find another route, but this time there was no dial tone. Just a distant sound, like drums.

Karen listened as the sound grew more distinct. Slow, heavy, methodical drums, like some type of funeral march. And someone moaning—very softly.

Her face paled. She dropped the phone and let it dangle from the cord. She didn't want to try again. She glanced at her ankle, but the blood was gone. Her knees shaking, she stepped out of the cubicle and moved back into the mainstream of pedestrian traffic.

She could barely think. She kept hearing the drums—and the soft moaning. She bumped into another passenger and absently apologized. Everything was the same, and yet something was different.

She found the plain, wooden door to the office that the guard had described, with an Authorized Personnel Only sign tacked to the outside, and peered in the glass inset at the top. A friendly-looking, dark-haired woman sitting at the front desk pushed a buzzer that unlocked the knob. Karen stepped inside, feeling her apprehension mount for no particular reason.

"How may I help you?"

"M-my ticket," Karen stammered. "There's something wrong with the flight number." She handed her boarding pass across the desk.

The woman looked at the number and checked it against a list she had in her drawer. "There must be some mistake. We don't have a Flight 253 scheduled to Kansas City." She smiled. "Just a minute, please." She swivelled her chair about and called to one of the other clerks. "Joe, you'd better page Mr. Howard."

Karen could feel her heart pounding in her throat.

The woman turned back, and her smile froze. "Miss, you're bleeding."

Karen looked down and caught a glimpse of red across her middle. It was spreading fast this time. Her fingers were sticky with it. She backed away from the desk and the friendly, dark-haired woman who was starting to panic.

"I have to go to the rest room," she whispered and yanked open the door.

She fled down the hall. Her body felt strangely flushed, as though there was a fire deep inside it, growing hotter. And there were voices, odd guttural tones she couldn't understand. War cries. A brief image of the magazine cover she'd seen in the lobby erupted through the chaos. Revenge for the dead.

The heat was becoming unbearable. Her legs . . . her whole body . . . tightening . . . swelling . . . the blood running faster. . . .

Her eyes met with those of a small child, a little girl the size of her own daughter. Karen stretched out her arms . . . and burst. Flesh and blood ruptured into a sea of red.

The child shrieked and closed her eyes.

The mother turned to her daughter, stooped and lifted her into her arms. "What is it, Holly? What's the matter?"

"She blew up, Mommy. The lady blew up." Holly pointed to the wall beside the rest rooms and a potted palm.

Her mother looked, bewildered. There was nothing except a few drops of blood.

THE SMOKING MIRROR

Dan Perez

THE SLEEK SHAPE OF THE AIR FORCE B-1B BOMBER ROARED through the darkness at 550 miles per hour. Descending slowly, its desert-camouflaged hull barely visible in the moonlight, the plane emitted a thin, nearly invisible stream of vapor from the underside of its fuselage.

In the cockpit, pilot Mack Arnett took a deep breath and slowly let it out, listening to the steady, muffled roar of the engine. The cool, oxygen-rich air flowing in his mask had a familiar rubbery smell and taste to it. He flexed his shoulders, then turned and spoke through his radio to his copilot, Patty Halpern.

"I'd better tell them." He flipped a switch so that the rest of the crew could hear his voice.

"Pilton, Gutierrez, listen up—we're losing fuel. It's nothing to panic about—the loss rate is steady, and we're watching it. But we don't know the cause, and it's significant enough that we can't risk turning back to Dyess. Next nearest base is Laughlin, and that's still too far. Dyess just sent Sierra Bravo clearance to land at the nearest civilian airport—"

Halpern cut in, "—which is Dry Plains International. It's plotted and in the computer. Twenty minute drive time."

"Any danger of fire, Capitano?" asked Ramon Gutierrez, the ECM officer.

"I don't know," Arnett said. "Let's all try to think good thoughts," he added.

"Cap'n," drawled Jake Pilton, the offensive-weapons officer, "ain't things bad enough? Do we gotta touch down at the spookport?"

Arnett cleared his throat and replied. "We're in a situation here, all right? I'm not taking any chances with this bird, its cargo, or any of its crew. If that means we touch down at Dry Plains, then we're damned well gonna do it and by the numbers. Am I clear on that?"

The crew acknowledged, and Arnett shut off the open circuit. They're too damned superstitious, he thought. But then too damned many crews were. In his fighter pilot days, Arnett had always carried his lucky cigarette lighter with him when he flew. But then he'd given up smoking, and that had been the end of that.

Superstitious or not, his crew was well trained. They weren't prone to panic in emergencies. Plus, they trusted Arnett to be straight with them—he always had. If he told them there was no reason to be alarmed, he was reasonably sure there wasn't.

Arnett shifted uncomfortably. None of that meant that *he* wasn't on edge. A fuel leak was always dangerous, but the timing for this one was particularly bad. As part of Operation Damocles, the B-1B's belly held twenty-four Short Range Attack Missiles, each tipped with a 200-kiloton nuclear warhead. They weren't armed, of course, and couldn't be without the permissive uplink signal from SAC or Looking Glass and the keys he and Jake Pilton carried around their necks. Even if the plane went down, a half-dozen safety measures would prevent the warheads from detonating.

So why am I nervous? he wondered. Maybe it was just having the missiles aboard. That was the idea behind Operation Damocles, after all—to keep the crews mentally accustomed to carrying a real nuclear payload, even as the cold war drew to an end.

Shrugging off his thoughts, Arnett glanced at the digital fuel gauge.

"We've lost six pounds of fuel since the last time you looked," said Halpern, her gray eyes solemn in the soft glow of the cockpit lights. "I've been watching it. You worried?"

"Nah," Arnett said, his tone aloof. He patted the console. "This old bird'll get us there."

He stared out the canopy at the moonlit West Texas desert sweeping past below, hoping he was right.

In the compartment behind the cockpit, Jake Pilton turned to Ramon Gutierrez and said, "Dry fuckin' Plains. The spookport. This gets better and better."

"Man, I've got to tell you," Gutierrez replied. "I feel bad about this one. Tezcatlipoca—" He trailed off.

"What was that you said?"

"Tezcatlipoca. He's an Aztec god."

"Anthropology major in college, right?"

Gutierrez shook his head. "I got a BS in physics, actually. But I took a bunch of anthropology and history. I wanted to know more about my ancestors."

"Like who invented the taco?" Pilton snickered, amused with himself.

"You're on thin ice, *chinga* breath."

"Naw, man, I was just kidding." Pilton slapped him on the shoulder. "I didn't mean to piss you off. Really. What does this Aztec guy have to do with anything?"

"Not a guy, not a mortal, but a god. The Smoking Mirror, they called him. When the priests in Tenochtitlán saw smoke coming from their obsidian mirror, they knew he was near." Gutierrez dug in a pocket and pulled out a gleaming black object.

"That's an Apache tear, right?"

"It's called that, but I got this one in Mexico City. Polished obsidian."

"Good-luck piece?"

Gutierrez nodded, replacing the black glass in his pocket. "You ever been to the Dry Plains airport?"

"Hell no. Not 'til now."

"Well, I stopped off there once, flying back into Texas from Mexico."

"And?"

"They've got this display of artifacts there that they found when they were building the airport. Most of it was Comanche stuff—flint arrowheads, beads, that sort of thing. But there was a small exhibit of obsidian knives and bits of copper and stonework that had been identified as pre-

Columbian. It was Aztec stuff. According to the exhibit, no one knows how the stuff got there."

"Did you call Indiana Jones?"

"Funny, *chinga*. Do you want to hear this or not?"

Pilton sighed. "Yeah, go ahead." At that moment, a red light gleamed on his board. "What the fuck?" he said.

Arnett listened to Halpern as she spoke with the Dry Plains tower: they were clearing a runway and hangar for the bomber, and placing emergency vehicles on standby. His eyes widened when a red light marking the permissive uplink signal flashed rapidly, then remained lit.

"Cap'n!" Pilton's voice was urgent in Arnett's earphones. "I just got a PU light on my board."

"Run a circuit test and stand by," Arnett ordered. He flipped switches, opening one restricted SAC frequency after another. He heard nothing but static as he cycled through them. It was the same on the NORAD Air Defense Emergency frequency. As he switched frequencies to contact Dyess, Halpern turned to him. "I've lost Dry Plains."

"This is fucking great," Arnett mumbled. Static hissed softly in his ears on the Dyess frequency.

"My board checks out, Cap'n," Pilton said. "Do we have orders?"

"We do not, repeat, do not have orders at this time, Jake. Stand by."

"Radar indicates normal commercial traffic," Halpern said.

"Gutierrez," Arnett said, "warm up your equipment. I think this is a malfunction, but I don't want to be caught off guard if it's not."

"Yes sir."

Arnett shut off the open radio circuit and tried the SAC and NORAD frequencies again. Nothing. He turned to Halpern. "What do you think?"

"If we were being jammed, the radar would be out." She shrugged. "I don't know what to think. Even if we got orders, how would we carry them out with a fuel leak? It'd be crazy."

"You got clearance from Dry Plains before we lost the radio, right?"

"Correct. No other traffic scheduled for that runway until after we're down." She glanced at the clock. "We're twelve minutes out."

"Then we're going in, and that's the end of it."

Gutierrez adjusted knobs and switches on his electronic countermeasures console. "You'd think we got a hot war on or something."

Pilton frowned at the glowing PU light. "Well, it sure ain't no fuckin' drill." He touched his chest, where the arming key hung on its chain. Then he shrugged. "It's got to be like the Cap'n says—a malfunction."

"I think you're going to want to hear the rest of my story," said Gutierrez slowly.

"Okay."

"I remember that it made me curious, seeing that stuff so far north from where the Aztecs were, so when I got home I did some reading at the library. I came across an anthropologist's account of this old legend. It says that a band of Aztec priests, led by one who named himself Xolotl after the evil twin of Quetzalcoatl, fled north from the Aztec empire. Xolotl had a vision of men with skulls of silver coming to destroy his people, so he and his followers fled, killing anyone who stood in their path: man, woman or child. According to the legend, Tezcatlipoca took fire from the sun god Toniuh, and cast it upon the desert, burning Xolotl and the other priests alive for their sacrilege."

Pilton frowned. "So you think those priests made it all the way to Dry Plains?"

Gutierrez nodded. "It makes sense, don't you think?"

"Man, I think you spend too much time reading," Pilton paused, then his shoulders rose and fell as he took a deep breath. "Goddamned fuckin' fuel leak, and then this shit with the PU signal. Just my luck." Turning to Gutierrez, he said, "You don't think the plane's going down, do you?"

Gutierrez's face twitched. "Like I said, I've just got this bad feeling."

"You're a real morale booster," Pilton said darkly.

They froze suddenly when they heard, filtering through their headphones from behind, a hissing, screeching, howling sound. For an instant, the cry sounded almost human.

They glanced back at the bulkhead which separated their compartment from the forward bomb bay.

"What the hell was that?" Pilton asked. He tugged one earphone off to listen to the cabin sounds. The bone-freezing cry came through again, and Pilton turned to Gutierrez.

"I've heard that sound before," Gutierrez said, his face ashen. "At the zoo. Central Americans call it *el tigre.*" He swallowed hard. "A jaguar. Tezcatlipoca can appear as a jaguar."

Pilton shook his head. "No fuckin' way, man. We were at altitude earlier. The bomb bay's not pressurized. No animal could survive back there."

"Not an animal," said Gutierrez. He took a deep breath and placed his trembling hands on the ECM console.

"It's wind through a rip in the hull or something!" said Pilton. "That's all."

Gutierrez's voice was barely audible. "They had another name for Tezcatlipoca. They called him End-of-the-World-Bringer. Every two thousand years he reached down to destroy the prideful world. He brought in the new sun."

The awful cry—a shriek followed by a low, reverberating growl—sounded again, and Pilton shivered. He saw Gutierrez go stiff against his harness, his eyes rolling, his lips drawn back across his clenched teeth. "Not me," Gutierrez murmured, then slumped in his chair, breathing heavily.

"What the fuck is going on, man?" Pilton said. "Are you okay?"

Gutierrez turned to him. He was pale, and a fine sheen of sweat covered his face. "I dunno—I think I may be sick."

"This is crazy," Pilton said. "When I get down, I'm applying for a goddamned transfer."

Gutierrez sluggishly reached into his pocket and pulled out the obsidian. He held it in his cupped hand, staring at it.

Pilton frowned. "What now?"

Gutierrez giggled and held out the stone. Pilton shrank back when he saw it. Tiny threads of pale, yellowish smoke issued from the glittering black glass, collecting in Gutierrez's palm. Tapping at it with his index finger, Gutierrez giggled again. "Not even hot," he said.

"This ain't happening," Pilton said. An alarm sounded on his board and he started. He turned to the board and saw a ring of lights indicating the rotary SRAM launcher in the forward bomb bay. The lights flashed red. A moment later the lights for the rear bomb bay lit up, one by one: first yellow, then red. They began to flash. Pilton shook his head. "That's fuckin' impossible!"

The captain's voice sounded in their earphones. "Pilton, I've got both bomb bays flashing armed here. Report."

"Same here," Pilton said, his voice wavering. "I—I didn't even use my key. There's something weird going on, Cap'n. We heard an animal in the bomb bay and—"

"What?"

Gutierrez laughed. His voice was slurred, drunken. "Not an animal. *El tigre. Tezcatlipoca.*"

"I don't know what it was," Pilton cut in. "But Gutierrez is freaking out back here."

"Now listen up," Arnett said sternly. "You *both* sound like you're losing it, and I won't stand for it. That's an order. Something's wrong with the plane and it's causing a shitload of malfunctions. Nothing more than that."

"All these systems are independent, Cap'n," Pilton said. "They can't all be affected, not because of one malfunction—"

"Jake! Listen to me. We'll figure it out after we touch down. We'll be landing in less than six minutes, and if you two don't get your shit straight, I'll do it for you on the ground. Got that?"

Pilton nodded weakly, staring at the two rings of lights on his board. "Yes sir."

"Gutierrez?"

"Gutierrez!"

"The sins of Xolotl and those who venerate him shall be cleansed again. The desert's black face shall mirror the sky." Gutierrez laughed and poked at the obsidian with his finger.

"Pilton," Arnett said quietly. "I want you to relieve him of his sidearm."

"But Cap'n—"

"Do it!"

Pilton reached up to hit the quick release on his seat harness just as Gutierrez—his face a wild, snarling thing—flipped the cover of the CABIN EJECT button open and pressed it.

"NO!"

Pilton's ears popped as the explosive bolts fired. He screamed as he accelerated up into the night, the bomber's engines a bellowing roar—receding to a whine as the wind slammed at his face and clothing. Dizzy, tumbling end over end now, Pilton clumsily got free of the seat and got his chute open. He pulled off his earphones and tossed them away. A sound reached his ears—high-pitched, tittering laughter.

"You spic sonofabitch!" he shouted out into the dark. "You just bought yourself a court martial!"

The laughing continued. Pilton worked the control lines of his chute, steering in circles, trying to find Gutierrez. There was only the drunken laughter in the dark. For a moment, he glimpsed the lights of the airport in the distance. "If I catch your ass—"

The ground came up suddenly, unexpectedly. Pilton hit hard, his left foot at the wrong angle. His ankle popped as he tumbled to the ground. He lay there, wheezing at the pain.

Suddenly the desert around him grew as bright as midday. Time seemed to telescope as he saw the shadow of his prone body in sharp focus before him; he saw the desert scrub and small boulders around him, colors lost in the harsh glare; he felt the heat against his back, his legs: it stung his exposed neck and ears.

The rumbling, thundering sound of the detonation washed over him as he rolled over, gasping in pain and fear, to see the twisting, roiling, glowing specter of the cloud rising over Dry Plains. At its feet, a curtain of dust rolled outwards, propelled along by the shock front.

As the rumbling died away, Pilton heard Gutierrez's footsteps behind him; he was still giggling uncontrollably. Pilton reached for his holster, but it was empty—his .45 had jolted loose somehow. The sound of laughter transformed as it grew closer, falling into a low, rasping, growling, rhythmic sound. Pilton froze, holding his breath and closing his eyes as it padded closer—on four legs now. Its breath grated in and out, the sharp smell of it flooding Pilton's nostrils. *El tigre,* he thought wildly, and then there was nothing but the sound of his screaming and the bright red pain.

SACRED WHEEL

Patricia Ross

We were lawless people, but we were on pretty good terms with the Great Spirit, creator and ruler of all. You whites assumed we were savages. . . . When we sang our praises to the sun or moon or wind, you said we were worshipping idols. . . . We saw the Great Spirit's work in almost everything: sun, moon, trees, wind and mountains. Sometimes we approached him through these things. I think we have a true belief in the supreme being, a stronger faith than that of most whites who have called us pagans. . . . Indians living close to nature and nature's ruler are not living in darkness. . . . Trouble is, white people don't listen. They never learned to listen to the Indians so I don't suppose they'll listen to the other voices in nature.

— *Walking Buffalo, 1871*

IT IS A GOOD DAY TO TELL YOU THIS STORY. THE WAYS OF OUR people are now being considered here. It was not always so.

You have asked me for the story of Stands A Lot and Wind In Hair. What you are really asking for is the story of how our people have learned, at least in spirit, to demand respect. That is the story I will tell you. It is the same as you have asked.

This was a sacred spot. The living and the dead were

uneasy in the years after the white man's airport was built here. Delegations came forward to try to prevent construction. But no regard was paid to the laments and protests of those in the tribes headed by Hunting Man and Walks Away. Shrill headlines describing treaty violations were splashed across the pages of neighboring communities' newspapers, side by side with bold stories of astronomical economic growth for both Mexican nationals and U.S. citizens.

Second page columns were given to tales of an old massacre perpetrated by the Comanche on this ground. Other fables of an even older battle, fought by the Aztecs, were still more vague. Both were true, but only in the sense that blood had been spilled there. Rivers of it had mingled and been absorbed by the thirsty earth. The true reasons for the battles had been long lost, like some secret treasure of yore.

Using their by-now infamous "weight of history" argument, the courts decided that since the Indians had historically lost their bids for retention or reclamation of treatied lands, that provided a precedent for ruling against them. They dismissed case after case with alarming rapidity. Protest was attributed to residual religious superstition or worse, to primitive nonsense.

Soon the issue was forgotten, fading to obscurity among the voluminous annals of voided treaties. Only within the circuit of those who waited did the airport incident remain in the fore. The shamans, the medicine men and women, they waited for the time to come.

Meanwhile, immigration laws changed. Tribal elders on both sides of the border predicted dire consequences. They sent their emissaries.

The time was now.

Stands A Lot arrived at the Dry Plains International Airport to travel on the great birds. While waiting to board their flight, Stands A Lot and Wind In Hair worked their way around the terminal, purifying it.

Both of them were familiar with the sudden incidence of white men being murdered, apparitional appearances in the air and on the ground, and of ghosts of the dead coming to reclaim blood debts from the white man.

Stands A Lot was a brave man. He was also a peaceful man. He did not believe all white men should die, as the slogans written in blood on the walls proclaimed. He knew these were the works of mischievous human hands, not necessarily all red hands, and not the troubled spirit hands of wronged Indians who occupied the territory.

As Stands A Lot continued purifying the terminal with smoke and whispered song, Wind In Hair guarded his steps by listening and watching for interference. The burning sweet grass excited speculations and aggravation among those waiting to fly.

An airport policeman, itching to exercise his authority, however small, sauntered up to Stands A Lot. Stands A Lot looked up at the large torso and waited expectantly for him to speak. He was not disappointed. "Chief, you can't be burnin' no incense in here. There's no smokin' and no open fires. C'mon now, you been out on the reservation too long. Put it out."

The policeman looked thoughtfully at Stands A Lot. He had discarded his first impulse to be brusque and rude. The old fellah looked kinda like his Uncle Buddy, God bless him, who now had to be cared for in a nursing home in Santa Fe. He patted the old man's shoulder and continued with genuine regret. "You gotta listen to me, now. There're a lot of people who don't like Injuns around here, and I ain't 'specially fond of 'em myself, ya know. You just remind me of somebody I know."

Stands A Lot looked at the high cheekbones, discounted the Texas drawl, and looked deep into the Texan's eyes, then at his name tag. "Handley, you are one of The People. Your uncle should have told you that. Do not hinder me now. This is for the lives of our people and your father's people. It is for the Great Spirit that I begin to call back these grounds."

Handley drew back from the old man's unflinching stare, and spoke a little more urgently, looking over his shoulder at the cyclops eye of the wall mounted video camera. His face paled. "Pops, ya gotta git outta here. My parents are both as white and Texan as they come. You're mistaken. I'm gonna lose my patience if you don't give it up, *now*."

He held out his hand for the offending partially burned

rope of sweet grass in the old man's hand. Stands A Lot shook his head and looked up at Handley sadly. "Grandson, ask your uncle what his real name is. Ask your mother what her parents names' were. Tell her it is all right now; your father is at rest."

Handley backed off, confused. With no further admonitions to the old man, he walked abruptly away.

Stands A Lot continued the purification ceremony and Wind In Hair completed her offerings of tobacco and joined him to wait for their plane to the Yucatan. She was elated. They were going to visit cousins who she'd heard about since she was a small child, but who she had never seen. They'd been studying the medicine way in the south. Stands A Lot had made it clear that more preparation was needed before the blood sacrifices could be stopped.

Wind In Hair recalled her excitement as Walking Bear had made his pronouncement last week. He had made many decisions in his one hundred eleven years, but this one had been different. The Lakota medicine man had received a twin vision, along with Stands A Lot. Stands A Lot, also a respected medicine man among his people, was to go to negotiate with the spirits at Dry Plains International Airport, for a peaceful settlement to the ever bloodier tribulations that had become their horrific routine. Wind In Hair was to accompany him. Wind In Hair was the granddaughter of Reindeer Eyes, the last great medicine woman of the tribe. As a small child, Wind In Hair had learned the medicine way at her grandmother's gnarled hands. This open joint venture was almost unprecedented in tribal history since before the destruction of the Sacred Hoop.

This day, Dry Plains International was busy. There were police everywhere, security everywhere. There had been too many killings with no explanation.

The situation had grown to such a pitch that the President had called in National Guard troops to patrol the corridors of the airport. There were many who hated the Guardsmen, many who showed their disdain for federal interference in what was clearly to them, a local matter. The Guardsmen were called bulldogs because they didn't let go of something once they sunk their teeth into it.

Other, more preternatural government agencies maintained a low-profile presence, protected by the umbrella of "national security." They had discovered a curious phenomenon among those people who were slaughtered at the airport: they were not Native Americans, not Indians, not redmen. It seemed all it took was a small quantity of bloodshed for the supernatural murderers to come forth. The Guard Battalion leader, who allowed the information on a need-to-know basis, said it was more than strange, it was conspiratorial. He said it gave new meaning to the term "bloodthirsty savages" and was heard to mutter old saws about who the only good Indians were.

All the Indian employees of the airport were under suspicion and surveillance. New video cameras were installed. No Indians were seen perpetrating any important crimes, but the suspicion persisted.

The Indian elders knew this was typical of the previous century's white soldiers, who did not know or recognize when they were wrong. Some things didn't change. Too far removed from their own spirits to acknowledge anything not felt or smelt or tasted, the airport phenomena only existed to the new soldiers and police when it took on the form of the physical.

Blood, torn flesh and horribly mutilated corpses turned up from time to time in the most unlikely places. There had been the headless body in the men's room toilet. Lab analysis of the toilet seat showed that he had been vomiting blood. Sanitation never recovered the head.

Then there was the lady in pink, on her period, in the midst of changing her tampon. The tampon was still in her fingers when they found her—that is, most of her. Other deaths had been less dramatic, but the victims were no less dead.

The Guard had papered the security office's blank walls with maps. Maps of all the Dry Plains facilities, even the parking decks, maps of the rat warren of service tunnels contained underneath the airport proper, maps of the new Tex-Mex Airlines terminal previously under construction.

National Guard personnel sat around smoking cigarettes, trying to look busy. Five and six grouped around video monitors, flipping the view from corridor to corridor, looking for trouble.

Airport security police glowered at the National Guard usurpers. This was their turf, and they were not happy with being driven off of it. They were the best of the rent-a-cops. The airport had only hired those with real honest-to-god experience. Eschewing the typical security services who contracted with many airport facilities, they had formed their own corps. They wooed numerous professional cops from their jobs and brought in a respectable percentage of Hispanic employees. They had spent a lot of money, too, and been ridiculed for it in the beginning. The laughter had stopped when Dry Plains International had been cited the safest major airport in the world. What came at them after the killings began had not been laughter. Morale was at an all-time low. They were pros, goddamn it. Now the Guard had taken over their territory for an "indeterminate length of time." To make matters worse, since the Guard had been deployed, there'd been no more killings. Guardsmen were heard singing the theme song from *Ghostbusters*. It was sung hopefully, without rancor. Like most armies of occupation, the majority just wanted to go home.

There were jealously hidden bits of information garnered by both sides, shared with none outside their own. Each side was determined to net the perpetrators first.

Handley went to the airport police office, now relocated into what used to be its storage closet. He was too upset to report his encounter. Something about the old guy ... almost movie cliché material. Seemed like he ought to hear bells tinkling when the old guy walked and talked. Something special. *Naaa*, he thought. *Don't be stupid. That damned old man's got you spooked. He's probably been doing that mindbending shit for years in his old tribe. How's an old man with probably no teeth and no job gonna eat these days? Forget it.*

"Hey, *Hoss!*" The jowly sergeant slapped his hand down on the table and elbowed three or four of his Guardsmen pals. "We saw you talking to that ol' redskin. Saw yer balls shrivel right up inside, too, when he stood up to ya. Whad he *say,* Tex? What was that shit he was burnin', anyway? Did he put an ancient Indian curse on ya? Haw, haw! You Texans are all alike. All talk, no fight."

Their laughter continued to echo in Handley's ears until he drank himself to sleep later that night.

As Stands A Lot walked through the terminal with Wind In Hair, he smelled blood and death. He was not alone in this. The ventilation system spewed a putrefying odor throughout the terminal. Wind In Hair grabbed Stands A Lot's arm. "Grandfather, it's like ice in here," she said. "The stench of decay is warm and moist, but it is riding on a cold venomous wind."

Stands A Lot looked at her fondly, abashed. "My daughter, you have the spirit of a great tribal storyteller. When this is finished, as it will be, *you* must be the one to tell it to the others. It will be good for all of us to hear your words and your vision."

Stands A Lot knew that Wind In Hair was afraid. But he did not want to dishonor her by encouraging her to dwell on that fear. It was not fitting that he should acknowledge it here, in front of strangers. *White* strangers. To do so would cause great embarrassment. He patted her hand secretly, and continued his slow stroll through the terminal's waiting area.

"I don't give a good goddamn where you *think* it's coming from. Uncle Sam doesn't pay you to think, shithead! Find it!"

Handley didn't feel any smugness watching one of airport security's primary tormentors getting his comeuppance from the sergeant. He felt only nauseated relief that he didn't have to go look for what surely must be a corpse in an advanced state of decomposition, judging by the stench that had passengers nearly in tears.

"Grandson, do you remember me?"

Handley spun around in his swivel chair and banged his knees into the side of the closet-cum-office. He could only nod at the old man and file away for future reference the young woman with the ancient eyes who was with him. "I need you," the old man said simply.

"Go away, Gramps," Handley croaked. "I ain't a social worker. And I don't think you want me to vomit on your shoes." Stands A Lot held out a bandanna to Handley. "Put this on your face, like a bandit. It will help you." Handley reached out and took the proffered bandanna, noting as he tied it the strong smell of sage. He immediately felt revived, and only smelled the decay as if from a distance. "Thank you, Gramps. But this don't mean I'm gonna help you."

Stands A Lot said nothing, but Handley thought he saw tears in the old man's eyes. Those eyes, their expression so much like Uncle Buddy's, made his stomach knot, and his throat tighten in response. "Aw now, shit, Gramps," he sputtered to cover his own emotion. "Don't cry on me. What is it you need?"

Stands A Lot looked at him curiously. Wind In Hair was smiling at him. He noticed that she had a pretty smile. Her eyes dropped when they met his. Handley blinked. The old man had the same maddeningly serene and kindly expression on his face that he'd had last time.

"Oh Jesus. *Great.* Now *I'm* seeing things. Are you here to kill *me*, Gramps? Am *I* next?"

"Grandson, you do not listen to the voices of the spirits," Stands A Lot sighed. "They are not going to kill one of the blood. They are not going to kill anyone who has not committed sacrilege on those places holy to us. I will wait while you check the records of the dead. That man over there in the black suit. He is with your FBI."

Stands A Lot had spoken softly. But the figure standing across the room turned to look at him. "He listens to his inner voice, Grandson," said the old man. "But he uses that voice to cause mischief and misfortune to others. Wakan Tanka will not be pleased with him. The Earth, our mother, may take his corrupt energy and resend it through a more positive being."

"What information do you want checked, Gramps? And whadya mean, he's FBI? He's just airport brass. The only thing good about him and his is that they hate the Guard's interference as much as we do."

The nattily dressed agent in question approached them warily, chewing vigorously on a toothpick. "Holdin' up a bank, Handley? The color is definitely you. What's Tonto doin' here?" He turned his back to Stands A Lot and Wind In Hair, speaking directly to Handley.

"Gramps here is a friend of my Uncle Buddy's," Handley lied glibly. "He passes through from time to time to talk about the good old days. He's harmless. This is his, uh, granddaughter. And you are . . ."

"Wagner." The man's expression hardened as he spat out the name, ignoring Handley's proffered hand. "See they don't cause any mischief then, Handley, or it's your ass." The dark man turned to leave.

Handley spoke quickly. "So, you with the FBI, huh?"

Wagner spun on his heel and pointed one long, bony finger at Handley. "What the hell are you talkin' about? Gettin' nosey all of a sudden. What do *you* care who I am?"

Handley chose to stand at that moment, his larger, more muscular frame looming over Wagner's slimness. "It's okay, Wagner. Nobody'll hear it outta me. I *don't* give a shit. Just hopin' to retire and move to Florida in a few years on a fat pension and sit on my future fat ass." Handley smiled as he spoke and Wagner's wary expression changed to one of contempt.

Wagner flicked the chewed toothpick at Handley's face and spat on the floor by his feet. Walking away, he taunted Handley. "Pussy rent-a-cop. Indians are all alike, if ya ask me. They're just tall gooks. Speakin' of which, Handley, lose your nerve after Special Forces in 'Nam? Smoke too much dope? POW camp take your balls? What a *joke*. Shit." Wagner exited through the doors of the private VIP elevator.

Stands A Lot waited in silence until Handley sat down again. "Grandson, I did not lie. That man is with your FBI."

Handley looked up at the grave old man, then grinned and shrugged. "Shit, Gramps, I know that *now*. How else would he know I was a POW? I never talk about it. *Never.* And it's *not* on my personnel record, either. And I'm not exactly high-security clearance, here. *Damn,* old man. Now I guess I'm gonna have to go and visit Uncle Buddy, too. But don't get any ideas. I'm not the Lone Ranger. I can't help you much."

Stands A Lot pointed to the desk next to where Wagner had been standing. "Grandson, the FBI has left the information you need *there.*" Handley walked over to the scarred metal desk and casually picked up the file. National Guardsmen were scarce in the wake of the latest incident. The video scanner was manned by one lone, bleary eyed operator, too nauseated to pay attention to Handley, who was more or less a fixture anyway.

Handley's breath came in short gasps as he jogged to keep up with Stands A Lot and Wind In Hair. Once outside the main terminal, the elderly man seemed to drop years from his age. Handley could swear he stood taller and straighter. He damn sure could walk fast. He and Wind In Hair seemed to walk as one person.

After looking at the file Wagner'd left behind, he'd decided to help Gramps. After all, this mess was weird, so why not let somebody who was weird and reminded you of old movies with tinkling bells and wise Indian types work on it? Who was he to say no? Just a shit-kicker with nothin' better to do. Some guys put big bumpers on their trucks to play chicken on the highways. Some loaded up their rifle racks and went hunting for freeway game. Some drank themselves into oblivion under the crotches of exotic dancers, like back home on the East Lancaster strip in Ft. Worth. What the hell.

"Gramps, do we hafta walk so damn fast?"

Stands A Lot grinned at Handley and kept striding silently down the tunnel.

Wind In Hair said, "His name is Stands A Lot," then ignored him, leaving him to his own thoughts.

"Shoulda been Walks Too Fast," grumbled Handley out loud.

The file had been gruesome in its detail and scary in its lack of concrete information. Depositions on ghostly Indian apparitions appearing just before each death occurred came from rich and poor alike: janitors, preachers, lawyers, doctors. The only thing missing had been an Indian Chief. Till now.

And all the old man had wanted was for him to use his security pass to get them through the catacomb of tunnels to the new construction site without hindrance. Once done, the old man had said Handley could go where he pleased. Handley wasn't sure he liked the idea of returning alone.

But he damn sure wasn't gonna stay for whatever ritual the girl and the old man were primed for with the blankets and bundles they carried. It was weird enough that all the victims had been anti-Indian on some count or other. From the Tampon Lady to the Headless Heaver, and more than a dozen less-publicized victims, they had either worked for a government agency screwing with Indians, or gone out of their way to make modern Indian life more miserable than it already was. Even weirder was the fact that all this started when construction began on the new Tex-Mex Airlines terminal.

They emerged from the tunnel, and into the night.

"Well, this is the proposed airfield. This musta been what it was like when they started screwin' with Egyptian tombs and curses, huh, Gramps . . . Um, I mean, Stands A Lot." Handley followed the elder's gaze to the murky green light on their left. Blue sparks danced on the edges of the haze.

"There," said Stands A Lot, "is what we are here for. It is a Sacred Medicine Wheel." Handley felt his heart speed up until he thought his chest would burst—there was a congregation of Indians in full regalia waiting for his companions in the center of a giant circle marked with stones. Even Handley could tell that many tribes and many times were represented in that intimidating gathering. Dog soldiers, medicine women and men, plains dwellers, desert dwellers, northern tribes, Aztecs. Just short of the circle was a backhoe, its bucket still poised in the air. Handley remembered that the first victim had been its driver.

As if that thought triggered a self-destruct mechanism in him, something snapped in the back of Handley's skull. It sounded like a walnut cracking open. He fell to the ground next to the backhoe's oversized tires.

He tried to sit up. His head felt like it was full of broken glass. *I musta had too much last night,* he thought. *Whata weird dream.*

Wind In Hair pushed his chest down and sat on him. "I will slit your throat myself, Handley, if you do not keep still," she hissed. Handley turned his aching head sideways. Stands A Lot made his way around the circle of multicolored lights. It appeared to Handley that as the old man approached each stone, he changed form, and changed again as he returned to the center of the circle.

The gathering of Indians inside the circle watched him, ululating cries going up and down in a rhythmic cadence Handley could feel in his bones, but could not understand. They looked as solid as himself now. Stands A Lot was changing into a bear. The bear looked out for a moment at Wind In Hair, in her position holding Handley down, and waved its paws in the air. Wind In Hair responded, making a series of animal grunts. Handley closed his eyes, afraid to look at Wind In Hair, afraid that she too might be a bear.

Eventually he could stand it no longer and opened his eyes. She was the same, only her eyes were shining in the turbid night, and Handley could see she was aware of him solely as a burden to hold down. She looked impersonal, he thought. No, *inhuman* was better.

Turning his head once again, Handley saw that Stands A Lot now resembled a buffalo. It snorted and pawed. Wind In Hair took a buffalo robe from the ground next to Handley and laid it over him. She blew her breath in his face. Her face, just above his, began to change. Her breath snorted out of both nostrils and her mouth in wide white tendrils, spiraling upward, dissolving in the chilly night air. Handley stared, opened his mouth to scream, and passed out again.

On and on into the night, Stands A Lot and Wind In Hair danced and sang and spoke with the Spirits. They were pleading for the white men and the men of all colors. They explained that the Wasichu, the white men, had blundered in their ignorance onto the ground of this Sacred Medicine Wheel. The White Men, the Spirits retorted, had been ruining things for far too long out of destructive ignorance. They are like children, Wind In Hair explained. She pointed to Handley and spoke. *"They are big and blundering. It is the white man's way, not their blood, that is bad. We have to show them a different way."*

The congregation spoke as one voice. "Too much has passed for us to allow the desecration of yet another power spot for our people. The white man's way corrupts even our own. Witness the one on the ground. Too much white man's blood runs in his veins. He is like something nature has rejected. He is neither one thing nor the other."

Stands A Lot smoked his pipe. He watched the smoke waft among the figures in the center of the wheel, some legendary, some young and hotheaded even in spirit. The elders nodded their wizened heads as strong words flew among them. Stands A Lot listened throughout the night. He, too, nodded his head with the others. The time had surely come to do something decisive. The Great Spirit knew that mankind was out of control. Mother Earth, Grandfather Sky . . . surely they had sent him because the time was right for all men to change. But blood could not be the answer. There was precious little Indian blood left to spill on the great Earth Mother's bosom.

"We have always had the power of destruction," said Stands A Lot. "But we have not always had the power to change things in a way to show our good hearts, while at the same time teaching the white man a lesson." The others in the circle nodded.

Wind In Hair kept her vigil outside the circle, tending Handley. She was a little resentful at not being allowed to attend Stands A Lot in the center, on the turtle's great back. She was able to hear all that was said, though. And occasionally she was asked her thoughts, which were considered with as much gravity and weight as the others. She saw her grandmother, Reindeer Eyes, looking at her from time to time, and her eyes misted over as she remembered the wonderful time of learning that had led her here. Finally she fell asleep, slumped over Handley's chest.

"Come, Wind In Hair. It is time to go. Come, Handley. Wake up. We have much to do." Wind In Hair jumped up with alacrity, pink cheeks revealing her embarrassment. Handley got up more slowly, holding his still-groggy head with both hands as if afraid to let go. They walked back to the main terminal together.

The end of the story is plain to you, Wasichu.

You are here as a visitor. Do you see any white employees? This airport is owned and operated by the United Indian

Nations. Stands A Lot showed the white men that the only way this airport could survive was to be given back to the Indians. Of course, they never would have agreed to that if Stands A Lot had not brought the airport fathers out here to the sacred circle and they realized then the error of their ways. Those white men did not want to lose all that money. And our people did not want to lose the chance to reclaim a piece of our heritage. The buffalo are gone. But the silver birds are now ours, and we have paid for them with your people's symbol, the eagle.

We have always had an affinity for birds.

BUZZKILLER

Clark Perry

JIMMY LEE KEMP TASTED BLOOD AS HE ENTERED THE AIRPORT. Sharp and sour, like an old coin in his mouth. He'd been chewing the inside of his cheek since stepping into the cab back at the hotel, and he felt foolish and bitter as he walked through the sliding glass doors. Sweating profusely, he made for the nearest men's room to rinse his face.

In the mirror, Jimmy Lee saw his own ghost, pale, gaunt, flickering like an x-ray in the harsh fluorescent light. Eyes hollow and wired, his mouth a severe line. A week with Valsen could do that to you. He shuddered and promised to get some sun when he hit Tampa, burn some color into his flesh.

Four sinks down, a businessman at a mirror—spiffy blue suit, brown hair—was brushing his teeth, executive travel kit propped smartly on the mirror's narrow shelf. A scene from an ad, Jimmy Lee thought. Two other men stood patiently at the line of urinals opposite the sinks and pretended to read the sports pages tacked to the walls before them.

Jimmy Lee disappeared into a far corner stall. He latched the door, hung his bag on a chrome hook and smelled it: prison. He was back there just like that. He looked down and saw that someone had left him a present in the toilet. He pressed the handle with his foot and watched it swirl away.

Trying to get a grip on himself, he reflected for a moment on how clean everything was. Even this black plastic toilet

224

seat, spattered with urine, seemed clean to him because he knew that someone would eventually come in and wipe it off.

In prison, the toilets would flood and overflow and you'd have to shower with your sneakers on, then rinse those off in the sink and leave them out in the yard to dry, hoping all the while that no one would come while you weren't looking and steal them.

Horrible things happened in prison bathrooms. The cold tile floor had been freshly mopped when they caught Jimmy Lee in there and held him, yanked down his pants and spread him wide. Three of them, but only one had his way with Jimmy, sliding in and out, in and out. And finally out.

They held a sharpened spoon to his throat and told him not to talk about it. Jimmy Lee had no problem; he was always talking to himself, but he'd long ago learned to keep his mouth shut while doing it.

He unzipped his fly and realized he didn't have to piss. What was he doing here? Chilling out. Okay. Fine. Plenty of time to catch that bird to Tampa. If he needed to hang here between the partitions and savor the isolation, he could do it.

He wiped the seat clean and sat, cupping his face in his hands. He and Valsen had been doing too many drugs the last few days. Booze, coke, the standard four joints for breakfast. Valsen had pills that would let him beat any urine test the probation officer might spring on him.

And then there was that new stuff, the stuff that had gotten its hooks into Valsen something fierce. As soon as Jimmy Lee thought about it, glittering little white spots flecked his vision. They burned, dazzled, and faded. Over and over, just around the edges of his eyes. *Blowback*. He had never experienced blowback before. He was amazed.

He stood and the white flecks increased in number and intensity. His ears popped and the sounds of the bathroom —running water, shoes on tile, the song hummed by the businessman—drifted away from his dimension, as if he'd been encased in a glass bubble.

The spots went off like fireworks. He leaned against the door and held both hands over his eyes to keep them out.

Jimmy Lee belched and bile rose up his throat. He turned, opened one eye, and spit into the toilet.

The water went dark pink from the blood.

He bent to his knees and looked at it, just to make sure. The flickering spots, as if sensing his distress, subsided for a moment, pulled back to allow him full view of a sight that filled him with dread.

His heartbeat hammered quick and loud in his skull, and the three million dollars riding stowaway in his stomach suddenly went cold, like a flash-frozen lump of ice.

"Condoms," Valsen told him. "Used ones work best."

"You gotta be kidding."

"I'm kidding."

The night before was a painful, beautiful memory of booze and sweat, the round curves of willing, well-paid women beside and beneath them. Now they were alone in the hotel room, because although Valsen made a lot of money he lived in a dump and didn't like to stay there on weekends. The orange curtains were parted to let in a little sun so Valsen could see what he was doing. In the middle of it all, a maid tried to come in and make the bed. Jimmy Lee hurriedly shoved bags and bottles of contraband into his travel bag as the door opened. His heart thundered with the fear of being caught. Valsen spoke calm Spanish to the pretty young lady, asking her to come back later. He kept laughing at how Jimmy Lee had panicked: "Man, was that a buzzkiller for you or what?"

They filled the rubbers using room service spoons from a discarded tray across the hall. The blue, sooty powder was so fine that they dared not breathe as they lifted each spoonful. They tied them off like balloons and stacked them like little cords of wood in the center of the table.

"So," Jimmy Lee said to break the ringing silence, "this stuff comes up south of the border?"

Valsen grinned. The morning light across his face revealed deep acne scars, the skin on his cheeks pitted like the surface of some small moon. In high school they'd called him Pizza. Now that he was one of the biggest dealers in the area, people called him by his name.

"Well, that's what I told you last night," Valsen nodded. "But there's more to it than that. I know people down there who are always looking for new drugs, the synthetic kind. Most of what they find is pure crap, but every so often they'll come across something really, really wicked."

Jimmy Lee tied off another condom and watched Valsen lean his big hangdog face in to sniff another line he'd cut for himself. One deep snort, a few seconds of silence as Valsen's face went slack and colorless. Then he was back, blinking and grinning at him.

"It's great stuff," Valsen said. "I've never seen anything like it. You can snort it, smoke it, shoot it, eat it. Different buzz, every time. Everything else pales beside it."

"So who cooked it up?"

"This batch was done by my lab boys, my own private chefs. But the recipe comes outta—hell, what's it called? Quintana Roo."

"Mexico?"

"Yeah, the Yucatan. Friend of mine, hacker chemist, gets wind of a scientific article that shows up in some magazine, all about how they deciphered some of that Aztec writing on some ruins down there and found out how to make this drug used in their ceremonies."

"What ceremonies?"

"Dunno. They were heavily into sacrifices, though. And this stuff is so potent I'd be surprised if they didn't worship it, y'know?"

Jimmy Lee tore open another foil packet and unrolled the condom. "Drugs aren't what they used to be, I guess."

"What do you mean?"

"Well, ceremonies. Drugs were like holy and all way back then, weren't they? You didn't get messed up just for the hell of it. You got messed up to talk with the gods."

Valsen stared at him. "Guess I never thought of that before."

"Who decided to call it Disney?"

"Oh, I doubt they called it that," he replied sourly. "But you gotta think in terms of marketing. 'Disney' makes you feel like a little child again, right?"

"How close is this to the original stuff, do you think?"

Valsen frowned and looked out the window at the sun-blasted city. "Hell, I dunno. This is pretty much it, more or less. I mean, there's some stuff we changed out of necessity, y'know? We couldn't get the blood of virgins for every batch, right?"

Jimmy Lee was about to scoop up more of the powder, but he stopped and said, "What about this batch?"

Valsen grinned again. "Oh, this is the *good* stuff."

Jimmy Lee believed in paying his dues.

Three years out of high school he got nabbed taking a trunk full of high-grade smoke from Arizona to Texas, a little weekend run for another dealer. Jimmy Lee was going to use the driver's fee to finance a run of his own and set himself up nice. He'd seen others—like Valsen—do it. Looked easy enough.

Someone had tipped off the cops, however. They waited until he crossed the state line so they could nab him for interstate trafficking.

He served his time, paid his debt, didn't even raise hell when they took him in that prison bathroom—he would've fought if one of them had wanted Jimmy Lee to be a punk, but nobody was interested in him after that. They'd broken him in, plain and simple; they hadn't even looked particularly excited when they'd done it. Just showing him the ropes. Clock in, clock out.

Once outside, Jimmy Lee stayed clean and low for almost three months. That was when old high-school buddy Bobby Valsen brought his Cadillac into the carwash where Jimmy Lee and two black kids wiped down windows and dashboards in sixty seconds or less.

Jimmy Lee almost walked off the job right then and there because he didn't want Valsen to recognize him. He didn't want to see Valsen shy away. That's what most of his old friends did when they saw him: smiled at first recognition, maybe even took a step or two forward. Then they remembered. He could see that very instant pass in their faces, the smile going slack with realization, the forced pleasantries and quick retreat.

Jimmy Lee didn't want to see Valsen's smile disappear.

But Valsen stunned him by offering him a job on the spot.

That day he picked him up after work, took him out for a few beers.

"You got hit hard," Valsen told him, his face a stroboscopic flutter in the lights of a downtown disco. "It's the fucking right-wing Jesus-sucking wackos out there calling the shots. The judge that sent you down the hole has let *child molesters* walk free." He shook his head and ordered more drinks. "Can't stand the thought of anyone having a good time. And they'll turn this country into a police state to prove the point.

"Fact is," he said, louder now, angry red lights spinning behind him, "in a police state you're either a cop or a criminal. No in-between, friend. No middle class. Things happen. You watch. Things happen."

This increasingly incoherent rant surfaced frequently, often fueled by the very drugs Valsen defended. Jimmy Lee wasn't sure about the politics, he'd never had a mind for subjects like that. But he picked up on the stuff that applied to him.

Yes, his sentence had been much too stiff. Even his probation officer had registered surprise when going over his file. You'd think Jimmy Lee had halved and quartered the Pope or something.

"I know a lot of people been in that big house," Valsen said once, carefully. "I know, man. I know. But it's okay. You're out here and you ain't never going back there again.

"If you want, I can put you to work making some big money. Your safety is guaranteed."

The plan: move the Disney fast before the feds had a chance to discover it, break down the chemical composition and post it on their schedule of illegal substances. Working in the shadows, Valsen could expect about a year of uninterrupted and mostly legal profits.

Stage one: float the word to the regional buyers, but not all at once. Build the base slowly, let the word spread, get people anxious about this season's big hit.

Valsen wanted Jimmy Lee to carry samples to his man in Tampa, who handled the Southeast. He had a whole network of people who worked for him——good, reliable people ——but he also had fond memories of Jimmy Lee buying nickelbags off him in the high school parking lot. He felt sorry for him. Jimmy Lee accepted this pity with an awkward grace.

"Salvador Dali Museum is about a half hour from the airport by cab. You'll meet someone inside the museum who will comment on purchasing the painting in front of you, whatever it is. Tell him you saw one just like it at Disney World. You both leave, go to a hotel and you feast on an Ex-Lax dinner.

"Now," Valsen said with a grin, wagging a finger, "it'll feel weird coming out. But it's not unlike what the Orientals like to do during sex."

"What? Take a shit?"

"They have these little steel balls tied on a string. Shove 'em up their butt and as they come, they start pulling them out really slow. They say it enhances the effect, prolongs the orgasm. Brings them closer to godhood."

Jimmy Lee wasn't looking forward to it. "Sure is a lot of stuff to go through, man. I mean, the museum and all. Why don't you just have somebody drive the shit down?"

"This is due in Tampa yesterday. Look, I know the feds are eventually gonna catch up with me here, but by then I'll have made my money and will be moving on to other things. I don't need them stumbling over this stuff before it's even sold."

Valsen was staring at him warily. Jimmy Lee offered a half-shrug. "Oh, I get all that. Just sounds more elaborate than what I'm used to. You know, secret code words . . ."

"These people have class, is all. Look, you want, I'll have them handcuff you to a shower stall and chainsaw your arm off."

Jimmy Lee grew more nervous the morning of the flight. He choked down the filled condoms, which wasn't as unpleasant as he'd been expecting. Valsen suggested they smoke a couple of joints and watch some TV, only they'd gone through the pack of rolling papers. "Can't believe this," Valsen said, jangling coins in his pocket as he headed for the soft drink machine down the hall. When he returned he emptied the can into the sink, flattened one side of it and, using the ballpoint pen from the nightstand, poked a small circle of holes into the flat side. "Haven't done this since high school," he chuckled. "Now where'd that bag go?"

Jimmy Lee found the loose baggie in his suitcase, where he'd hidden it from the intrusive maid. The bag, sealed with a lick of Valsen's gray tongue, was loose and some pot had spilled over Jimmy Lee's change of clothes. He shook them out and Valsen handed him the can with a little pile of pot covering the holes. Jimmy Lee took the makeshift pipe and sucked in through the can's popped top.

Valsen tried to hide it, but Jimmy Lee noticed his friend filling his long black pinky nail with Disney and sprinkling it on the pot before he smoked. Jesus, he thought, he's really hooked on this stuff.

Okay, he said to himself in the bathroom stall, white spots swarming around his head again, *gotta figure out what's happening. . . .*

He boldly considered the worst: The condoms in his belly had ruptured, maybe the Disney had eaten right through them. He pictured the blue dust coating the inside of his stomach, dissolving it. . . .

No, he told himself. No, there's not enough pain for that. That would really hurt, wouldn't it?

Okay. Then there had been some Disney dust on the outside of the condoms. It rubbed off on his stomach, some minor bleeding, no big deal. This also explained the huge rush he was getting.

But he'd swallowed the condoms over two hours ago. Valsen had wanted to make sure he wasn't going to throw them back up or anything. Why had it taken this long to affect him?

He spit again. More blood. Not much, just a red thread in his saliva.

He shouldered the bag and left the stall. The businessman was slapping on aftershave with precise, brisk pats and the alcohol aroma cut through the curtain of haze and fear that surrounded Jimmy Lee. He wanted a drink but knew the alcohol would probably eat through the condoms. But there was really nothing preventing him from having bread or crackers to help soak up the Disney dust in his belly, keep him from freaking out.

He wandered the vast carpeted corridors but could only find stand-up coffee bars and hot dog stands. He wanted to sit down and rest and calm himself, and more than anything he wanted to get a grip on his senses. Things were fuzzy in his periphery, but the center of his vision provided a narrow tunnel through which he could navigate his way. He realized he would have to proceed further into the busy airport to find what he wanted, so he found his ticket, walked toward the nearest gate, and stood in the line there.

The line was slow enough for him to fix on the hectic moods of those around him: harried travellers, people looking haunted by things inside their heads. As he edged closer he also noticed the high security that had been placed on this gate. Two armed customs agents were searching carry-on luggage with a black toothy canine that drooled.

Jimmy Lee just wanted to get past them all. He stepped forward and dropped his shoulder bag on the x-ray conveyor belt, then walked through the metal detector and paused just beyond to wait for the bag.

The dog snarled when Jimmy Lee's bag slid down the chrome chute. One of the armed men came to Jimmy Lee's side and began to unzip the bag while the other kept a firm grip on the dog. The conveyor belt had stopped and the people in line waited tensely.

The customs agent held the bag open and let the dog prod around inside with its wet snout. It growled louder and finally erupted with a series of sharp angry barks.

Jimmy Lee shrugged and shook his head. "I don't understand, is there some sort of—"

The agent took him forcefully by the arm and pulled him aside. People had paused in their passage to stare at him, only he couldn't see them clearly. They were shrouded in a thick gray haze. Beyond them, however, Jimmy Lee caught brief, uncanny glimpses of people who stood outside the haze, watching him.

The agents were moving him away from the conveyor belt, down a dimly-lit side hallway. Jimmy Lee could hear the other agent and the dog not too far behind. He knew he should be saying something, perhaps making a joke out of the whole thing, but his lips were locked tight. He was afraid of what his mouth might say, and shocked by what his eyes were beginning to see.

Shapes shuddered in the green corduroy wallpaper as he passed; the curved lines appeared to assume shapes and then dissipated as he approached. Things moved there, and when Jimmy Lee tried to cast his eyes downward at the marbled tile he saw jagged hieroglyphics forming in the blue-black veins there. He hadn't found his bread, and the Disney was really kicking in.

"Step in here please," said the agent who had his arm, thrusting him without further comment into a plain white room that held a table and chair. Jimmy Lee slumped into the chair and blinked around. The other agent entered with the panting dog and locked the door.

"Now would you mind showing us what's in the bag, mister?"

Jimmy Lee shrugged and tried to focus on them but they were blurring out of his vision. Darker figures loomed behind them, parts of faces—one wide eye, the twitching corner of a thick-lipped mouth, the ear of a bald person. These were clear when he did not look directly at them; when he did, they too wavered just out of range. "I don't have anything," he finally gasped, painfully aware of how desperate he sounded.

"We'll just have a look then," said the voice. The bag was turned upside down and the contents fell onto the table. Jimmy Lee could barely see the shirt and shorts Valsen had given him, Day-Glo tropical prints, real tourist shit.

"Ho, ho, nice outfit."

"Hey, waitasecond," said the other agent. "Look at *that.*"

Hands scrabbled around inside the bag. The clothes were unfolded and searched, then searched again. "Hey, I'm not finding anything," the agent said. "You think it's *that?*"

"No, *that's* bullshit," said the other. "Sandy doesn't know that stuff!"

"Well, let's put her back on it." The dog's growl grew louder and it barked again. The noise was terrific in the small room. Jimmy Lee could barely see the table before him. All he could do was shake his head *no* at what was happening.

"Yo, what's going on?"

"Sandy is not a narc, goddammit! There's something else in here!"

"But she's smelling *that,* Roddy. Watch her!"

A shadow leaned in and took a fistful of Jimmy Lee's shirt. "What's in the bag, asshole? Where is it? You got plastique sewn in the bottom or what?"

His eyes fluttered, seeing nothing that was there and several things that simply could not be. The strange figures were more fully formed now, pressed against the far walls and instead of their features Jimmy Lee saw what they held: dark stone blades, sharp spears, scepters carved like serpents. The customs agents were featureless and threatening. In the distance the dog barked and growled.

"Why," pleaded Jimmy Lee," why is it so *loud?*"

"Cause she smells whatever you got in the bag, asshole."

"Nothing—in the bag—"

"Well, there's *this,* which is enough to haul your ass downtown," and something was held beneath Jimmy Lee's quivering nostrils. Inhaling deeply, he recognized the pine scent of Valsen's marijuana. *Oh shit.* He must've missed something, perhaps a loose bud that had slid into an interior pocket. "We'll check the bag out ourselves."

He tried to stand up and protest, this wasn't fair, weren't they saying that the dog couldn't smell it anyway? Then how did they know? Why did it bark? But two strong hands pushed him against the wall and he felt himself being cuffed and frisked, then seated again. He couldn't look at the dog because when he did it wasn't a dog anymore. Out of the corner of his eye, he could see the great black jaguar casually licking its lips, watching him.

Someone made a phone call, and within minutes the police arrived.

Handcuffed in the back of the car, he could not see the cops through the thick wire mesh; there were patterns in the mesh, shapes that formed and swirled and fell away. Some of them looked like people, tan faces with exotic features, wide impassive eyes.

They thought he'd been smuggling a bomb. Someone had said there'd been an explosion at the airport. The cops couldn't wait to book Jimmy Lee and get back out to Dry Plains International. They cursed the terrorists and regarded Jimmy Lee as nothing more than a nuisance who kept them from achieving their true glory.

The sounds of the crowded station were deafening, amplified: the clicking of typewriters sounded like horses' hooves thundering past. Voices boomed like thunder. He smelled sweat, smoke and fear. They couldn't book him yet because most of the force had been called out to the airport, so they led him straight to the holding cell.

Long and white, a tank with rows of steel benches running down the walls. There were about a dozen people in there, sweating and stinking because the air conditioner vent had been stuffed with someone's shirt. "Motherfuckas better gimme my *smokes!*" a barechested black man blurted every few minutes. "Ain't supposed to take nothin' offa me till I'm *booked,* goddamnit!"

Jimmy Lee sank to the bench and lay there. Closed his eyes against the hallucinations, only they kept right on going against his eyelids. The phantom people were clearer then, sharper, as if the images of the outside world diluted their existence.

A face floated nearby. Sloping forehead, brown skin, wild swirls of paints across the broad cheeks. A half-smile, teeth sharpened into points, and decorated, careful tracings of figures and faces so intricate they invited Jimmy Lee to lean forward.

"Well, ain't this just fuckin' great!"

The face receded. Another appeared. Jimmy Lee's eyes were open; he was looking at Valsen.

"What the fuck *happened?"*

Jimmy Lee tried to sit up but Valsen shoved him back down hard. The back of his head thudded against the bench and white sparks exploded. Valsen was yelling at him, punching a stubby finger into his chest. It started to hurt and Jimmy Lee vainly slapped at his hand. Valsen cocked back a fist and punched him.

The world cascaded past him in the glaring pain of the blow. A couple of guys were holding Valsen back, talking cool to him, calming him down only it didn't sound like it was working. Jimmy Lee rolled over to a sitting position and rubbed his eyes. Strangely, the punch seemed to clear his head for a few seconds.

"Valsen," he said, and saw how pale the man looked. Slicked with the nervous sweat of a junkie. "Why are you here?"

"Me? Why am *I* here?" He came at Jimmy Lee again.

A large bald man planted a fist squarely in Valsen's chest and held him there. "Be cool, c'mon," he said. "You freakin' on something, the both of you."

"What happened to *me,*" yelled an exasperated Valsen, "was that little bitch maid who tipped off security! She comes back and sees me skin-popping and before I can get out she's got security up there! Now why the holy hell aren't *you* on that plane?"

"Listen," he muttered, "I gotta get this stuff out, there's something wrong—"

"You just fucked up real bad, son!"

"I'm spitting up blood, man! I gotta get this out of my stomach, there's something happening, I think one of 'em's come open. . . ."

The bare-chested man bent down to Jimmy Lee and stared at him. He was flicking a lighter in one hand. "What you swallow, my man?"

The face wavered and smiled. Large black eyes, sharp teeth. The man's thumb scraped sparks from the wheel. Jimmy Lee's vision blurred again and he felt tears streaming down his face. "Look, I've got to throw this up or I'm gonna die. . . ."

"Yo, yo, hey, hey," sang the man to the others. "Someone give us a hand here, I think we got a sick mule."

Someone: "What's he carrying?"

Another: "I'll have a taste, whatever it is."

Valsen shrugged free and grabbed Jimmy Lee's shoulders, pinning him against the wall. He was shouting but the words were all wrong. They weren't in any language Jimmy Lee could recognize. His ears popped like a gunshot, and he was removed entirely from that space, as if encased in a glass bubble. Beyond the bubble he could see the holding cell, the men moving in around him, Valsen's pitted face hovering before him.

But on the surface of the bubble, like oil, danced the

leering faces and half-naked figures that had haunted him since the airport. They moved faster and faster in a celebration of some sort. They spun and kicked and held their arms to the sky.

His stomach began to cramp. He pulled his shirt from his pants and loosened his belt. In a distant corner of his mind he heard a voice telling him to get a finger down his throat; the voice was his own but it was too hysterical, too frightened, and he didn't want to hear it.

There was another way.

Valsen's eyes shone like wet black marbles. He was staring intently at Jimmy Lee, as if he too could see the phantom figures and what they celebrated. The men behind Valsen were smiling and laughing, excited. Valsen was nodding slow and sure. His mouth was open and he drooled.

He gently lay Jimmy Lee back on the bench. "I'll take care of it," he said clearly through the din. "I'll help you."

Jimmy Lee grasped the bench slats above his head as they pulled off his shoes, his pants and underwear. A voice screamed again from a distant place in his mind but he was able to shut it out. Faces orbited him like tiny planets; they hungered for him but there was no malice, no anger. Only desire.

Visions of ceremonies flashed in his skull. He saw obsidian blades plunging through the chests of sacrifices high atop stone altars. Children falling into deep stone wells while their parents watched from far above. A heart plucked free, squeezed triumphantly by a slick red fist. He saw himself struggling on the prison bathroom floor, held down and ridden by brown-skinned men with shaved heads and pierced noses.

His legs were spread apart and he felt Valsen's rough stubby fingers probing him, sliding deeper and deeper within him. Jimmy Lee felt the pain as nothing more than a dull ache, and as Valsen made a clutching fist deep inside his bowels he realized what was happening and almost smiled.

Valsen withdrew a length of intestine and pressed it flat, letting it drain onto the floor. Someone rubbed Jimmy Lee's temples as others pressed firmly down on his stomach, emptying him. The stench was strong and sweet.

When he was sufficiently emptied, someone took a sharpened belt buckle and traced it gently over Jimmy Lee's stomach. The others looked on and nodded their approval at the pattern traced there.

The blade punctured his stomach like a cold kiss deep inside him. Using their shirts they wiped the blood away from the holes, which formed an unusual but ancient pattern.

The sour white walls of the holding cell dissolved, and his eyes beheld great stones that stretched away from him, forming monuments and altars whose edges he'd never see. Sparks. The lighter. The hazy figures had merged with the ancient ones, and they bowed to partake of the sacrament. For just a moment an image flashed before him, that of the soda can in the hotel room. As the flesh of his belly caught fire and smoke was pulled through him and deep down into Valsen's aching lungs, Jimmy Lee Kemp gently began to laugh.

The gods gave him that.

SACRAMENT

Brian Hodge

IT WAS THE CALL SHE HAD NEVER RECEIVED, HAD ALWAYS dreaded, had always expected would eventually come. Inevitability worked in its favor, and against peace of mind.

Concourse B security office. Come quick. Aid and comfort for someone in . . . well, in bad shape.

Details were unavailable, but that it was a victim of some sort was obvious. The taut urgency in the voice of tonight's ranking officer on duty told Ally Pendleton as much as she cared to know this soon. Imagination took over once she cradled the office phone she shared with half of Dry Plains' rotating staff of chaplains. It was better not to know, according to Senior Chaplain Fulbright, an elderly Methodist minister. Fear the worst, he would tell his neophyte volunteers from area churches; envision it as terribly as you can. And by the time you arrive . . . well, perhaps the grim reality will actually be a relief.

With luck, and God's blessing.

Ally grabbed a palm-size crucifix from the single desk drawer allotted her in the division of communal space. As a Lutheran, she set no undue ceremonial store by it—it was no more and no less than a symbol of her chosen faith—but there were plenty who did, so for their sake it was best to be prepared. This close to Mexico, great numbers of Catholics passed through the gates and terminals.

She left her office, to find the night's other chaplain doing likewise. The two offices faced each other across a narrow hallway branching off the concourse of Dry Plains' main terminal. A little farther along, and the adventurous or the pious would come to a small nondenominational chapel.

"Concourse B?" Ally asked. "Did they call you too?"

Baxter Hanley nodded. "They did."

"Tell you what's going on?"

"They did not." Baxter buttoned his suitcoat around him and quickstepped beside her. "Regardless of Brother Fulbright's feelings on protocol, I, for one, do *not* appreciate being kept in the dark on situations such as this. I like to go someplace with both eyes open, if you know what I mean."

She looked at him out of the corner of hers. "Oh, come on, Bax. Where's your sense of adventure?"

He didn't answer, nor did Ally expect him to. Baxter Hanley was never less than cordial, in a grudging Southern Baptist fashion, but she knew he did not care much for her in any sense other than his obligation as a sibling in the eyes of the Big Boss in the sky. Baxter was fiftyish, and a traditionalist who wore his salvation on his sleeve, as well as his car. She had seen the bumper sticker, *This Vehicle Driverless In Case Of Rapture.* Then there were the vanity plates, the seven-letter limit editing his message to U NED GOD.

They had never discussed it, but it stood to reason that she represented everything he secretly found appalling: the Lutheran, the liberal, the reformer. Woman clergy, of all things, a travesty of God-given roles even to some among her own denomination. How unthinkable would this be for still harder-headed hardliners? This *was* Texas, after all. And she wasn't even a native.

Or did God even recognize state boundaries?

Concourse B's security office sat behind an unmarked door, across from a row of gates serving United Airlines. Ally knew from her initiation tour last year that such unidentified quarters were less for the public's convenience than for Security's. Everyone from suspicious travelers to passengers made hysterical by sudden eerie frights could be whisked out of the flow, and hidden away until the situation was resolved.

Ally and Baxter stood before the door for a moment; behind them the pace of life went on unhindered. Arrivals and departures, and those who came to say good-bye or hello. They all walked with the same hurried pace that could be seen on a downtown street of any city, eyes staring as blankly as the rows of monitors charting flight information. As strangers they lived, and as strangers they would fly.

Ally rapped on the locked door and they were admitted by a young uniformed officer whose nameplate read PRYOR, and whose face had gone sweaty and pale.

What had he witnessed this past hour, Ally wondered, to leave his eyes so glassy, so lacking in the "I've seen it all" assurance natural to security guards?

Whatever it was, it lay beyond yet another door, a holding office from which drifted the occasional moan, and small warbling cries gone weak with traumatic dementia.

Our Creator who art in Heaven—

"We picked him up on the gangway, just off the plane . . ."

—let me be ready when I see this.

". . . I didn't know a human being could *do* this to himself . . ."

Ally led the way to the door, past another pair of security officers leaning against desks, as they dragged on Marlboros. At her heels, Baxter Hanley was puffing from the brisk walk, clutching his Bible to his belly as if it were a shield.

She opened the door. And stared. They both wrinkled their noses at the sudden whiff of decay.

Three more guards, sweating more than the cool air warranted, stood around a desk swept clean to serve as a medical examination table. A pair of nurses from First Aid worked on their writhing patient, but clearly he needed more than they could provide.

"Oh merciful God in Heaven," Baxter murmured from behind her.

"He's in shock," said one of the nurses. "So we don't dare sedate him. But he's not . . . cooperating."

"You've called an ambulance, haven't you?" said Ally.

"Ten minutes ago, soon as we saw what we had." This from Nuñez, the ranking security officer. "But we got ground fog out there tonight, and you know what that does to the traffic."

She nodded, and tried to switch to breathing through her mouth so she might avoid the worst of the smell. It didn't help, because then she thought she could *taste* it, an overripe gray-green odor.

He was young, perhaps twenty, with the dark skin and black hair and features of Mexican descent. His pants lay heaped on the floor, and he wore silken briefs, and a shirt fully unbuttoned over his torso. His chest rose and fell with rapid, shallow breaths, and his limbs trembled rigid as he strained. The pain must have been horrendous, if in some small way he was not beyond it already.

He had been deeply incised four times. An eight-inch slice along each inner thigh, and a four-inch cut just outside either armpit, over the outer edge of the pectoral muscles. None looked to be fresh wounds; they had been made long enough ago to have all but quit bleeding. The flaps of cleaved flesh were puffy and curled and gangrenous.

He may have seen Ally, and he may not have. With fever surely curdling his brain, there was no guessing what he saw. They could be angels clustering about him, or devils come to rend his soul. If he fought them, the nurses would obviously be little help before the ambulance arrived. And it would do him no good at all for Security to wrestle him into submission every time the nurses needed to touch him. Signs of struggle were already evident: one guard had a swelling eye, and a hypodermic was lying on the floor with a bent needle.

While the young man chattered garbled Spanish—ravings, for the most part, to her comprehension—Ally left Baxter Hanley standing agape, and drew a rolling deskchair across the floor so she might sit at the boy's side.

"Are you Catholic?" she asked softly, leaning in. *"Estas católico?"*

A wild fist glanced off the side of her ear, smarting and jarring her vision for a moment. Ally waved back a couple guards who sought to do the macho thing and protect her. It wouldn't hurt if she didn't let it, and everything was about control now, wasn't it? Let him understand he was with *one* friend, at least, and need not fight. Need not scream. Need not weep. Need only relax at the soft press of her fingers upon his trembling forearm.

"Shhhh, shhhh," Ally soothed, and leaned in further to sing so soft and low he might be the only one to hear.

She held the crucifix above his gaze so that he might see its pewter gleam, like the mobile she had hung a few years ago over her infant daughter's crib, and that had proved so fascinating to eyes that saw all things as new.

He saw, he recognized, he stilled perceptibly. . . .

Even as her eyes strayed too far, following her nose. The gray-meat incisions, yawning open like diseased mouths every time he flexed a limb, made her stomach roll, for surely things were not *moving* in there, he was not that far gone, was he?

Her lullaby was forgotten in mid-verse, and the crucifix was beginning to slip from her fingers when the young man suddenly reached up to seize it, bring it sharply to his lips for the most reverent of kisses. He sobbed, once, very loudly, and fell as still as he was likely to stay.

The nurses moved back in while Ally rolled away in her chair, knowing it would be a few minutes before she would trust her legs beneath her. Maybe she could have Baxter wheel her all the way back to her office. She left the crucifix in the young man's hands while the nurses worked at disinfection and antibiotics.

"Thanks, Pendleton," said Nuñez.

"What in the name of Heaven happened to that fellow?" asked Baxter. "I have *never* seen wounds like that on a living soul."

Nuñez crushed out a cigarette and squirmed in vague disgust. "This kid comes in on a flight from Guadalajara. They had already radioed in about him. A flight attendant noticed him almost from the moment he boarded. Was walking real stiff, like he had legs like Frankenstein, right?" Nuñez demonstrated. "Walked the same way every time he went to the bathroom, and he went a *lot,* they say. Plus he's sweating like a whole *herd* of pigs."

"High on dope," said Baxter, and sadly shook his head.

Ally hoped he wouldn't see her roll her eyes. Baxter seemed to suspect everyone under age twenty-five of the same thing. She supposed he was the kind of man who functioned best when he had plenty to frighten him. Thirty years ago he would have been seeing Communists. Three hundred years ago, it would have been witches.

Nuñez went ahead with his explanation. Once the flight had landed, and the gate extended for passenger offloading, a security crew intercepted the young man as soon as he stepped off the plane. They wanted no scenes inside the terminal. When the flight attendant pointed him out, and Pryor and two others detained him, he offered no resistance, just a renewed outpouring of sweat. A quick patdown revealed a bulge along each inner thigh, and they thought sure they had a smuggler on their hands, with something taped beneath his pants.

Well . . . yes and no.

They had ushered him off the gangway and into Concourse B via restricted passages. Got him in here, got him to strip. And found that the bulges weren't just beneath his pants, they were beneath his skin.

Each incision had been stuffed with rolled plastic packets of powder, the infected wounds covered by strips of shipping tape. The guards were already on the verge of losing dinner when they found the rest: flat packets slid into the incisions along his pectorals.

Nuñez pointed across the room to an evidence tray, smeared with congealed blood. There the packets lay, six in all, plus curled strips of tape clotted with scabs and hair.

"I'd say he was carrying about a pound and a half, total," said Nuñez. "Maybe a little more." Could it be possible he was *enjoying* this? "I peeked. Looks like Mexican brown to me. That's heroin, by the way. But hey, I'm no expert. Heroin's making a big comeback, I know that much." He shook his head, fumbled for a cigarette, cast a pitying glance behind him. "Not exactly a rocket scientist, huh? Just when you think you seen everything. . . ."

Baxter Hanley had more than paled, he'd gone greenish. "Never have I heard . . . of a more wanton violation . . . of the Lord's temple."

Oh, give it a rest, Bax. Ally shut her eyes, concentrating, mind over stomach. It was a repulsive thing this boy had done, yes, but she found herself wondering why he had done it at all. It couldn't be merely greed; such extreme measures to conceal his cargo was more an act of desperation. Where he had come from? What family had he left behind, and were they counting on the money he was to have made? She pitied him.

Especially when he began to shriek loud enough to shred his lungs.

Ally was a helpless witness. This boy's ordeal of flesh and infection were beyond her ministrations. His seizures redoubled in fury and strength, adrenalized, the anguish of every cut unleashed. If anyone could be driven mad by pain, clearly he was proof.

"Él viene, VIENE! Tequihua!" he cried, whipping his arm. Ally blinked as something whizzed past her face, and heard it hit something just beyond her. A high cry pierced her ear, and turning, she saw Baxter Hanley, wide-eyed—

With the ornately beveled top end of the crucifix imbedded high upon his forehead. It stuck a moment, like a dart, then fell loose to the floor, and Baxter wiped dumbly at a trickle of blood that seeped to his eyebrow. He staggered back into the wall.

"Oh, *my,*" he said, and slid to the floor without once losing that glaze of surprise.

"Tequihua!" the boy screamed again, to the ceiling, to an unseen sky, and he bowed his back in strain against four pairs of hands, then collapsed at once, silent.

Ally knew he was dead even before a nurse confirmed it. CPR was administered, but she hoped it would fail to bring him back. *Let him go, he's past his pain now, let him keep that gift of God.*

Let him give up the ghost.

Ally helped get Baxter off the floor, occupational therapy, she *needed* to be needed to get through this. He trembled all the way to a chair provided for him. Poor Baxter, shaken. The cut in his forehead was cleaned, then bandaged, and was not deemed serious enough to warrant stitches.

Nuñez was looking as if all the fun had gone out of his evening. He snapped his fingers at one of his guards, then pointed at the young man's body.

"Find something to cover him up with until the ambulance gets here for the body." Shaking his head, hand plunging in pockets for a cigarette. "What a mess."

Ally touched his arm. "What was that he was saying at the

end? 'He comes, he's coming,' that much I got. But that last word, I wasn't familiar with that."

"Tequihua . . . tequihua?" Nuñez hunched his shoulders. "You got me there."

"Tequila?" suggested one of the guards. "Wasn't he saying something about tequila?"

Nuñez scowled. "Oh, don't be a bonehead, you don't even speak the language. That was a *w*-sound at the end of that word. Like in, weapon or whack-off."

"Maybe he had trouble with his *l*'s," offered another guard.

Nuñez waved his arms. "Who's he look like over there to you, Elmer fucking Fudd?" To Ally, then: "Pardon my Español."

She nodded, weakly. "Consider it pardoned."

"I've always liked that about you. You're just one of the guys." He nodded in Baxter's direction, where a nurse had given him a painkiller; Baxter swallowed it gratefully. "Not like him. One wrong word, I can count on a lecture like I haven't heard since my grandmother was alive."

Ally couldn't help a wan smile, then lost it as she glanced back at the dead boy. "What if he wasn't alone?"

"Mmm?"

"With what he was carrying, don't you think someone might have been waiting on this end for him to step through the gate?"

"Oh. That." Nuñez nodded. "I was running that through my head a minute ago. Yeah. Maybe there is. I'll leave some of the guards here, till the police and the ambulance show up. Whenever *that* happens." He crossed over to the window, peered around a curtain, mouth curling. "Ground fog, just what we needed tonight."

Ally couldn't take her gaze off the boy. He would have had such captivating eyes, such long lashes. "I always meant to have Father Pedroza teach me how to give the last rites. Just in case something like this . . . ever . . ."

Nuñez patted her shoulder. "Leave the dead to us; you work better with the living. Me? I don't think Baxter over there should be wandering around alone."

She nodded. "You're right, I should get him out of here."

He clucked his tongue, then chuckled. "The holier they are . . . the harder they fall."

Ally walked Baxter to their offices, with one hand loosely holding his arm, and he seemed not to resent it. Baxter Hanley was returning to reality as a different man. Gone was the proudly militaristic stiff-backed strut. His shoulders were rounded, sagging toward the floor, and he said nothing.

Ghastly though it was, how it had been brought about, a little more humility was an altogether welcome change.

Ally stood with him for a moment outside the office doors.

"Are you going to be okay, Baxter?"

"Yes. I shall." His voice belonged to a beaten man. "I just . . . I think I should be . . . alone for a time."

She patted his hand. "Why don't you go on home. There's no reason you should stay here after that. Go soak in a hot tub, or let Rebeccah rub your shoulders, or put some Brahms on the stereo. If anything else comes up tonight, I can handle it."

He was nodding, eyes lowered, lips pursed. "Perhaps that would be for the best."

"Besides," she said, trying to coax a smile from him, "we're volunteers. What can they do, dock your pay?"

He wasn't biting. "I . . . I have a sacred obligation here, you know. I . . . do *not* take that lightly. Please don't think I do."

Baxter shuffled into his office. Ally retreated to her own, turned on the desk lamp instead of the ceiling light, and adjusted it for lowest wattage. There, dim and soothing, the shadows felt softer. Ally sunk into her chair and reached for the picture of her daughter she kept at the side of the desk while on duty. Four years old now, exhibiting her own unique personality at an unprecedented rate . . . and surely the most eloquent case for the existence of God that Ally had ever known. No seminary could compete with it, or better define it.

Five hours. Five hours and Ally would be back home, and could stare at her sleeping child as long she needed to to set herself straight again. Such a paradox, children. Despite the way they could turn your life upside-down, they were stabilizing in times of turmoil. It was their true gift in return for life.

Way to go, God.

Baxter Hanley was tapping at her door within five minutes, and declined to sit after entering. As if by standing he refused to admit any need to be here, keeping his escape options open.

"I'm, ah . . . I'm having some . . . difficulties, you might say." Baxter kept his voice almost as low as his eyes. "I dropped to my knees in prayer in there, and I asked God to help me understand why He would allow a thing such as this to . . . to *happen* to . . . well, to me." Baxter rubbed at the bandaged wound. "I prayed hard, Ally. I truly did. And I don't feel I—I got an answer. None at all."

Ally, in the moment, could not rebuke him for his occasional pomposity. Underlying it was likely a great deal of pain he might never acknowledge. And here he seemed to have, without realizing it, tapped into the fundamental difference that separated them.

"Do you think it's possible," she said, "that you might be expecting a little too much from God?"

Baxter looked clearly surprised. "I beg your pardon?"

She would clearly be treading thin ice here. "Why do you have to assume God had anything to do with it at all?"

His head twitched, and he backed a half-step away, as if in retreat into himself. "Perhaps . . . perhaps He meant this as a test for me. This is some obstacle I'm to overcome, yes . . ."

"And maybe," she said, "it just happened. Without any reason other than you standing in the wrong place at the wrong time. One foot to the left or right, and it would have missed. Bax . . . I can't believe in a God who would throw a crucifix at anyone, for any reason. I *can* believe in a very troubled boy who was in too much pain. He may have known what he was doing, and he may not. Either way, Baxter, that's the essence of free will. And for better or for worse, the consequences."

Ally watched him carefully . . . Baxter, close to trembling, clutched at his shoulders as if chilled. He shut his eyes for a few moments, and when he reopened them, he looked as if he had decided to sidestep the issue entirely.

"We *do* see our share of repeat travelers through here, you know," he said. "Business folk mostly. I've been volunteering my services here longer than you, and I have come to recognize many a face. And in their faces I recognize needs. Their loneliness, their godlessness, their sorrows. I can tell those times when they don't even mind a layover between flights, because it gives them a chance to come down here and unburden their souls."

"I know who you mean," said Ally. "It really is rough for some people, being on the road like that, away from everything."

Baxter was nodding, then gazed into space. "They come back to you more than they do me. That I've noticed as well. They like you better. I tried to tell myself that I was telling them . . . well, what they needed to hear. That you must have been telling them only what they *wanted* to hear. And that I was doing them more good in the long run. Now . . . I have to wonder."

"Jesus never told one person they were a sinner." Ally smiled and hunched her shoulders. "My views about things may not be the most traditional, or even liked by everyone, but I don't see my job as being about inducing guilt. Or rules that a lot of ancient priests came up with centuries after the death of someone they never even knew. I've always seen it as being about loving your neighbor, Bax. That's all. Love and free will. The God I can believe in gave us the ability to think for ourselves."

"Perhaps mine should get together with yours sometime . . . and settle it once and for all."

Her eyes widened. Coming from Baxter, it was a truly shocking statement. "If I'd said that? You *know* you would have accused me of blasphemy."

He rubbed tired eyes, wincing as he massaged the skin around his bandage. He looked older than Moses. "I never could believe it was as simple as you say it is, Ally. I was not taught that way. Not raised that way. Those weren't the lessons I had . . . beaten into me." He fell more tightly into himself and suppressed the tiniest of shudders. Then touched the doorknob with the look of a man torn. "I looked into something's face over there in my office. I believe it was a devil. And I believe it was laughing at me . . .

"Goodnight, Ally."

He shut the door behind him, softly, and she listened to his footsteps receding down the hall. She had welcomed the advent of humility? Perhaps she had been hasty. A pompous Baxter might have been preferable to a broken Baxter after all. Men and women such as he were the great tragedy of blind dogma. When confronted with a challenge to their preconceptions, rarely could they bend to accommodate it. They rejected. And if it was too forceful? More often, they broke.

She had to wonder then whether Baxter, sacred obligation or not, would even be back.

Ally sat upon the floor and meditated awhile: Restore me where I am weak. She found it lacking; the face of the mutilated boy tended to drift before her mind's eye. Mantras of calm were no match for his convulsions, his final ravings, and, yes, even Baxter's devils. Surely the former had inspired the latter.

Whatever *tequihua* meant, Nuñez hadn't thought it important, but she wasn't so convinced. There was, naturally —or unnaturally—much that remained resolutely unexplainable at Dry Plains. Nuñez would not be the first to confront it with denial. While she could, academically, allow for it all.

Reverend Fulbright was much of the same mind, if less open about it; she had surmised this during conversations with the man. In his office he had compiled a minor library devoted to helping him comprehend those things which might arise here, like ghosts of a past that was never truly buried.

Ally now entered his office; he left it forever unlocked in his absence. She scanned titles, many of which were devoted to myth and legend and tribal lore. Ancient history and history that never was . . . at least on this particular plane of existence.

She knew only what was already common knowledge, and shared among airport employees with the same fearful glee as seen in children telling stories around a campfire. Their waking minds refused to believe, even as their shadow minds accepted the irrational because they knew, on some level, that to speak of it at all was to admit, yes, it *could* have happened.

Tequihua.

Recalling the inflections in the dying voice, the word did seem less Spanish than, perhaps, Indian. Certainly that was in keeping with circulating rumors of Comanche and Aztec legend. Like so much of New World civilization, Dry Plains was figuratively built atop the bones and mummies and heritage of far older races. New could supplant Old in ways that turned out to be less design than mere accident. Where numbers and force of will might fail, an insignificant detail can serve as the pivot on which fortunes spin, or sow the seed that brings downfall and conquest.

Take the Aztecs. Mighty warriors who ruled the whole of ancient Mexico, they could have easily decimated Hernando Cortez and his conquistadors were it not for one thing: the timing of his arrival perfectly coincided with a long-prophesied arrival of the great Aztec god Quetzalcoatl, the Feathered Serpent. Cortez was greeted with the respect due a god. By the time the Aztecs had realized their error, Cortez had put together an allied force of tribes subjugated by the Aztecs, and who lived in mortal fear of them. Their final downfall came less from military might than a weakness inherent in their own bodies. The Spaniards brought with them smallpox, and Aztecs who could brave lance and sword had no defense. Besieged on their island capitol of Tenochtitlan, their extinction was assured by a primitive form of biological warfare: smallpox-infested blankets were lobbed by catapult from the shore of the Lake of the Moon, into the city.

Ally found it a worthy lesson: It was the little things that could prove your downfall.

Tequihua. She found it after twenty minutes of searching through glossaries and indexes and text. Immediately she dropped the book and grabbed the phone to have Nuñez paged out of the central security office.

"Where are you?" she asked.

"Concourse C, carry-on screening," he said. "Why, what's up?"

"Did anyone ever show up to take care of that boy's body?"

"Don't think so, I was waiting for the call, but still haven't got it yet." He groaned. "You taken a good look outside lately, toward the highway? Ground fog got worse, got a pile-up out there, eight cars at least. They're probably right in the middle—"

The weather again. How terribly fortuitous it seemed. Could restless spirits influence even the weather, to suit their own purposes? And fog came from earth instead of sky, did it not?

"Who did you leave with the body?" she said.

"Pryor, it was his collar. Plus a couple others. Listen, Pendleton, you got a point here you're trying to make, 'cause—"

"See if he's all right. Just check if everything's okay there."

Ally could hear him grumbling at the other end of the line. Heard the crackle of his radio, then his voice, removed, calling for Pryor on Concourse B. Again. Again. Static answered, nothing but static.

"He—he doesn't . . ."

"I'll meet you there." Ally hung up the phone and thought, *May this be no more than a wild thought in an overactive mind. Please.*

She was off again for Concourse B, alone this time, and could move much faster without Baxter to slow her down. The airport was beginning to clog with frustrated travelers whose flights had been delayed, and welcoming parties with smoldering tempers. To them, Ally was sure, she looked like one more driven soul hurrying to nowhere.

She wasn't the first to arrive back at Concourse B's security branch. Approaching from midway along the terminal, she could see a swarming knot of airport uniforms—apparently Nuñez had radioed for those closer than he to converge.

And apparently, there was good reason.

Shouldering her way through, Ally saw faces both paling

and reddened. All the varied reactions to tragedy: here was rage and shock, grief and revulsion. Here were people whose thresholds had been forcibly broadened.

Some bending . . . and others breaking.

Hands upon her shoulders, one of the guards who monitored the luggage x-ray stopped Ally. She shook her head at Ally. "You don't want to see this. Believe me, you *don't*."

As if it were a choice? Ally had none, and muscled ahead. She looked. She saw.

And could understand why even Nuñez was trying his best to hold back bitter tears while desperately striving to remain in control of a situation gone to hell. Past hell? Perhaps it was.

Heaven and hell may well have become immaterial here. Perhaps some unknown agent had been at work. She could be certain of nothing, could only trust her senses. Her eyes . . . and nose.

The charnel smells of blood and meat were quite potent.

Where one had died, now lay four. Pryor and another guard lay in haphazard jumbles on the floor, a third left stretched atop a desk. All had bled from bludgeoned skulls, and their chests were yawning cavities which had surrendered their hearts. All of which sat in one of the evidence trays.

And the passenger, responsible for bringing her here to begin with? He remained, though considerably less whole than he had been.

He still lay upon the desk where he had died. And where he had been skinned. Of course, he had made it easy for whoever had done it, given them a start. Those incisions? Just slip a hand in, grip firmly, and peel the rest free.

Too much; this was past even her tolerance, and she lurched away with her stomach heaving at the back of her throat. She would deny it its traitor's victory, and Ally steadied herself against a wall outside the offices. Beyond her, a pair of guards with more presence of mind were herding away the curious.

She had much to tell Nuñez, but he had much to do even as the world fell upon his shoulders . . . and perhaps it would have been of no value now, anyway.

She only knew that, once again, she needed to be needed to get through this. And there were those around her whose uniforms were but a wall, through which the men and the women inside were never seen. But who hurt nonetheless, and were desperate for answers, and lacking those, were willing to settle for comfort.

Oh, they knew, all right. Knew this place was home to something whose idea of holy was far different than her own. Though no less legitimate was its claim.

Ally took a breath. She touched one arm, then another. She met the eyes of the grieved.

She did her job.

Morning light: dawn as seen through the last vanishing swirls of ground fog that had wreaked havoc near and far. The police had made it through hours before, to finally descend upon Dry Plains in numbers fit to contend with multiple homicide. Their disdain for airport security had been typical and maddening, scoffing at these little rent-a-cops scurrying around getting themselves killed. That Nuñez had managed to control his temper so well lent him a new level of respect from Ally.

They shared the dawn, and coffee, and the reddened eyes of veterans after a losing battle.

"You wanted to tell me something," he said. "Would it have made a difference earlier? Would they still be alive? I gotta know that, Pendleton. Would they?"

"I don't know. Probably not. It's only clear to me now, after . . . after the fact."

He nodded and lit a cigarette. Smoke curled around him like a laurel to herald defeat rather than victory.

"*Tequihua* is an Aztec word. It was an honorary title given to warriors," she said. "It meant 'Master of Cuts.' It was earned by those who captured three enemy prisoners and brought them back alive for sacrifice." She wondered what it would have been like to grow up in a world where your gods asked this of you. Demanded it. "Aztecs didn't fight to kill, in war. They fought to subdue. They had more use for prisoners than casualties."

"Why are you telling me this now?" Nuñez was plainly the most miserable person she had ever seen.

"I don't know." Then she amended: "I suppose, in case we ever hear the word again."

He was shaking his head in denial. "You can't expect me to believe this. It was Colombians, they *do* shit like this, they *thrive* on it. They're big on making a statement like this, when something doesn't go just the way they plan." He ran his hands through his hair. With his head lowered, she noticed for the first time that his hair was thinning on top. "You were right earlier. That cut-up kid had people waiting. They woulda known he walked on that plane in Guadalajara. And when they didn't see him walk off . . . they went hunting."

Ally couldn't contradict him. Certainly he made a persuasive case. And part of her wanted to believe this was what had actually happened. Still . . .

Which to believe in: the humanly repugnant, or the irrational? Between the rock and the metaphysical hard place.

"How could he have even known about the Master of Cuts?" she asked. "Something like that, it's hardly common knowledge. And even if he did . . . why *then?* If you knew you were dying, wouldn't you want to communicate something that was at least important?"

Nuñez laughed, weary, bleary. "He was talking about tequila."

Maybe he was. Maybe so. Still . . .

"What about the skin? I defy you to come up with a reason why a group of smugglers would bother taking it with them. Wouldn't they leave it behind? Whatever statement they were making, it would already have been made."

"Well, now you're talking something interesting." Nuñez scrubbed a hand across his cheeks, his chin. His night's growth of beard was quite heavy. "It didn't get up and walk away on its own, now, did it?"

She shut her eyes against the sting of smoke and wondered. Over the past several hours, she had gotten *awfully* hard to surprise.

Ally was able to distance herself from the night by virtue of job description. As a volunteer with a once-per-week shift, she supposed she was entitled to leave it behind upon returning to her home, her own church, her own congregation, her standard duties of births and quiet deaths, comfort and counsel and celebration of sacred and mundane. All these hallmarks of Protestantism that were beginning to increasingly resemble pieces of a much larger puzzle left incomplete.

She kept in touch via newspaper, and a few telephone calls to Chaplain Fulbright . . . enough to learn that the wheels of justice rolled slowly. The police, it seemed, were faring little better than the airport security they had so mocked. A few leads, a few speculations, and no arrests.

When she returned a week later, ready for the next troubled voyager or full-blown crisis, it was almost as if it had never happened. Ally supposed that airports the world over were much the same, exporting their memories of tragedy on flight after flight until none remained, and all was forgotten.

It was an exceptionally quiet night she passed, with ample time to peruse Chaplain Fulbright's library. She read again about this dead civilization that seemed to have left such an imprint on our own. Historically fascinating, theologically unsettling.

Rituals, even for peeled skin. Imagine: every last one of them was walking around in tender sacrament.

She read until she could tolerate no more, and shelved the books with mild shame. But past was past. Regardless of the nature of the agent provocateur, she could not undo what had been done. And too much knowledge was such a burden on those ill-equipped to do something about it.

Quiet night . . . lonely night. Solitary; she found she could even miss Baxter Hanley's frowning disapproval. As she'd speculated, he had not returned. Perhaps the news of what had transpired after his departure had been too much.

The next morning, she decided to pay him a visit. Volunteer or not, if he was leaving Dry Plains, it should at least be made official. Mostly, though, she supposed she just wanted to make sure he was all right. Such a sad thing, clergy in despair. To whom could they turn when even God seemed strangely silent?

His parsonage sat beside his tiny church, in a residential

neighborhood of mostly retirees, where even the dogs seemed old. Ally parked on the street; here, too, all was quiet, as if life went on only at a distance. The wind was all that stirred.

She walked up the front walk, past a matted yard of overgrown grass, stood on the porch and prodded the buzzer, rattled at the locked door. Nothing. Nothing. Windows gave no clue, and when she found one at the side that hung cracked a few inches along the bottom, she pressed her face near to call in.

"Baxter? Baxter! It's Ally! Are you—"

She drew back, slapped in the nose and pit of her stomach. One whiff of putrefaction, and you remember it for life.

Ally ran around to try the back door. Locked as well, but she would not take no for an answer. Baxter was a trusting soul at heart, and if he didn't wholly trust every fellow man, he at least was the type to trust God to prevent anyone from finding a hidden key. Her fingers probed crevices along the back porch railing; she finally found a key beneath a pot of petunias dying of thirst.

The stench hit her like a wall, and Ally hung in the doorway until her gag reflex ceased to clench. Praying by rote, she wondered why she didn't just hurry to a neighbor's down the block and phone the police from there? It was obvious someone had died *here*.

Then again, even distressed preachers were entitled to vacations—during which refrigerators and deep-freezers could fail, and meat spoil. Oh, she would feel quite the fool then.

She walked slowly, room to room. This was her first time here, and all was new, raw. Her footsteps clicked on wooden floors; the irritating buzz of flies swirled in her ears.

She called out, her voice made loud and brittle in a stillness pregnant with anticipation.

It must have been Baxter's wife that she found at the kitchen table. Whether she died there or was put there afterward, Ally could not tell. She was just a dead woman staring, her gray bloodless face thick with blisters, one limp hand resting near a mug of coffee scummed over with mold.

When Ally went for the wall phone, she found it smashed, with a furious deliberation, as by one who had grown tired of hearing it ring.

And was there the faintest stirring elsewhere in the house? A shift of weight, a breath? She was not given to fooling herself.

She followed the sound through the dining room, into the living room, and from there she confronted the dim, reeking interior of what she assumed to be Baxter's den. With the shutters slatted and the curtains drawn, sunlight was a weak intruder here, rimming the spines of books and a broken cross hanging skewed on one wall. From the darkest corner came the thick buzz of engorged flies.

"Baxter?" she whispered. "Are you—"

"Go away!" The voice was a roar, pained and enraged and so very very frightened. With it came a cloud of flies, black specks that arose to churn about the center of the room, stirring with their wings a stink of graves violated.

Their sacred obligation was to minister to the sick, the dying. Had Mother Teresa ever wanted to run?

Ally stepped forward, then stopped. No farther. No. "Baxter, please, let me help . . ."

Shadows thickened, clotted, rose to unsteady legs in the corner, and began to shuffle toward the center of the room.

Her first impression, of silhouette and shading, was a man in the only clothing he'd owned for years. Now tatters and rags, trailing from him—but that surreal sagging of his face, was that even Baxter at all?—and then a piece tore free and hit the floor with a thick slap, like rotten leather.

A cold floodrush of understanding.

"Oh, Bax," she whispered. "You didn't . . ."

"I'm . . . not alone," he croaked in that shattered voice. "They just . . . just go to sleep, sometimes. Inside me. They're not devils, I know that now. They're just . . . enraged."

Ally took a step backward, for the door. Suppose they awoke, in the middle of his sentence, these spirits and their sacrament of flesh. And their motives.

It had been ancient ritual, each spring, for Aztec priests to skin alive a drugged sacrificial offering to the gods, insuring a bountiful crop of maize. The peeled hide, still warm and moist, was worn by a warrior as a second skin. For days on end he wore it, until it rotted and fell away and the man beneath was revealed afresh, a living symbol of new growth bursting through the skin of the seed, new life emerging from the death of the old.

But for what harvest did they hunger now?

Baxter was reaching. "Help me, Ally. They won't let me help myself. *Help me* . . ."

Thresholds crossed . . . and Ally met her breaking point. The flesh was willing, but the spirit was weak. She turned and fled, and from behind came the sounds of clumsy scramble, and a boiling cloud of flies.

She reached the front door before him, unlocked it and made it through. Blessed sunshine, air sweet and fresher than she ever hoped to breathe. Once off the porch and on the walk, Ally turned and saw Baxter hang in the doorway, and as a scrap of old face fell away, his skin beneath was revealed, aflame with thick scarlet blisters. She got one glimpse, then he fell back, blind to the glare of the Texas sun.

Ally was heaving by the time she got to the still-deserted street, and she sagged to her knees upon burning pavement. She gazed skyward, into that scorching yellow eye that so terrified and so blessed ancient men and women, some of whom were no doubt fed with such strength they refused to wholly die.

What harvest were they now intent on reaping? She wondered . . .

Had—nearly 500 years ago—some brave warrior lay dying of smallpox in a Tenochtitlan street, as walls crumbled under cannon fire, and had he looked forward through the years to this day, when he might pay back his European conquerors in kind? Or had such dour visions driven him north to escape, only to fall prey to other conquerors?

Oh yes. Behind her was the dying proof.

Behind her and around her, and down the street, and in other houses, while before her fell the shadow of a steeple topped with a small cross. She was bathed in a wind that gathered out of the stillness of this desolate neighborhood, and on it was borne a scent of pestilence.

The sun slipped behind a cloud, and before her, the shadow of the steeple disappeared. Perhaps the Age of

Miracles was no more, and a new Age of Savagery was poised to begin.

Other houses, other streets . . .

She could have proclaimed it aloud, could have warned them.

But she feared she would only have been preaching to the converted.

PASSING THROUGH

Steve Rasnic Tem

AT THE FAR END OF THE NEW CONCOURSE, THE TILE FLOORING appeared to be awash with a viscous red light. Clayborn figured it was a trick of those new neon bulbs the maintenance people had put in. He returned to his mopping, struggling to regain the steady back-and-forth rhythm which would get the job done. But he was distracted tonight—the steady work of cleaning which was usually so soothing now filled him with anxiety. He didn't like mopping tonight; he didn't like touching these floors. He'd never be able to get them clean. He might as well be mopping the bare Texas dirt.

Clayborn was agitated by the number of people passing through the airport—great masses of them moving in groups as if they'd been sewn together from incompatible parts. They were making noises which were angry and loving at the same time, bird-like and bovine-like and likenesses that were unrecognizable.

If this was humanity, he could not identify with any part of it. Not that this was any great surprise. He had never "identified." He had never even understood the concept of *identification*—it must, he thought, be some philosopher's fantasy.

He had never felt like a "janitor," although he supposed that was his occupation. He had never felt like a "father," although that had been his most important identity for years before it was ripped away from him. He had never felt "Indian"; he had never felt "Comanche," though not feeling

261

Comanche seemed like a terrible betrayal of all those who had come before.

But his ancestors, too, had simply been passing through. They'd tried to stay; he gave them that, with almost two hundred years of continuous war. Clayborn thought they should have been happy just to be passing through. Long cold winters and unbearably hot summers, dry as bone—this had been no place to linger. They should have been relieved not to have to stay.

He looked back down the corridor. There was something gray on the floor there, or was it brown? A piece of cloth. Someone's hat, that's what it was. Someone had left their hat on the floor of the new concourse, the one they weren't using yet. But it didn't look like a workman's hat. It was a fancy dress hat. As if it had blown there from another concourse. But the airport had no wind.

Sound rose in a roar from the concourse next door, the overcrowded one this new one was supposed to supplement. Through the glass walls that separated the two concourses, Clayborn could see the masses of people pushing each other, anxious to get out of the narrow passageway. Tanglings and twistings and wreckings of people, their voices together made a screech and a scream, although individually none of them was screeching or screaming. They were a great crash of broken-throated instruments. So many of them undulated in the throng that their faces blurred together into ovals and lines of color, floating above scarves and overcoats, the overcoats jostling one against the other in mysterious urgency, gloved hands clenching and unclenching. Almost no looking around—the hour was late and the overcoats had some more distant destination in mind.

"Hi, how are you? Lovely evening . . ." He greeted as many as he could, trying to make contact, trying to let them know that there were still friendly voices in the world, and faces to go with those voices.

Passing through. Endless destinations. No time to stop and talk. As if there *were* things to talk about. As if there were some contact to be made, relationships to hold on to. Sufferings to share. A recognition that they might all be in the same predicament. But their wounded voices were far too loud for such subtle communications.

Then, almost as suddenly as the explosion of sound had begun, the voices were gone, as if the passengers had all suddenly realized where they were, and they were feeling stifled, wary of this place. He could see their eyes shifting slowly, uneasily above their scarves. Dry Plains had this effect on people. He had seen it a thousand times before. Now there were only the hollow echoes of their shoes, anxious to get out. And the muffled caress of overcoats.

He looked back down the length of the new concourse. A shiny red scarf had joined the hat, and he could see more of the hat: a fancy one for sure, definitely brown, with a smooth blue silk hatband. At some point he'd call the supervisor about it, maybe even security. The new concourse was off-limits to passengers until the gates had been completed. Security would want to know if there'd been any violations.

People were still passing through the concourse next door. Double the usual number, he figured. Clayborn had vaguely heard reports of a series of snowstorms in the midwest resulting in massive delays, and he had the impression that news stories had been making quite a bit out of all this. His memory of such things was hesitant. Unlike the others on the late-night cleaning crew who followed delays and cancellations as closely as an air traffic controller might, he paid little attention to such things. To him, it simply meant some minor fluctuation in the numbers of people who passed through, their eyes furtive, not meeting his, their mingled scents lingering after their bodies had passed on. A few more footprints to erase, that was all. A few more cigarette butts to scrape up, magazines to toss, love letters to read and discard, bloody tampons to remove from out-of-the-way corners. There was always such a mass of them on the move he supposed they thought no one would notice when they dropped such things.

He knew some of them, recognized particular patterns of behavior seen over and over again. All his observations were made quickly, of course. It wasn't as if any of these passengers lingered for long in Dry Plains. Airports were passageways, like sidewalks or highway interchanges. Who cared how many passed through? Except perhaps for those responsible for cleaning and maintenance.

A little boy stumbled and scraped his knee. Clayborn rushed over and helped the little fellow up. He had his handkerchief out instantly to pad the boy's knee, a rag to mop the blood from the floor, although blood tended not to last long on these floors. "Now now, don't you fret. I used to do this for my own child—she used to scrape her knees all the time and I'd be picking her up, talking to her . . ."

The boy's parents grabbed the child and pushed him along, staring at Clayborn as if he were crazy.

Everyone was simply passing through. No one noticed. No one lingered. No one stopped to comment on the job he had just done. No one stayed behind to talk, or touch. They all rushed through these halls, disappearing into distant doors and other concourses, sometimes all too quickly for comfort.

The floor of the new concourse flickered redly once again. He thought he saw a brief spark in the shadows. The sudden explosion of a match, his daughter running, screaming, begging her daddy to put the fire out. Begging him to make it stop hurting. He closed his eyes. Maybe he should call maintenance. If there was a fire, he'd be blamed. Then he opened his eyes and gazed at the hat and scarf. A coat had joined them, one of those nice designer raincoats, like it had just floated up out of the floor. He'd definitely have to call security now.

But maybe he should wait. It didn't pay to overreact on this job. Especially if you were old. They'd give you early retirement—they were looking for any excuse. And then where would you be?

"Having some bad weather up north? Well, you won't be needing those coats much in Texas, I guess." He chatted inanely to the passersby, persisting with the small talk although no one seemed to be listening. But there was always the possibility one of them might feel comforted by it, someone too shy to answer.

At about three A.M. he heard the last of the passengers descend into the baggage claim areas below. Their stench faded from the concourse. Their echoes were absorbed by the slick, seamless walls of the passage. The moving walkways below would take them out even farther into the distant arms of the airport substructure, to where the rental vans and taxicabs ran all night, obsessively, even when there were no passengers to retrieve. A few stragglers looked over at him mopping, just to have something to look at, he supposed.

Don't bother saying hello to an old man. Don't bother to smile. Never mind that he, too, had had a destination once, a job that meant something, a family waiting for him. No more. No one wanted to listen to his stories anymore. Not his supervisors. Not his coworkers. Certainly not the endless stream of travel-dressed transients and late-night wanderers. No requests to hear about what he had seen. And what he continued to see.

The smooth tile stretched out into glistening nothingness beyond the frayed aura of his mop. He could never seem to keep the floor wet enough. It was of a peculiar material, this floor, the way it drank up the water. Like Texas sand at the end of a long drought. Watching these floors soak up the water like that always made his own mouth dry, necessitating countless and almost obsessive trips to the employee's watercooler.

But he had hours more to clean. Then a few hours sleep on the narrow bed in the rented room in the small boarding house on the edge of the airport grounds. Then back here to this place-between-places, chasing the dirt away like some medicine man.

Surfaces in the new concourse looked clean, but they were not. He cleaned everything every day, and yet he knew that no matter how much he cleaned some dirt would always permanently adhere. Even when no passengers passed here.

Clayborn could see that, out on the floor of the new concourse, a pair of gloves had joined the rest of the clothing. He really ought to call somebody. He imagined somebody running around in that new section, tearing off their clothes a piece at a time and leaving them in a pile in the middle of the passage.

That must be it. Somebody was playing a trick on him. Most of the cleaning crew was far younger than he. There had been a few older, but after one of those old-timers had been found dead after he'd cleaned a washroom mirror the rest of that shift refused to work, and the supervisors had sacked them all, replacing them with still younger men and women who had no knowledge of dirt, untutored in the history of filth and decay, their faces as smooth as the new floors.

The man who'd died was old, the supervisors said. Heart attack. It could have happened at any time. It didn't pay to get old. If he'd fallen for this little joke they would have watched him and found any excuse to fire him. The supervisors didn't want old people working for them anymore.

They didn't yet understand that if you live long enough, everything becomes old and dirty. Dirt gets in the narrowest of cracks and you never can get it all out. Live long enough and everyone you know will sicken and die. Dirt finally has a way of taking us all. After Clayborn's daughter had perished in the fire he should have expected his wife's death, but he had not. After that shock had worn off, though, he had settled into the inevitability of it all. Dirt would have its way.

Losing a child was like losing yourself. Now every month it seemed he lost someone, an old friend or relative died, and he lost another piece of himself. And nothing surprised him anymore.

Clayborn heard footsteps out in the farthest reaches of the new concourse. Probably the practical jokers, waiting to see his reaction, waiting for him to make some mistake. Or maybe Security. Security personnel at the airport had been jumpy of late, going everywhere in pairs, their eyes red and sleepless, their feet quick and stumbling. Additional patrols were scheduled seemingly without purpose. Most of the officers carried additional weaponry: a baton, a second firearm. Accidental discharges became almost commonplace. Every night Clayborn heard at least one ambulance arrive late in the evening, then speed away with a frantic siren.

All this rebuilding at the airport, planning and unplanning. People were always hoping something better would come along. Cleaner, happier passengers. Passengers with pleasant destinations in mind. Couples on their way to new marriages. Families on their way to reunions. Parents with small children, all of them travelling together, sisters and brothers seated at the banquet of time.

Beyond, the pile of clothing in the new concourse the floor

glistened wetly. But Clayborn had not mopped there. There was no point—they hadn't finished building there yet. The dark plains stretched out beyond the windows. And the floor glittered with red.

But his eyes had been giving him trouble for months. He couldn't say anything about it because he knew they'd use that as an excuse to retire him. Clayborn couldn't afford to retire. He couldn't live in his single room all day without even the presence of those who merely passed through to distract him from the memory of his daughter's screams.

The shiny floor reflected the light. The floor glistened red. And there was a smell like spoiled meat.

In the distance was the sound of hydraulics suggesting another plane arrival, but Clayborn knew there were no more flights due. The redness of the tile deepened and shimmered. A faint, harsh chorus of pneumatics sounded in the distance, but then he realized it was in fact a chorus of whispers and muted conversations.

The pile of clothing gathered itself together and began to rise. Someone was there now where there shouldn't have been anyone. He couldn't tell how tall the figure was because it seemed to be growing right out of the floor, its legs becoming longer by the moment. The figure's shoes were oblong blurs at the ends of the baggy trousers. As the figure—man or woman, how could he tell?—walked toward him, the blurs of the shoes changed shape, flattening out then bulging into mishappen growths, twisting so far sideways he expected the figure to tumble. Then suddenly it increased in height again so that he wondered if the figure might be a woman wearing extremely high heels.

The shadows at the far end of the concourse began to warp and breathe. Clayborn stared at the figure as it tried to hurry its way down the long passage. *Don't be late!* Clayborn thought anxiously, *Don't miss your flight!* and fought down a nervous giggle.

But then the figure began to slow, as if its shoes were sticking to the floor. Without thinking Clayborn moved forward to help. The lighting in the concourse changed suddenly, making the raincoat appear to soften and run. The blurred shoes sank into the floor without a trace. The redness of the tile deepened. Clayborn was now only a yard or two away from it. The raincoat fell slowly open, revealing the redness of meat, the hide removed from the body. The figure collapsed in slow motion into the floor, and shallow waves of scarlet light rushed Clayborn's way.

As the red wash of light reached his feet, Clayborn looked down and watched as viscous strings of blood wrapped themselves around the toes of his boots, crawling over his ankles and creeping up his legs as if in a desperate struggle to become flesh. He looked down the concourse and saw other figures: coats and scarves and hats of indistinguishable gender rising up out of the floor, striding forward then struggling, sinking at varying rates into the bloody floor, the cloth falling away to show musculature and circulation, red meat which liquefied as it sank beneath the tile.

Clayborn pulled away from the dripping edges of flooring, and tossed his mop to the fingers of plasma.

Always just passing through. Never saying hello. Never staying behind.

He had been wrong. Some had stayed behind. Some who had finally realized the lateness of the hour, who had destinations, families to meet them, and now refused to rest until their trips had been completed.

THE TELLTALE HEAD

Adam-Troy Castro

AT 9:23 P.M. LOCAL TIME, THE PRETTY WOMAN IN THE BRIGHT blue blazer came out to tell them that the connecting flight to Los Angeles wouldn't be taking off for at least another hour. Technical difficulties, problems with the runways, bombs set by strikers, or some such thing. It was the third such announcement, delaying a flight originally scheduled for 6:07, and though nobody took it well, only one of the passengers, one Cary Walters of Sweetwater, Texas—a pale, thirtyish man whose sparse blond hair had been plastered to his scalp by sweat—saw the scaly fanged things taking bloody bites from the woman's face. There were three of them, at the moment: they had glowing red eyes and funnel-shaped ears and razor-sharp fingernails they were using to tear the flesh from her cheeks.

According to the little rectangular badge she wore on one side of her chest, the pretty woman's name was Sandi. She probably dotted the "i" with a little circle. The little circle like a wheel, going round and round, spraying sparks like beads of sweat, hi-ho.

"Technical difficulties," she said, and Cary's fellow passengers moaned in unison. The fat man in the business suit muttered something irate; the two little kids screamed that they wanted to go home; the balding man with the walrus moustache muttered something to himself and turned the page of his Ed McBain novel. Other scaly fanged things were ripping gobs of flesh from their own faces; the same scaly fanged things that had been devouring everybody in the

269

world, for years, but which nobody but Cary could see. Blood dripped from their serrated fangs, and when they laughed, they sounded like psychotic hyenas.

Sandi—the "i" in her signature like a staring eye seeing right through him—said that refunds and travel vouchers were available to those passengers who wanted them. As she spoke, little clawed hands shot out from between her lips and dug deep into the ragged skin of her face. Another scaly fanged thing, being born.

"Do you *believe* this?" asked the balding man with the walrus moustache.

Cary did. He'd been believing it for a long time. He said, "Excuse me," which was unnecessary because he wasn't travelling with anybody who would care if he left, but came naturally anyway because he'd always been an uncommonly polite man. He said, "Excuse me," and got up to go to the bathroom, taking his overnight bag with him. It was a heavy bag, not just in terms of mere weight but also because it contained a human head. His mother's head. He'd wrapped it in aluminum foil, placed it in a brown garbage bag, placed that garbage bag in another garbage bag, and padded the sides of the overnight bag with rolled-up newspapers, but that didn't matter: he could still hear her speaking to him. She wasn't saying much of anything that made any sense, but she did keep up a long incoherent monologue, mostly consisting of demands that Cary clean up his room. He was pretty sure nobody could hear her speak except him, but he was unable to shake the fear that it would push aside all the padding and fling itself against the side of the bag with such a distinctly headlike thump that all his fellow passengers would shout, "Head!"

Despite that fear and the sounds of rending flesh so close behind him, he moved slowly and carefully, with the walk of a man who knew the ground could change shape under his feet. The men's room was right next to a candy-striped cart that when he last passed this way had been doing a brisk trade in peppermint sticks and chocolate-covered peanuts. There were no peppermint sticks or chocolate-covered peanuts there now. The scaly fanged things must have eaten them all. The red blotches on the wall behind it—blotches that kept changing shape and size the more he looked at them—must have been all that was left of that kid who'd been manning the cart. The thought of scaly fanged things burrowing under that kid's skin, till the blood ran down his white trousers in spiral patterns just like the red-and-white peppermint sticks he sold to travellers who didn't realize they caused Elephant Man's disease, brought the gorge back up Cary's throat, and he uttered a little whimper as he barrelled into the men's room looking for a place to throw up.

The men's room was a double row of five stalls apiece. An assembly line for the production of excrement, behind a double row of sinks providing another assembly line for the washing of hands. The two rows of sinks faced each other, so the mirrors above them also faced each other and reflected an infinite number of Carys, all wild-eyed, all bathed in sweat. He walked right past eight empty stalls to take one against the far wall, so he'd only have to guard against scaly fanged invaders crawling in on one side. Fortunately, the one he picked was uninhabited by scaly fanged things. He placed the overnight bag on the floor and kneeled by the toilet and pulled the lever to flush.

The water spiralled. The Coriolis effect. More circles. Just like the dot over the i in Sandi-with-an-i. Or was that "with an eye?" He opened his mouth wide, so wide he could almost feel the top of his skull zip open to reveal the soft spongy brain inside. He tried to puke. Nothing came out, not even a scaly fanged thing. He knew why, of course; they were living inside him like tapeworms, they ate everything he ate, and left him nothing *to* puke. He flushed the toilet again, to cool his sweaty face with the wind of its passing.

Somebody knocked on the door of the stall. "Hey, you okay, fella?"

"F-fine." It sounded strangled. Like there were little scaly things writhing in his throat. "Just a little sick." As if sick was fine. Did that make sense? He supposed it did. Sick was always fine as long as it was body-sick and not brain-sick. Body-sick was Mother with the cancer wasting her limbs to matchsticks and her cheeks to sunken hollows and brain-sick was Cary needing but not taking the daily medication that kept his body chemistry balanced so the scaly fanged things didn't come out and start chittering on the walls. But body-sick was body-sick and brain-sick was just plain crazy, and people could deal with body-sick but they couldn't deal with just plain crazy. He sensed the man still standing outside the door and he said, "Something I ate," and there was something hysterical about the way he said "ate," something that sounded like hate, that reminded him of the scaly fanged things and drove his nausea into high gear.

"Oughta sue the airport," advised the man who'd knocked on the stall, before clopping away to his own stall and leaving Cary alone with the swirling water and the overnight bag containing his mother's head. He oughta catch some sleep, is what he oughta. He'd been awake almost forty-eight hours now, much of the last twenty-four of them spent staring at Mother's body, after she clutched his wrist for the last time and in the depths of her own delirium said the last words she'd ever said to him, which were "Take me to heaven." He wasn't a hundred-percent sure she'd said that, at least not in so many words, especially since he hadn't been a hundred-percent sure of anything since the money had run short and they'd had to choose whose medication they were going to continue. There had been times in the last few months when he hadn't been sure if it was day or night or whether he'd remembered to eat anytime in the last week or whether it made sense for the phone to still be ringing when it had been disconnected for nonpayment a year earlier. When Mom was lucid, and not drifting in and out of coma, he relied on her to tell him these things, taking another in his steadily diminishing supply of chemical balance pills only when the words she spoke came out too foggy for him to even understand what she was saying anymore. But he was pretty sure he'd heard her correctly when she said, "Take me to heaven," because that was the sort of thing she'd been saying all along, and since she now needed his help to just get from room to room it seemed only reasonable that she'd now need his help to get to heaven, which was after all much farther. And then she heaved her last breath, and the scaly fanged things burst from her body like maggots who'd eaten everything else there was to eat, and he went crazy—well, crazier—trying to figure out how he could take her to heaven without physically dying himself, until something reminded him that Los Angeles was the City of the Angels, which wasn't exactly heaven but was after all what heaven was supposed to be, the city of angels, and though you can't fly a plane to the afterlife, this would at the very least be a start. He hoped that's what he hoped, since the one-way ticket had cost him almost all the money he and Mom had had left . . .

. . . when something chittered. The scaly fanged things, finding him. Little green hands crawling under the stall, probing at the air, looking for him, they couldn't live without tormenting him. There was a face in the bowl, grinning up at him: a malevolent carnivorous face only slightly blurred by the nauseous movement of the water. He stood (the rush of air to his head making his head spin round and round, like little wheels, or little circles, or Sandi-with-an-i, hi-ho), grabbed the overnight bag (Mom's overnight bag, the one she'd used on her one-and-only trip to Hawaii, sometime during those two years Cary was married, Cary married, Cary marry, hari-kari, hi-ho) and stumbled out to the double row of sinks to splash some water on his face. His face looked no less wet before the water than after. He looked at the infinite number of reflections of himself, extending from here to infinity, and wondered if they were all thinking the same things he was, or if some of them had their heads on right, the way his had once been, once upon a time, a long long time ago.

Then the man in the cowboy hat announced himself with an amused, "Heh," just like that, just like it was a statement in and of itself. Heh. Maybe it was. Cary turned, grateful for the chance to face something other than the mirror, saw a man dressed like one of the singing cowboys his mother had loved to watch on TV. (Roy Rogers, stuffing Trigger, using sawdust to fill the places once filled with red whinneying horseflesh. "Happy Trails," Roy's ass.) There were no scaly fanged things taking bites out of this singing cowboy. None at all. And as Cary took a step back, not sure whether this apparition was real or just his own personal reality taking another giant step into the ozone, the cowboy flashed a big broad smile with big white teeth. "Sorry I scared you, friend," he said. "I just wanted to help. I saw you had a problem, and if it's the problem I think you have, I wanted you to know I can help."

". . . help?" Cary managed.

The singing cowboy laughed gently, almost paternally, so much the adult to Cary's trembling child that for a second Cary was horribly afraid the man would call him son. "Whatever you need," he said. "You got the cash, I got the stash."

Cary's cash wasn't much of a stash, it was only fifty-seven dollars and some odd cents, pocket money really, but much more change than you'd expect to get after buying your dead mother a one-way ticket to heaven. But for what he needed it would be a bargain. And what he needed, as he saw it, was one of those little yellow caplets that he hadn't been able to afford since Mom took sick. They had a long chemical name that he'd never been able to remember, which is why he'd always privately thought of them as the Go-Away pills, since they made the scaly fanged things do just that. He said, "Sure," and he took out his wallet, and he removed the fifty-seven dollars from the wallet, and he gave it all to the cowboy hero without even asking for his prices, and the singing cowboy smiled and smoothed out the crumpled bills and placed them in his own wallet and glanced around and asked, "Anything in particular?"

Cary opened his mouth, muttered something incoherent.

"Come on, you've got to know what you want."

Cary knew exactly what he wanted. Really. The problem lay in getting his mouth to form the words. All of a sudden, everything he said now sounded like the meaningless gibberish natives chanted in jungle movies. Hummubuwa. Mubbugawa. Mummmuna mummuna. The severed head inside his overnight bag and the toothy mouths lining the singing cowboy's jacket providing accompaniment, like the backup singers in a schizophrenic's band.

The singing cowboy brightened, clearly having one of the most amazing ideas anybody had ever had. "Hey, I know." He reached into his loud jacket—literally loud, for Cary, since the pockets were all little toothy mouths babbling at him in tongues—and withdrew a little black vial of the sort used for carrying 35mm film. (Film, fill him, kill him. Hi-ho.) He opened the vial and tapped a single yellow caplet into Cary's palm. "Something special," he said. "Something new. Just got it from my L.A. supplier. Trippiest shit since acid. Hasn't even hit the street yet, but you look like a fella interested in exploring new horizons, and fuck, the way this airport is run it may be the only way you'll ever get to take off. Check it out."

The caplet was oval and stamped with little red letters, like a peanut M & M. (M & M. Meaning Mmmmmmm? Or, more likely, Mom? Maybe this was the pill that would take her to heaven. It was, after all, labelled MIRAC, as in Miracle, as in Cary Needs A Miracle, as in "You look like a fella interested in exploring new horizons." As in Heaven. As in "Check it out.")

He popped the caplet and swallowed it whole, without benefit of water, and the singing cowboy clapped him on the back and said, "Pleasure doing business with you, son," and there it was, the man calling him "son." Cary thought about what his real father, who'd skipped out on the family when Cary was fifteen, telling him he'd never amount to anything, about the pleasure Cary had taken in starting a career and proving the old man wrong, about the despair he'd felt when his mind started to go and proved dear old Dad right after all.

He felt a wave of cold, as if a window had just been opened between him and the arctic; shivering, forgetting the presence of the singing cowboy now humming and combing his hair a couple of sinks away, he bent over a sink, turned on the hot water, and let the steam rise from the basin to warm his face.

There was something wrong with the water.

It swirled around the sink in little circles, Coriolis effect, like the circles Sandi used to dot her eyes, and there were circles inside those circles, and smaller circles inside those circles, and smaller circles inside those circles, and so on and so forth an infinitely receding number of circles like the infinite number of Carys reflected in the bathroom mirrors, and it was like seeing the entire universe at once, in one eye-blink, and while Cary often saw sights like this in what passed for his everyday life, he had never seen anything this vivid. It looked real in a way nothing he'd seen in years looked real. He knew, somehow, that it had something to do with that new buzz in his head, the buzz that made him feel simultaneously very, very powerful and very, very frightened.

He turned away from the sink . . .

. . . just to see the spigot the singing cowboy was using disgorge a scaly fanged thing that immediately attached itself to to the other man's arm.

The singing cowboy cried, "Oh *shi-iii-ii-ii-iiit!"*, the catch in his throat giving the word a multitude of extra syllables, each one higher-pitched than the one before. He staggered back, his eyes bugging, his mouth opening wider than the human jaw was supposed to be able to hinge, and the scaly fanged thing coiled back and flew at his face. The attack itself was too swift to see, but it drove the singing cowboy to the ground, and once it was done the thing's jaws had widened enough to swallow the singing cowboy's head whole. As Cary watched, it flexed, drawing the singing cowboy deeper into its throat. The man stiffened with the last muscular convulsion before death, then went limp. The scaly fanged thing continued feeding, a contented look on what passed for its face.

Cary was not impressed by the attack itself; he saw and heard even more outrageous horrors every moment of his waking life, and didn't see any reason why he should consider this particular one worse than any other. What bothered him was the way this particular scaly fanged thing seemed to lack that disconcerting quality of . . .

. . . of . . .

. . . well, for lack of a better word, transparency . . .

. . . that he'd always been able to use to distinguish his visions from the reality that people without his problem could see.

The scaly fanged thing burrowed deeper into the singing cowboy's chest, with great circular slashes of its razor-sharp claws fanning sprays of blood against the tile walls. Cary's stomach made a raspberry. He turned away, looked at the mirror, saw somewhere among the legion of receding Carys one that resembled a cleaner, brighter, younger version of himself. This Cary was the Cary who'd graduated college, and held a job, and had friends, and gotten married; the Cary who had actually possessed both a life and a future, before the chemicals of his brain ran amok and started showing him menacing things in dark corners. The Cary in the mirror was actually wearing a tie—a tie he remembered as the last one he'd ever worn, the one he'd been wearing the day he freaked out at work, the one he'd been wearing when in a rare moment of lucidity he told his wife he'd realized he wasn't ever going to get any better, and that she should leave him and get herself a life while she still had a chance. The Cary in the mirror had the same begging tone in his voice as he implored his present-day counterpart, *Run! Get out now, you stupid bastard! Get yourself somewhere where there aren't any other people!*

The message penetrated. Cary grabbed the overnight bag and staggered from the bathroom into the cold cool air of the terminal, a place composed of solid lines and right angles and not bubbling shifting shapes at the corners of his vision, a place that for a change resembled the world of the days when he'd been functional and sane. He did not take comfort from the feeling. The world had always looked this way before the Go-Away pills wore off: like a place utterly devoid of scaly fanged things, as if they were really gone and not just lying in wait the way it always turned out. And as he rushed past his gate, where his fellow passengers sat forlorn and fuming waiting for the flights that for some reason were all refusing to board, he saw all around him the signs that this respite of mere seconds was now about to end: the strange darting movements at the corners of his vision, the way his overnight bag shifted in his hands, even the chittering and grumbling sounds from behind the plain white walls and the way the floor itself kept shifting like the ocean during a storm.

Somewhere behind him, somebody yelled.

Cary was tempted to call it a scream, but it wasn't quite a scream, it was too early for screams, I scream, you scream, we all scream for ice cream, *no dammit,* (this last part said in the angry but sober voice of the Cary he used to be), *focus, pay attention to what you're doing, keep an eye on the real world, if you freak out here you'll never get away and a lot of people are going to die* which made no sense to him because of course they were always dying, they were always being eaten alive by scaly fanged things, they were always having the eyes gouged from their skulls and the cheeks ripped from their—*No they weren't, you sorry bastard, listen to me, this is not business as usual,* but they never noticed, did they? No, Cary was the only one who—*LISTEN TO ME, DAMN YOU! This is something else, something's happening, something that has something to do with that hallucinogen and something to do with your fucked-up brain and something to do with the airport itself, somehow alive and WANTING something horrible to happen, I don't know what it is, I don't claim to understand it, but it feels powerful as all hell, and whatever else it's doing elsewhere it's also taking your delusions and making them pop from your head for REAL* and this new voice demanding his attention was so insistent that Cary screamed back, "Shut up shut up shut UP!"

The overnight bag hit the floor with a dull thud, and then tipped over with an even duller thud. Mom's head emitted a flurry of irate gabbles. Cary took a step back, horrified, about to shout that he was sorry, that he hadn't meant to do it, that he was just frightened, that's all, he hadn't meant to drop her like that . . .

. . . and then the screams behind him grew so loud that he had to turn to see what they were about.

It was a man. Cary recognized him as one of the people who'd been waiting with him to board that long-awaited flight to L.A.: the one he'd pegged as some kind of travelling salesman. He was staggering around by the entrance of that men's room, his arms pinwheeling as if he thought that by spinning them fast he could take off and fly away from the scaly fanged thing that had leaped out the door and ripped into his groin. Not a good idea; the newspaper he'd dropped in the first moments of the attack was already so sticky with the blood of his emasculation that the loose pages stuck to his shoes as he staggered about trying to escape the monster he'd found.

The salesman wasn't able to scream very loudly, anymore, but there were plenty of people around able to take up the slack for him: everybody close enough to see it happen or come running when they heard the screams. There must have been two dozen, all told, and they stood around him, at distances ranging from five feet to fifty, paralyzed by the conflict between the need to help and the need to turn tail and run like hell. Cary recognized several of them as ticket-holders from the same flight to L.A.: the balding man with the walrus moustache, a sixtyish woman in a flower print dress, a fat man with the bell-shaped head. And of course the rep from the airline, Sandi-with-an-i. They were all wide-eyed, all shouting, all frozen, all certain that they were next, all wholly unaware that the walls were bubbling with more scaly fanged things ready to come out.

Cary registered all of this in an instant. And even as the Cary he had been screamed from inside him, *See? See?*, he reacted in the only way he could: by leaving his overnight bag behind him and running back to help. He ran the way people run in dreams, on floors that surged up to grab him, but though they closed on his feet they couldn't stop him, they could only pull off his shoes. He ran shoeless, his arms stretched out before him to shove aside anything that might get in his way, and though there was something awfully courageous about his charge, the only soundtrack music he got to hear was not the William Tell Overture but the voice of the man he'd once been somewhere inside him screaming *No, No, NO, NO, NO!*

Cary launched himself at the scaly fanged thing, seizing it by the long wormlike tail that was the only part of it still showing through the ragged hole in the salesman's belly. The tail was smooth and hairless, almost impossible to grip, so well greased by blood and other juices that it slid right through Cary's fingers as the thing evaded Cary's grasp to seek refuge deeper in the salesman's body. The salesman took a step back, trying to fall down and die but so trapped by the agony of the moment that he was unable to. Cary moved with him, reaching in deeper, finding the scaly fanged thing, grabbing it with both hands and refusing to let go. The thing squealed and dug in deeper, toward the upper abdomen, pulling Cary in as it went: the steaming viscera tumbling down on top of him like hot sausages as he suddenly found himself elbow-deep in the last few moments in the life of a human being.

Then all he knew was white-hot pain, and he pulled out his arms, which were glistening red with blood and spotted black with other things, and there was something wrong with his left hand, and he scrambled back, the salesman's intestines falling off him in coils. The salesman threw his head back and geysered forth a fountain of blood before his jaws pried apart and the scaly fanged thing emerged from his mouth with three of Cary's fingers clutched between its teeth.

Oh, you've done it now, moaned the Cary that had been, *you're hurt, you're involved, they'll never let you out of here.* Not that he could run even if he wanted to; there were altogether too many other people doing that. Just about everybody in sight, all the folks willing to endure delay after delay just so they could get to Los Angeles had suddenly decided to cancel the trip and were instead hauling ass by the dozens. Most were running in the direction of the main terminal but some seemed to have trouble remembering where it was and one or two were just running around in circles as if looking for the sane world they'd misplaced on this spot only a couple of seconds earlier. Only three remained just where they were: Cary, who still lay on the floor at the salesman's feet, wondering just when the hell the man's legs would get the message that he was dead . . . the balding man with the moustache, who remained frozen, goggle-eyed, unable to understand what was happening . . . and Sandi-with-an-i, who was frantically opening a little glass door in the wall.

The salesman sank to his knees, but otherwise remained upright.

The scaly fanged thing spat out Cary's fingers, one at a time—ptoi, ptoi, ptoi, like that—licked its great bulbous chops, and lazily looked about for somebody else to kill. It glanced at the balding man with the moustache, evidently decided naaah, not him, not yet . . . made eye contact with Cary, made the expression of a gourmet who'd already tasted something and found it wanting . . . and then leaped at Sandi-with-an-i. But Sandi-with-an-i had more than an "i," she had a fire extinguisher already inverted and aimed, and as the scaly fanged thing leaped the few short feet separating them she gave the bastard a solid blast in what passed for its face. Its shriek and hers were wholly identical. Clouds of white smoke billowed around the two, like dry ice at a disco, turning her and the scaly fanged thing into silhouettes joined together in a sort of distorted dance

(Sandi's dance with ants in her pants won't enhance her survival chance, hi-ho).

Cary realized he was standing up. That was surprising. He didn't remember standing up. He remembered being sprawled across the floor wearing more of the salesman's innards than his own clothes, pressing his mutilated left hand under his right arm to contain the bleeding, but he didn't remember standing up. Something seemed awfully wrong about that. If somebody started doing things like sitting down and standing up without consciously deciding to, who knew what kind of trouble he could get into? He—

Goddamn it you crazy bastard get it together NOW!

And the sound of his past self cursing at him was like a bucket of cold water being splashed in his face and it made the world snap back into sharp focus for just a second and that was just enough time for him to see the hundreds of other scaly fanged things just beginning to coalesce at the corners of his vision, under the seats and behind the picture windows and behind the ferns and on the wall just behind the place where the balding man with the moustache stood still paralyzed trying to get his legs to move for Chrissake MOVE.

Cary concentrated very, very hard on making the scaly fanged things GO AWAY.

The mist cleared. Sandi-with-an-i was still holding the fire extinguisher, and for a second it looked like everything was going to be all right, because the scaly fanged thing wasn't on top of her flaying the skin from her bones. In fact, it wasn't anywhere to be seen. She wasn't dead, not even hurt. The flecks of blood dotting her pretty face like the little circles over the i in her name weren't hers, but splatter marks from the death of a salesman.

(Death of a Salesman, heh, that was a good one, Cary couldn't remember anything even remotely like this ever happening to Willy Loman, though the unusual angst— "What happened in Boston, Willy?", "Well, a ravenous monster escaped from the head of a crazy man burrowed into my body through my crotch"—would have certainly enlivened the play, hi-ho.)

The walls began to bulge again. The indistinct voices inside his head began to gabble again. Cary felt the floor beneath him curve upward around him, all pink and translucent like the world glimpsed through the inside of a tulip. Sandi-with-an-i and the balding man with the moustache shouted as the sudden change of architecture engulfed them. Cary bit his tongue hard enough to draw blood, forced himself to concentrate on the pain and nothing else, again restoring the world to what it should have been.

The balding man with the moustache asked, "Is it gone?", in the absurdly conversational tone he might have used to ask whether it was going to rain.

"I don't know," said Sandi-with-an-i, her tone that of a woman on the wrong side of hysteria.

Cary felt weakness oozing through his body in waves, from blood loss he supposed, which was good, which was definitely good, if he passed out he wouldn't be thinking of, thinking of, well, the things he shouldn't be thinking of, just concentrate instead on the crisis being over, on getting past this rough spot and going back to the relative sanity of a world where his dead mother could jabber at him from inside her shroud of Reynold's Wrap and her coffin of American Tourister.

The balding man with the moustache said, "Jesus."

After a pause, Sandi-with-an-i said, "Oh no."

And it was too much to expect that Cary actually keep his eyes closed with that much provocation to open them, so he opened them, and saw both Sandi-with-an-i and the balding man with the moustache facing his direction, but not looking at him, looking past him, behind him, at something that clearly astonished them both.

Cary did not want to turn around to see what they saw.

He looked anyway. The remains of his overnight bag now looked like a cannon had gone off inside it. The cannonball, Mom's head, sat about twenty feet away, the garbage bags shredded into confetti on the floor around it. The aluminum foil was still intact, but carefully peeled back to reveal her pale white face, which steamed oddly, like a baked potato that was now done. As Cary watched, she opened her mouth, and spit out a stream of angry gibberish. He reeled. His control shattered, and half a dozen scaly fanged things clawed through the tile floor around her.

The salt-and-pepper pair of cops running up the corridor

behind her wore the expressions of men who sincerely wished they could get their legs to stop.

"This is major league fucked," the balding man announced unhelpfully.

And as if things weren't bad enough, Sandi-with-an-i chose that moment to start screaming again.

Cary whirled and saw why: the scaly fanged thing she'd been fighting had just made its reappearance, clutching the fire extinguisher that was still in her hands. Its claws were so firmly embedded in the metal cannister that it couldn't release itself to go for an immediate leap at her throat, but its face, bobbing at the end of an absurdly elongated neck, leered at her from a distance of two inches. Sandi-with-an-i hurled the extinguisher away from her with all her strength, crushing the scaly fanged thing between it and the wall. Blood spattered, making a purple Rorschach pattern that even as he watched resolved itself into the symmetrical shape of a butterfly.

Cary's Mom jabbered something approving.

The balding man with the moustache stiffened, stumbled back against the wall, and simply came apart, that's all, the six or seven scaly fanged things coming to life inside him burrowing from his flesh to join Cary in the more-or-less real world.

The salt-and-pepper cops arrived, their guns drawn, their faces aghast at the sheer number of scaly fanged things bursting from the walls and floors and ceiling, and though the cops were armed, there were hundreds of the bastards, thousands, more than could be counted, more than the stars, and they were all laughing like hyenas, and there was nothing that could be done against them except . . .

. . . except.

. . . except, except, except.

All at once Cary knew the *except,* and it was such an elegant *except* that his heart leaped from the simplicity of it.

The white cop fell to the floor noisily, his feet severed from his legs by the claws of the scaly fanged things that had just emerged from the floor beside him. The black cop fired his revolver at nothing in particular, his shout a futile attempt to drown out the noise of his approaching death. Cary's Mom rolled a little closer, gabbling something about a promise to escort her to heaven. Sandi-with-an-i, the i dotted with a circle, pressed herself flat against the wall, eyes tightly shut, to block out the sight of the scaly fanged things surrounding her on all sides.

Except. Hi-ho.

Cary sat on crossed legs, in the blood of the butchered salesman, and extended his arms.

"Come back," he said.

The fanged scaly things froze.

"Come back," he said, and wherever they were, whatever they were doing, the scaly fanged things turned toward him and saw in him the diseased brain that had given them birth.

"Come back," he said, and they came back: first one or two of the bravest, then a dozen followers, then, with increasing eagerness, all of them. They dropped from the ceiling and burst from the walls and hopped over the furniture and converged on him, the center of their universe, the place that had conceived them.

"Come back," he said, and the closest one among them drew its claws and punched a hole in the center of Cary's forehead, a hole that it immediately dove through head first, its reptilian feet squirming as it struggled to get in all the way despite the tight fit. The one behind it chose a different entrance, forcing Cary's jaw past the breaking point, then squirming in through the mouth, shattering his teeth along the way. After that they came in waves, so tightly packed that the weaker ones were crushed to liquid as the bulk of them forced their little bodies through the few available holes. The tunnels they dug through his eyes and ears rendered him both deaf and blind, and the pain of his overstuffed skull expanding to accommodate them destroyed what little remained of his sanity. He was incapable of thinking anything, feeling anything, except for that one thought repeated over and over and over again: the one thought he needed to think, which was, "Come back."

They kept coming. His head kept inflating, taking on the look of a canvas bag stuffed with wild cats. His skin rippled and bulged from the violence of the scaly fanged things fighting for dominance inside him. Every once in a while it bulged with the shape of one of their faces, trying to chew its way out; then smoothed over, and bulged again, in the shape of an arm, or a leg, or a claw, pinned against the inside of Cary's skull.

They filled him up, and they kept coming, and as the sides of his head encountered the ceiling and the walls, they flattened out like a liquid, to conform with the shape of their container. The growth had to continue laterally, down the corridor, flowing over the benches and the water fountains and the newsstands and the cylindrical silver ashtrays to continue its inexorable advance on both the main terminal and the greater world beyond. The windows of the boarding area exploded outward in a rain of shattered glass. The flesh pressed against them bubbled outward and continued to expand. The millions of scaly fanged things emerging from the ground everywhere from here to the horizon started swarming in Cary's direction in waves.

He was only dimly aware that both the black cop and Sandi-with-an-i, the i in her name dotted with a little circle, had both been pinned against the nearest wall by the explosive growth . . . and that they were both messily (and, by this time, gratefully) suffocating. It didn't matter. What mattered was that cacophony of little gibbering voices was finally making sense to him: they, too, wanted Cary to take them to heaven.

Something heavy dropped by a scaly fanged thing landed in his lap; he had to explore it with his fingertips to determine what it was. His finger brushed aluminum foil. Of course. They didn't want Mom to be left behind when he finally took off.

He wondered how long it would be before they finished boarding.

PIRANHA

Stephen M. Rainey

THE MAN WHO HAD KILLED RAMON ESCALERA'S BROTHER STOOD six-foot-five in a skeletal frame, with sunken eyes and hollow cheeks that gave him a distinctly corpse-like appearance. Thin, greasy black hair swept back from a tall forehead that might have insinuated wisdom if the face were not so cruel. A jagged scar like a bolt of white lightning arced across the right cheekbone to the bridge of the aquiline nose. The one incongruous feature was his mouth: a small, pouting "O" with dark red, feminine lips, always slick and wet-looking, hiding a row of tiny, pearl-hued teeth; no doubt it was this mouth that had earned him the dubious epithet "Piranha."

The mouth of a cocksucker, not a killer.

Jack Crutchfield emerged from his hotel room with the squat, waddling Frank Mundy in tow like a cowed mongrel. The tall man's deep-set but glittering eyes scanned the hallway, falling briefly on Escalera at the water fountain, then moving on. He started toward the elevator, Mundy following faithfully, ignoring the young man stooping to take a drink. The killer had no reason to suspect or even recognize Ramon Escalera. As the tall, stiff-looking figure passed, Escalera caught a strong whiff of musky cologne. The pudgy Mundy, however, reeked of a week's worth of sweat and cigarettes, unrelieved by so much as a single bath.

Crutchfield pressed the elevator button and stood back to wait with his arms crossed in relaxed fashion, eyes dropping briefly to regard his companion with obvious distaste. Mundy fiddled nervously with his wide, flowered tie, oblivious to his boss's expression of contempt. Escalera rose from the water fountain and strolled nonchalantly toward the pair, pulling a handkerchief from his pocket and wiping his mouth gingerly. He wore an ivory-colored suit, the jacket of which concealed a snub-nosed .38 revolver, his appearance that of a well-to-do Mexican businessman, perhaps newly arrived from Mexico City. The air-conditioning in the Dry Plains Hilton wasn't the best, and he was hot even in the lightweight outfit. Discreetly, he mopped his brow with the handkerchief, not wishing to betray the slightest hint of nervousness as he approached the waiting pair.

He *was* nervous. While his brother might have been ruthless, Ramon had never even contemplated killing a man before. But in his time Jack Crutchfield must have escorted countless numbers to their appointments with El Dios, without hesitation or remorse. Escalera must respond in like fashion, for the skeletal white man deserved to receive nothing more or less than what he had given.

The elevator doors opened, and the three men stepped into the dimly-lit cubicle without acknowledging each other's presence. Neither Crutchfield nor Mundy carried a briefcase, so they were not likely heading to a business meeting. It was almost 5:30; chances were, they meant to dine in the hotel restaurant before meeting whatever contacts were on tonight's agenda. Pity, they would not be able to keep their appointments.

At that moment, a sharp "Wait, please!" echoed through the hall, and a bulldog-like figure scurried toward the elevator, just as the doors began to close. Crutchfield very kindly held them open and smiled at Philippé, who stumbled inside bowing his head effusively. "Gracias, señor. Thank you." Crutchfield nodded politely in return, then punched "L" on the control board. The doors closed and the elevator descended.

Escalera did not look at his partner, but kept his eyes on the illuminated numerals above the doors. Philippé was not so nicely dressed, and his long hair was unkempt; they would appear as strangers to the unsuspecting Americans. Still, Crutchfield would be by nature wary, and one must not underestimate his wile. Escalera was tempted to make use of his blade right now—he preferred it to the gun for obvious reasons—but it would not do to step out of the elevator in front of witnesses with a pair of dead men on the floor. No, he and Philippé would wait for the right moment, which might come in the next few minutes, or later, when the drug dealers left the hotel, as they inevitably must. Patience was the key.

When they reached the lobby, Escalera found it even hotter, for the front doors were constantly opening and closing for guests on their way to and from the airport terminal, just across the wide access boulevard. But the body odor of Frank Mundy had become stifling in the cramped elevator, and at least the hot air of the lobby smelled of nothing more offensive than jet fuel. Crutchfield and his man turned right and, as Escalera had anticipated, made their way toward the restaurant at the rear of the building. He followed at a reasonable distance, while Philippé headed for the gift shop, where he would browse with eyes alert for his partner's signal to move.

The hostess greeted the Americans at the door and led them to a table near the windows. Escalera sat down at a barstool and ordered a Dos Equis beer. From here, he could see the pair quite adequately, while remaining in virtual shadow. His mind whirred with his plotting, constructing and evaluating scenarios, assuring him that he would be able to seize and utilize the right opportunity once it presented itself.

His beer arrived, and the bartender took his money with a lingering gaze. *Damn it!* he thought. He needed to remain invisible, and the last thing he wanted was to appear the least bit suspicious to a potential witness.

The bartender gave him change, still staring. After a moment, the young man said softly, "You have haunted eyes."

Escalera regarded him with restrained hostility. The bartender had shiny black hair, sun-darkened skin, and slightly almond-shaped eyes. Of Indian origin, but not pureblood. He was White American from many generations back. "I lost a brother," Escalera said softly.

"I'm sorry," said the bartender with a slightly abashed nod. "I sensed a troubled spirit. One sees many of them in my position."

"Yeah, I'm sure."

"What happened to him?"

Escalera took a hard swallow from the bottle. "His heart."
The barman shook his head regretfully. "You were close?"

"Once, we were."

With another lingering, sorrowful look, the bartender stepped away to wait on another patron. Escalera surreptitiously eyed his marks, who were ordering their dinner. He glanced around at the restaurant, taking note of the kitchen entrance, the rest rooms, the windows. Except for Crutchfield's, all the booths along the windows were empty; it was still early for dinner.

The waitress left the Piranha and his partner to sip their margueritas. Escalera hated the way Crutchfield's tiny lips parted and his pink tongue licked the salt around the rim of the glass. The gringo hardly even looked human. No, he was a filthy predator, fit only to be slaughtered, like a rabid animal.

It wasn't that Ramon had approved of his brother's chosen trade—dealing cocaine and heroin in the barrios of Mexico and L.A.—but Enriqué had not deserved to be ignominiously butchered by Crutchfield as a matter of "business." Crutchfield thought of himself as a big-time mobster, a man of great position and respect; in truth, he was just a white-collar hoodlum, a second-rate appendage of the much bigger South American drug lords, who at the first slip would cut him off as flippantly as he'd cut Enriqué. In time, no doubt, he *would* slip, and his bosses would rid themselves of him, with far less risk to their skins than Escalera was assuming for his own.

But he could not wait for such an event. His brother must be avenged, and by his own hand. Before his death, Enriqué had begun to wise up, had seen the end of the road he'd been running for the last five years. He'd wanted out. He could never undo the harm he'd done or repay the people he'd hurt—and yes, even killed—but the important thing was that he had changed. He was ready to break all his connections and move away, without so much as a whisper against his former employers. Yet Crutchfield had been unable to accept the possibility of Enriqué confiding in the law at any future time, so he'd dispatched the younger Escalera by carving out his heart and stuffing the hole in his chest with his severed testicles.

An example to others. A warning.

And now that man sat in a booth a couple of dozen yards away, comfortably sipping a drink in a hotel restaurant. He'd been fingered by Philippé Enfantino, once a good friend of Enriqué's who'd done some small-time dope-running several years back. He knew about Crutchfield, though the mobster had never known him, which worked distinctly to his advantage. Together, he and Escalera had made enough contacts to learn that the American would be making a run to Colombia after handling some business in Dry Plains. They'd driven here from their home in El Paso, intending to make their own appointment with Crutchfield.

Escalera saw the toad Mundy rise from his seat and make his way toward the rest room. The whole side of the restaurant where Crutchfield sat now appeared empty; no servers, no other patrons, and Escalera's heart kicked into overdrive, his instincts screaming that this was the moment. He peered at the rest room door after Mundy, barely able to believe what was happening inside him. He tried to think above the rush of blood in his head. His hand slid into his jacket pocket, touched the cold steel of his blade.

No, it was not yet Crutchfield's time. But it was getting late for him. Very late.

Escalera stood up, and slowly began walking toward the men's room, forcing his rubbery legs to remain steady. He glanced back at Crutchfield, knowing that he had to move quickly. The knife found its way into his grip.

Entering, he happily saw that no one besides Mundy occupied the rest room. The toad stood in front of a urinal, relieving himself, paying no attention to the new arrival. Forcing himself not to hesitate, Escalera lifted the blade in his right hand and suddenly lunged forward, aiming at the exposed nape of Mundy's neck, just above the collar. Steel bit into flesh, cutting through muscle and sliding between vertebrae, squirting hot blood over Escalera's hand. Without even a hiss of breath, Mundy jerked once, and went rigid as Escalera slid his left arm around the man's neck. He twisted the shaft, and felt the cylinders of bone momentarily separate, allowing the steel to sever the spinal cord. Mundy's rank-smelling body relaxed and tottered backward, kept from falling by Escalera's supporting arm. A final jet of piss sprayed the urinal as thick, red wetness spilled over Escalera's right wrist.

He hurriedly pulled Mundy into the nearest stall, awkwardly maneuvering the heavy body onto the toilet seat. The toad slumped forward, nearly toppling over, but Escalera pushed the torso up and back, so that the body rested against the top of the fixture. Satisfied that the dead man would not slip from his seat, he jerked the knife from the corpse's neck, wiped it clean with his handkerchief, then stuffed it forcefully into the open fly of the toad's trousers.

He locked the stall door, and carefully slid under the partition, taking care not to upset the body as he propelled himself with his feet. He stood in front of the mirror, breathing heavily, trying not to hyperventilate, then washed his hands thoroughly, disturbed to find that a large red blob stained his right cuff. And his jacket was streaked with grime from the stall floor. With a frustrated hiss, he pulled the jacket off, which was heavy with the weight of his gun. His pants had also gotten dirty, but at least he couldn't see any telltale red stains. He ran a comb through his hair, took a last look at the floor to make sure he hadn't left any blood.

He hadn't. Draping the jacket over his arm, he appeared respectable enough, certainly nothing like the killer he'd now become.

It had been so easy. He'd had no idea what it would be like, how much force it would take to drive a knife into a man's body, how much blood would spill from the wound. It had been so quick, and relatively clean. *So damn easy!*

And he'd left Crutchfield a warning.

No. A foreshadowing.

He quickly left the rest room and hurried toward the restaurant entrance, trying to appear relaxed, glancing at his watch to rationalize his rush. As he approached the door, the hostess's eyes fell upon him, face all smiles, wishing him all her best.

"Thank you, sir, and have a good evening."

"You too," he said, smiling as naturally as possible. Still, the skin of his cheeks felt tight and hot. He nodded politely, then moved toward the door. Perhaps later there would be remorse. Not now.

Then his blood froze, for behind him, a familiar voice called, "Oh, sir! Just a minute!"

Keep going.

No. If he did, he would immediately arouse suspicion. Stiffly, he turned, trying to maintain his smile.

The bartender gave him a little wave. "My condolences on your loss. I hope your spirit will find comfort."

"Thanks," Escalera mumbled. "Thanks so much." He turned back to the entrance, but not before catching a glimpse of Crutchfield casting a concerned eye at the men's room door.

Something between terror and elation roared through his veins as he returned to the hotel lobby. Within minutes, he would learn his adversary's reaction. His instincts had led him to gamble that, once Crutchfield found his partner dead, he'd try to leave the hotel at once, without involving any police. A man in his position could not afford to have even a passing association with the law. No, he'd be frightened, abort his mission, and in his initial shock, leave himself vulnerable.

Philippé sat on a bench near the concierge's desk, reading a magazine. He looked up as Escalera approached, then appeared to return to his reading. Escalera casually leaned against the pillar close behind him.

"Mundy is dead."

"And the man?"

"Get upstairs and wait for him. He'll go to his room first. The only other way out is through the kitchen, and he won't draw attention to himself."

Philippé closed his magazine and stood up, heading for the elevator. He patted his trouser pocket to indicate the slight bulge there. "You're sure of this?"

Escalera glanced back. As yet, no sign of Crutchfield approaching from the restaurant. "He'll have valuables in his room that he cannot abandon. I'll come up in the car after him. Or if he does decide just to split, I'll have him in sight."

The doors opened and Philippé disappeared. Escalera remained behind the pillar, out of direct line of sight from the restaurant entrance. The concierge noticed him and asked if he needed any assistance, but he said, "I'm just waiting for a friend." The young clerk nodded and returned to his chore of filling out baggage tickets.

Then, the tall, skeletal figure came out of the hallway from the restaurant, his face pale, eyes darting around the lobby, obviously aware that he was danger. Expecting him to go straight for the elevator, Escalera was surprised when Crutchfield approached the concierge and said, "I'm going to need some help with my bags. Can you send a porter up with me? I'm on fifteen."

"Of course, sir."

With a silent curse, Escalera scooted out from behind the pillar, where he would be seen when Crutchfield turned around. He should have counted on the man to remain sharp. He wasn't going to go up to his room alone, where an assailant would most likely attempt to move on him. It would probably be some time before Mundy's body was discovered. Crutchfield would want to get out of town quickly, for indeed he would be the prime suspect in the murder. He had rented a car at the airport, Escalera knew, and it was parked in the hotel garage. He might try taking the car and running, or possibly grab the first taxi he could find. Even more likely, he would go straight to the airport and book himself on a flight back to L.A., where he'd be on safe, familiar turf. He'd have to be stopped before he could gain safe passage out of Dry Plains.

When the elevator doors opened, Crutchfield boarded, followed by a porter pulling an empty baggage cart. The moment the car left, Escalera punched the call button and waited for the next elevator to take him up, knowing he'd have to take extra care not to be seen. Philippé would be at the door of their own room, keeping watch, so at least the Piranha wouldn't be out of their sight except while he was en route between floors.

When the elevator arrived at fifteen with an annoying "ding," Escalera stepped out with assurance, wishing to convey no furtiveness should anyone be waiting in the hall.

To his relief, the corridor was empty, but the baggage cart stood in view just outside of Crutchfield's door, midway down the corridor. Two suitcases had already been loaded on it.

He began walking slowly toward the open door, knowing Philippé would be watching from the peephole of his room just behind him. He slowed down as he approached, and at that moment, the porter stepped into the hallway, carrying another pair of bags, which he placed on the cart. Crutchfield then appeared at the door, and Escalera walked past without breaking stride, utterly ignoring the suspicious glare from the American's beady eyes. He was just a Mexican businessman returning to his room after a couple of drinks.

He rounded the corner and drew to a halt, turning to peer back in the direction from which he'd come. Crutchfield and the porter were heading toward the elevator, cart wheels squeaking piercingly. Suddenly, at the far end of the hall, Philippé emerged from his room and began stalking toward them with a purposeful glare. "Goddamn!" he shouted, and Escalera's heart leapt. "There's a fucking rat in this room. You!" He pointed to young porter, who stared back with an expression of disbelief. "Come here right now! What's the goddamn idea, a rat in my room?"

The porter glanced up at Crutchfield apologetically, unsure how to react. He called to Philippé, "Sir, I'm assisting this gentleman just now. I'll be happy to help you in just a few minutes. If you'd like, I'll notify the manager and he'll be right up."

"The hell with that. You come here. Right now!"

"I cannot leave a guest I'm helping, that's hotel regulations, sir. But I will get the manager up here immediately."

Crutchfield glanced toward Escalera's concealed position, aware now that he'd been set up. Philippé was almost upon them, eyes set on the porter, making no sign that he was a threat to the hotel guest. Escalera feared Crutchfield might grab the porter and use him as a hostage, but then, his assailants were not police. Still, neither Philippé nor Escalera wanted innocent blood on their hands.

"You come and take my bags right now," Philippé said in

a venomous tone. "And I do not expect to receive a bill. What kind of place is this to have rats in the rooms?"

"Sir, please. Let me finish assisting this gentleman, and the hotel will be more than happy to make amends."

Crutchfield's right hand moved toward the inside breast of his jacket. His sunken eyes were wide with apprehension; he could not likely take out both of his adversaries without being killed himself. But then, with a swift movement, he spun and shoved the porter into the wall, grabbing the baggage cart and ramming it straight into Philippé's stomach. Caught by surprise, he went down with a yell, as the cart toppled over, spilling suitcases to the floor. Escalera, gun in hand, leaped around the corner and broke into a run, as Crutchfield sped down the hall toward the stairway. Escalera did not slow to assist his partner, knowing he could not let his quarry escape. But glancing back, he was gratified to see Philippé pulling himself to his feet and hurrying after him, though obviously with a considerable degree of pain. The porter, winded, and aware that he was in a deadly situation, lay prostrate on the floor with his hands over his head.

Smart man. And one not likely to be able to identify the attackers.

Crutchfield rounded the corner to the western wing at surprising speed, the pursuers dogging his heels. A small gun, probably a beretta, appeared in his hand, but at the moment, outgunned, he was intent on escaping. The stairwell lay at the far end of the corridor, twenty or so yards ahead. If he got there and began making his way down, they'd have a hard time getting a bead on him. From behind, Escalera heard Philippé cry, "Ramon, move!" He sidestepped as the stout young man went down on one knee, arm raised, glittering blade catching the fluorescent light from the ceiling fixtures. In a flash, the dagger went spinning through space toward Crutchfield, and a split second later came a sharp screech as the weapon found its mark. The handle of the knife protruded from Crutchfield's right shoulder, and the tall man staggered, but did not go down. Escalera saw the beretta come up and point in his direction, and he dropped, burning his elbows on the carpet. A second later, the report shattered the silence of the corridor, and Escalera braced himself to take a bullet.

But it never came. Instead, he heard a low grunt from Philippé, and saw his partner pitch forward and fall face-first to the floor. His nose struck the floor with an ugly crunch, and a gout of blood splattered the floor around his head.

"Oh, God, Philippé!" he cried, but knew he could not help him. Crutchfield had done it now, using his gun, which Escalera had hoped to prevent. Everything was coming apart. Philippé must surely be dead!

Crutchfield shoved the door open and hurled himself through, miraculously remaining on his feet. But Philippé's dagger had done its work, and Escalera heard a crash and a loud cry as the wounded man fell on the stairs. He thought he heard the metallic clatter of a gun striking iron somewhere below.

Picking himself up, he tore down the hall to the stairwell door, leading with his .38. He threw the door open, and saw an abstract, crimson swath leading from the landing down the first flight of stairs. He heard a movement just below, and hugged the wall, in case Crutchfield still possessed his gun. The sound of tortured breathing reverberated up through the stairwell. It was time to end this horror; if he had to use his gun, so be it. He would pay the consequences. Justice would be served, one way or another.

He took a deep breath and started down the stairs. Unsteady shuffling came from the landing just beneath him, and he thought he heard a hoarse cry as Crutchfield realized how close his pursuer was. The scrambling below became more frantic.

The Piranha was probably trying to reach his gun. Escalera bounded down several steps at a time, grabbing the rail at the landing to assist his pivot down the next flight. There . . . there he was! Halfway down the stairs, on his knees, clutching the railing to keep from falling headlong. The knife handle still jutted from his shoulder, where a large dark stain spread like blotted ink. Escalera aimed his gun directly between the beady, terrified eyes.

"Why are you doing this?" Crutchfield groaned, raising his hands as if to ward away the bullet.

"Because you took my brother's heart, and still you have none."

The man shook his head. "I don't know what you're talking about."

"You son of a bitch. You don't even remember the men you kill. I am Ramon Escalera. Does the name mean anything to you?"

It took several seconds for understanding to register in Crutchfield's face. "Enriqué Escalera. So you're a grieving sibling. Don't you know your brother deserved what he got?"

Escalera leaped the last few steps and planted a solid kick into Crutchfield's chest. The bony figure screamed in agony and pitched onto the next landing, curling into a fetal position, rolling back and forth as if to escape his pain. Blood spilled anew from the knife wound.

"Bastard. You butchered him. And now I am going to butcher you."

The skeleton's eyes widened as the foot drew back to kick him again, then his jaw dropped in a silent scream as the blow drove the breath from his lungs. Then Escalera pocketed his gun, reached down and jerked the knife from the ruined shoulder, to the accompaniment of a weak gasp.

He knelt and gazed directly into Crutchfield's pain-reddened eyes. "I want you to know this isn't business. It's personal. And it's a pity I cannot make this last longer." With that, he waved the dripping blade in front the Piranha's face, slowly, deliberately. Then, when he was sure Crutchfield could not mistake what was coming, he thrust the knife directly into the gaping, fish-like mouth, forcing it up through the upper palate into the nasal cavity. The man's head jerked back, and blood spewed through his flared nostrils. Escalera gave the handle a final push, and the blade dug deeper, finding the brain, perforating it. Crutchfield died too quickly, flopping onto his back with legs twitching, eyes bulging from the sunken sockets. A crimson flood washed over the floor from the open shoulder wound.

Escalera stood up, completely numb, not sure whether or not to believe what his eyes saw on the landing before him. Compared to this, the killing of Frank Mundy was a fiesta. This was the real thing: a horrible bloodbath which he himself had wrought, so vicious and calculated that he must deny that he was its instrument; deny it or go mad. Could he really have done this? *This?*

Upstairs, Philippé lay dead or dying. A shocked porter might at this very moment be notifying the police. No telling how many guests had heard the shot that Crutchfield had fired. Probably by the time Escalera could reach the ground floor, the hotel would be sealed. But Philippé! He could not abandon the young man who'd helped him and followed him with such faith.

With a superhuman effort, he tore his eyes away from the dead thing on the floor, and rushed back up the stairs to fifteen. Tugging on the door handle, he found to his surprise that it was securely locked. What the hell? What if all the doors were locked from the other side? There would be no hope for him. He hurried down to fourteen, checked the door. Also locked! What good was this stairway if you couldn't get from one floor to another?

He descended another flight, to the landing where Crutchfield's body lay, still twitching slightly. He averted his eyes, and hoping against hope, tugged on the door handle. It wouldn't budge. "Shit!" he moaned, trying to keep himself from staring at the body. This was the landing for the thirteenth floor, he realized, seeing the stencilled numerals on the metal door. The hotel had not skipped numbering that floor, as most did.

Unless he found a way out of the stairwell, he was destined to be apprehended. Very soon, the police would be swarming through the building.

"So be it," he said. He deserved to pay for this act he had committed. He would pay in a court of law, probably be jailed for the rest of his life, if not executed. But he had considered all this before. His brother was avenged. What came after made no difference.

So he'd told himself.

He took off again, propelled by the fear that had begun to gnaw at his numbness. Eleven. Ten. All the doors locked. By the time he reached seven, he was winded. His gut ached, and he had to slow down, grasp the railing for support. Taking a few deep breaths, he forced himself onward. Every wasted second increased his chances of being caught. Only now that the possibility had become so real, he realized how much he valued his freedom.

His footsteps echoed endlessly in the shaft. Looking down into the rectangular space between the flights, he saw only darkness, as if the stairwell descended into infinity. Above . . . the same. Panic fired his blood and despite his fatigue he began running in earnest, hurtling down the stairs like a terrified rabbit. Four . . . three . . . two . . . he stopped at the first floor, looking over the rail to find that the stairs still continued far below. How many sub-basements could this building have? He reached for the door handle, and not unexpectedly, found it sealed tight. But his heart sank; how could he get out of here? Would he have to beat on doors until somebody opened one for him—probably a cop?

He looked down again, then up. The stairwell was endless, in both directions. Cold chills began to shake him, for this was a nightmare! He had to get out of here. Resolving to push on, he began trudging downward, into the basement levels. The doors were no longer marked with numbers, and all remained locked.

And below, the staircase extended on and on.

"Bullshit! This is bullshit!" he cried. Then, in desperation, he remembered his gun, hiding in his back pocket. He drew it, aimed it at the doorhandle of what had to be the fourth sub-basement. His thumb drew back the hammer. And he pulled the trigger.

The blast was like the concussion of a grenade in the enclosed chamber. His eardrums must have shattered, for the sudden pain in his head was almost unendurable. Sharp, ringing tones filled his brain, sending pain down his neck and into his shoulders. And when the smoke cleared, and his aching eyes saw that the doorhandle remained undamaged, Escalera screamed.

He dropped to his knees and wept. This was madness; his mind could not accept the murders he'd committed. But no . . . this *was* real! The solid weight of the gun in his hand, the ringing in his ears. The blood on his hands.

When the sounds in his head began to clear, he started down the steps again. He could barely breathe, and a cramp in his abdomen almost doubled him over. But the stairs went on, ever downward, with no sign of an end. What if he went back up? He'd go to the lobby floor and beat on the door until someone opened it, even if the entire Dry Plains police force waited on the other side. He had to go back. Now.

He turned and gazed upward. My God, it was so far. How long had he been running? He'd never make it, not in this condition.

Then he heard something moving above him. The softest of shuffling sounds . . . perhaps a hiss of breath. Had someone else entered the stairwell, come looking for him? He leaned over the railing and peered upward, almost expecting to see a blue-suited police officer leaning down to look at him.

What he saw caused his knees to buckle, and he tumbled to the floor with a hiss of pain. But panic sent him flying down the stairs again, blindly, his mind rebelling. *No! It wasn't there! It wasn't there!*

A low whisper drifted down to him, indistinct syllables like someone mumbling in his sleep. Slowing again, he could not prevent himself from looking up, to give his eyes a chance to prove they'd lied to him.

No. There it was, drifting through the rectangular gap between the ascending and descending flights, closing steadily on him. A dark, shadowy shape, like some kind of huge fish swimming through the air.

He screamed, and broke into a final, agonized retreat down the never-ending staircase, into the layers of shadow that seemed to rise up to greet him. Above and behind, the pursuing thing gained on him, its whispery voice calling out nonsensical supplications. The voice began to rise, louder and louder, until it sounded like a freight train approaching through a tunnel.

No . . . his mind must have completely snapped. He could *not* be alone in this darkening shaft with that fast-approaching shape . . . the floating shape with sunken, beady eyes . . . and its mouth! The wet red lips, those pearly, shining teeth . . .

SOUL CATCHER

Wendy Webb

THE LITTLE BOY, CAUGHT IN THE AMOEBA-LIKE MOVEMENT OF A
mass of angry deplaning passengers, hitched up his leather
backpack in the shape of a bear that threatened to slip from
his shoulder, and fought to keep up with the great strides of
the grown-ups as they hustled across the runway to the
airport.

Heat waves vibrated, danced, and stretched lazy oscilla-
tions of air high into the sky where they merged and hung as
aberrant gray clouds refusing any promise of rain. A corner
of his worn, pastel baby blanket touched the sticky asphalt
and caught the pointed heel of a shoe belonging to a lady
who twisted free, then set her sights on the door to the
building without so much as a glance at him.

A grim-faced man mopped his sweating forehead with the
sleeve of his designer suit, tugged futilely at the stiff, tight
collar and mumbled a bad word under his breath. The little
boy mimicked the act. His bare arm touched his face and his
fingers took a quick swipe to the neckerchief that curled
beneath his chin, Boy-Scout style, and was held in place by a
pewter clasp that captured a crude rendering of a bear paw.
Claws and all. He considered mouthing one of the bad
words he had heard grandaddy speak this latest visit, but
decided against it. Too risky. His parents would be waiting
inside the airport for him and they would, well, *know*.
Parents always did.

The edge of the pulsing crowd reached the door and

spilled into the airport lobby fighting for the best position at the one open counter to register their complaints. A tight-lipped woman in a uniform droned mechanically, "The airport is closed until further notice."

The woman in heels pleaded her case. "You don't understand—"

The PA system sputtered a continuous loop, a static-filled monotone message, ". . . events out of our control . . ."

A dark stain spread under the arms of the suited man as he pushed through to the counter. "Listen, you witch, I need to get to New York and I need to get there now."

"The airport is closed until further notice."

The little boy searched the crowd for signs of his parents, spotted a familiar back and ran to it. "Momma?"

The woman turned at the word, gently smiled and nodded.

A mistake. Not her. Not his mother at all. He backed away with a mumbled apology.

She took a step forward, reached out to him, her smile frozen in place on her face. "You can be my baby. Yes, that would be just fine. Come to Momma, little one."

"No, I . . . No."

She touched a finger to his cheek, ran her hand through his hair then pulled ever so slightly. "Come on now. Momma's waited long enough."

He stumbled over the edge of his blanket, caught himself and skittered just out of her outstretched grasp. He winced at the sore place on his head where she had pulled.

Her voice turned hard. Glass cold. "What's the matter? I'm not good enough for you? I'll show you what's good. Come here and I'll show you."

He plugged his ears with his fingers against her rising, tortuous voice and ran. The blanket whipped around his legs, as the crazy lady pulled it. He fought against it, snatched it free with a backward glance at her, and tripped over some new unseen obstacle.

A strong, tanned hand offered immediate assistance. "There now, young man, that was quite a fall. You OK?"

The little boy looked into the man's friendly dark eyes and nodded.

"Good." The man tucked a loose strand of long black hair

into his ponytail and began righting a box of spilled chalk pieces the child had just tripped over. A tattoo of a bear crept out from under the sleeve of the man's tie-dyed T-shirt.

The child stared openly at the tattoo, glanced at his own bare arm, then returned an envious and impressed gaze to the animal that dipped from view then reappeared with every muscular act that strained its cotton cage. "Wow."

The man captured the last chalk piece, tossed it into his box, then rose. He winked at the boy, pushed his sleeve up over his shoulder and flexed. The bear moved forward as if attacking, then retreated. Back and forth, forward and back again while the boy watched.

"Neat." A small smile played across his lips. "I like bears best."

"I can see that." He smiled with bright even teeth and offered his hand. "Put it there, my man. Anyone who likes bears is certainly a friend of mine. Call me Mack. All my best friends do. What's your name?"

The little boy tucked his small hand into the man's massive one and shook. "Winston, I'm almost eight, and I hate that name."

"Then Little Bear it is. What do you think?"

Winston thought about it for a milli-second and made up his mind. "Yeah." He stroked the pewter clasp of the claw around the neckerchief and smiled back. "Yeah. I like it. An Indian name. Are you an Indian?" He puffed up his chest and stuck out his lower lip in his best imitation of a grown-up. "I'm part Indian. Least that's what Momma says. Grandaddy says it too. He made me this pack when I was just a kid."

A high-pitched, amused cackle split the air and drew their attention. A skeletal old woman with high cheekbones sat behind the newsstand. She threw back her head and laughed until tears popped into her filmy white eyes, as white as the skin of an egg, then dabbed at them with an embroidered handkerchief. She ran her hand through her gray hair tied into a knot at the back of her neck. The laughter stopped abruptly, but something else—something the newly named Little Bear couldn't quite catch—danced and glittered in the fathomless eyes. She hesitated, then formed the words with her lips before speaking them. "Finally. After so very, very long—"

Mack raised a hand to stop her. "Perhaps . . ."

"No," she argued. "This one. He's brought them home. Where they belong. I can feel it."

"There have been others, old woman. You have forgotten."

"This one's different." She reached out, slowly, tentatively, toward the child, as if she were touching the contours of something soft and elusive. The little boy shivered. "Yes, different."

"I will know when it happens. Not before."

The old woman snorted, growled under her breath, and stared sightlessly. The glimmer in her eyes faded to dull. She withdrew into the shadows of the newsstand and waited.

Little Bear gasped and spoke in a loud whisper. "Can she see?"

"Not like you and me. But just as clearly all the same."

"But how . . .?"

Mack pointed to the floor. "What do you think of this, Little Bear?"

The boy saw the chalk drawing then. A complicated and intricate design of lines, circles, squiggles and curves bordered by a large square on the bland, chipped, and scarred floor of the airport. Bright colors formed patterns that seemed to change and move with every blink of his eye. He squinted at the empty oval space in the middle where the dirty floor peered out like a suspicious eye. "What goes there?" he asked.

"Something very special."

Little Bear walked the perimeter of the drawing, tilting his head for a better look here, toeing the edge of the chalk line with a scuffed sneaker there, and stroked his chin like his grandfather did when he was formulating a careful response. "A bear? But it'd have to be pretty small."

Mack looked deep into the drawing and barely found voice for his answer. "Maybe. May be."

"When will you know?"

He turned his gaze on the little boy and scanned him from head to foot. "Soon, my little friend. The matter is out of my hands."

The boy glanced around the airport for sign of his parents, saw none, and pulled the blanket tight under his chin. Two fingers slipped into his mouth.

Mack squatted next to the box of chalk, pulled out a raspberry-colored stick, and added a stroke to a corner of the drawing. "Don't worry, they'll come." He held up the box. "Do you like to draw?"

Little Bear considered the tempting offer, looked around once more for his parents, then reached for a blue chalk piece. No. Green was better. Prettier. He dropped his backpack by his side and hovered over the drawing. "I don't know what to do."

"Whatever you want to."

"I can make a stick man."

"A green stick man. Well now, that'll be just fine."

"Nah." Little Bear shook his head. "It's stupid. Wait. I got a better idea." He grabbed his backpack, unzipped it, and rummaged around inside. His hand hesitated, then produced a half eaten pack of peanut butter crackers. He popped one in his mouth, and offered one to Mack who declined. Back into the pack, his hand dipped and pulled, recovered tissue wrapped objects and rejected them until he found it: the cheap, silver plated charm bracelet his mother gave him for good luck. He peeled away fine layers of tissue, fingered the tarnished charms, and examined each one closely. The bell? No, too small. The heart then, or the little house with a door that opened? Nah. Too dull. The bird. That was it. Even better, the little feather that hung next to it. Yeah, that was it. He'd draw the feather.

Tongue planted between his teeth, Little Bear carefully placed the bracelet on the floor just inside the chalk square, and stretched out to begin drawing. He nudged the open backpack out of the way with his foot and ignored the protruding neck of the wrapped bottle and the lint covered jelly bean that rolled away and disappeared under a chair.

First the outline of the feather. Too skinny. He erased it with his fist and started over. Now it was too fat. His hand turned a dusty green with his thwarted efforts. The charm was just too small to copy, but there was something else he could use. Something better, bigger. The real thing.

He sat up and reached behind him for the pack. Reached

further. He twisted in place and scanned the space behind him. Empty. The pack was gone. "Hey." He crawled to where he had kicked the pack aside and looked. Nothing. He stood and frantically searched under a row of empty chairs. Gone. It was gone. Panic tightened his stomach and roared in his ears. He couldn't lose it. Just couldn't. All his neat stuff was in there. Everything he had collected over his entire life.

Momma was gonna be really mad.

And Grandaddy.

Grandaddy had made him promise that he would never, never, *never* lose the bottle. Never. And now it was gone, inside the backpack.

He had to do something, had to find it and quick.

Maybe his friend Mack knew where it was. Sure he would. He would have seen where it went, maybe even put it some place safe. That was it. Safe. The bottle and everything else. "Mack?"

The raspberry chalk stick rolled in a slow arc, then stilled. No hand moved it now to make the dirty floor come alive with color. Mack was nowhere to be seen.

A cackle split the air and punctured the deafening roar in his ears. He spun on his heel and saw the old, blind woman behind the newsstand rock gleefully in her chair. The lips on her skeletal face peeled back as the pitch in her voice rose. She grabbed herself around the chest and laughed that much harder.

Little Bear caught a slight movement from the corner of his eye. There. Next to the stand. A man he had never seen before. The man who had stolen his backpack. "Stop."

His little legs propelled him forward. The man stopped him with an unexpected outstretched hand to the chest that knocked the wind out of him and sent him sprawling into a pile of bound yellowed newspapers.

"Now then. Let's just see what you got in here. Might be something I can use." The man spit at the boy's feet, wiped a line of spittle from the corner of his mouth with the back of his hand, then hitched at the stained overcoat that slipped from his hunched shoulders. He scratched his weeks-old graying beard and returned his attention to the contents of the backpack that he held up by one bear ear.

Little Bear gasped for breath and kicked out at the man. "It's mine. You can't have it."

The man swung the pack, lodging a blow to the side of the little boy's head. "That ought to keep you shut up for awhile. Well, well, what's this?" He unwrapped an object and tossed the tissue to the floor in a crumpled ball. "A baby rattle for a little baby." He snorted in disgust, dropped it, then dipped into the pack again and tore away the paper to a collection of wooden sticks covered with bird feathers and little blobs of white glue. "What the hell? Feathers?"

The newsstand woman's laughter choked to a sudden stop.

The child rose to his feet. Anger burned red splotches in his cheeks. He tightened his fists. "Those are mine. Give 'em to me."

The man eyed him. A mean smile split his face. "You want them? Here." He threw one at the boy, then another in rhythmic precision. The boy cringed and turned and covered his face from the assault. "What's the matter? Your daddy not teach you how to catch, or maybe you don't know who your daddy is? I wouldn't own up to you either." He snapped a stick lengthwise and pointed the sharp edge at Little Bear. "Ever play darts? I think I know just where the bull's eye is, too."

"No." The boy threw up his hands and ducked, but it was too late. The point of the stick lodged firmly in one palm. He squeezed his eyes shut against the sharp pain.

The old woman started her chant then. Barely audible, scarcely spoken.

Little Bear stared at the feather-covered stick in his hand, then, with a quick gasp, pulled it out and watched as blood formed a growing dark red bead at the injury. His eyes widened in shock. His knees wobbled and threatened to drop him. He whined and turned to the old lady with his outstretched bleeding hand. "Hurt. He hurt me."

She reached out to allow his hands to touch hers. He met her and was surprised at the softness, the warmth, the comfort her old hands offered. Her fingers curled gently over his little ones, then tightened.

"You're hurting me." He tried to squirm away.

Her hands became a vise grip of surprising strength. She

continued the chant as her eyes rolled into the back of her head and left only corneal white.

He turned and pulled. Her bony fingers held, left imprints on his soft skin. He screamed then, as loud and as long as he could. Just like his momma had told him to do. Someone would hear, someone would come and help. He scanned a line of people sitting in a row of chairs just yards away and added an extra bolt of volume until there was no more air, no more scream available to him.

A mother turned the page of her magazine and took a cursory swat at the toddler begging attention. The baby crinkled its red face in preparation for a wail of his own, then let loose.

Silence.

He couldn't even hear the monotone announcements of the airport PA system.

All sound seemed to stop as if a transparent wall had imprisoned and separated him from the others in the airport. Most others.

"Stop your caterwaulin'." The old man spat a large wad, wiped his mouth, and studied the last object in the backpack. "Huh. Who would have guessed the little shit carried a bottle? No one deserves a snort more'n me."

Little Bear twisted and writhed in the woman's grasp and tried to free himself. Blood from the wound rolled down his wrist and spattered the wood of the newsstand. "Let me go." He directed a new shriek to the business man from the runway who was walking by. The man never even blinked, never acknowledged anything amiss in his determined stride.

An impenetrable wall. All around him. A prison. And he was the almost-eight-year-old prisoner held against his will.

The old man turned the bottle around and around in his hand, and smacked his lips.

There was no one to help him. No one at all. Little Bear's voice betrayed his helplessness. "Grandaddy gave me that bottle. It's mine. No one can open it but me. 'When the time is right,' he said."

"Did he now." The old man eyed the green glass bottle suspiciously and sucked his teeth. "Well, then, time's now." He popped the tip of the cork in his mouth, pulled, then spat it out. He sniffed the contents, grunted, and turned the bottle upside down. "What the—" He shook the bottle as if the act would free up its contents, then turned accusing, rage-filled eyes on the boy. His words came out in a measured, barely contained tone. "I'll kill you. That's what I'll do. Kill you dead for tricking me." He took a step forward, the bottle clenched tight in his fist.

Little Bear jerked away from the blind woman who let him go and disappeared once again into the shadowy depths of the newsstand. He stumbled backwards matching step for step that of the old man.

"Kill you. That's what I'll do. It'll be a pleasure. Pure and simple."

The little boy whimpered. "I didn't do nothing. Anything." Two bloodstained fingers snaked their way to his mouth. "I promise." He pulled his blanket toward him. Chalk dusted the threadbare edges of the cloth. He looked down and saw that he stood in the empty oval of the drawing.

"Like hell." The old man wiped his mouth, stared at the boy and stepped to the edge of the drawing. His eyes widened in surprise as a small ripple, barely a shiver, coursed through his body. The shiver turned to a tremble then to violent shaking as if a lethal electrical current had found an entrance and was actively seeking an exit point.

The wind started then. Howling, gusting currents of air that screamed and shrieked and deafened.

Little Bear cowered against the sound and pulled his blanket closer to him so that it would not be yanked away by the wind. It hung at his side. Still. Lifeless. Even the feathers glued to the wooden sticks remained unruffled.

The old man twitched. Color drained from his face and turned it to an ashen gray. The bottle flew from his grasp and fell to the floor unbroken. He stared at it and opened his mouth in an agonized howl. The sound was lost.

The bottle finally spewed its contents as if under pressure, releasing them willingly to the still air. Undulating waves of wind screeched and roared in a vortex of their newfound freedom.

The mantra of the old woman was an almost-subliminal undertow to the fast moving current of the wind that battered and swirled all around them. "Ancient spirits. Home. Ancient spirits. Freed."

The little boy pulled the blanket to his face and peered out through chew holes in it that he had made as an infant.

Then the wind shifted. A pull rather than a push. Something was happening. Something . . .

The old man.

. . . bad.

A thin strand of spittle escaped the corner of the old man's mouth. His tortured scream found voice, then spent itself. Terror drained from his eyes. Resignation and his own helplessness registered there.

The wind turned to a sharp intake of air. The bottle vibrated, hummed.

"Ancient spirits. Freed. New spirit . . . lost." The old woman's voice trailed off.

The old man shrugged, a last gesture, then collapsed in a crumpled heap.

Then the wind stopped. As suddenly as it had started.

The airport PA droned in a bored monotone ". . . events out of our control . . ."

A toddler wailed and tugged at his mother's hem followed by a soft *thwack* of a magazine.

Suddenly, Winston noticed that Mack had returned. He corked the bottle, wrapped it in tissue, tucked it into the bear backpack and handed it to the boy.

Little Bear reached for it, then stopped at the sight of his hand. He stared at it. Confusion formed little wrinkles on the bridge of his nose. "It's not hurt anymore."

"No. You healed it." Mack waved his hand expansively around the room. "And them. They're back where they belong now. They were here long before there was an airport. And will be long after this place is gone."

The boy looked up and saw her then. "Momma?"

Her voice rang with worry. "Winston? Thank God you're all right. I was worried to death." She knelt and scooped him into a bear hug. "Your dad's waiting out front. The traffic is horrible. Just awful." She kissed him, tousled his hair, and brushed away a tear. "You're all right. Thank God, you're all right."

Mack slid the backpack over the little boy's shoulders and

shook his hand. "Take care of your medicine bundle, Little Bear. I had one like this a long time ago. But not near as special."

Winston nodded and took his mother's hand as she led him away.

"Newspapers. Magazines. Tobacco."

The little boy looked over his shoulder at the newsstand. The old woman was gone. Instead, a beefy, heavyset man stood behind the counter hawking his wares. "Get your newspapers here."

Mack waved, then winked.

With the pastel baby blanket dragging behind, a hint of chalk dust coating the worn threads, Winston winked back.

I AM NO LONGER

Nancy Kilpatrick

I AM NOT THE SAME WOMAN I USED TO BE. EVENTS ALTER ALL OF us. Sometimes irrevocably.

This journal began the day they delivered the computer. It's been a slow agonizing process, practicing for hours, hitting the modified keyboard with a touch stick clamped between my teeth. The spot where my jaw is hinged still aches much of the time, as do the muscles at the side of my neck, but I've got the hang of it. Those areas of my body are strong.

The computer is essential. It's vital that I write everything down. Somebody has got to keep a record; *I* have to keep a record. For now I have nothing else to do.

I never dreamed I'd end up in a place like Dry Plains. On the other hand, no nightmare ever warned I'd be paralyzed from C-7, the seventh vertebra down, my voice box severed in the six-car pileup outside Houston. That the newly conceived fetus inside me would be miscarried. That I'd spend the rest of my life talking to myself and what's left of the world through modern technology, the same technology that used to confuse and annoy me. But then I've come to understand and accept many things recently. I'm not the person I was.

By the time the hospital sent me home, the bills had piled to the ceiling and Terry was at his wit's end. The recession hit the factory where he was a manager. Recent trade agreements had taken a lot of work to Mexico. The baggage handler job in Dry Plains was all he could find. At least the bungalow near the airport was cheap.

Terry's life insurance paid off the mortgage. And bought the computer. I need the computer to keep Terry's truth alive. He knew what was going on at the airport. About all the "accidents." The flights where more passengers disembarked than the plane held. About the Indians. I'm one-quarter Comanche myself. On my mother's side. Maybe that's why I believed him. Now I believe him for other reasons.

I had a premonition of Terry's death. I get feelings. Always have. Like my grandmother. My vision blurs, I hear echoes. Sometimes a headache slices into the middle of my brain. Before the accident, my backbone used to feel as if someone had rammed an icy steel rod down it.

I tried to tell him: don't go, you're in danger. Back then I only had the letter board and pointer to spell out a warning. It was tedious, I was always frustrated, the stick in my mouth, fumbling to point to the right letters, Terry having to figure out the words and then make sentences. He was endlessly patient, but that night he was late for work. He only got half the message: "Don't go."

He paused at the door in his midnight-blue coveralls and looked at me with eyes brown as fertile soil that always reminded me of the harvest back on my grandmother's farm when I was a girl. Of plenty. Of happier times. What I couldn't say with words, I told him with my eyes. His turned fearful. "Got to go, Meg," he said, covering it up with forced cheerfulness. He kissed my mouth with his generous lips and smiled, his teeth so white, one chipped. The scent of musk from his aftershave lingering. "'Rosanne' is on to-night. Why don't you watch it?" The door closed. I remember the cold empty feeling in the house; I swear I felt that rod up my spine.

His kiss left an invisible imprint on my lips; it caressed my skin through half the night, that and the thick tears coating my cheeks.

It was late when the world exploded. Even the dead must have felt the bomb tear up the runway. It was as if the earth had been slashed to the core. Hell fire shot skyward until the flames licked heaven's gate. The house grew frigid. I knew the moment Terry left the earth; the scent of musk vanished. His body was never found. That night I changed again.

Soon I started seeing them. Before they'd been just rumors. Talk Terry brought home from the airport. He didn't tell me, of course. He wouldn't have wanted to frighten me. I overheard him talking to his buddies. About the passenger who died of a sudden heart attack and then, two hours later, got up and walked, shoe soles not making a sound as they contacted the floor, skin too grey and mottled to be called living. About the red-headed Mexican twins, children really. They followed a black woman and her daughter from Atlanta into the washroom. And never came out. Two bodies were found, one adult, one teenage, the skin stripped off the way a hunter peels the hide from his prey to get at the carcass. Stories about hideous babies with yellow eyes and red teeth, who resembled stone demons, who sucked blood from engorged nipples. About half a dozen old men who carried tomahawks into the smoke shop, hacked the attendant to pieces, scattered tobacco all over the tarmac . . . And all the while it was business as usual at the airport.

I heard the stories and believed them. And now I see the spirits myself. Just like my grandmother used to. All day and all night. They roam the fields surrounding the airport, passing the house. One paid me a visit. That's how I know they're ancestors. And how I know they are not wholesome spirits. They aren't here to help but to punish. For deeds long forgotten. To exact revenge on the sons of the fathers, and their sons. And the mothers and their daughters.

"I am Tacomaak." He said that without opening his mouth, our brains like two modems, connected. There was something hollow-looking about him yet sturdy. He was solid enough to break down the door all by himself but he could walk through walls, which I suspect is how he got inside my house. Maybe, in the past, I'd have been scared. But that part of me dried up and blew away with the parched earth of this desolate place. In my new widow's grief, I transmitted the message: Why are you here? Why now?

He was two heads shorter than me when I'd been able to

stand. Dirty skin and hair, prominent nose and cheekbones slick with sweat stinking of mesquite. Maniacal black eyes glared through me, reflecting distorted images from the spirit land he came from. He knew I was paralyzed but I doubt he'd have found me a threat even if I could defend myself. From the way he stood rooted to the earth, I knew he didn't feel threatened by anyone.

Right away I sensed he was Comanche, although I can't say how I knew that. My mother did not like to talk about our native blood. I've seen movies, though. He was dressed warrior-fashion, fierce ochre and red clay face-paint, natural leather headband, a tomahawk and stone knife hanging from a beaded belt decorated with what I believe were scalps. Thick swatches of hair dangled in a row, shades of brown. One blonde. Like Terry's. Dried blood clinging to it. Staring at those blond strands and then into Tacomaak's eyes, suddenly I understood everything. The bomb had not killed Terry. I knew why he had come here.

Any dry dust motes of emotion that remained in me were moistened by my tears. They quickly turned into a mud slide that swallowed me. I never would have imagined myself pleading, but I did, in thought. He showed no mercy. His sharp knife gouged deep into my chest over my heart. It was not a wound that leads to death but a calculated mutilation of pure savagery. His mouth clamped onto my breast. Physically I could not feel his obscene kiss, or the brutal rape of my disabled body that followed—for that I am grateful to any benevolent spirits who may still exist. But physical pain is not the worst kind. Loaded into my cellular memory banks was an image. For a second two faces superimposed one over the other. A glitch. Mesquite and musk clogged my nostrils. I became irreversibly numb.

Generous lips smile. White teeth, one chipped. Smeared with red gore. Blazing hatred in inhuman eyes scorches me. He despises my mixed blood even as he greedily steals it.

I am not the same woman. I cannot feel the twisted thing growing inside me but I sense its coiled, warped energy draining my life force. My existence is a flat computer graphic. RAM memories keep me alive: a blond man who loved me with all his heart; my grandmother who blessed me. I am driven. I must delete something. If I do not, who will?

When the reincarnated demon crawls from my womb like a maggot, I will drive the plastic touch stick I have sharpened into its callous heart. And if I fail, if my body expires as this malevolent being seizes life, you who read this must act.

Do not be fooled—the spawn is not human. It is no friendly ancestor returning to guide us in our time of great need. It has come to destroy us. All of us.

Kill it!

I write this easily and with absolute certainty. The word mercy is not in my program.

I am no longer the person I once was.

PLANE SCARED

Douglas D. Hawk

My passenger strapped in the seat next to me was bleeding like a leaky bucket. The plane was pitching and bucking and rolling and it was all I could do to keep the damned thing in the air.

Outside, the fat rain clouds were thick as sea poop or pea soup or some such.

And it was dark out there, as dark and wet as a lake bottom.

This was stupid. This was fucking insane! What the hell was I doing flying in this kind of crap?

Making a living.

Yeah, right.

I did better when I was flying those nasty Colombians from Belize to Santa Rosa, New Mexico. They paid good money and I didn't ask any questions.

And the plane, my new, previously owned, twenty-years-past-its-prime plane, had all the grace and maneuverability of a barge. I'd bought it just last week from some weird guy at Dry Plains International. My other plane, a real beauty, was lying out in the Mexican desert in a dozen pieces. I counted myself lucky not to be rotting out there with it.

The crash had been pretty bizarre. I'd been flying some young guy back from Mexico City. He looked familiar. I knew I should know him, but damned if I could place his face. Right after sunset, the plane just went dead. Engines stalled. I radioed a Mayday, declared an emergency, and dead-sticked the thing down. We hit hard, bounced along the desert floor forever, tore up some shrubs, and destroyed my plane.

I was coldcocked. When I came around, I was alone. My passenger was gone. *Poof!* Just me and a dead airplane and lots and lots of desert.

I walked out, found a road and caught a ride with an old guy headed for Brownsville.

Thinking back, it was all sort of weird. I found no trace of my passenger. No footprints leading away from the plane. No note. No nothing!

And when I checked, nobody had heard my distress call. But, what the hell, I figured the guy was some light-footed drug smuggler and maybe I'd been on the wrong frequency.

I didn't really care. I was alive. Sans plane, but alive.

An old buddy said some guy at Dry Plains had a twin-engine Beechcraft for sale, cheap. I checked it out, even though I hate Dry Plains International. A lot of bad stuff goes down there. People die. Planes crash. Some controller flipped out and two commuter planes kissed each other at five hundred feet.

But the plane was a steal. The engines had just been overhauled, the fuselage was freshly painted and as tight as a drum, and the price was bargain-basement low.

The seller was a little strange. Like my disappearing passenger, he looked familiar. He had a face I'd seen before. Somewhere, a long time ago. He was a big guy. Fat. And he dressed funny, like he'd gotten all his clothes from a rummage sale. A long time out of style. But he was friendly enough and eager to sell.

So I bought the plane with the last of my cash reserves.

When I flew it out of Dry Plains, I had the oddest sensation . . .

. . . like there was someone on board with me.

Of course, it was all bullshit. It was just me, heading back to Roswell.

And then, lo and behold, the first time I've got a passenger, he gets shot and I get stuck in the worst desert rain storm I've ever seen.

I couldn't get above it and I sure as hell couldn't get under it. But it was funny, you know? It came up quick. Too quick.

All of a sudden we went from sunshine to storm. It happened so fast, I had no time to try to navigate around it.

And to make matters worse, the fucking instruments were going crazy. The altimeter was shot. The fuel gauge read empty, which was bullshit, since I'd topped off the tanks that morning. And the compass was spinning around like a propeller.

No wonder the price was so cheap. The plane was a piece of shit.

So there I was, flying blind in some ungodly storm over Texas with a passenger carrying an ounce of lead in his guts and bleeding all over my Beechcraft.

Bleeding a *lot*.

In the almost constant lightning flashes, I saw his pasty face. He was in bad shape. Terrible. He'd probably be dead before I could land. Shit, the FAA wouldn't be too impressed. But with me, they never are.

Miles Gilchrist. That was his name. A rock and roll promoter. He was an old guy, pushing seventy I'd say, although he looked pretty fit and trim when I'd met him earlier. Fit and trim if just a little nervous. He kept checking outside the hangar, watching for someone.

I should have been suspicious, but when he flashed a wad of bills the size of a softball, I figured what the hell? He wanted to fly out of Roswell right then.

Fine by me.

Only problem was, about the time we were in the plane and getting ready to take off, a big black limo came screaming out onto the runway. Some joker in the back with a wicked automatic pistol started taking shots.

Gilchrist started screaming. I started screaming. And then I put my crate in the air. It wasn't like I could stop and have a rational discussion with the shooter. People who use guns are not, in my experience, rational.

I didn't realize Gilchrist had taken a slug until he started moaning and groaning and I saw the blood.

Jesus, there was a lot of blood.

I started radioing, but all I got was static.

So, okay, I'd just head to the next airport. I knew the area, I could set down in some podunk junction and get Gilchrist to a doctor.

Only the storm hit and all of a sudden I was flying without instruments, with a busted fucking radio and a dying passenger.

"Trent," Gilchrist wailed.

I looked at him and about peed my pants. In a flash of lightning, I swear to God, his face looked like a . . .

. . . skull.

A skull with big eyes and bloody teeth.

But I blinked and he just looked like an old guy with a bullet in his gut.

"Hang on," I said.

He shook his head frantically and looked at me in wide-eyed terror. "You gotta get me out of here!"

"I'm trying. Shit, I'll be lucky I can keep us in the air."

He motioned with one bloody hand. "No, you don't understand. *They* are coming for me!"

I glanced at the dark spreading stain on his shirt. "I think they already came."

"No," he said desperately. "Not those guys. Not the guys that did this . . ." He looked at his wound and shuddered and gritted his teeth.

"Well, ain't nobody going to get us up here," I said. Except, maybe, the Flying Nun. If she had water wings.

"Those guys back there," he breathed, "that was something else. A different deal."

"You sure aren't a Dale Carnegie graduate are you?"

His eyes were big and wide and the whites were showing all around the dark pupils.

"They'll get me up here!" He closed his eyes. "I shouldn't have flown! It was . . . stupid!"

I thought so, too.

"I . . . I haven't in years," he went on, panting in fear and pain. "Not since I did the album . . ."

That made no sense. But I wasn't looking for sparkling conversation. I wanted to get the hell on the ground.

He persisted. "I . . . I wasn't really tryin' rip 'em off, you know? I mean, they were dead. Who cared?"

"Let's talk about this later . . ."

"NO!" he shouted and his bloody hand grabbed my arm, leaving a gooey red print on my best shirt. "No, you don't understand. I ripped 'em off and they . . ."

He stopped talking and started groaning. Then he was quiet. When I looked at him, his eyes were closed. I thought he was dead. I chanced taking my right hand off the controls and felt for a pulse. He had one. It was weak and erratic, but he was still alive.

I tried the radio again. There was a lot of static and then I heard a faint, garbled reply. I was able to catch a few words. Dry Plains International. Which was weird, because I had been flying away from Dry Plains. It was as if the storm was . . .

. . . pushing me east, toward that stinking, dangerous airport.

I tried them again, but now everything was static.

Then we hit turbulence. It was bad. A roller coaster without tracks. We dropped maybe a thousand feet and I was fighting the stick, expecting to kiss the ground at any second. In the clouds and rain, without gauges, I didn't know if we were at ten thousand feet or right on the deck.

When I was finally in control again, I fished out a cigarette and started looking for my Zippo. There was a flare of light behind me and a match appeared right in front of my face . . .

I spat the cigarette into my lap and let out a scream. It was real loud. Wake-the-dead loud.

I whirled around in my seat. There was a dark shape sitting back there. Just a shadow.

"Who the hell . . . !"

Then the lightning flashed and I was looking into a black, grinning skull face.

I've seen people after they were incinerated in a fiery crash. Skin all black and crisp and shriveled like burned bacon. This looked worse.

And *it* was wearing glasses. Big, black-rimmed glasses that were a little melted around the edges and with cracked, spider-webbed lens.

Flashback!

It had to be. Flying Colombians back and forth I'd partaken of some illegal substances.

A lot of illegal substances.

Obviously, too many.

I don't know if I screamed or not.

Gilchrist did. He wailed like a banshee.

The plane pitched and I turned around and spent the next few seconds fighting the stick and when I turned around again, there was nobody behind me.

"They . . . they're coming," Gilchrist gasped. He was alert again and his eyes were wide and he was staring behind me.

"You . . . saw that?" I asked.

He bobbed his head up and down. "I told you. You gotta get us down, Trent. You gotta get us on the ground right away."

"I've got to get us the hell out of this storm first." I pounded on my gauges. They were still dysfunctional.

So was Gilchrist. He was still holding his side, but his face was all screwed up, and he was crying like a baby.

"Hang on . . ."

"No," he cried. "You don't understand. It's because of the album."

"What the hell are you talking about?" I demanded.

"Fire in the Sky," he said, like I knew what it meant.

"Just relax."

"Fire in the Sky, the album," he said, frantically. "Songs by rock and rollers and some country singers. Dead ones!"

"So? A bunch of dead musicians. So what . . ." I paused and looked at my passenger. Still looking scared, he nodded.

"Trent, they all died in plane crashes."

I swallowed the lump in my throat. I didn't want to talk about plane crashes. Hell, I'd already survived one. The way things were going, it looked like I was about to have another.

Then I thought about my passenger from Mexico City. He was a kid. Hispanic. Good-looking. Had a nice smile and seemed kind of shy and . . .

. . . and when we were about to crash in the desert, he was as cool as a corpse.

A corpse!

Fuck me runnin'!

"No way I'm buying into that shit, Gilchrist!"

"Ghosts!" he bleated. "They're all dead, but they're back. I . . . I ripped 'em off! I pirated the songs. Black market. Lots of money. The CD went like hot cakes. I made a bundle. And . . . and now . . ."

He started moaning and blubbering again.

Quick like, I got back on the radio. I screamed into the mike. I called people out there who might be listening a lot of foul names. I wanted the hell down. I wanted the hell out of this lousy, stinking crate and away from this dying lunatic.

"This is Dry Plains International tower." The voice was clear and crisp. I whooped.

"Mayday, Dry Plains!"

"State your situation." The controller was very calm and cool. He could afford to be. He was sitting down there with his fat ass in a padded chair and I was stuck up here with some shyster record producer and a bunch of really pissed off . . .

. . . rock 'n roll ghosts?

"My situation?" I yelled. "Listen, I got a guy bleeding to death. I've got no instruments! It's raining so fucking hard I need sonar! My situation? *My situation . . . ?"*

"Try to remain calm."

I sucked in a deep breath. Calm! Right.

"Okay, Dry Plains. Sorry. Little spooky up here."

"Roger that. I've got you on radar."

Hallelujah!

The controller gave me my coordinates. I was fifty miles out at four thousand feet.

"Stay in radio contact," he said.

"Roger."

I sighed.

Gilchrist screamed.

He was looking behind me again. I turned.

Mother-grabbing, crotch-biting, rat-turd-eating bastards!

There were three of them back there now. Dark shadows. And then, in another flash of lightning, I was looking at two god-awful, ugly, hideous burned skull faces with big round eyes in black eye sockets and both grinning big, toothy grins and the third face was all swollen and bloated with big, bulging eyes.

There was the one who had tried to fire my smoke and another that might have been a woman if it had had a face, although its head was framed in a halo of long, soft hair. The third one, the only one not a crispy critter, was a black guy, bloated and swollen and looking wet, like he'd just come out of a shower . . .

. . . or a lake.

"NO!" Gilchrist screamed.

One of the things made a dry, crackling sound like a chuckle, and reached down with a black, skeletal hand and touched the blood on the floor.

Gilchrist shrieked and shrieked and shrieked . . .

. . . and maybe I did, too.

The thing looked at the sticky blood on its fingers and then licked his bony digits with a black tongue and made, I swear to God, a *yummy* noise.

"You better do some fast prayin'!" I yelled at Gilchrist.

He just kept screaming.

Thinking back on it, I'm surprised I didn't simply lose my shit and crash right into the hard desert floor. I mean, I wouldn't have been like I murdered anybody. Gilchrist was as good as dead and the folks in the back . . .

. . . well, let's just say they'd seen better days. A whole lot better.

But I didn't crash. I gripped the stick and looked straight ahead and got back on the radio. My voice must have sounded a little funny, because the controller asked me if I was having any medical problems. I told him no, while my brain was screaming, no, no, I'm fine, I'm just up here with a bunch of deep-fried zombies who probably want to suck out my brain.

No. No problem. Everything is peachy-keno, A-OK, you overpaid, dumb-shit bureaucrat!

But I didn't say any of those things because this was the voice of the guy that could get me down and pissing him off would be really stupid.

Then I felt movement behind me and I didn't want to look, but I did and I screamed, too, I think, and, Jesus Christ with kittens, all three of those things were dipping their boney fingers in Gilchrist's blood and licking them and making noises of approval.

And poor old Gilchrist was burbling and gurgling and keeping his eyes squeezed shut really tight.

I needed a drink. I needed a big gulp of Mexican tequila, the kind with the dead worm in the bottom.

And wouldn't you just know it, all of a sudden, a black, burned hand shoved a bottle under my nose. The glass was sooty and smokey and the label was singed beyond readability, but the liquor and worm inside looked okay . . .

I mean, what are you gonna do?

I took it and pulled out the cork and swallowed a big pull.

It burned all the way down but felt good and real and normal.

I needed some normal right about then.

After that, everything happened fast.

All of a sudden, I had full instrumentation. The storm died down, the clouds sort of evaporated, and in the distance, I could see the lights from Dry Plains.

They gave me a priority clearance to land.

I didn't look behind me. Although Gilchrist was still moaning and wailing and I could hear those fucking monsters making yummy noises.

I just aimed for the runway lights and put my head on automatic pilot.

"They got me! They'll kill me!" Gilchrist managed to scream. Then his voice got high-pitched and hysterical and everything came out in a weird, pleading rush. "I didn't know! I didn't know they'd care! They're all dead! Otis and Buddy and Patsy and Jim and the Bopper and Richie and . . . and all the rest of them! They're all dead!"

I ignored him. Fuck him and his cigarette-smoking, tequila-drinking ghosts and his corrupt little plans and . . .

. . . and why did *they* keep making those damned *yummy* noises and happy grunts when I was trying to land my plane?

The controller had me coming in on the runway furthest from the terminal. I figure they didn't want to take a chance on some little plane smacking into their big building.

The wheels touched down and the plane rolled along the runway smooth as glass. Smoother. Like I was on a cushion of air.

Piece of cake. Easy.

Never mind I had a guy bleeding to death and a bunch of zombie rock and rollers hanging out in the back.

Never mind any of that shit. No sir, we were on the ground.

And then things got a little fuzzy. It's kind of hard to

remember this part. Hard to remember because I'd rather forget.

I stopped the plane, opened my door, and jumped out. I hit the tarmac hard and rolled and there was a lot of pain in my ankle.

But even through the pain, I could see Gilchrist climbing out the other side. I still don't know how he found the strength, because he had bled more blood than I thought a human body could hold. All the same, he scrambled out like a scared rabbit looking for its hole.

And then . . .

. . . and then I saw a lot of dark shapes sort of rise up out of the ground. Right out of the fucking ground. And the three in the plane were on the wing. Black skeletons with burned clothes, one in a tattered dress, and the bloated black guy and they were howling and moaning and . . .

. . . and it was god-awful.

Gilchrist stumbled off the wing and fell hard and started screaming. And then those shapes were all around him and he was bawling and bleating and blubbering . . .

I've never seen a pack of wolves attack a lone deer, but I hear it's fast and brutal. Well, think of ol' Gilchrist as the deer.

He vanished beneath those screaming, howling things, and I looked away, thinking, quite naturally, I was in the midst of a very ugly nightmare. Another flashback.

When I looked again, I just saw Gilchrist. His arms were flaying in the air and his mouth was open, leaking streamers of dark gore, and half his body was already in the ground. Right in the tarmac. He was being sucked down like he was in quicksand.

For one long, awful, terrible second, he saw me and reached toward me and then he was gone . . .

. . . and I faded out.

When I came around, lights were flashing and people were yelling and I was being wheeled on a stretcher to the back of an ambulance.

"Where's my passenger?" I demanded, my voice a little ragged and a lot shaky. I asked because I knew he hadn't gone underground. That would be . . . insane.

"Passenger?" one of the medics asked, shaking his head.

"Just you. Jesus Christ, buddy, what happened up there? How'd you survive the fire and all? How the hell did you land that thing?"

"Wh . . . what are you talking about?"

"That," he said, pointing. The gurney came to a halt.

I propped myself on an elbow and looked toward the plane.

Yeah, definitely, I did too many illegal substance way back when.

Way too many.

The plane I'd bought from the guy—*the guy who looked a lot like that fat fifties rock and roller who died in the plane crash in the Dakotas with those others*—was nothing but a burned out, rusted hulk. A shell. There was no glass in the windows, no doors, no new paint. Nothing. It was just a battered and beaten and . . .

. . . and this was crazy!

I couldn't have *landed* that thing, because I never could have gotten it off the ground and . . .

. . . well, I don't know what.

I mean this was Dry Plains International. Bad things happen here.

And way back when, I did too many drugs too many times . . .

Of course, now I figure ol' Gilchrist just flat-out fucked-up. He ripped off the wrong folks and now he's down there—wherever that is—paying them back, because—well, it's like the song says, "Rock and roll never forgets."

SCALPS

Chet Williamson

IF THEY FOUND HIM, THEY WOULD KILL HIM.

Oh, they would give him a trial first, but the result was a foregone conclusion. They would either execute him, or sentence him to a living death, alone in one of those cells way in the bottom of some dungeon. He had seen the movies, that one with Jodie Foster and that Englishman. That was the way they treated people like him.

He had liked that movie, though. That Englishman was so smart and clever that he tricked them all at the end and got away. Got away to kill another day.

Just the way Jeremy Delver did.

Well, not quite, Jeremy thought. Jeremy had a mission. Jeremy was a collector.

Jeremy collected scalps.

He lived in Roswell, sixty miles east of the Mescalero Apache Indian Reservation. His family had lived in New Mexico as far back as his great-grandfather, who had fought the ancestors of the same Apaches who lived on the reservation now. Fought them until he died, horribly mutilated, parts of his body missing. Jeremy's grandfather and father had never told him which parts, but he could guess.

Both Jeremy's grandfather and father had served in the Army, Jeremy's grandfather in the First World War, and his father in the Second. At their urging, Jeremy had enlisted and spent a total of two and a half years in Vietnam.

Even though it had been twenty years ago, he still missed

it. He had grown up on the stories of his father and grandfather, so instead of fighting Vietnamese, he saw them as Apaches. Apaches were what he fought, and, since he knew how, he kept on fighting Apaches when he got home.

The Indian he had just killed was his fourteenth in the last fifteen years. The first had been when his father died back in 1978. The old man had been run off the road by a van full of Indians. The police had tried to tell Jeremy that his father had been drunk, and that he had crossed the line and hit the Indians, but Jeremy knew better. His father could hold his liquor, and the authorities were all the time covering up for the damn Indians. They were probably the ones who were drunk. Jeremy went to see a lawyer, but he turned out to be as bad as the police. So Jeremy decided to take a scalp for his father.

It was easy. At sunset, he picked up an Indian boy about sixteen years old, hitching a ride back to the reservation. When the kid got in the car, Jeremy smacked the back of his head with a hammer he'd stuck between the seats, drove down an old side road, killed him with a knife, took the scalp, and then buried the boy deep in the sand.

Gone forever. Had he run away? Maybe. No one would ever know. And although they might search, the desert was a big place. But this time, with fifteen years of killing under his belt, it might prove too small.

The policeman had seen him driving out the old trail this time. It had been dusk, dark enough to need his lights, and when he saw the police car parked by the side of the road, it was too late to douse the lights and stop. He put on his right turn signal, and was about to pull onto the main road when the cop held up his hand through his open window.

Jeremy gave a little wave and kept going, but the cop gestured that he wanted him to stop. Jeremy did, pulling over on the sandy shoulder, and the cop got out of his car and walked casually over.

"Whatcha doing back there?" the cop said disinterestedly.

"Taking pictures," Jeremy said, gesturing to his camera gear in the back seat. "Desert at sunset."

"Didn't see a girl anywhere?"

"A girl?"

"Indian girl. About fifteen. Disappeared."

Jeremy shook his head. "No sir. Didn't see a soul back there."

The cop nodded and gestured for Jeremy to drive on. Jeremy watched the cop in his rearview mirror as he pulled onto the road. The man watched Jeremy's car in return, and Jeremy thought he saw him pull something out of his pocket.

Writing. The son of a bitch was writing down his license number.

It wasn't hard to figure out what he'd do if they didn't find the girl—follow Jeremy's tire tracks over the old trail road, stop where he stopped, see that the sand wasn't the same shade as the rest of the desert, start digging . . .

Jesus, he'd taken too much time with this one. If only he'd done her fast, taken the scalp, and rushed away. But she'd been pretty, and he'd taken hours, tying her up, making her bleed until she fainted, then waiting until she woke up again, until finally she didn't wake up anymore.

Oh Christ, if only she hadn't been so pretty. If only she hadn't been so *strong,* she'd have died faster, and he'd have gotten away before anyone started to look for her. If only he hadn't discovered that he liked doing women more than men, doing things to their scalps before he took them.

If only he hadn't discovered the glory of blood.

It was what he liked to see more than anything else in the world—the blood coming out of the skin, seeping through thin slices, emblazoning the symbols of his power on tan flesh; or pumping upward from the deep wells, bright red ejaculation of his will.

He didn't like the touch of it, and hated the taste of it. He took wet paper towels with him every time, and used them. But the sight of it took him beyond himself. Even the artificial color of the photographs and videos that he took and looked at later in his home could send him into blissful states of excitement where he felt both weakened by his worship and strengthened by the majesty of what he saw in the clear pictures and grainy videos.

And now they would find out, and they would come to his house and arrest him and go through his things and find it all, and take him away forever.

Before he would let that happen, he would kill himself,

cutting his flesh over and over again, and watching his own blood run out until he was too weak to watch any more.

But there was still a chance to escape, and as he drove home to Roswell, he worked out his plan.

Jeremy didn't drive right up to the large house he had inherited from his father. Instead he parked several blocks away, and walked through the alleys, coming upon the large yard from the rear, and entering the back door of his house. Once there, he looked out the front windows, but saw nothing suspicious. Then he quickly gathered the only things he would need—the $20,000 in cash he had tucked away for emergency money, and the box of scalps. Everything else was expendable, even the photos and videos. They already knew, so let them see it all.

His father's second car, a 1977 Dodge Dart, was still in the two-car garage behind the house. It had been there since his father's death. Jeremy started it every few weeks, kept the tires filled, and the fluids at the proper level.

He went across the yard into Mrs. Tork's driveway, crouched behind her 1982 Crown Victoria, and screwed off the plates. Mrs. Tork used the car once a week to go to Golden Memories Club every Saturday. Today was Wednesday, which gave Jeremy plenty of time.

In the garage, he attached the plates to the Dart, and tossed the briefcase and the envelope of money into the front seat. Then he started driving toward the road that would take him south out of Roswell, to Mexico.

Three blocks from his house, he passed two police cars, their lights flashing but sirens quiet, undoubtedly heading toward his house. They had found out then, checked the plates, found the fresh grave at the end of the tire tracks. He could not try to drive across the border now. By the time he got there, they would have his picture and be watching for him.

No, he would go somewhere else instead, somewhere even the police feared to go.

Dry Plains Airport.

"We gotta be crazy to try and fly out of here." Dan Gaines shook his head, looking at the low, flat desert landscape, broken only by the control towers, the hangars, and the terminal building.

"It's the closest," Frank Evans said, his eyes on the road in front of him. He tried to keep his thoughts away from the things that were happening and had happened at the airport ahead. Instead he filled his mind with their mission. He thought about the chilled human heart in the back of the Medic-5 van, about the young American woman who was waiting for it in a hospital bed in Mexico City, about how the fastest way to get the heart there from Alpine was to fly there, and how the closest airport was Dry Plains. It sucked, but it made sense.

"It shouldn't be that bad," Evans told Gaines, but knew he was only trying to convince himself. "It's not like we'll be in the main terminal."

Evans swung the van down a side road that led to a hangar adjoining the terminal, where a chartered plane was supposed to be waiting for them. There was no guard at the gate, which was standing wide open, but after Evans drove through he saw in the rearview mirror a man in a guard's uniform sitting on the pavement on the other side of the fence. Froth bubbled from his mouth, and his thighs were a sodden mass of red. He seemed to be cutting into his own legs with what looked to Evans like a pistol clip.

He didn't say anything to Gaines about it. Gaines was spooked enough as it was.

Evans drove past Hangars Four and Three, then pulled up next to the door of Hangar Two and turned off the motor. He turned and looked at Gaines, who looked back at him. Gaines had sweat on his forehead, in spite of the air-conditioning.

"Let's do it," Evans said, and pushed his door open so that the heat swept into the cab. As he climbed out, he thought about the last time he had flown out of Dry Plains. It had been Hanger Two, and everything had gone smoothly. Davis and Coletti, the same pilots he and Gaines were to meet today, had been friendly and professional. He hoped that they were professional enough today not to let the madness at Dry Plains stop them from doing their jobs.

Gaines opened the back door, and Evans reached in and

grabbed the heavy white case with large red letters that read MEDICAL SUPPLIES—DONOR ORGANS. They walked toward the small door inset in the larger hangar door, and went through.

When Evans saw Davis and Coletti standing near the small Beechcraft Duchess, he knew right away that something was wrong. Davis looked as though he was trying to make his grin cover his entire face, even though it hurt him to do so, and Coletti was standing slack-jawed, his eyes red-rimmed, staring at nothing.

"Holy shit," Gaines whispered, and Evans clenched his teeth and decided to see it through.

"Hi, guys," he said to the pilots. "All ready?"

"Ready for what?" asked Davis. The death's head grin narrowed a bit when he spoke, but sprang back to its full width in the silence.

"The flight. The flight to Mexico. With the heart?"

Suddenly Davis's grin vanished, Coletti seemed to shake himself, and both men looked awake, relieved, terrified, and sane, as though they had just awakened from a nightmare.

"We'll never get there," Davis said, and his voice shook, not in madness, but from fear.

"What is it? What's wrong?" said Evans.

"We're crazy," Coletti said.

Jeremy had no problem getting to Dry Plains. All the way down 285 and across 20 he had watched for police, sweating every time a police car appeared on the road. But none of the officers pulled him over or even gave him a second glance, so that by the time he headed south on 90, he had relaxed enough to switch on the car radio and sing along with the oldies.

In the airport short-term parking lot, the gate was stuck in the up position, and no ticket came out the slot, so Jeremy drove straight through and parked. He took his money from its envelope and wedged it in his front pants pocket, left the keys in the car, and walked to the terminal with his briefcase.

There were several people picketing outside the building, but their hearts and minds didn't seem to be in it. They were merely standing there, their arms down, signs at their sides so that Jeremy couldn't even read them. He walked past and into the building.

Jeremy felt his skin grow clammy as he looked at the mob in the waiting area. It was composed of men and women who looked nothing like Jeremy's previous experience of commercial air travelers. They were grim and sullen and swarthy, and appeared to be a ragtag collection of thieves, smugglers, and fugitives, who, like himself, possibly saw the nightmare of Dry Plains as an escape from something worse—if they could get a plane out, which, as Jeremy quickly learned, was no small trick.

Every ticket counter showed the same thing. Nearly all arriving planes had been cancelled, and all departures without exception were listed as delayed. Jeremy got into a line of angry, shoving people, and stood waiting for an hour, listening to the people ahead of him shouting at the clerk and the clerk shouting back.

When there were only three people between him and the clerk, the woman at the front of the line went berserk, and attacked the clerk, slashing at his face with long fingernails. A few other clerks intervened (there were no security guards to be seen), and hauled her, biting and screaming, through a door, after which a louder, more agonized scream was heard, and then a relative silence.

By the time Jeremy reached the front of the line, the clerk was touching the cuts on his face, looking at the blood, tasting it, going back for more.

"Excuse me," Jeremy said, excited by the tracks of blood on the clerk's face, in spite of himself. "I need to get to Mexico."

The clerk gave an automatic grin. "I could use a vacation myself," he said, and giggled shrilly.

"Yeah, well, can you sell me a ticket?"

"I can, but it won't do you any good. There haven't been any planes out of here since last night." He touched his cuts again, examined the blood on his fingertip, made a mark on the back of his other hand, then glanced up at the departure screen. "See for yourself."

"There's gotta be some way," said Jeremy. "It's important. I'll charter a plane if I have to—I've got cash."

The clerk's expression suddenly became surly. "Cash don't mean shit. *Nothing* means shit. Nobody's going nowhere."

"Where are the charters?"

"Find 'em your fucking self!" said the clerk. A second later he lunged at Jeremy, who leapt back, dropping his briefcase. He kept one foot on it while he pushed the clerk back over on his side of the counter, then quickly picked up the case and scurried away.

The cafe was open, and Jeremy went into the bar, where he sat on a stool and ordered a shot of Wild Turkey to steady his nerves. He felt a wild mixture of emotions, including elation at the blood he had seen shed, and a mixed terror and fury that he would not be able to leave this place. He knocked back the shot and ordered another.

As he nursed the second drink, he became aware of four men sitting at a table in the corner of the bar. They were snorting and giggling, and when Jeremy turned around to look, he saw that a short-skirted cocktail waitress was being held by two of the men while another rubbed her stockinged thighs and the fourth cupped her breasts from behind. They seemed to be trying to pull her onto the table on her back.

"Hey!" Jeremy shouted involuntarily, and the cry got their attention long enough for the girl to wrench herself away from their grasp. They sat there as if too relaxed to get up.

"You *bastards!*" the girl shrieked, then wheeled about and ran through a door into what Jeremy assumed was the kitchen. Jeremy glanced at the bartender, but he was ignoring the situation, and seemed to be looking at himself dazedly in the mirror over the rows of bottles.

"Whoopsie-doo," said one of the four men languidly. "Got caught with our hand in the cookie-nook."

"Sorry, pardner," said another. "Didn't mean to offend. The little lady just asked me what I wanted to eat, and damned if I didn't want to show her."

"Pussy," said a third.

"Gar-on-teed," added the fourth.

"You like to eat pussy, pardner?" asked the second man. Jeremy said nothing. "*We* sure do. Our fav-o-right dish, 'specially when it don't wanta be eaten, when you gotta chase it down and *ketch* it." The men laughed. "How many we ketch so far today, boys?"

"That'da been the third," one of the others said. "Think we made a mistake tryin' to grab her too much in the open. Disturbs the citizens."

"Well," said the second man. "We won't make *that* mistake again. The Knights of the Open Sky will just have to do their huntin' more subtly."

Jeremy didn't get it. They were in their fifties, and all were wearing well-tailored suits, white shirts, and conservative ties. They looked like typical businessmen, not rapists. But there they were, their expressions like the cartoon satyrs in those old *Playboy* magazines Jeremy's father had bought.

"Knights of the Open Sky?" Jeremy said tentatively.

"That's what we call us," said the man who seemed to be the leader, and then laughed at his non-joke. "Four hot studs bound together by business in Mexico and a desire to scarf pussy. Takin' to the air when we can get us a goddamn plane, but havin' fun in the meantime. Care to join our merry band?"

In reply, Jeremy finished his drink and walked out of the bar, ready to swing his briefcase at them if they followed. He heard their voices fade:

"Ah, fuck that homo . . ."

"Let's git that Air Texas clerk, the one with the big melons . . ."

"Why not go back there in the kitchen and finish what we started . . ."

They disgusted Jeremy. A bunch of goddamned dirty old men who had no style, no tact, no class. He felt nausea. Such things should be done secretly, and should not be shared with others. Such things should be done with a man and a woman alone, far away from the world, under a dark sky which looks down on them alone. Pain and blood are private things, personal matters.

Jeremy began to wander aimlessly through the throngs of people, frequently patting the wad of bills in his pocket to make sure no one would lift them, and always clutching the briefcase handle, the briefcase filled with all the evidence of his love and hate that he would ever need, the items that encompassed his life to date.

After a while, he began to hate the closeness of the sweating, waiting, unwashed bodies, and began to steer himself to wherever the human tide lessened, until he finally found himself alone in a dimly lit gray corridor. He walked down it, his heels echoing, until he came to a door on his right.

He pushed it open and saw the interior of a hangar, a small plane, and four men. Two of them were sitting on the cement of the hangar floor, and the other two, dressed in bright orange jump suits, were talking heatedly to each other. A large white box sat on the floor next to them. Jeremy caught the end of the taller man's sentence.

". . . gonna just turn around and go back?"

The shorter man, who was much stockier than the tall man, answered, "Hell, they know what's been goin' on here, it's not our fault we can't get out. Shit, nobody could get out of this nuthouse, and we oughta damn well *drive* out while we can, before we go nuts too!"

Just then the tall man saw Jeremy. "What do *you* want?"

"I'm, uh . . . looking for a charter."

"Yeah? Well, we're looking for a pilot."

Jeremy nodded toward the two men on the floor. "What's wrong with them?"

The two orange-clad men glanced at the two on the floor, then walked over to Jeremy. "They're crazy," said the tall man. "It comes and goes. But we can't be sure that they won't drift off just as we *take* off."

Jeremy shook his head. "I heard this place was bad, but I didn't know it was *this* bad. What are you? Medics?"

The tall man nodded. "We're supposed to be going to Mexico City with that." Here Gaines gestured to the white box. "Organ transplant."

"What is it?" Jeremy asked, stirred by the thought of a living human organ inside the box.

"Heart," Evans said, and was going to say something else. But he was interrupted by a clattering that resounded through the hangar.

Jeremy saw the white box vibrating, jiggling, almost dancing, back and forth across the floor. Then it began to skitter toward the three of them, shaking its way until it was only a few feet away. Gaines and Evans stood there open-mouthed, their eyes wide. The two men on the floor did not move.

The box stopped shaking. It sat for a moment, perfectly still.

Then it burst open.

Jeremy couldn't tell whether it was wrapped in ice or gauze or some material that he'd never seen before, for his mind seemed as cloudy and translucent as the heart. It lay there inside the box, and as he watched it he knew that he saw it pounding, pounding, and now he could hear it too, like the sound of a yellow-brown hand coming down on a drum of animal skin.

He didn't even feel the briefcase slip from his hand, nor hear it strike the floor. He stood entranced by the vision before him, for vision was what it had become. The heart was no longer in a white box, but in an irregular container with ripped and ragged edges, and the ice or gauze had become a red pool.

It was something Jeremy had seen before, and in another awesome instant he knew that he was gazing into an open chest in which a heart was alive and pumping.

Jeremy scarcely heard the moans of terror from the others, or the retching, or the spattering of their vomit on the floor. Over all of that he heard a chanting, and the pounding of more hearts, louder drums, and something inside him revelled in the sounds and the sight of what lay before him. There was madness in this place, but he was not mad. No. On the contrary, he felt blindingly, violently sane.

He felt as if he had come home.

Not scalps, but hearts. These were the core of life, the essence of death. This is what he had unknowingly come to Dry Plains to learn.

And this was how he would leave.

He understood. No voice had to say *Do My Work*. No hand had to guide him further. He had not come here to be destroyed or to be made mad, but to destroy, and cause madness in others, to fly away, spreading the plague of Dry Plains into the south, into another country.

He looked, and only a few yards away was a mechanic's tool box, filled with sharp and magical things.

Now all he had to do was find the proper tool.

The suit fit surprisingly well. Jeremy zipped up the front, thinking how fortunate it was the suit was orange and not white. It hardly showed the blood stains at all.

He patted the pocket in which he had placed his money, then picked up the closed white container, stepped out of the darkness into the bright hangar, and walked toward the plane.

"All ready, sir," said Davis, the pilot.

Coletti, the copilot, nodded his head, smiling. "Checks out great. Oughta be in Mexico City in a little over four hours."

They climbed aboard, and Jeremy followed. Even though they were the only plane to leave Dry Plains Airport that day, there was no delay whatsoever in getting off the ground.

As they lifted into the air, Jeremy looked down at the airport. It seemed fitting, he thought, that an airport was built over whatever was there or had been there. An airport, from which the glorious red madness could fly out into the world.

The weather was clear. The pilots were flying the plane. The way to Mexico was open.

Dry Plains knew how to take care of its own.

"You hear that?"

The Knights of the Open Sky cocked their heads like so many idiot dogs. Then they scuttled down the long, gray hall toward the sound.

"That was a broad, I'm damn sure of it."

"Yellin'!"

"Screamin', y'ask me. Let's go give 'er sumthin' to scream about!"

"Knights of the Open Sky—attack!"

"Eat that pussy, *yeah!"*

When they got there, the small, brightly lit hangar was disappointingly empty.

"Hell, I'm *sure* it come from in here . . ."

"Let's look around. Looka that door there."

Together they walked toward an open door that led into a dark room. Next to the door, one of them saw a briefcase lying on its side. When he picked it up, he seemed surprised at its lightness. "Empty?" he said as he opened the latches.

The lid fell open, scattering a dozen items made of black hair and dried skin.

"What the *hay*-ull," said one of the men, who stooped and examined the things. "They wigs or what?"

Now the others were looking too, trying to identify the strange yet somehow familiar objects.

"They're like *scalps*," one whispered. "But there's . . ." He took a pen from his suit coat pocket and rearranged one of the things on the floor. "There's like a *hole* in it." Realization dawned on the man then, and he drew back in disgust. "Aw *Jee*-zus, that ain't *head* hair, that's a god-dam—"

But he didn't finish. The things began to move, the individual hairs trembling like prairie grass in a heavy wind. Then they seemed to individually compress, tensing for a greater motion that came when they bounced into the air, straight for the faces of the four Knights of the Open Sky.

The men reeled back, but the things remained in their faces, blinding them, flapping like hairy bats. When they opened their mouths to scream, the things entered the wide holes of flesh, forcing themselves further into the men's mouths, pressing in and down past teeth and tongue, and into the throat.

The Knights of the Open Sky clawed at their mouths, raked their lips, broke their own jaws, choked, turned blue, and fell. One stumbled through the open door before he went down, and tripped over something that he saw with his eyes, but, in his agony, could not identify as the bloody bodies of two men, one still wearing a bright orange uniform.

And in a few terrible minutes all four men were as dead as Evans and Gaines, as dead as the matted hair and flesh that clogged the throats of the Knights of the Open Sky.

In Mexico City, the box had arrived, and everything was ready. The doctors, the nurses, the anesthesiologists were prepared. The patient, drowsy but still awake, lay on the table, ready for the anesthetic. The box was brought in.

And opened.

Nothing covered the three hearts that lay inside, all of them beating of their own volition.

Everyone in the operating room stared at the hearts, speechless. And in another moment, all that anyone in the room could think about was whose heart to take next.

Then they understood, and looked to the chief surgeon.

He took his scalpel, but not by his fingertips as he usually did. Instead he wrapped his fingers around it to make a clenched fist, and thrust it eagerly into the patient's chest.

Far below, on the street in front of the hospital, Jeremy thought he could hear a scream. He smiled, filled with dark joy, then walked into the busy streets, plague spreader, proselytizer, worshipper and priest, come home at last.

IN THE STILL, SMALL HOURS

Charles Grant

A SLOW STRONG WIND TOOK TO THE SKY AFTER MIDNIGHT, DRAG-ging litter from the corners of every corner of the airport, dancing with the debris, mostly tattered paper, until it tired; and when it tired, it moved on, dragging grit across the windows like the clatter of muted hail, stinging the cheeks and closing the eyes of those who wandered outside because the inside was too quiet; snapping a flag on the pole near the terminal's main entrance, the ropes slapping and whipping against the pitted metal shaft to ring a tuneless hollow bell; gusting now and then across the nearly empty parking lots, across the deserted entrance road, across the runways and grass between, startling pilots, wobbling planes, and moving on without a sound.

It should have been cold, the wind that scoured the night-stained tarmac, and it should have had a voice—at the very least, a thunderstorm.

The best it did, however, was a monotone hum as it slid across the panes of the observation deck, a sound so low and constant Lucas barely even heard it.

But it was enough.

It could have been a moan.

And he shivered, only once, and blamed the faulty air-conditioning that, like everything else, was scarcely working these days. The only place he could find a small measure of peace was in this place, tucked away in the Dry Plains terminal that served the smaller, local flights.

He lit a cigarette.

The room was little more than a fairly wide corridor two-and-a-half stories above the ground, blank plaster wall on one side, an inward canted wall of glass on the other, and at their junction above his head a spotty row of fluorescent bulbs. The floor was carpeted, the carpeting worn, and at the north end, a heavy metal door with a small window, no handle or bar on either side, just a strong push to get it open. Although a waist-high metal rail ran the room's length, no one had thought to install chairs or benches. To watch the landings, to watch the take-offs, as he did most every week, he had to stand.

A chilly place.

Unfriendly.

Deliberately so, he gathered, because there was no money to be made here, no concessions, no machines, no poster advertisements, not even a water fountain.

He didn't care.

He seldom stayed for very long, just long enough to watch the lonely three o'clock flight from Dallas make its landing. When it had taxied to its destination—a long extension from the main building off to his left, rounded at the end to accommodate a dozen gates—and the jetway umbilical made its connection, he would watch the handful of passengers ghost along the glass-wall corridor back toward the exits.

He would watch, but he'd never see her.

Tonight would be no different, yet there was a difference anyway.

He was no expert, neither an engineer nor a former pilot, just a man who rented floor space in brand-new empty buildings, but he could tell that the aircraft coming in this summer night were having more than a little trouble. They landed more like stones than gliding birds to a welcome pond. They'd drop onto the runway hard, tires smoking at frantic brakes, and once, not an hour ago, a 727 fishtailed and he'd held his breath, hoping it would make it.

It had.

But only barely.

The wind slapped the pane, shimmered it, and he blinked.

A glance at his watch; he had an hour to go.

Though the lighting wasn't bright, barely bright enough to

see the floor since only every other narrow bulb was lit, he squinted as he tried to make some sense of the still-black morning sky. There were stars, the moon long gone, but he couldn't see a single cloud, or a blank spot up there that would tell him a cloud was passing. Nothing, as far as he could figure, that would signal unsafe weather.

Nothing but the wind.

Then he saw himself in the glass and gave himself a nod and smile.

In all the months he'd been coming here, no one had ever stopped him, no one ever asked why an ordinary-looking man in a decent suit, a decent tie, would make his way so late to this place just to watch the planes. And precious few of them there were these days, he thought as he crushed the cigarette beneath his heel. From midnight to one, an even dozen; from one to two there were only eight; and from two to dawn he'd be lucky to count them on the fingers of one hand.

One night there hadn't been any.

A week ago, one had crashed on take-off, thankfully out of his sight.

He leaned lightly against the railing, looking westward toward the main terminal. Lights and dim shadows and the glint of steel and polished plastic. It made him nervous; especially now. When he had arrived tonight, just after twelve-thirty, there hadn't been a single soul inside. The ticket counters had been deserted, the shops closed and locked, not even a man with a broom working over the mirrored floor.

Nothing.

No one.

He hadn't heard a sound.

As he hurried toward the covered walkway that led to the smaller building and the observation deck, his footsteps had followed him, echoing faintly, faintly mocking, until he'd found himself virtually on his toes, so as not to break the silence.

And once he had arrived, he had almost stumbled and fallen, not realizing until he touched the cold railing for balance that he'd been holding his breath most of the way.

He had shaken his head then, and he shook his head now,

frowning, wondering what the hell was going on. If Joan had been here, she would have poked him in the side, teased him about omens, portents, the stuff that she claimed to believe, although she had never tried to force him to share her beliefs.

"Either you believe or you don't," she had said that last time, the last night they had been together, waiting in the reception area for the call to her outbound flight. "But sooner or later, you're going to have to admit that there are coincidences, and then there are coincidences that only look like coincidences." Then she'd kissed him good-bye, a sisterly brush on his cheek, and he had hurried over here to watch her leave for Dallas, and points west.

He did believe in one thing—that she would be back five days later, briefcase filled with papers that would make her richer than she already was.

He also believed he still had a chance, had to have a chance, to somehow win her back.

He believed it implicitly until the moment he saw the ball of flame the following week, an amateur video filling the TV screen with dying color as the reporter on the scene tried to explain what had happened fifty miles west of its Texas destination. It had something to do with an engine valve and a fuel leak; the reporter wasn't very good.

It really didn't matter.

That night he stayed home, flicking aimlessly from channel to channel, waiting for the awful error to be admitted, the flight number to be corrected. He watched, he didn't weep, not until dawn and the call from her mother, weeping herself, begging him to help her put Joan to rest.

He had.

What was left of her.

None of them ever knew; the coffin had been closed.

And one night, no night in particular a handful of weeks later, he found himself dressed and in his car, heading for Dry Plains, found himself looking out the airport window, waiting for her plane.

He never asked why, never asked anyone if maybe he was going crazy.

He just did it.

But now, tonight, he thought he knew.

It didn't make him happy.

In fact, it made him feel . . . almost nothing.

A sigh, a silent scolding for being so damn melodramatic, and he watched a small, private jet slip swiftly out of the stars, out of the dark to his right, and aim for the runway. Its noise was muffled, but he knew instantly something was wrong with this one, too. The engines sputtered, and the aircraft, so unbearably tiny and pale, began to slip from side to side. He put a palm against the glass and leaned closer, feeling the rail press into his stomach.

Side to side.

Moving so slowly as it drew even with his position that he couldn't imagine what held it up. It couldn't have been more than twenty or thirty feet above the tarmac. Side to side. Abruptly dropping like a stone just before the gate arm blocked it from view.

He held his breath, waiting for the explosion, the scream of the emergency vehicles, the race of workers from their caves beneath the building.

There was nothing.

Thank God, there was nothing.

He sighed loudly, closed his eyes for a moment, and let the relief ease him back from the rail until he heard a noise in the hallway, as if something large had fallen onto something not quite soft. He turned, head cocked, listening for a curse or a call for help.

There was nothing.

Just the door.

He stared at the door's small window, but all he could see through it from where he stood was a square piece of the cinder block wall, painted a faded green. He supposed the color, when it had been originally applied, was supposed to be restful, but it only reminded him of a hospital.

A quiet noise, then, deep in his throat.

All right, he told himself, all right. Not just any hospital; the hospital where Joan's mother had been, recovering from a mild heart attack. In the hall, the pale green hall, outside the woman's room, Joan had suggested in a whisper that when she returned from her next trip, perhaps they ought to consider not seeing each other for a while.

"We don't seem to be getting anywhere, Lucas," she had

said, expression regretful, voice calm and laced with reason. "It's almost a cliché, isn't it—it doesn't seem like either one of us is ready to commit to anything else but more of the same."

He probably should have argued, if only for the sake of his ego. He probably should have done a lot of things. But as always, he didn't.

She was right.

She was, when he thought about it, always right. Just as she always made the decisions, the big ones, the small ones, the ones he never found the energy to care about and so deferred to her with a quip and grin.

A puzzled frown then, when yet another plane, this one much larger, maybe a DC-10, wallowed over the far end of the runway. Though he couldn't make out much of its body, the swinging lights on its wings told the story, and once again he held his breath until it had touched down safely, and much easier than the small jet that had vanished a while ago.

Weird, he thought; they were coming in as if it were the middle of the day.

The door opened.

He didn't turn right away, but he was surprised to realize he was annoyed. This deck was his place this late at night—or this early in the morning—and he resented someone disturbing him. A foolish notion, perhaps, but he had been alone here for so long, nearly six months to the day, that he supposed the reaction was fairly natural.

"Well, damn."

He looked toward the voice, and wasn't sure how to react.

The man stumbling through the doorway was tall, easily a head taller than he, and large. Almost huge. A soft grey blazer with something gold pinned to the lapel, black slacks, black shoes; a white shirt with tiny specks, and a tie that matched the jacket. What was left of his hair was dark and slicked straight back, not quite reaching the blazer collar. Thin mustache. Thick eyebrows. His jawline was fleshy, not many years to go before they began to sport some jowls.

"Damn."

The man shook his hand vigorously to one side as he crossed the floor, blowing on the palm now and then, his puffed face alternately folding up, smoothing out as he pulled his lips away from his teeth and muttered, "Damn," a third time.

"Trouble?" Lucas asked.

The newcomer stopped, obviously surprised to see Lucas there, grimaced again and came over. "Damn stairs," he complained. A mound of fat pressed against his shirt, pushing the buttons to their limit, and his tie was twisted and skewed to one side. "Not watching where I'm going, you know what I mean? Can't even see my goddamn feet, they hook a step, I fall like a kid that can't handle his stupid beer." He stomped his foot once. "You'd think they'd put some carpet down out there, you'd think that. Cheap bastards."

He shook his hand again, and Lucas realized the specks on his shirt were droplets of blood. Startled, he checked his own clothes, and saw a drop on his breast pocket. He wiped it off with a quick grimace as the man held out his hand for inspection, skin harshly abraded and nastily red.

"Here," Lucas said, reached into his hip pocket and pulled out a handkerchief.

"Grateful," the man said, shook his hand one more time, blew on it one more time, and wrapped the cloth gingerly around his palm. "Tell you, buddy, this place is turning into one goddamn obstacle course, you know what I mean? Jesus." He shook his head, took a breath, and propped a hip against the railing. "You waiting on someone?"

Lucas nodded before he thought.

"Daryl," the man said, jabbing a thumb at his own chest. "Daryl Rayman."

"Lucas Nelson."

They shook hands; Rayman's was soft, hot, moist, and strong.

"Hell of a name, ain't it, Luke," Rayman said, easing back a few steps, gazing out at the runway. "Hippo like me with a name like Daryl. 'Course, my momma didn't plan on having a hippo. Think she was hoping more along the lines of something like a basketball player." He snorted a laugh, stared at his bandaged hand. "Didn't plan on tearing myself up either, come to that."

"Maybe you ought to get it looked at."

Rayman shook his head. "Here? You're kidding. This place's going to hell on the express, buddy, and I wouldn't trust a hangnail to those idiots down the First Aid Center, swear to God." He shifted until his stomach rested on, folded over the railing. "My last night tonight," he said, voice lower but without regret. "Thought I'd take a last look around, you know what I mean? Over ten years, but I ain't gonna miss it, not anymore."

He flicked a finger against the gold pin, which Lucas realized now was the stylized shape of a soaring airliner—it was a Dry Plains Courtesy Crew badge. He had seen it several times, usually on women, and assumed that the company representatives spent their shifts wandering around the terminal, answering questions, directing lost passengers, handling complaints, spreading cheer, and softening tempers. But he had a hard time imagining this one walking all day; he looked as if he had barely made it here without passing out. His face had the sheen of a man preparing to explode in sweat, and he wheezed softly, breathing through a slightly open mouth.

Movement outside caught his attention, and another plane swooped in, this time without trouble, and turned almost immediately to the gate arm on the left.

"Amazing, ain't it?" Rayman nodded toward the airliner maneuvering along the blue-lighted runway sidepaths. "Ten years, I ain't seen so many come wandering in this late." He glanced at Lucas. "Kind of like they want to get it over with, you know what I mean?" He shook his head, smacked his lips. "Hardly anyone showed up tonight, you know." He gestured vaguely toward the main building. "It's kinda like New Year's Eve, after twelve—nobody flying in or out, you have the whole place practically to yourself."

"I guess."

Lucas followed the plane to its gate, squinted, but could see no one inside.

"Ain't no guess about it, buddy. This place is dying."

The lights went out.

It happened so abruptly, no flickering or buzzing, that he gripped the railing tightly as the glass wall vanished and the outside lunged toward him, clearer now, details no longer blurred by reflections or ghostly smears. He swallowed heavily against a rise of vertigo, looked up at the ceiling, and made a face. It wouldn't have been so bad had he been alone, he supposed, just a little startling, but the shadowed hulk of Rayman only a few feet away made him inexplicably uneasy.

The outside glow gave the man's face a sickly yellow tinge.

"What'd I tell you? Place is going to hell."

So leave, Lucas thought sourly. You don't like it here so bad, leave, and leave me alone.

Figures in coveralls scurried around the parked aircraft, unloading luggage, blocking the wheels, fussing here and there with open hatches on wings and undercarriage that he didn't understand. A check of the corridor that led to the terminal showed him nothing; it was empty.

If there's luggage, he thought, where are all the people?

From someplace in the warrens beneath them, another worker appeared, this one pushing a long and low empty handcart across the runway toward the plane.

"Feels like them pictures you see in school," Rayman said quietly as he followed the handcart's progress. "You know. The gods on that mountain?"

"Olympus," Lucas said automatically.

"Yeah, that's right. You always see them looking down, dropping some lightning on some poor guy's head once in a while, butting in when they're bored, or just watching, doing nothing. Wearing sheets or robes or whatever." He chuckled, and plucked at a lapel. "I don't think this sorry outfit's gonna make it, do you?"

Lucas couldn't help it; he grinned.

One by one the little men finished their jobs and deserted the plane, hand signals directing them to one place or another, vans and electric carts speeding away into the dark.

Lucas lifted his wrist and peered at his watch—close to two-thirty.

Joan's plane will be in soon.

His eyes closed, and he felt a faint sting there, not as bad as those first nights, but far from leaving him forever.

That's when he decided this would be the last time. It had

to be. Whatever therapy he supposed he had thrown himself into either wasn't working, or it had worked and he hadn't known what it would do. Either way, this was stupid. He had an office to run, a life to get on with, and there were still those photographs in his desk at home. He wondered if it would have been worse had they been married.

He didn't think so.

"Son of a bitch," Rayman said. "Look at that fool."

"What?" Lucas scanned the shadowed area below the window, around the parked airplane, not seeing anyone who didn't seem to be belong.

Then he spotted the man with the handcart.

He was pushing it straight for the runway.

"Damn fool." Rayman leaned farther over the railing, his forehead nearly touching the glass. "That boy's just walking there, Luke. He's just walking there."

Lucas snapped his gaze to the right, not really wanting to see if there was another plane on the way in, and was relieved when he saw nothing but stars out there.

Until two of them moved.

"Jesus," he whispered.

"Boy's got trouble."

Lucas looked around the room. "We have to tell someone, find a phone." He took a step toward the door, looked out, and changed his mind.

It was too late.

The worker had already reached the runway.

The airliner, another DC-10, had already touched down.

There was no sound but the whine and roar of engines, muted only slightly by the thickness of the panes.

Lucas couldn't watch the plane, and he couldn't stop watching the man and his empty cart.

Oh my God, he thought when the plane was less than a hundred feet away; he whirled and stared at the blank wall, swallowing hard, fast, one hand pressed to his stomach, one clawing at his shirt. Sweat curled down his left cheek from his temple. For some reason, he expected to hear the squeal of brakes, the crunch of metal against metal, as if it were an automobile accident he could witness from his porch.

The roar rose swiftly, peaked, and instantly faded.

Rayman said nothing.

Wheezing filled the silence.

Lucas ordered himself not to look, just turn and go for the door. He didn't need to stay. Joan's plane would land or it wouldn't, and she wouldn't be on it, and this kind of grief he didn't need tonight.

He did turn.

He did start for the door.

But curiosity made him look, and astonishment made him stop.

The worker was alive, pushing his handcart on the runway's far side, and Lucas watched him shrink, fade, vanish into the far dark, not a shadow left behind. He clung to the railing while his legs decided if they were going to work or not. He wanted to laugh, giggle a little, maybe scream once just to be rid of the pressure that had expanded to fill every cell in his chest; he wanted to throw up; he wanted to grab the fat man's arm and demand an explanation.

Instead he simply stared.

"Know her, you know," Rayman said, still looking out at the deserted tarmac.

Lucas paid him no attention. As the shock wore off and his heart stopped its heavy thumping, he figured he would take the day off, stay in bed until his back ached, take himself out to dinner, and maybe do a little downtown cruising. It had been a while. Over a year, as a matter of fact. A couple of bars, a couple of beers, and if he didn't get lucky it wouldn't really make any difference. What mattered was the effort. He didn't believe there'd be a miracle, like the guy there with the handcart, but maybe just a glimpse of a pretty lady, maybe a pleasant smile in his direction, would be another step, maybe the last, toward whatever they called it when mourning came to an end.

"Hey, Luke?"

The first step had come on the drive out here tonight, when he finally admitted to himself that, heartless as it may seem, Joan's dying had spared him the trouble of agreeing with her decision. The moment he had seen the fire, heard the reporter, heard the sirens, some part of him knew that he wouldn't have to tell her that she was, as always, right.

IN THE STILL, SMALL HOURS

What they had left from their year together wasn't really love. It might have been, once, but if so, it had withered, or faded, or whatever love does when it doesn't feed properly and isn't properly fed.

They had both been cowards, each waiting for the other to take the first step, both knowing it would be her because that's the way it was.

That realization, harsh and horrid, had made him sick enough to pull over and wait until he was sure he wasn't going to throw up.

The coward saved by an act of God in the form of a faulty valve and a fuel leak.

Jesus.

"I know her."

Lucas passed a hand over his face, drove away the demon. "Excuse me?"

Rayman still wasn't looking at him. "I know her. Joan Becker, that right? Some kind of commodities broker, something like that?"

He couldn't find the words.

The fat man gestured outside with a lazy crooked finger. "Them boys out there, they're gonna strike soon, you know. Heard them grousing about it the other day. Stuff going on around here you wouldn't believe, buddy, and they're getting a little riled. Bet if you came back in a couple of days, this place'd be shut down."

Noises in the hall, people laughing, someone talking.

Lucas looked to the door, looked back at Rayman. "You knew Joan? But . . . how?"

Rayman turned his head slowly, one side of his face yellowed, the other blanked in shadow.

One eye.

He could only see one dark eye.

Another plane landed, engines screaming, tires blasting smoke into the slow night wind.

The door squealed as it opened.

"This time of night," Rayman said, "it's kind of special, you know what I mean?" He sighed contentedly. "Peaceful. Real peaceful."

Lucas couldn't see his lips move.

He could only see the one dark eye.

Suddenly the fat man straightened, taller, his face all in shadow despite the reach of the outside glow.

Lucas took a step away, and though it was yards behind him he could still feel the doorless wall at his back, no escape.

Then a voice, a woman's voice, as someone stepped into the room: "Daryl? Daryl honey?"

Rayman turned quickly, slapped a joyful hand against his thigh as he laughed heartily, and hurried over to the small figure hesitating on the threshold. "Momma!" He wrapped his arms around the tiny woman, gave her a smothering long hug, then turned them both around. "Momma, this boy here, he's Luke Nelson. He's waiting on someone, just like I was waiting on you."

Lucas smiled politely, and took a few steps forward, not sure if he should extend his hand, or simply nod.

"Who's he waiting for, Daryl?"

›Before Lucas could explain, Rayman said, "Joan. Joan Becker. She was on your plane, remember? Cute little thing, blonde hair, big blue eyes?"

"Oh . . . yes. Yes."

The lights flickered, bright and dark.

Lucas averted his eyes and squinted, as if the room had been touched by lightning.

"Momma, look, we got to go. It's a long drive, you know that, and I don't want to speed. You know how you hate when I have to speed."

The woman nodded. "He's just terrible, you know, Mr. Nelson," she said gaily as Rayman steered her gently toward the door. "Eats me out of house and home, speeds like a demon, you don't know what a chore it is just to make him behave. He's terrible!"

The fat man laughed.

A dark hand fluttered in the air. "But you know, I don't think he can live without me, poor soul" A laugh of her own, hoarse and woman-soft. "Not that he'd admit it to the Devil, the big oaf."

The lights flickered again just as Rayman, laughing harder, pushed the door open.

Bright and dark.

"Hey . . . uh . . . Daryl?"

"Nice to meet you, Mr. Nelson," Mrs. Rayman called. "You get home safe now, y'hear? Find yourself a nice girl, a boy like you shouldn't ought to be left alone, the time of night like this."

Lucas felt his temper spark, but he didn't move, couldn't move when Rayman waved good-bye, and his mother glanced over her shoulder to give him a wave as well.

In the corridor light, just before the door closed, he saw her clearly for the first time.

Her clothes were shredded and black; there was nothing left of her face but charred bone.

The door closed.

Slammed.

Another plane landed, and he checked automatically, just in time to see it veer off the runway onto the grass, swing around violently and hit the runway again. Somehow it managed to straighten out before skidding off the other side, and when it rumbled past the gate, Lucas sprinted for the door and slammed it open with his shoulder.

The corridor was empty.

Sixty yards of it in four sections marked by steps, and no doors except the one he propped open with his foot.

The Raymans were gone.

He put a hand to the side of his neck and rubbed the skin there until it burned.

They were gone.

They couldn't be.

"Daryl!"

No place to hide.

"Mrs. Rayman?"

The other voices, the other people.

Nothing left but the light, and dark hand-smudges along the wall.

He stumbled back inside and took hold of the rail, lowered his head and waited until he could think again, until he could stand alone. It was the lighting, of course, and probably not a small amount of guilt at not feeling worse for Joan's dying. All this time he had been kidding himself— the tears, the glum expressions, the solemn nodding when his friends passed condolences and sympathy his way . . .

some of it was real, most of it was sham. And Mrs. Rayman there, clearly loving her son as her son clearly loved her, had only underscored the acting he'd been doing all along.

In a way, the admission, like the admission in the car, was a relief.

He still felt like a monster, like something less than human, but it was still a relief.

Burdens lifted, he thought, and all that psychobabble crap.

So when Joan's plane landed smoothly at precisely three o'clock and taxied to its gate, he blew it a kiss and wished it well, smiling as he watched the unloading proceed without a hitch.

Rayman was right.

The silence here was peaceful. Restful.

These still, small hours of a day yet unborn were indeed something special; wasting them here would be a sin.

"Okay, you heard the lady," he said to his reflection in the glass. "Get your sorry ass home."

He grinned.

He pushed the door open and saw Joan waiting at the corridor's far end.

Suit black and shredded.

"I've changed my mind," she called, smiling broadly as she waved.

Face more bone than flesh.

"She's right, Lucas, darlin'. You shouldn't have to be alone."